First published October 2024

To my best friend and soulmate, Diane,

I couldn't have found a better partner to share my life with.

PART I – FURY

CHAPTER ONE

She was invisible again. Ageing had wrapped its cloak of invisibility around her.

A soft wetness spritzed her face. Umbrellas popped up in unison to dome all around her as a flash of yellow split a distant cloud. She plunged her vein-mapped hands deep in the pockets of her trench coat, her fingertips digging at the stitching.

Limping, with unsteady gait, her left foot dragged behind her. Battling for space she squeezed between bodies, toward the stony faced buildings. She adjusted her headscarf, tucking grey fringe curls from the downpour as an unapologetic elbow rebounded her arm and brolly prong skimmed her head.

Amidst a blur of headlights and amber flashing signals, angry horns blasted their frustration at the fast slowing traffic. The sidewalk was a cacophony of panicked stomping. Like the wildebeest migration they surged relentlessly on.

Arabella turned onto a side street where it was calmer, and at the next turn it was quieter still. By the time she reached Silver Mews Terrace the clattering human bustle had all but gone and the pathway was her own. The rhythmic drumming of feet was replaced by the thudding angry torrent bouncing back hard off the shiny-stone surface.

Here, a more menacing darkness lurked. Two of the Narnia style street lanterns at the end were out, the others barely offering a silvery hue. The cobbled terrace was lined by chest high spiked railings, shielding properties that boasted flower boxes below their sash windows. The residential mews, dating from the Dickensian era, appeared frozen in time.

Her sodden shoes squelched their ruin with each laboured step, oozing as she stopped at the end house of the Victorian terrace. She squirrelled an inner pocket, before scuttling the bowed stone steps, worn from generations of footfall.

The door creaked a noisy welcome, before squealing its displeasure at her careless closing slam. The distant patter filtered slowly into the silence inside, where a mustiness of abandon hung thick in the air. A Tiffany lamp sat alone on the parquet floor offering but a glimmer of the wood-panelled hallway that surrounded it. Over bended nail she hooked her drenched coat and peeled her sopping headscarf.

Arabella ankle-flicked away her saturated shoes, whilst sliding bony fingers into her thick grey locks to remove a bobby pin. Her wrinkly face grimaced as she dug again, prising more tightly-clasped grips as she made her way to the galley kitchen at the back of the house.

A mirror and packet of tissues lay on a picnic-style folding table below a run of wooden cupboards. Arabella slumped to the moulded plastic chair alongside it, pulling the mirror to meet her aged reflection. The hideous face of a witch, a gypsy fortune teller of a hundred years.

She grinned, watching the creases of her brow lift and furrow, rippling in dance across her eyebrows as crows feet joined her crooked smile. A toothless gap accentuating her tombstone-like, discoloured teeth. She took a long black-eyed gaze at the repulsive image, eyeing the bony hook of her nose, the wiry hairs sprouting proud on her chin.

Like picking at sellotape for its invisible end, Arabella dug hard at her temples, nails digging, scraping her skin. Finding traction, three deep wrinkled lines peeled smoothly from her forehead. Scratching behind each ear, a flimsy film lifted, pulling the creases from cheeks and eyes. The masking concertinaed to meet at the hooked bridge of her nose, released in a skin-tugging suck, leaving a youthful pinked complexion.

Bella folded the prosthetic into tupperware before plucking the mole and peeling bushy eyebrows. Squeezing her eyeballs released two dark lenses that plopped into the box. Lifting the curly grey hairpiece revealed bleach blonde hair that lay slick to her head.

Tugging at the pouch of wet wipes, she flannelled them three-thick rigorously around her face and neck. Rubbing the membrane on the back of each hand, the blue-veined mapping rolled away, leaving smooth pink skin. Bella finger-poked, wiping each tooth to clear sharpey marks and leave stunning straight white teeth. Peering into the mirror, her sparkly blue-eyed beam broadened, winking at her transformation.

Clicking to seal the container, she slid it with the wig into a cavity behind a strip of loose skirting. From the recess she pulled a phone that she tapped into life. A dial tone echoed.

"Airport Carz," a monotone voice announced.

"Hi, could I book a taxi to Heathrow for six thirty tomorrow morning, please? Under the name of Maxwell."

"Address please," the operator replied sharply.

"Yes it's, 35 Silver Mews Terrace, Plaistow."

After a moment of silence. "That's all booked for you," the telephonist declared, robotically repeating back the address and time.

Bella unbuttoned and yanked off her threadbare brown cardigan before hip-shaking to slip off the ankle length skirt. She stood half naked in the kitchen tapping at the phone. As it rang she wriggled, peeling thick brown tights and unfasten her blouse one-handed.

"China Panda, can I take your order please?" came an enthusiastic voice.

"Hi, yes, could I order Szechuan Duck for two, a special fried rice and mushroom chow mein, please. Under the name of Maxwell."

"Collection or delivery?" was the high pitched response.

"I'll pick it up in about half an hour, if that's okay?"

"Yes, yes, order for Maxwell ready in thirty minutes, thank you."

Bella strode back into the hall and clicked the socket at the foot of the stairs. A wire dangling bulb on the landing tinged, flickering into life, illuminating the paint-peeling staircase. She bound the stairs in twos, pausing halfway, breath-held with head cocked.

The shriek of a police siren stunned her, heart-pounding; too soon surely? Her momentary paralysis softened, replaced by electric-like tingle running through her. Her forearms pimpled as she hurtled the remaining steps and darted for the bathroom.

Ten minutes later the lamp-lit hallway filled with the clacking of heels across the hardwood floor. Bella's still damp blonde bob glistened, framing her perfectly round face and porcelain-like cheeks that shone like a china doll in the moonlight. Her transformation from aged crone, to elegant young woman was breathtaking; Bella radiated a vibrant, natural beauty.

In white turtleneck and dark knee length pencil skirt, she cut a professional, authoritative figure, only belied by the flush of youth. An innocence, an inner warmth sprung from her sparkling pale blue eyes as she tapped gently at the screen of her iPhone.

"Hey Carl, I'm running a little late, so I'm picking up Chinese on the way," she said, behind a lip glossed beam.

"Sounds good Bella. I've been delayed anyway, its gridlock around the Cheveley estate. There's blue lights everywhere!"

"We'll have to catch the news later and see what's happened," Bella said, capturing a concerned tone. "Remember I can't stay over tonight, early flight!"

"Yeah, I know," he grumbled. "Gonna miss you. And *we won't* be watching the news! See you at the flat as soon as."

Bella slid on a waist-skimming black leather jacket and threw her handbag strap over her head, before palm-pushing one of the oak panels, *click-clack*. It bounced smoothly from the wall, revealing a gloomy passageway behind it. Ducking inside she tugged at a dangling cord before disappearing into the shadowy space.

Re-emerging moments later, she pushed the panel too, to disappear instantly into the wall of dark wood. Bella gingerly rolled the bloodied severed finger, sealing it carefully into foil. She exited from the back door, crossing the little courtyard and vanishing into the myriad of murky alleyways at the rear of the property.

CHAPTER TWO

THE OLD BAILEY – FIVE MONTHS EARLIER

Courtroom number one was heaving with warm bodies as a feverish intensity built. International media reporters and the public had merged to cram all available space. Sticky air hung overhead in the cavernous expanse between pillared white walls and high domed ceiling.

His Honour Lord Danton presiding cracked heartily his gavel. With the greyed complexion of a battle weary Major, he nodded sternly at the bench below, granting permission for the prosecution to proceed.

Outside, the protests that began on the opening day of the trial had grown exponentially in a clamour to witness the conviction of these abhorrent men. Inside they stared-on, transfixed in silence, their faces set as one as the drama of the last six weeks drew to a climax. Those without seats shuffled seven or eight thick across the rear wall. Mostly men, all now jacketless with top-buttons released, few amongst the perspiring throng were without a visible dampness of shirt.

"Your Honour, ladies and gentlemen of the jury, the decision to be made by you within these hallowed walls is of historic importance. Beyond your deliberations there are life changing laws that await your judgement. Given the magnitude of their egregious crimes, I implore you to convict these men, and, on behalf of female-kind say, ENOUGH."

The distinguished, horse-haired King's Counsel, whilst senior in years, carried a youthful demeanour. Theatrically energetic in gesticulation and commandingly eloquent in delivery, he held the famed court one at his every suspense filled pause. From the Kray twins to Brady and Hindley, to Peter Sutcliffe, its notoriety held morbid fascination, cultivating an unnerving atmosphere.

"ENOUGH of the degradation. And it has always been that, at its root. From the belittling everyday remarks, where generation and gender stand diametrically at odds. Many remaining ignorant of their societally unacceptable behaviours and the damage they cause."

Both benches sat in stony silence behind him with eyes to the front, save for one clerk who remained scanning the jurors faces intently. It appeared juror number nine, Mrs Bateman, was dozing again as she had been on multiple days. Junior barrister Bella Maxwell slid a note to her senior with an ear-whispered word that was met with a dismissive shake of the head.

"The kernel planted in homes now germinates our streets, where a sickening misogyny abounds unfettered, pandemic-like. From construction sites and offices, to places of recreation, our pubs and clubs, to gymnasia and openspaces. Public transport remains riddled, where deviants lurk in great numbers," he said, before sipping from his glass.

In the dock, three men of widely differing appearance but with faces matched in scornful, dismissive expression. Two wore ill-fitting dark suits, with necktie knots that had strayed far from their collar.

Suitless, the muscular thick-set, shaven headed Roman Darcy, released his familiar mocking smirk, chortling behind it. Wide-necked, his head was the shape of a big toe, with a single crease running the length of his forehead. A celebrity DJ and leading aficionado in electro-house and trance, with a fanbase of millions across Europe. He had the build of a Bison with shoulders that tested the tailoring of his shirt.

"It is time to reclaim our streets, to rid ourselves of this vermin!" he said, staring at the dock. Half-turned back to the Jury's pews, he wagged a stubby finger in the direction of the three men. "And of this, new breed, trolling the internet highway. This coercive, controlling strain, a hybrid sewer rat, spawned from our broken society," he added, glancing at the public gallery.

He flapped to unfold a crisp white handkerchief from his breast pocket, dabbing it daintily at his temples. The late afternoon swelter was intense; the air conditioning had failed some days earlier. Compounding matters three of the eight free-standing fans had been removed given their incessant rattling and Mrs Bateman being unable to hear the witness evidence.

Finger-jabbing at the accused, he blasted. "These are truly the worst of our species, shameful, men-of-our-time. Societal defects, allowed to prosper and flourish by our nonchalant acceptance of them. Shrugged off as, boys will be boys!"

The eyes of the courtroom simultaneously travelled to the dock where the men shuffled uneasily, momentarily detached from defiance by the wave of ill-feeling cast upon them. The weaselly dark haired man with deep-set furtive eyes, twisted, eyeing the wall of faces behind him. His pitted cheeks glistened under a sweaty film. Pierre Lebouf, billionaire financier, a monetary manipulator and hedge fund fixer. His cufflinks glinted as he pinched to straighten his collar.

Despite custody officer's behind each of them, the three had sat throughout, wide legged and indifferent, contemptuous. The powerfully built Roman Darcy crossed his chunky arms, furrowing the crease in his baldness with an incisor-flashing, lion-like snarl at the barrister.

"Three men; the banker, the DJ and the sportsman. The money, the means and the wherewithal; a financial facilitator, a global influencer and billionaire footballer. Dubbed the TikTokTrio, a triangle of evil guilty of the abduction and sexual exploitation of women."

Outside, protest groups Reclaim the Streets, MeToo, and TimesUp were all active, their chants now audible inside the courtroom. Brilliant sharp rays pierced the elongated windows that ran the wall, high above the Judge's bench. Despairing of the dizzying swelter, many relentlessly fanned their faces, wafting the claggy air.

"Teenagers, trafficked to a remote island, dehumanised by men whose barbarity knew no bounds in the massacre of these girls." Counsel turned with hardening face, directing a chubby finger at the dock.

"Their mutilated bodies found strewn across a private island," he said with an arm arching his back bench team. Bella Maxwell swivelled in her chair, casting narrowing glare at the odious men.

"The only three survivors, so frantic in their plight, that they would throw themselves down a disused well. Barely surviving the fall, to lay hidden, buried among the rotting corpses of fellow victims," he said with the sorrowful eyes of a Basset Hound.

"And of the three, Tamara sustained a catastrophic brain injury in the fall, and Jasmine remains with psychogenic mutism as a result of her trauma." Staring emptily at the Jury he added, "Sadly, neither were able to tell us their story."

"But from Marcie Stone you have heard, a first-hand account of a ruthless regime of trafficking, sexual exploitation, and of cold-blooded murder. Marcie's powerful testimony sits beyond challenge, in evidence of these women's tortuous imprisonment."

Bella Maxwell had met frequently with Marcie Stone, the only survivor able to recount the horrors of the women's enslavement on the tropical isle. Bella had devoted the last year of her life to the case, befriending families of these once confident, spirited young women. She cemented a deep personal attachment as vicarious-witness to their harrowing demise.

"I call upon you the Jury, to say Enough! To speak as one, that we will no longer tolerate them, or their ilk. On behalf of your wives and mothers, sisters and daughters, I implore you; let us cleanse ourselves of this scourge of evil."

Counsel turned, clearing his throat under a hand-cupped cough and lifting his near empty water to his lips. A refreshed jug was swiftly passed forward by Bella. He nodded his gratitude at the young lawyer, as he wiped his sticky palm down his black robe whilst folding it back. He rested a knuckle-tucked hand on his hip, flashing pinstripe waistcoat and sparkling gold-linked watch chain.

"But more than that.," he continued, glancing up at the Judge who sat with elbows spiking his desk and chin resting on his fingertips returning an impatient grin.

"More than anything, we ask that you deliver the right verdict in memory of those lives lost, and for the survivors, who remain mentally fractured, psychologically crippled by their trauma."

Bella tugged at a yellow-tagged bundle from a stack of psychiatric reports, opening the summary. She peeled and passed a single page to the front bench before fixing her gaze back on the jurors. Old Mrs Bateman remained slumped against the side on the top pew, head-lolling as her drowsiness deepened. 'Unfit to serve at seventy five,' was the view of the prosecution. But the Judge, 'to balance demographics,' had sided with the defence.

"For those killed at the hands of these monsters, I say their names should never be forgotten.." He voiced each with a growing passion, extending the pause between names, he narrated with the sincerity of loss.

Bella dabbed a finger below her eyelid and blew heavily. The families' tear-spoken impact statements remain embedded in minds as names echoed the walls, cutting chillingly through the silent courtroom. Leaning back hard in her seat, Bella cupped a hand to her mouth, bottom-lip biting. But resistance was futile, at each name she welled, before watering over at the next. Meandering trails weaved her powder-blushed cheeks.

Bella peered up at the dock, the middle of the three men instantly captured her glare. A smile tickled at the corners of his lips as he fleeted her a subtle wink. Tall and elegant, with chiselled features and advertiser's approved physique, he had been the British media's focus throughout the trial. The Premier League superstar with the world at his gifted feet; Jamal Jackson. Modelling deals had projected his fame to the global stage.

"And of the three who survived., each is described as irreparably broken, withered shadows of their former selves," the barrister paused, glugging from his glass. "..As empty vessels, gentle shattered soles, unable to function in this world, their minds hot-iron branded by the worst of humanity. They exist, marooned in anxiety, vacantly trudging the corridors of their support facilities."

The barrister re-acquainted his glass with its coaster, tore a reluctant post-it from its page and gazed mournfully at the Jury with his hands clasped high on his lapels.

"Hauntingly, one psychologist characterised the girls as being, 'those around which death has wrapped its cape, but neglected to fasten it.' They are, 'the tender dead.'"

The following morning the three men were discharged from court having been pronounced, despite all expectations, Not guilty. Released via a rear exit, they walked free to resume their lives.

CHAPTER THREE
PRESENT DAY — CHINA PANDA, EAST LONDON

Ceiling length halogens glared a brightness akin to strobe lighting but without pause from their gleam. The two plastic chairs in the far corner were taken, so Bella Maxwell remained standing at the service counter.

An angry fat-splattering sizzle crackled through from the door-wedged opening to the kitchen. A spicy-sweet aroma wafted into the waiting area.

The fake yucca's leaves were unmoved as the China Panda's door clattered open. A chilly breeze lassoed the space as a chubby balding guy in scruffy anorak stepped inside. Head down, seemingly avoiding eye-contact, he stood by the menus at the far end of the long counter.

"I wouldn't say no," a young voice whispered, turning to face the lad sitting next to him.

He poked his tongue hard into the side of his mouth, bulging his cheek. Repeating the motion as they shoulder-rocked their shared amusement.

Bella eyed them from the mirrored display cabinet sitting on top of the counter. It held some still grease-dripping battered fish and three cherry red sausages. The boys only looked late-teens, one with heavy acne wore a baseball cap pulled low.

The other, fresh faced kid slid his hands through gel-styled black hair, interlocking his fingers behind his head with elbows wide. He leaned back on the rear legs of his chair, looking Bella up and down, his eyes resting on her rear. Both sat with legs-splayed in casual trackware and sneakers.

"Two minutes please, Miss Maxwell," a squat woman shouted from the kitchen doorway before noticing the new customer. She shuffled over and took his order before disappearing into the back of the shop.

"I'd slip 'er one," the capped boy said, winking at his mate.

"You'd better join the queue pal," the dark haired guy responded, moistening his lips. Returning his seat to the floor he smirked up at Bella, who remained with her back to them. He rubbed his hands rapidly up and down his thighs. "She can park it right here!" he said, a little louder now.

The motion prompted a burst of laughter from his excitable friend as Bella tightened the strap of her handbag, taut to her shoulder.

"How much you charging, luv?" he shouted over, instantly changing the atmosphere.

Slipping her hand into the waist pocket of her jacket Bella eased apart the velcro strip inside and clasped the smooth hilt of a flick knife, placing her thumb gently over its release button.

"I said.. How much, bitch?" he snarled.

Bella glanced over at the anoraked man and nodded, flashing him a knowing smile. He looked uncomfortable, dropping his face to the floor and turning away to fidget with a pile of magazines.

"Fink she's playin' hard to get, Milo," the boy in the baseball cap scoffed.

The eye-probe camera fixed above the door to the kitchen was directed at the entrance to the takeaway and covered the service area. Bella peered over the counter, checking the picture on the box-screen; the men seated in the far corner were out of shot.

"Muggin you right off mate!" cap-boy teased, sporting a gormless grin.

Bella peered into the glass cabinet, noticing the distinctive shape of steel in their trackies, she released her grip on the knife. Pinching her fingers along the velcro, she re-sealed the blade into its hidden pocket.

"The bitch, fuckin betta not be!" he barked, spittle firing towards the back of Bella's head.

Bella rolled her shoulders slowly, feeling a little light headed as a now familiar warming wave flooded her. A building surge of blood rushed to her head, burning behind the eyes. She turned to face them, leaning back on the counter, laying her arms along it.

"Think she's up for it Milo," cap-boy said, tilting his peak. "Nice pair on it too."

Bella blew heavily through flaring nostrils, fixing a loathing glare at them. The two smirked, the bolder lad head-cocking with pursed lips in mocking kiss. She clattered her heel hard into the metallic walled counter behind her, pushing off it.

"Dear, oh dear, here we go again!" she muttered, headshaking. "Yet more walking wet dreamers, another couple of *BC's* from the underbelly."

"Wad de fuk, you say!" the greasy-haired boy squealed. Both sat with jaws dropped, confused by the insulting volley. "B, C, fukin wat?" the other spluttered with a rooster-like head jerk.

"*Brainless, Cretins*; you two, lowlife losers," Bella declared calmly, peeking at anorak man. He seemed to be enjoying the show; an excitable grin lit his plump face. "Same old story of school-skipping, respectless, sexist morons!" she added, her features darkening in scowl.

"Mindya mouf bitch.."

"What., I'm not speaking the language of zombie-tranced teens with a head full of fantasy-porn?" Bella hissed, glaring a venom beneath hooded eyes that flitted between them. "Yep, I've seen your sort before; goggle-eyed fantasists fresh from your *kill-em-quick* games!"

The men eyed each other, stiffening in their seats. "We're warnin' ya.."

"Except you're not dead., and you keep seeping out. You're like a plague!" loathing fired from her every word.

"You fuckin' what!" the dark haired guy snapped, finger jabbing up at her. "I ain't havin' that.."

"*Shut the hell up.,* Milo!" she shrieked, in a powerful surge of unpredictable rage that boomed back off the tiled walls. Her wrinkling nose met capillary shot eyes, firing revulsion at what slouched before her. "And what have we got this time.. *The Tweenies!*" she blurted, spluttering her hatred into their faces.

The guy mouthed expletives at his mate, pissed that she knew his name.

"You've had your say, and guess what.. I've heard it all before. It's as boring as you two juvenile delinquents, spouting your testosterone-fuelled threats," Bella shook her white-knuckled fist in the air, "Jesus Christ, give me strength!"

"Order for Miss Maxwell please," came a small voice from the entrance to the kitchen, with a bubbling crackle behind it.

"Just pop it on the counter, please," Bella replied over her shoulder.

The dark haired guy slid his hand to the pocket of his joggers, easing a flash of silver from them as he lurched to his feet. "Yoos wan suma this dooya, bitch..."

"*Sit down Milo!*" Bella ordered, whilst burying her foot deep in his crotch.

Milo screamed, stumbling backwards and clattering into his chair that collapsed with him to the linoleum. He lay curled squealing in agony, cupping his groin and panting hard at the air. His light grey trackies were rapidly red-spotting.

"Now, I know your name and I know where you live," Bella said, in hushed tone.

Returning to the counter, Bella peeled a napkin from the pile, bending to carefully wipe her blade-edged stiletto. She strode back over to the boy who remained in foetal position with eyes tearing.

"Start showing some respect boys, or I'll be back," she said, pointing at cap-boy. "I might lose my temper, next time!"

He rocked back, rearing his chair legs and flashing his palms.

Increasingly large burgundy pools were merging around Milo's crotch as he lay in painstriken, staring desperately at his blood glistening hand. The razorblades protruding from the rim of Bella's stiletto had slashed easily his fleshy thighs before severing the tip of his penis.

The lady behind the counter and a cleaver-in-hand chef stood with mouths ajar as Bella scooped her takeaway bag by the handles whilst apologising for the bad language. Throwing a headshaking tut at anorak-man, she strolled out.

The cool breeze of the city street was refreshing as Bella stepped from the curb with an arm aloft. She hailed down a yellow lit taxi cab and jumped in.

CHAPTER FOUR
CHEVELEY ESTATE, EAST LONDON

The crumbling Cheveley estate had wrap-around scaffolding to its north, south and east towers, where snail-paced cladding works continued, years after they were due to be finished. The site comprised four thirty-storey blocks that had been erected in the 1960's. Dilapidated by time and lack of investment, many of its tenants remained forever in ill health from their damp and mould.

Tom Broad wasn't the tallest of policemen and was struggling to see what was so interesting to the team, who were peering over the closeboard fencing into the storage area. With fingers curling the fence, he bounced up and down Tigger-like, before embarrassed by the sniggering of his officers.

"Can one of you get that bloody gate open, with or without a key!" Tom barked, behind a darkening grimace.

"I think there's a footstool in the car boss!" DI Neil Turvey jibed, to the chortle of the officer next to him. Turvs, the high pitched scouser was always first with a quip.

"Yes thank you Turvs, I don't think this is the occasion for your childish jokes," Tom retorted with head-cocked. "Save it for your wedding!"

"He's only pissed 'cause I found out about his other job," Neil whispered to the group. "Yeah.., he's got a part time job standing on wedding cakes!"

The coppers' burst of laughter was cut in two as DCI Tom Broad's tone changed sharply.

"That's enough Neil. We've got a crowd of onlookers building by the minute and the media over there, zooming in." Tom jabbed a finger toward the slither of open space behind them.

A taxicab, with engine whirring, had slowed to a crawl with its passenger rubber-necking the scene.

"Now get me access to this storage unit, whilst I speak to the press," he ordered.

Above them, the freshly re-clad west tower stood proud, in stark contrast to the deteriorating trio of blocks around it; a rose amongst thorns. Extensive repairs had been effected to its top floor flats and communal areas. Even the lifts now shone silvery bright, graffiti-less and more importantly, they worked.

Tyrone Saunders lived on the fifth floor of the refurbished block, and had been walking his dog across the estate when he discovered the body part. DI Neil Turvey accompanied by his junior attended his flat, fist-thumping the doorbell-less door.

"Fuckin 'ell," Tyrone complained loudly as he approached and turned the latch. "It ain't me that done it guv!" he added.

Having been kicked from its hinges and reattached numerous times, the ill-fitting hollow front door rattled noisily against its frame. Tyrone swung it wide, and stood with belly sagging beneath his holey-tee, frowning at the coppers in front of him.

"Yeah sorry sir, bit heavy handed with the knocking there," Neil replied with a cheek lifted grin, not wanting to get off on the wrong foot. "I understand that you're the chap who found the body, sir. Do you mind if we come in and take a statement?"

"Cock and balls!" Tyrone announced with a gormless grin.

"Sir?" Neil quizzed.

"It was only his dick and bollocks that we found, innit. That's why I've been saying it's 'cock and balls' to everyone," he said, smirking at the officers. "You know, like a cock and ball story!" he added, before releasing a broken, Boycie-like cackle. "Got 'em wiv it again, Mand," he shouted through an open door behind him.

The officers shuffled into the flat where they met Tyrone's other half, Mandy, who was strewn across a small sofa, with knees hooking its armrest. She smirked up at them before lumbered to her feet and offering them a cuppa. She disappeared momentarily, before returning with two chipped mugs of very weak tea.

Tyrone had explained that 'Fury,' their terrier, named after the boxer, had been 'playing up,' and wouldn't come out from the ditch behind the disused park. When Ty finally managed to drag him out, he saw that the mutt had a penis and testes, hanging from its slavering jaw.

"Looked like he was gonna eat it! All covered in blood and everything it waz!" Tyrone said.

"No ID on it, but he'll be a big fella!" added Mandy, with a wheezy titter. Tyrone's head rocked back, in a nasal snigger.

Neil's colleague took down a statement from Tyrone, whilst he got some background about the Cheveley estate from Mandy. She mentioned some of the estate's problem residents; names that were already known to the Met, for drug and knife crime.

From police records the estate had been almost crime free over the last six months, save for two minors for drunk and disorderly offences. Mandy revealed that local dealers had left the area a while back, and it had been peaceful ever since then. Tyrone advised that the drug gang had been forcibly removed from their top-floor flat, from where they had operated.

"Dead quiet up there now," he said, pointing at the ceiling. "Not like us poor sodz down 'ere. We still got fuckin reggae blastin' fru the walls every night!" he added, at an increasing volume at the wall.

Tyrone told the officers that it was only, 'old misses B' up there now, and she'd got a 'knock-fru' on the back of it.

"Livin' in luxury now, Bernie is," Mandy said, with a toothy smile.

Tyrone explained that the top-floor flat belonged to an elderly resident, Bernadette Bateman. It had been extended into the properties on either side of it. They had all been told that it was, 'council approved,' to compensate for the seventy-five year old having to live so high up. It was also on account of her, 'disabilities'.

"She might need wheelchair access, grab rails and all that stuff," Mandy interrupted.

The pair confirmed that Mrs Bateman would have had a better view over the gully from up there, of where the 'cock n balls, waz found'. They advised that she'd be at bingo tonight as usual, but that the cops should definitely speak to her.

After enduring further jokes, including an offer to join the couple for 'sausage and meatballs,' the officers left to join the rest of the team on the ground. The entire estate had now been taped off and floodlighting erected alongside a humming generator. White sheeted tents had been pitched above a narrow shingle pathway that sloped away from the open green space at the foot of the west tower.

A police search team had been deployed, and were engaged in the fingertip exploration of an area inside the broken fenced play park. Three of them were on all fours, their attention focused on a patch of asphalt beneath the frame of two swingless swings.

CHAPTER FIVE

Confrontation was exhausting, and it seemed to be happening all the time now. Attention that, in its infancy, had seemed harmless and flattering, was clearly perverted and sinister. Being slight in figure had accentuated her curves from an early age, increasing unwanted male scrutiny. It had been the one thing Bella longed to be rid of.

"Marylebone Heights please. Could you possibly go via the Cheveley estate?" she asked politely.

With petite, delicate features Bella exuded a natural, effortless beauty; she was stunningly attractive. Her wide heart-lipped smile lit a youthful exuberance that beamed from her sparkling blue eyes.

"Can do, but it's a longer route, luv," chirped the driver, with beady eyes peering back from his rearview mirror.

Her aesthetically appealing features had become something of a curse. At times she had wished she'd been born of plainer look; it had to be easier than this, daily torment. The Silverback at London Zoo got more of a break.

"Yes, that's fine. I don't mind thank you," Bella replied, easing back in her seat and releasing a breathy puff.

From her first day working in the city, and the incident at the building site, Bella's life had become a battle. From the flippant, demeaning remarks to the openly sexist, humiliating commentary, excused away as, 'banter.'

To the uncomfortable 'followed' feelings she often had, to the very real groping and endless body brushing Bella experienced as she journeyed across the capital. The packed tube train harassment was relentless, where many would grabble; as if checking ripeness. And more recently this, the verbally aggressive men, threatening physical confrontation; even when picking up a takeaway! Bella's patience was exhausted.

"Tough day, sweetie?" came another chatty-eyed glare from the mirror.

"Yeah, you could say that," Bella replied, hoping he was just being friendly, a nice guy. She'd ignore the patronising, 'sweetie' jibe.

His eyes remained on her a little longer than comfortable. '*Look at the road, not at me,*' she transmitted behind a cold smile.

Wearing less make-up, and eventually none at all, hadn't changed a thing. Altering her wardrobe from mini, to long skirts, from spaghetti straps and halter necks, to long-sleeved tops and jumpers, and latterly wearing suit trousers and jackets. From her much loved boots and heels, to flats and trainers. The waist hugging coats, replaced by those that skimmed her calves or ankles. But none of it had made a difference; the lecherous harassment was incessant.

"Not a great night for those heels, darlin," he thin-lipped smiled, as he adjusted his mirror toward the back seatwell.

She met his gaze with a sarcastic grin. '*What the hell - he knows what shoes I have on!*'

Bella aired the comment, letting a tense silence fill the juddering taxi. On the carpet of the cab she surreptitiously cleaned the razorblades embedded into the sole of her shoe. Wiping specks of blood from the shiny strips of blade that jutted either side of the toe. She glared head-on, staring-off yet another furtive glance, deflecting it back on the traffic.

"They-err, 'ad a bit of bover over the Cheveley estate earlier," he said, reading her coldness and changing the subject. "Old bills still got it cordoned off," he added as they approached the neighbourhood.

Bella shuffled to the edge of her seat, peering out of the window. Small groups had gathered on the open space. Scampering shadows of children flitted between them in the fading light. The cab shuddered slowly along the road that ran parallel to the westerly block of flats. It stood proud of its shabby, scaffold-clad neighbouring towers.

"Have they said if they've found anything yet?" Bella blurted, a little too enthusiastically.

"A cabbie mate of mine said body parts," he replied, with widening eyes in the mirror.

Bella stared out at a shadowy area of playground, beyond which the west tower was brightly lit. The nearby side road was clogged with media vehicles. Blue lights flashed intermittently across the entire scene, illuminating a soft play area in the foreground. An asphalt pathway led off it, running alongside a shallow gully beyond.

"Could you slow down a bit please!" she said, without thinking how that sounded.

"What..? You some sort of grief tourist or summat."

"No, no. ...it's just a-er, a friend of mine. She's a journalist, and might be covering the story," she stammered. "Thought I might just-er say hi," she bumbled to explain.

He smirked as he slowed to a crawl, inching-on alongside a gaggle of chattering girls as they meandered past his window.

"You want me to stop?" he said as the taxi trundled on.

"No-no. Thanks, that's fine, I can't see her car. Please drive on," she said apologetically, as she sat back from the window.

The cab whirred noisily as it sped from its crawling of the curbside. Bella sat crossed legged with head down, swiping at the phone in her lap, hoping that the conversation between them was over. She tried to distract herself from the unnerving feeling of another dark-eyed stare. The uncomfortable silence had returned.

Seconds later his mirror-filling glare was back as he chirped, "You off to see your boyfriend?"

Bella ignored him, keeping her face in her mobile.

"The Chinese takeaway bag!" he sought to explain. "Looks like it's for more than one. Nearly full I'd say," he chortled. "And it don't look like you're a big eater, luv, not with that figure; am I right?" he winked. "Not a lot gets past me, sweetie."

"Sorry. Work stuff," Bella replied, waggling her mobile at the cab's screen. "Emails, emails, you know," she sighed.

"Luckily, I don't," he said. "What is it you do? Something professional I'd wager.. Accountant, Lawyer.., or something in property," he probed, his slanty eyes widening a little.

"Sorry, but I really have to deal with this," she said, with a hint of impatience.

"Definitely right then, aint I. Emails, all dressed up and can afford taxis, rather than buses," he blurted, whilst cutting across traffic to make a hard left.

His narrow eyes fixed back on her, as the car straightened-up, unashamedly trawling her legs.

'*All dressed up*,' what the hell. Bella was struggling to hold her rising temper.

"Look I'm really sorry but I don't want a conversation with you. I just want a quiet taxi ride, which I will happily pay, *and* tip you for!" she said, with an open face.

"No need to get shirty about it! What is it, time of the month?"

"Pull over, you fucking arsehole," she snapped.

"What, you can't take a joke."

"I said, pull the fuck over. Now!"

"You feminists are all the same - wound too fuckin' tight!"

The cab swerved into the curbside, with a squeal of brakes.

"You're out of a job in the morning, dickhead," she announced, whilst taking a photo of the driver's ID card that was fixed to the cabs perspex screen.

He half turned, putting his arm across the front seat's backrest. "For what..! Chattin' to a customer, cracking a joke," he scoffed. "All the best wiv that luv!"

She could see him now; thinning grey hair that draped his shoulders, meeting a webbed tattoo scrawling his scraggy neck. Studded earrings and a gold neck chain, insufficient to detract from the spirograph of lines that filled his weather beaten face.

"From the casual sexism and misogyny, and now the unveiling of the chauvinist. You're a dinosaur, and I'll see to it that you're made extinct," she shot back at him.

"Pay up and get out of my cab, you mouthy slag," he ordered, yanking the handbrake hard.

"You're an insidious sex pest, that's barely hiding paedophile tendencies, for the full predatory set. I'd better add that to my complaint," Bella declared matter-of-factly, as she jumped out of the taxi.

"Don't you fuckin-well dare. I ain't 'avin that!" he said, pointing angrily at her.

"By the way I'm in the legal profession, if you must know," she said, slamming the door behind her. "So rest assured, you won't be working again after this," she added, as she strode away.

He fumbled in haste with his door handle before stepping out of the cab.

"Oi! That's £17.50 you owe me. Get back 'ere, you little bitch," he bellowed, at the back of his fast disappearing fare.

CHAPTER SIX

Carl Turner stepped from the shower, towel rubbed his helter skelter hair and peered into the bathroom's single mirror tile. His blonde locks flopped Alpaca-like, curtain-parting his face. He palm-wiped the steam filling tile, suddenly clutching his chest.

"Jezz, don't do that.. you're like a silent assassin!" he said, head shaking. She was there, in the reflection. He puffed into the fast re-steaming tile, "Wow, love the new haircut," Carl said, dropping his towel. He turned to admire his stunning girlfriend. "Are you sure you're not with the SAS, you're so bloody sneaky!"

"Babe, I can be whatever you want me to be," she said, running her hands down his back and settling on his pert buttocks. Definitely his best feature. "Aww.., you don't look ready for me!" she teased, her eyes rolling down his stomach.

Bella wiggled out of her skirt, letting it fall to the bathrug. Carl eased the curls of her bob from her face, tucking them behind her gold studded ears and tilted her head, gently kissing her full lips.

"God you smell so good, I could eat you," Carl whispered in her ear, feeling a twitching of his penis. "But I did think we might have that Chinese you promised me first. I'm starving!" he winked.

"Oh, yeah, about that.. There's some bad news, I'm afraid," Bella said, her eyes widening. "I left it in the back of the taxi coming over here," she explained in a doe-eyed apology.

Carl interlocked his fingers with Bella's and walked her into the bedroom, sitting her on his small divan. She kicked off her shoes whilst peeling her top.

"Well, that's kinda decided then," he announced, cupping her cheeks in his huge hands. He kissed her softly with a sweet tenderness that made her melt. "It's you, for starters, main and dessert, my gorgeous girl."

Parting her lips a little, they kissed as they lay down on the bed, his cock stiffening quickly. Bella rolled on top of him, her nakedness brushing his arousal as she straddled him, her toned legs clamping his. His fingers fondled the fullness of her breasts, slipped around her hips, squeezing her silken buttocks as she slid his throbbing manhood inside her.

The sex was average and over in a moment, as it always was. Her scent, her warmth, her smooth shapely body caressing his was overwhelming. Her sweet plump lips and soft welcoming tongue was often all that it took. Bella was beautiful, and Carl felt lucky to be with her. It was fair to say that in looks, he was boxing well above his weight.

But Bella was happiest when with Carl, her loveable, easygoing lump of a man. Carl was no Adonis, but he was her very own superhero who had saved her on the first day they met.

Carl Turner had worked for the council for a little over five years, having joined straight from school, initially as a bin man, or 'waste controller' as he liked to call himself. Leaving an inner city school with just one qualification meant that he had to take various courses to gain promotions, or achieve departmental transfers. But he had climbed the ladder quickly, becoming a hugely likeable team-player.

Carl left the flat to pick up dinner from a local fast food outlet. Whilst he was gone Bella returned the keys from the Cheveley estate that she had taken from him, link-chaining them back onto the bundle dangling from Carl's rucksack. She slid his staff pass and inspection docket booklet into the front zipped pocket.

"Gotcha a strawberry milkshake, Bel," Carl declared as he clattered back through the front door.

He passed her a small cheeseburger and a cone of fries, with a lip-kiss, before settling alongside her on the battered two-seater sofa.

"And..err, drumroll..," he declared, digging in his back pocket. "I've got us tickets to Miss Saigon, for the day you get back."

"Oh wow, that's fantastic! I don't deserve you," Bella sighed, laying her head on his chest.

"Hey, I know, I know. What can I say," he said, shoulder shrugging. "Now let's eat; we gotta feed you up before your flight tomorrow. That airline food is rank."

Carl jabbed at the tv remote before burying his face into a burger that oozed its fillings, slapping to the crispy wrapping on his lap. Bella picked at her fries dabbling them delicately into a small pot of sauce.

"I remember how much you loved it the last time at the Garrison," he added between mouthfuls. "Not sure I can get backstage this time, but I'll try. Council 'VIP' privilege and all," he added, with a wink.

"You're the best babe. I'd love that," Bella beamed as she took the remote, switching channels to BBC news.

Carl had journeyed from garbage collection, to building site inspection, and currently, estate management. He often received invitations from local businesses that the council had worked in partnership with. The Garrison Theatre was one such enterprise that they had saved from permanent closure, following the pandemic.

Bella had met Carl in the first week of her new job at Diamond Law Chambers, Lincoln's Inn. Having suffered an increasing torrent of verbal abuse from the construction site workers that she passed each day, Bella had decided that enough was enough. She took matters into her own hands.

It started on Monday, when some indiscriminate shouts mixed with a chorus of ear piercing 'wolf-whistles'. They were swiftly joined by some vile, sexually suggestive hollers and raucous mocking laughter. Bella reddened, tugging hard at the hem of her skirt, and quickened her step to shorten her rising discomfort.

But Tuesday was so much worse; they were waiting for her. Many more yellow-vested, hard-hatted oglers lined the scaffolded platforms. They bellowed down their lewd suggestions with matchingly crude gesticulation. The sexual references were now far more explicit, and increasingly vulgar. Each workman seemingly daring the next to go further. Their abusive chants filled the building site's wide entrance.

Bella strode on defiantly with face to the opposite side of the street, until she heard a slur that included the word, rape. Bella stood and turned to face them, her humiliation instantly replaced by a burning desire to put a stop to this unjust barrage of foul-mouthed obscenity.

Bella marched toward the front gate area and a red striped vehicle barrier. "I want to see the site manager," she demanded, to a thickset shaven headed man, who was standing inside an upright coffin sized box.

"Do you now sweetheart, and who is it that wants to see him?" he replied, head-cocked.

He glanced, beaming up at his workmates, who increased the volume of their blunt, suggestive chants. Now neanderthal-like in their grunting.

"I f-fucking well do!" Bella spluttered, furious at the gatekeeper's indifference to the abuse being shouted down at her.

His chalky face grinned dismissively at her in an arrogant, self-satisfied mocking smirk.

"Now then luv, there's no need for bad language," he said, shaking his head slowly. "Have you got an appointment," he added loudly, engaging his co-workers.

"Are you hearing this!" she yelled, pointing a finger at the second floor platform that was still filling and rocking slightly.

He picked up a clipboard from a narrow shelf behind him in his box, tapping a biro against it as he stepped from the booth.

"Well if your name's not down here, then you ain't seeing no-one, darlin'!" he announced, now playing to the gallery. "I'm afraid I'll have to escort you from the premises," he added, wrapping his tattooed forearm around her waist.

"Get the fuck off me!" Bella screamed.

As she twisted from him, he slid his hand down over her skirt. Roars of approval rose to the man's lewd action, in a colosseum-like atmosphere.

Stumbling to get away, Bella's ankle buckled to the ground as her heel gave way on the rubble-ridden surface. Cheers erupted as she half-fell to the floor, one hand saving her from a gravelly landing. Teary and in pain, Bella hobbled with broken stiletto in hand from the site with the jeering hoard filling her ears.

The next day, Wednesday, would be different.

CHAPTER SEVEN
SCOTLAND YARD

"So, behind the bin storage area, we have the decapitated body of Jamal Jackson, initially identified from documents on his person." Tom Broad opened to the slowly hushing briefing room. "The lab has since verified that tissue samples taken from his remains confirm a DNA match."

"Not only was Jackson decapitated, but he had also been castrated. Cheveley residents reported finding his penis, in the gully area, here," he said, directing his laser pointer at a blown-up google earth image of the estate.

"Must've been hard for them, guv!" DI Neil Turvey said, with his familiar quick scouse wit.

"Yes ok Neil, let's not start with this, shall we.," Tom said, through some tittering. "This was a savage killing that was very personal in nature. He was targeted by someone who knew him."

"Balls, sir!" Neil interjected, whilst grinning across the room. "Don't forget the balls."

"Yes, thank you Turvs; Mr Jackson's penis *and testes* were found together! Now, a little focus if you will," Tom said sharply.

"The body was hidden here, behind these locked gates," he redirected the laser pod light to a rectangular fenced area with large containers inside. "Now, who would have access keys?" He looked across the faces of his colleagues.

"You mean besides every resident on the estate, guv!" Neil replied, with more than a hint of sarcasm. He had a grin that filled his cheeks.

"Yes, besides *some* resident's, thank you Neil. Please bear in mind it is only tennant's of the West Tower who had access; it was their garbage store," Tom said.

"That keeps it to just the hundred-odd suspects then boss!" Neil quipped, glancing around the room for shared smirks. There were none.

"Sixty one!" Tom barked back. "There are only sixty one occupied flats on the west wing; a number remain vacant on the upper floors and five bottom floor apartments are undergoing refurbishment. And the top floor has, rather oddly, only one resident! A misses..,"

"Mrs Bateman boss, she has a 'knock-thru' apartment on account of her age and disabilities! Apparently," Neil helpfully, interrupted.

"Yes, Mrs Bateman. Thank you Neil, good work," Tom nodded at his number two, pleased to see him now fully engaged.

"So, sixty one doors to knock-on. Six of you first thing in the morning; usual probe please. Their last access, who has use of their key and anything unusual they might have noticed in the vicinity in the last twenty four hours. Neil, allocate that would you please."

"Will do boss. Should we establish other, outside access?" Neil said, enthusiastically. "Maybe landlords, maintenance contractors, or on-site security."

"Landlords yes, but workmen wouldn't have needed access to the bin storage unit, and there isn't any security on the entire estate. So just landlord's please guys," Tom instructed.

"What about council employees, for refuse collection, guv?" Neil added whilst scribbling in his pocket book. "They must have a key."

"Yes, good point Neil. Check with the local authority and find out when the bins were last emptied and who has access."

"They were overflowing when we looked over the fence. Not sure if you noticed that boss," Neil said, beaming over at the crew that witnessed Tom Broad's toe-bouncing antics earlier that evening.

Tom furrowed his brow at the now tittering room. Neil was such a good copper, but a real pain in the arse. "Yes, ok thank you Neil; just check with the council."

"More importantly! We still need to find the victim's head, before someone else does. Search teams are booked to resume at first light and a quarter mile square has been cordoned off." Tom said. "This will no doubt be headline news; Jamal Jackson, nickname 'JJ' was a high profile footballer.."

"Not the best striker though, guv, southern softy really," Neil interrupted. "Good in the air, mind.., maybe that's why they took the head guv.."

"Neil!" Tom barked. "There's no place for that sort of comment."

Tom continued after a stern look silenced the room,

"So, this is a Premier League player, with no known connection to the Cheveley estate. You will see from the briefing pack that Jackson, along with two other men, were the subject of prosecution at the OB in the summer. There's almost certainly a link there, so I've added the trial Judge's summary to your packs to refresh memories. A little bedtime reading, please guys."

Tom winked at Neil, who was clutching the one inch manilla binder and shaking his head.

"Didn't they all get off, boss?" someone hollered from the back of the room.

"They did indeed! Much to the shock of all that followed their trial following the massacre of seventeen women. It's a horror story you'll be reading this evening. And everything is, as ever, *'for your eyes only'*. I need total discretion with this one please, guys," Tom stressed.

"Didn't the prosecution allege witness intimidation or something?" Neil said, frustrated by his only faint recollection of one of the biggest cases in recent times.

"'*Jury fixing*' was levelled but found to be unfounded, on investigation," Tom corrected him.

"What about the victims' families, they must be looking for revenge. Surely that's our angle here, boss?" Neil said.

"Very possibly Turvs, and that's why I've requested additional support from the Chief," Tom replied. "We may need to widen this out, with so many families wanting these men dead!"

"This could get complicated, guv!" Neil said.

"Yes, I'm sure it will," Tom replied, with arched eyebrows that matched his number two's.

CHAPTER EIGHT

JAKARTA, INDONESIA

The deafening engine whir was softened by the comforting breeze and brilliant crystal skies that welcomed Bella. Warm air engulfed her senses, as taught shoulders dropped at every breath of the balmy air.

Sliding her DKNY shades from her head, she strolled from the plane. A shimmering heat danced across the runway, distorted images hovering over the blistered tarmac. In both escaping England, and its shuddering cold, a warming calm now filled her.

The last few hours had been arduous; from the mistake of playing peek-a-boo with the small child sitting in the seat in front, who wouldn't accept it had an endpoint. To the ongoing arm-rest battle with the large American lady sat beside her, and the repeated turbulence alerts. Bella had barely slept in the last twenty four hours. The hum of crickets populating the bushes that hugged the terminal building was a welcoming, hypnotic sound.

With hand luggage only, Bella's journey to the Grand Plaza was swift. She might have dropped off in the taxi if it hadn't been for her recent experience. Thankfully there was nothing more than an initial gaze from the elderly driver, who had to be in his seventies. He switched without pause between chatting loudly with his controller and croaking along to country and western music. Despite her head lolling and eyelids folding, Bella was jerked back to life as his gravelly tone grated at the chorus, and she was deprived of a much needed cat-nap. The stunning, undulating landscape rolled by, boasting lush forest carpeting rising peaks to her left. Contrast with turquoise still seas skimming wide sandswept coastline to her right.

The huge marbled foyer of the deluxe hotel was refreshingly cool. A wide-eyed girl shuffled over, with an arched head-gesture at the shiny tray of sparkly drinks she was holding. Bella took a pithy orange one with a nod of gratitude as she flopped her carry-all to the floor and slumped onto a high-polished circular bench that rounded a number of thick-trunked cacti. She took in the opulence of the place; its decor, from gold-leaf trimmed ceilings to multi-teardrop chandeliers that hung high above a sweeping staircase. Beyond that, she could see a plantation-like display of large-leafed plants, dotted with vivid blooms, set in a white pebblestone bedding.

Bella sat yawn-stifling as she waited for the couple that were standing at the shiny reception desk to finally receive a keyfob, before stepping forward. It was tiring to stand up now, her body seemed to be aching all over; crying out in surrender.

Despite her polite 'thank you, I'm fine,' and dismissive hand waving, the little man in a crisp white shirt and tan chino shorts was insistent. Taking her bag and beckoning her to follow him. Thankfully he led her only a short way to a golf-cart type vehicle that was open at its sides. They whizzed along a narrow tarmac path whilst Bella adjusted to the hot leather seat at the back of the cart.

The three minute ride took in fabulous views across the hotel's private beachfront and mountainscape of an island beyond. Infinity pools appeared at every turn, with thick cushioned loungers and tree strung hammocks, sprawled around them. It seemed quiet, with only a handful of book-clutching couples braving the intense heat, albeit beneath huge white parasols.

"Villa 105 for you pleez, miss Maxewells," the little guy said excitedly.

He dug into his surprisingly deep pockets, before opening the ornate grooved wooden door with a key-card. Bella, planting some notes in his hand, lugged her bag inside and clunked the heavy door shut with a breathy sigh.

Dropping her bag to the shiny-tiled floor, she peeled off her damp tee, heel kicked away her white pumps and wriggled out of her ripped jeans. Slipping beneath the cool cream sheets of the super-king, Bella was asleep within a minute.

CHAPTER NINE

"Could you tell me the flat number, please?" the operator asked again.

"It ain't gotta number, it's jus' *top floor* - Mrs Bateman's place!" the caller replied impatiently.

"An ambulance is on its way now, if you could remain with her please."

"I told you, she ain't answering the door. We bin banging on for the last ten minutes!" the man stressed.

"I understand. I'm dispatching a police unit to assist," she advised. "Could you tell me a little more about how it happened please?"

"Alls we know is what we err'd. A scream from the ol girl, then a thud like she's collapsed or summut. Sounded like she took a table down wiv err!" he explained.

Two emergency service vehicles had been dispatched under blue lights to the top floor apartment of the West Tower of the Cheveley estate, following the reported incident involving a senior citizen. Emergency access to the property was sought, given the area was already held in lockdown due to the major incident earlier. Tom Broad's investigation team were procedurally alerted of the call to dispatch.

DI Neil Turvey jumped in the back of the squad car, behind two front seated officers. "Bagsy, I do the door!" he chirped, clasping the handle of the steel door-ram that lay alongside him.

Twelve minutes later they made their way to the top floor via the stairwell. Paint fumes clung to the officers' throats as they pounded each flight. As Neil bounded the open corridor, he glanced down at the recreation ground with a pathway cutting through it, to a gully beyond. To the left was the waste storage unit, where Jamal Jackson's butchered body had been discovered earlier that day. A middle aged unshaven man with deep sunken cheeks stood ahead of them.

"Stand clear now, please sir," Neil directed the guy who'd called it in, to step back.

The scruffy looking neighbour nodded his compliance, lumbering a couple of paces back from the doorway, as the three burly officers approached, with door breaker in hand.

"Proper fuckin door this one buddy. Not like our shit-wipes downstairs," the guy advised.

"Yes thank you, sir. You can return to your home now," Neil said.

"I'z been shoutin 'er fru the letterbox," he complained, disappointed by the officer's dismissive tone. "But I couldn't see owt fru there," he added.

"You've been most helpful sir, thank you," Neil said whilst adjusting his hold on the door-ram. "Now stand well back please."

Neil swung from shoulder to waist height, as the heavy tool smashed a huge hole above the handle, jutting the door partially clear of its frame. It held firm from collapse, whilst revealing a number of heavy linked chains behind it, refusing to break. On the second swing an inner panel splintered and the metal links *pinged*. Neil thrust his size twelve, steel-toed boot into the heart of the door, below its lion's-head door knocker.

Battered, it swung jerkily in submission; they were in.

CHAPTER TEN
INDONESIA

The blackness took a moment of adjustment. Disorientated, she fumbled a hand across the artex wall beside her. Above the bedside cabinet, her fingers slid over a smooth square with a number of raised switches. She clicks them all downward and yellow light flooded the room.

'Shit, what time is it?' Bella's squint shot to her wrist. She leapt from the bed. 'Fuck, fuck, fuckety-fuck!'

Bella clattered across the slatted shutters to stand like soldiers at horseguards parade, either side of the floor to ceiling patio doors. She peeled back the flimsy voile netting that fluttered, wafting in motion with the cooling breeze pumped from the large vented wall unit. A low moonlit sky lit the rattan furniture symmetrically placed on the terrace.

She scanned the expansive suite, hardly recognising the space from her arrival. A wood carved bowl, overflowing with an exotic looking array of fruit, sat on an elongated table. An oversized flat-screen floated on the peachy wall directly above it. A voluptuous two seater button-back sofa was set opposite. A matching cushioned desk chair with bureau-style desk sat neatly in a shallow recess in the far corner.

Bella bit into what she thought was a peach, or possibly mango, chin-cupping as it oozed its sweet flowing juices. Its flesh melted on her tongue, releasing a wetness that instantly quenched, flooding her sand-dry tongue. The artwork filling the walls had more than a hint of the hedonistic, amidst a mass of sensual bodyform imagery.

The bathroom was similarly lavish, with floor-to-ceiling tinted mirrors on two sides. Bella stepped into the rainforest themed wet area and showered quickly. Towel wrapped, she unpacked her few clothes and trouser-pressed her yellow maxi dress, whilst she worked the safe. Before leaving the room she tore a map from the inside of the welcome folder.

Bella stepped out to a chorus of crickets; long-legged in violin melody, a grass-trembling thrum. Paired with the all-enveloping warmth of the evening and soft sea breeze, the tropical soundtrack was intoxicating.

Bella's Gucci heels clicked rhythmically along the palm-lined pathway. Its spotlights illuminating the flower-filled borders between the trees and thick-bladed grass in the shadows beyond. She breathed it all in, enjoying the moment of tranquillity; casting aside, what she knew was to come.

The path climbed a little, curling off to the left away from the coastline which had come fleetingly into view. Over a brow it led onwards through an archway between villas, towards the hotel's main building and complex. Bella leaned down at the pool, trailing her fingertips. The water was warmer than the night and as soft as the breeze. She wanted to sit for a while at its edge, to dangle her legs; but time was pressing.

The pungent aroma of freshly grilled fish took the air as she approached. Lights dotted closer, as pathways converged. Bella dangled her fingers at a skinny-looking cat that appeared from nowhere. It purred, head-rubbing her hand. Ahead, faint chatter merged with the mellow sound of jazz, drifting to the star-filled sky.

It felt like heaven, and yet the devil was near.

CHAPTER 11

CHEVELEY ESTATE

It was nothing like any inner-city flat that the officer's had ever seen before.

"Hello, Mrs Bateman? ..Mrs Bateman, it's the police."

The hallway was three times as large for a start. It was square, with towering display cabinets on each side. Behind their tinted glass a vast collection of dolls stood, dressed in colourful costumes, each representative of a different country. China, India and Russia were amongst those occupying the top shelves, along with some brightly clothed African dolls. A Welsh one with dragon emblazoned tabard and a Scottish red headed doll with tartan skirt that took prominence in the left hand dresser opposite.

"Jeez., kinda spooky looking bunch!" Neil Turvey whispered.

A high-polished hardwood floor ran through to the open rooms on either side of the hall. With a nod in each direction from their superior, the two officers ventured through whilst Neil clasped the gold handled door in front of him.

"Hello, is anyone home?" he shouted. "It's the Police, Mrs Bateman. We're responding to a concerned neighbour.. Hello."

It led to an expansive, state of the art kitchen, the extraordinary Tardis-like size of which was baffling. A huge marble-slabbed island sprawled at its centre, dominant with a five ring hob built into its counter, and brushed steel extractor hanging above. Four leather upholstered, high backed stools were tucked neatly into its breakfast bar opposite.

Behind the central unit a double oven was set amidst an array of purple, sheen-finish cupboards with glass fronted display doors. A long-hosed silver tap curled, snake-like, high over a two bowled steel sink. To the farside was an American-style fridge-freezer. One of its chunky long handled silver doors was ajar.

It was implausible that such an expensive kitchen could be found here. Or anywhere outside of an extensively refurbished mansion house in the leafy suburbs of west London. Certainly not in this, a 1950's tower block, on the dilapidated Cheveley estate. The hallway's hefty furnishings aside, the weight of the kitchen's extensive appliances and marble fittings should be a concern for residents below.

In the open-plan space to the left, a huge low slung gaming chair was directed at a sizable gold framed screen on the wall. Voluptuous floor-to-ceiling red velvet curtains cloaked the back wall. Neil parted the drapes at their centre, revealing patio-style doors with a narrow balcony behind them. The door was locked.

It seemed odd as none of the blocks on the estate had balconies; they were designed not to have them. Neil took in London's nightscape. It was impressive, the financial district's square mile illuminated; peppered with white specks, with the blue-lit Shard beyond.

The oversized Smeg stood commandingly to one side of the Kitchen; like a general about to inspect his troops. The bulky door opposite the ice dispenser compartment hung open. As Neil stepped around the kitchen island towards it, the toe of his shoe caught heavily on something.

"Guys. Guys, kitchen please," Neil called out, with a calmness that surprised himself. He knelt over the frail, gaunt-looking Mrs Bateman, pinning two fingers to her wrist, that fell limp.

"Mrs Bateman. Mrs Bateman, can you hear me, my love. I'm with the police, my name is Neil." He repeated a little louder, "Can you hear me, Mrs Bateman?"

There was no response as he tried for a pulse under her jawline. He tossed a large saucepan out of his way and placed a finger below her nostrils. A shallow breath tickled its hairs.

"Can you chase up the paramedics for us?" he said to the officers as they entered the room.

Slightly taken aback by the space, it took a moment for the officers to actually locate Neil. One peered over the counter where he was kneeling alongside the elderly woman. He patted the radio on his shoulder, cocking his head as he side-mouthed a request into his inter-com. Whilst stressing urgency he strode to the far end, turning to admire the kitchen.

"Err, Guv,.. Guv?" the other officer said to Neil, who threw him a quizzical glance. "You might wanna take a look in the fridge!" he said, throwing an eye-nod toward the Smeg.

Neil laid the old lady's arm across her middle before he rose to his feet and stepped over her, and peered around the door of the fridge. The jagged, neck-hacked head of Jamal Jackson sat, wedged between shelves, gazing back at him. It sat on a blood coated glass shelf, below a rack of premium bottled beers.

His familiar coiffed hair and handsome high-cheeked features were unblemished, instantly recognisable from his footballing fame. But as if enraged from being stuck fast between the shelving, a burning rage seethed from bulging dark eyes that stared back at Neil. An anger frozen from his moment of death. The still blood-pumping veiny entrails from the crudely slashed throat flooded the shelf, dripping onto the 'thick n creamy' yoghurt cartons on the tray below.

"Ice cold finish from the striker., I'll give him that!" Neil said, eye rolling.

Ninety seconds later, the paramedics arrived and managed to revive the estate's eldest resident, before strapping her to sit upright on their stretcher. She was taken to Princess Margaret Hospital, where she was scheduled for immediate surgery.

Bernadette Bateman had broken her hip and wrist in the fall, and was treated for shock; she could barely speak upon arrival. Babbling incoherently, she struggled to remember her own name.

CHAPTER 12

36 HOURS EARLIER

The doddery pensioner looked up at the strapping guy, who was strolling in her direction. His thick thighs stretching his skinny bleached jeans and muscular frame oozing his white tee.

"Couldn't be a luv and help me with this, could you?" she said.

Jackson always parked his Lamborghini behind the maintenance office, and walked to the flat past the bin storage unit. He threw a cursory glance at the dishevelled, frail old woman hunched over the large black sack that lay at her feet.

"You're not Bernie's grandson are you.. the footballer?" she added quickly, seeing a wrinkle harden his brow. "Jamie.., is it?"

The old dear looked so weak, it was a wonder that she'd managed to drag the bulky refuse sack to the gate of the waste shed.

"Jamal.. Yeah, that's me. Not a problem.., any friend of Grans!" he said, beaming his trademark, blindingly handsome smile.

He grabbed the sack one-handed and eased the heavy wooden door open.

"You've done well to get it this far!" Jamal said.

"Thought I recognised you from the telly," she said, softly. "Your gran's always going on about you. You're a red, ain't you?"

"Footy fan are ya?" he said, marching toward the brown lids at the rear of the large storage area.

49

She wobbled jerkily as she followed him into the refuse unit, pushing the wooden door closed behind her and sliding its bolt into the barrel.

"Ooo yes, I certainly am. But bingo first, my luv," she said, smirking a crease-cracked grin.

"Ahh, of course, yes! Bingo night aint it," Jamal replied, realising the old woman must be one of his grandmother's many 'games-night' mates.

He finally found space under the fourth lid that he lifted and tossed the black sack inside. As he turned he almost bumped into the elderly lady, who was now standing right behind him. He instinctively raised his hands, wincing as a sharp piercing pain hit him as he stumbled to one side to stop himself falling onto her.

"S-sorry, I didn't see you there," Jamal blurted.

"Don't mind me, love. I heard you like grabbing defenceless women," she snarled.

Her voice was instantly different. Its crackly weakness was gone, now youthful and vibrant. It was hate-filled; aggressive with loathing. Jamal stared at the haggard looking woman, his face flickering with confusion.

She stepped back, her eyes fixing on his chest. His Levi's tee was darkering quickly, glistening at the gushing wound. It was deep, the steel had slid easily to its hilt.

From her shrivelled face he glanced down to her wrinkly hand, that clasped a thick bladed knife. It's steel sheened ruby red, dripping from its tip.

"You fuckin, old crow," he said, puffing hard.

He lurched forward as his left leg gave way. His hands clutched at his chest, as a breath-stealing agony merged with a limpness as he crashed fully to his knees. Bella stepped back swiftly, two, three, four steps, as he tumbled toward her.

Jamal's rib cage had been pierced, his inner organs punctured. A whiteness seeped his features as the rhythmic gushing pulse flowed between his gold ringed fingers that now clamped to his chest.

"Who the fuck,.. are you!" he demanded, between an air sucking wheeze, as he collapsed fully to the floor.

"I'm Bella Maxwell - your prosecutor, judge and jury," she said.

She strode toward him, as he lolled in the dirt, slipping her headscarf and grey wig from her head.

"And you will pay for your crimes, Jackson," she whispered, leaning over his half dirtied face.

"Wh-hat the f-fuck..," he blurted.

Hauling his chest from the ground, he swung an arm to grab her, but stronger, agile and surefooted, she kicked it hard away. Propping from his elbow, he looked up at her; the old hag was gone.

"You th-that - lawyer b-bitch - in-in court.." he said, smirking, as he panted between words.

"That's right! The jury might have made a mistake, but I won't. They should have convicted you and your scheming mates; they should have brought back the death penalty for you lot!" Bella snarled.

A wide smile filled Jackson's face as he chortled. A little blood spluttered from his mouth, reddening his gleaming white teeth.

"You lo-lost.. You fuckin lost, b-bitch!"

"You fixed it you mean. You think I don't know about the old lady, juror number nine. Bernadette Bateman; your fucking grandmother!" she said, matching his smile.

"Don't.. you.. dare…t-t-touch… her," he wheezed.

"You're gonna wish you had been jailed, because I'm gonna destroy you, like you destroyed those poor girls," she said, stepping over his flailing arm.

His hand grasped feebly at her ankle. The powerful, muscle clad premier league footballer, weakening by the second, his blood draining fast and with it, his life.

"I said ENOUGH," she said, into his whitening face.

Bella stabbed the blade into the side of his neck, plunging it deep into his throat. Blood spurted high as his eyes bulged in their sockets for an instant. Jackson lay slumped on the ground as a thick crimson tide gushed, darkening the asphalt. Like a volcano spewing lava, it relentlessly flowed, covering all around him.

Stepping back and unlocking the gate, Bella peered around it. It was quiet. As with her previous visits, there was no-one around at this time of day. Over the course of the next twenty minutes Bella set about the butchery of Jamal Jackson's body. Retrieving the black sack from the bin she took out a plastic jacket and cap, shoe coverings, goggles and mask.

From a selection of knives and hacksaw, she finished beheading him. She scythed easily through his neck. Juddering slightly in severing the windpipe, and sawing bone of his spinal cord, before the slashed removal of Jackson's penis and scrotum.

Adjusting and refixing her disguise Bella disappeared into the darkness, planting the body parts strategically around the Cheveley estate. She left

Jackson's partially flayed torso in a pool of blood, inside the bin storage area. Using her boyfriend's council issued keys, she padlocked the unit shut.

With the key that Bella found in Jamal Jackson's Armani jeans she accessed his grandmother, Bernadine Bateman's top floor flat. She knew that routine meant Bernie would be out at bingo and she had time to place her grandson's severed head in her fridge. A nice surprise for the old lady when fetching the milk for her malty bedtime drink.

Bella was awash with a deep sense of satisfaction at her work. The killing of Jamal Jackson had been so much more enjoyable, than the abduction of Pierre Lebouf. Despite the heinous nature of Jackson's murder, she had felt a pleasure, beyond anything that she had anticipated.

The removal of two individuals, representing the worst of humanity, could be no bad thing and was easily justifiable in Bella's mind. With Jackson dead and Lebouf now incapacitated, it left just the ringleader, Roman Darcy to be dealt with.

CHAPTER 13

PRESENT DAY – INDONESIA

The brightly-lit main bar was crowded, and most of the tables that arched around it were taken. Bella stood eye-sweeping the space before she went any further. She sensed a number of body scanning stares on her, despite the lecherous culprits being sat alongside their partners.

Stepping to a side wall she panned the lounge-bar area, from the drinks counter and waiter's service point, to the far-corner where bi-folding doors opened to a pool area. There he was, tucked away at the back, sitting at a two-seater green baize table. Her eyes rolled in relief as she weaved chairs towards him; she wasn't sure he would come.

"I knew you wouldn't let me down!" she lied, in appreciation of him being there.

Pascal glanced up furtively, eye-nodding up at her and offered his hand. Bella's face lit up as she took it, releasing her wide smile.

"You change!" Pascal said, in his comfortingly familiar gravelly voice.

Bella's usual wavy brunette locks had gone. Her round face now perfectly framed by a slide-rule fringed blonde bob, that curled neatly at her cheeks. She beamed back at him, tucking one side behind her tiny ear. Her gold stud twinkling, like her Cheshire-cat grin.

"Well, you know what they say about blonde's having more fun!" she winked.

He grinned, brow-nodding his approval, before a deepening frown expelled it.

"Look, I no-want to be here longer than tonight," he said, under his thick spanish accent. "It still very dangerous for me. You know this!"

Bella folded her slimline body into the seat opposite Pascal, tucking her short dress under her bum.

"I know, I know. But you must realise that I wouldn't have asked if I didn't have to, Pascal. I need you, my friend!"

"You wan drink Bella?" he asked, noticing a waitress passing by.

"Just a coke thanks," she said, nodding her energy filled face at him. "Did you manage to get what we need for tonight?"

"Dos cola por-favor," he grizzled at the girl, who scribbled onto the pad on her silver tray.

Pascal tucked his seat a little closer, as the girl strode away, hip-swinging between untucked chairs around empty card tables. He leaned over their baize-topped table, his raspy tone a little more hushed.

"Listen, Bella I is still easily recognise here, from before. I has boat and will take you to the island tonight, if that is what you still want," he said, with a ridging brow. "But that it!" he added, his index finger digging into the felt.

"That's great, but I need you to come back for me," Bella said, her lips drooping, sad-emoji-like. "You know what he did here, Pascal! The courts wouldn't deal with him, so it's down to us now," she added.

"But, Darcy!" Pascal said, shaking his head slowly. "Darcy, is much worse than before," he said, hush-toned, glancing over her shoulder. "You need to think carefully, Bella, about what you do next!" he said, scolding her like a naughty schoolgirl.

Her face softened, as she turned out her plump bottom lip, accepting the warning. They sat in silence as their drinks arrived and Pascal hovered his card over the waitress's pin-pad.

Pascal had been a key witness in the trial of the TikTokTrio, providing crucial evidence in the prosecution of the three men. His testimony had described the illegal activities of Roman Darcy, the owner of a chain of nightclubs across the Indonesian islands. Pascal had been the subject of a witness protection programme for some months.

She nodded in appreciation of his concern, cupping his hand in hers. Bella had met and interviewed Pascal many times, believing his evidence would prove decisive in seeing Darcy and the other men convicted. She liked Pascal a lot, he was a simple, big-hearted family man.

Their discussions had nearly always been interrupted by his gorgeous children running in and jumping on his lap. Bella took time out to play with the children, always staying for dinner after their lengthy sessions. She had become a family friend.

Pascal had moved here over twenty years ago from Spain, starting a water-transport business, ferrying tourists between the islands. There was a property boom at the time and holiday resorts on the islands were expanding. New hotels and villas were being built apace. Pascal's island-hopping boat buses were in such demand that he had tripled the service, and his profits, within three years.

"I just need to hear all that you know about Darcy's resort, on El-Marney. If you can take me to his island and get me back, that's it," she said, with her familiar, all engaging wide eyes.

"Thiz is very dangerous for us both. You know, after trial I haz to leave here; to sell everything. People iz still recognising me here, Bella!"

Pacal leaned back in his seat, his face, a crumpled picture of worry. He jiggled his ice-filled drink to his lips, barely sipping it.

"Pacal, you know what happened to those girls! You have to help me," Bella pleaded. "Just one last time and then, that's it, it's over. I will do what I need to, and then we're away," she added, offering a reassuring eye-nod.

"But what evidence do you need now? Trial is done. We lost. Iz over, Bella!" Pascal protested in a hushed croak.

"Please believe me, Pascal," she half-smiled. "I just need to do one more thing.."

"But what you do. I don't understan.."

"You have to trust me," Bella interrupted, fixing his gaze.

The two sat for a moment, sipping their drinks. A deep-ridged anxiety remained etched across Pascal's face.

"Ok, ok, I trust you, Bella. But pleez be careful, this man is no-human. You know this!" Pascal said, breaking their silence.

Bella quizzed him about Roman Darcy's team and their operation. A number of Pascal's former employees were now working for Darcy, either in transport or security. Pascal had kept in touch with one guy, Jonah, who's role it was to transfer selected girls from Darcy's nightclub on the mainland, to his private residence, on El-Marney.

"After the trial they no longer traffic from England. It too dangerous for them now. They target and isolate single girls, then sedate them," Pascal explained.

And the beach raves were back; it was as if nothing had happened. The Old Bailey seemed a world away from this tropical haven, and its music filled golden beaches. People were either oblivious to the trial in England and the accusations, or they took the 'innocent of all charges' verdict as gospel. His followers never believed them anyway, not of their hero, Roman Darcy. If anything Darcy's fame and popularity had soared, once exonerated.

"Johan says they select those who iz on holiday alone. They get passports and belongings from the hotel they stay," Pascal said, to Bella's rising eyebrows. "Reception, iz easy to bribe, they make so little money," he explained.

Darcy's main operation was run from the Isle of El-Marney. Its expansive beaches were regularly filled with euphoric, amphetamine tranced revellers, boated over from the mainland. Their drug induced moronic state allowed easy pickings for Darcy's team, who shipped back the rest at sunrise.

"He can't have many held over there. It's only been six months since their release!" Bella argued.

But with the trial now firmly behind them, it appeared there was an unabandoned freedom. It was no longer necessary for the TikTokTrio to organise and fund kidnappings from the UK, or elsewhere.

Here, they sold tickets like a 'holiday excursion,' for a fun-filled, clubbing experience like no other. Once vetted, the youngsters (under 21's only), were taken on party boats to El-Marney, with the promise of a 24 hour music festival, featuring famed celebrity, DJ Darcy.

On the ground, the operation was run by Roman Darcy and funded by Pierre Lebouf. The third man, Jamal Jackson, gave the enterprise credibility, and a global, superstar standing. Between the three of them, they attracted huge numbers to the island.

Like crocodiles to the wildebeest crossing, their fellow sex-slave trading moguls soon slithered back over. Behind their mounting wealth an untouchable status was legitimised. Bribery and corruption were bedfellows here, that remained in wedded-bliss.

The trial had established that the trio had underworld connections across four continents, including North America. Interpol had partially decrypted hardware from the offices of Pierre Lebouf, evidencing a link to the dark-web. A paedophile-linked, pornography exchange was traced to source, but found to be inaccessible and that aspect of the prosecution was dropped.

Bella stroked her bob, finger-twirling nervously at its curly end. It was a child-like fidget and the first sign of doubt that Pascal had ever seen in her. She was always so self-assured and confident, so authoritative. He teethsucked a grin in a feeble attempt to reassure her that only reaffirmed his own disquiet about what she was about to do.

Pascal held huge admiration for Bella; she had done everything possible to put these men behind bars. He felt a deep pride in her, she was like family to him. Bella had always been so diligent, so careful, and yet this was so reckless, so dangerous.

CHAPTER 14

SCOTLAND YARD

Tom Broad's team had only been working on the murder of Jamal Jackson for twelve hours when it was paired with the investigation into the disappearance of city financier Pierre Lebouf. That case was link-transferred given their connection.

"The link here is obvious," Tom announced, as the last of his team bustled through the door into briefing room one.

The muttering petered swiftly as the lights were dimmed and the back wall illuminated with three police photofit images.

"It's the TikTokTrio. Our guy, Jackson, murdered yesterday. This chap, Lebouf," Tom said, redirecting his laser pointer. "Is missing, feared abducted, in the last few days. And we're tracking down this, third man.., a Roman.."

"Roman Darcy, guv!" Neil Turvey interrupted, enthusiastically.

"Yes, thank you, Turvs," Tom said, with an eye-roll.

"Somekinda celeb-DJ. He lives on some paradise Island, in Indonesia, I think.." Neil said.

"Yes, yes, thank you Neil. That is all actually in the briefing pack on the desks in front of you!" Tom said, panning the room, before setting a hard stare on his number two. "Background information, including extracts from the trial transcript are all in there. As are the statements of each of these men, taken at the time of their arrest."

The room became a cacophony of paper shuffling, amidst excited murmuring.

"Suspects," Tom boomed. "We need to focus on suspects. That is our immediate focus, please people."

Tom clicked the box in his left hand before directing his laser pointer behind him, as the room settled. A colourful chart outlining the men's career paths, and their interconnection filled the wall.

"Who wanted these men dead, and who stood to benefit? They were cleared of all charges of sex-trafficking and murder at the Old Bailey; so who wasn't happy about that?" he asked, the now silent room.

"Half the population of this country!" DI Spencer, the only female on the team, yelled.

"Thank you, yes!" Tom said, squinting around the room, but failing to locate his heckler. "And I have ordered prelims into the victims' families."

"Now, the brutal attack on Jamal Jackson; a successful Premier League footballer," Tom continued.

"That'd be motive for every centre half in England, boss!" Neil said, in his familiar scouse squeal, as the room erupted in laughter.

"Thank you, Neil," Tom said, with raised palms that hid a grin curling his lips. Glancing at the door he clocked the late arrival and familiar waddle of Jeremy Forsythe, the criminal psychologist.

Over the last belly laugh, Tom turned attentions to Pierre Lebouf, taking his team through the circumstances surrounding the city mogul's recent disappearance. Forensics were awaited from the Lebouf's home, from where his mother had been tied, gagged and injected with a substance that had put her to sleep. She remained at St. Martin's hospital in a severe state of shock. Getting a statement and description of her assailant was considered a priority.

"Jamal Jackson's murder was brutal. To take the time to behead someone, is truly savage. It indicates something more personal is at play here," Tom said, nodding at professor Forsythe, who was now at the front of the room. "Who harboured that level of hatred, or stood to gain significantly, with Jackson out of the picture?"

"The blue's might get the three points on Saturday, boss!" Neil said, winking at one of his colleagues.

The tittering faded swiftly as Tom barked orders, allocating officers duties from CCTV reviews, to verifying victims' family members' movements. Door-to-door enquiries were to be widened from the Cheveley estate. Undercover operatives were to be deployed across the manor.

"But let's also widen this out a bit from a purely vengeance-based motive, shall we. Let's consider the business empire that these men have created, and with it of course, significant wealth!" Tom said. Tech specialists were tasked with a deep-dive into the men's financial affairs.

Roman Darcy, the third man, was considered to be in immediate danger. Despite all attempts to contact him on his private island, he remained unreachable. Arrangements were made for two officers to travel to Indonesia to interview Darcy and offer him protection, as a British citizen.

Despite DI Spencer's protestation that a female officer should attend, it was decided that Neil Turvey would fly out with SIO Tom Broad. Neil had been most insistent that both his availability and skill-set warranted his attendance. Aside from that, his Hawaiian shirt needed another airing. Spencer was left with instructions to liaise with the criminal profiler, Jeremy

Forsythe.

Tom slipped on his suit jacket and exited at the side door of the briefing room with Neil. They headed for St. Martin's hospital to interview Pierre Lebouf's mother, Patricia, to confirm details of his abduction. Her affluent son remained missing and the police were still without a much hypothesised ransom demand.

CHAPTER 15

INDIAN OCEAN

From the smoke filled city streets, the sea air was refreshing as it breezed across Bella's face. A salty taste wafted from the bow as it broke the tranquil warm waters. The dull hum of the small boat's engine was the only sound, as she leaned back, breathing it all in, admiring the brilliance of the star-studded night sky.

Bella sat behind her friend Pascal who steered a direct line to the tropical island paradise of El-Marney that now protruded proudly into the dimming sky-line. Steep cliff faces stood prominent on either side of a deep valley into which carpeted vegetation flowed, to its tree-crammed centre. Its awesome, majestic beauty appeared like a marine oasis, luring their little boat in.

Within a kilometre, Pascal steered hard to port, heading for the denser cover that overhung a shadow filled rockface. Bella rummaged in the rucksack that lay at her feet, pulling tight to her head a black baseball cap and zipping to her chin a dark windbreaker. As the boat skirted the island's reef she completed her change into leggings and sneakers, both black.

"Where's that?" Bella quizzed, pointing at a smaller, low-lying Isle, barely visible in the semi-darkness.

The tiny island lay to the east of El-Marney, a fraction of the size of its huge neighbour.

"Makam-Raja," Pascal said, steering one-handed, as he half-turned. "It means, 'The King's Tomb.' Legend has it that it was King Raja's final resting place, and that of his Queens.

"'Queens',.. plural?" Bella said, with furrowed brow.

"Yes, he had twelve!" Pascal said, with eyebrows mirroring Bella's expression. "After his burial, at the island's highest point, tradition commanded that they, 'szanil o-pastri'. They remain on the island to grieve for the rest of their lives," he translated. "It was many centuries ago, of course. It's uninhabited now, and has been reclaimed by nature," he added, returning both hands to the wheel.

The boat foamed the ocean a little more, as it squared to fashion a starboard steer, toward a narrow sandy inlet. Bella checked her bag, before tightening its straps, pulling it taught to her back. Pascal glanced back, fleeting a limp smile that offered only warning of the dangers ahead.

"Don't worry!" Bella said, smiling at her friend. "I know what I'm doing."

"The moon won't help," Pascal said, his face to the skies.

It was almost cloudless as the little boat beached. Wispy shadows drifted across the huge moon that sat in splendour amidst the star-speckled sky. The boat's bow reared-up as it mounted the incline onto a spit of pristine white sand, half-hidden in the shadows of the cliffs that surrounded it.

"You remember the passage that I showed you," Pascal whispered. "Climb to the left, as high as the bruja bushes, then follow that ridge to the clearing at the top. Head toward the coconut palms, then work your way down through the forest."

"Yes Pascal, I know the route. Please don't worry!" Bella said, shrugging at her friend.

Bella lept from the boat, splashing to her calves. The water was amazingly warm, almost comforting as it filled her pumps.

"Listen for the waters of the fall, they will guide you," Pascal said. "Remember, climb down the waterfall on the left hand side, where the rock is. Is.. how do you say?"

"Where the rock face protrudes, like the Spanish Steps. You've mentioned it at least ten times!" she said, with a wonky smile.

"You are so brave, Bella," Pascal said, returning a cheek-pulled grin.

He, and his words were filled with admiration and pride in his friend, this young girl that sought to tackle evil, head-on, and alone.

"I will see you in twenty four hours," Bella said, with a heavy exhale as she shoved the boat back clear of the sand.

It bobbed silently back into the turquoise, sun-baked waters, before the gentle engine hum returned. Pascal spun the wheel and it drifted away from the narrow shore. Bella headed for the larger rocks that lay at the foot of the cliff to the left and began to clamber easily upwards. Within minutes she had reached the bushlined halfway point. The climb was easy, just as Pascal had said it would be.

With its larger rocks lower down, the elevated ridges of the cliff had created what seemed like a natural pathway; a stone-ladder to the top. Bella's thought of Jack and the Beanstalk, the book her mother had read her a hundred times, the only book in the house. It had become her 'comfort blanket,' after her mum had died. She loved Jack and what he stood for; courage and cleverness, 'good over evil.' Bella was always mesmerised at the part where the giant searched frantically for Jack. But their size difference didn't matter now, it helped Jack.

Bella's thoughts were broken by the pitchy whirring sound of a speedboat, bouncing through the waters below her. From her high vantage she could see it clearly, sweeping around the curve of the island, before swerving off in the direction of Pascal's vessel in the distance. There were four men on board, rocking in unison with the boat as it slashed through the waters, weaving white foaming trails at its rear. Voices in harsh foreign tongue were shouting as they closed in on Pascal's little boat.

Bella lay flat to the rockface, her hand clutching a branch of one of the many bushes that had sprung from cracks in the stoney headland. Her limbs shook at the sound of gunfire as its explosion lit the night sky. They powerboat sped in a circular motion around Pascal's boat, which sat bobbing in surrender at the centre of their sea-churning wake.

A week ago she had a normal life, work, boyfriend and a routine where everything was simple. Now she was a fully fledged criminal, clinging to a cliff face. Bella felt her heart pounding her chest as she looked up and climbed on. In the space of seven days, she had planned and executed the abduction of one man and killed another.

The murder of Jackson had been easy, and surprisingly enjoyable. Stabbing and dismembering a man that she had loathed for so long triggered an adrenaline rush, a triumphant high. And with it came an overwhelming feeling of abandon; she no longer cared about consequences. Bella was fully prepared to sacrifice her life for the destruction of these monsters.

Jackson was the little boy blessed with both an aesthetic and sporting advantage. The kid that skipped schooling to concentrate on his ball skills. Jamal Jackson 'JJ' was a jackass halfwit, living in his own reflection.

Roman Darcy was in a similar bracket to Jackson. Uneducated, he had left school mid-teens to begin a career in the drug trade. A courier that advanced to pusher, before upgrading to wholesale seller and importer. His only 'talent,' the ability to mix Electro-House and Trance, served with an addictive narcotic cocktail.

Behind these underclass dimwits was the key to their success, Pierre Lebouf, undoubtedly the mastermind of their operation. Without his financial muscle, there was no business. It was his money train that had to be stopped. Witness evidence at trial had revealed a rapid growth in their organisation; it was clear there were other key players involved.

From people smugglers and sexslave traders, to the dark web fantasists, all had clambered to affiliate. Innumerable, unidentifiable sexual deviants were now dining at the table of the TikTokTrio. An endless queue of depraved sycophants, desperate to join the party.

It was Pierre Lebouf that Bella had removed first, to be broken; like all the women he had trafficked. A simple, quick death wouldn't be anything like justice. He would suffer the physical pain, the humiliation and loss, as his victims had. But more than that, Lebouf, the multi-millionaire trader, would pay financially too.

Bella hauled herself up onto the grassy headland that rimmed the top of the rockface. Staying low to the lush vegetation she ducked, darting to disappear out of view from the water, thrashing on into thick woodland. A shuddering fear for Pascal took hold at the sound of further gunfire that echoed the tall trees that surrounded her. Swinging the rucksack to her lap, she slumped to the ground and glugged heavily from the water bottle.

Bella adjusted her cap to sit tight to her temples and sprung to her feet, marching on. Within ten metres she instantly froze, ridged in alarm at a distant clamour of voices. They were deep and aggressive in tone, their intent seemed clear. A sense of panic took her as the men's bellowing was suddenly joined by the excitable barking of hounds.

Bella yanked hard at the straps of her rucksack, pinning it tight to her back as she sprinted off, swerving between bushes and trees. Her pounding heart and feet thudded in synchrony as she zig-zagged, weaving an untrod pathway through the thorny thicket.

An all-consuming trepidation swamped her, a sense of foreboding. This distress was immediately familiar, this panic-building anxiety. She had felt before; the night her mother had died. A childlike yearning, a desire to go back, to rewind the clock, screamed inside her as an increasing desperation grew.

But Bella's previous life was over, changed irrevocably. Bella blew heavily, filling her lungs as she thrashed on, relentlessly bounding the weed tangled undergrowth.

PART II – VENOM

CHAPTER 16
SEVEN DAYS EARLIER

Cavendish House was a development of luxury apartments, exclusively owned by multimillionaires. Wealth dripping magnates from their inherited business empires, or international tycoons who sought a prestigious UK residence.

Twenty four lavish suites, situated just off the Kings road, a Javelin throw from Harrods. The penthouse, offering a three-sixty panoramic vista, was owned, for tax efficient purposes, by Patricia Lebouf, mother of Pierre.

It was Patricia's sixty fifth birthday on Saturday and gifts had been arriving at reception since Tuesday. Security had delivered the parcels to her suite each day, but as a traditionalist, she wasn't going to open them until the 'big day.'

At just after three on Friday afternoon reception phoned through confirming her expected guest, Margaret Cooper, had arrived. She was a friend from childhood that Patricia hadn't seen for years, who had got in touch through Facebook.

Margaret sat waiting patiently in the foyer. She had moved to the capital last year following her husband's promotion. Recalling how she and Patricia had often shared joint birthday parties as children, she was keen to catch-up given their advancing years.

"Please do send her straight up," Patricia said excitedly, aware that Margaret might overhear her from the loudest of intercom systems in reception.

Margaret, wearing a beige cashmere turtleneck, sat in the centre of the middle settee, one of three red leather button-backs. Her lambswool overcoat lay draped to one side, with a huge bunch of multi-coloured lilies and reeds on the other.

"Thank you, please madam," the top-hatted, elderly man said whilst rounding the concierge desk.

He beckoned Margaret forward, having received a stern nod from the younger man that was standing at reception, replacing the telephone receiver.

"You like, come this way, please Misses Coopers."

"Thank you," Margaret replied, slipping her coat across her forearm as she rose to her feet.

She was ushered under exaggerated gesticulation and bowing, toward a shiny lift door that opened with an efficient ping. A similarly grey morning-suited man, although hatless, appeared. He stepped, soldier-on-parade-like to one side, inside the elevator.

"I take you up to the Penthouse suite now," the attendant enthused, with a wide pulled smile.

Margeret nodded politely and slid on her oversized sunglasses as the lift rose effortlessly through floors. She lifted the large bouquet to her chin.

"Patricia Stimpson!" Margaret boomed, as the lift door slid open, with its ping still reverberating.

"Err, Patricia Lebouf, if you don't mind," Patricia announced, with a widening beam as she stepped toward the elevator.

"Of course, Lebouf," Margaret said, smiling. "It's been too long!"

"For you. Happy birthday!" Margaret said, passing her the flowers.

"They are simply stunning, thank you," Patricia said, whilst waving a queen-like limp wrist, at the elevator attendant. "Do come through to the sitting room, Margaret."

The attendant grinned a nod at Mrs Lebouf, finger-touching his temple. The shiny silver door slid across, pinging loudly again, before a soft hum as it faded in descent. The two women walked through the open double doors into a living room that boasted a shoulder height redbrick fireplace.

"It's been far too long!" Patricia said, striding across the deep pile cream rug, to the floor-to-ceiling windows. "Now let's get some light in here."

A gold framed canvass of Patricia and her son Pierre hung proudly above the mantle. He wore a red sashed black robe and mortar board, and was grinning like a teenager on his prom-date.

Patricia laid the bouquet on a circular side table, before easing the red velvet curtains a little further to their sides and fussing with their tie-backs. Sunlight flooded the plushly furnished space.

"Views across Queen's parks with the Palace just on the left there," Patricia said, with an arm aloft. "I've been very lucky, you know," she added, admiring the vista.

Margaret slid her sunglasses from her head, tossing them onto the large mahogany coffee table that sat central to two emerald green sofas. She removed a syringe from her coat pocket and placed it alongside her shades.

"It's all down to my wonderful son Pierre, you know," Patricia said, turning to her friend.

Margaret flung her coat to one of the sofas, and sat down on the other.

"What on earth is that?" Patricia said, taken aback at the sight of a large needle on her coffee table.

"Can I suggest you take a seat, Patricia," Margaret said, her voice different now; younger, and assertive in tone.

Margaret slid her hand through her grey wig easing it off, revealing a short blonde bob that lay slick to her head. Picking at her temple she peeled away a transparent film from her face that took clean-away all the wrinkles from her forehead and eyes.

"What.., what is this," Patrica said limply, with widening eyes. "I-I don't understand."

Patricia stood frozen, statuesque in shock, staring at the transformation occurring in front of her eyes. Bella threw the prosthesis and wig to the coffee table and marched over to Patricia, clasping and twisting her wrist hard up her back from the elbow.

"With me!" Bella said, shuffling Patricia into the kitchen and shoving her onto a chair.

Rifling drawers, Bella clattered through silverware, tossing cutlery, before finding a knife that suited her.

"I., I'm really not sure what all this is about," Patricia said meekly.

"I don't want to hear from you, until I say so!" Bella said, with the command of a drill sergeant. "Now let's get back in there and get your phone."

They returned to the living room, where Patricia was thrust into one of the high-winged armchairs and passed a note. Seeing that Patricia was trembling as she passed her the iPhone, Bella repeated the written instruction back to her.

"You've had an accident. You need Pierre's help. Him alone and no-one else!" Bella said, pointing at the note that was shaking in Patricia's hand.

"That's the gist of it, but say it your way. You're not reading a fuckin script - right!" Bella said.

"But he'll j-just t-tell me to call m-m-my d-doctor," Patricia said.

"Well you had better explain that you don't need a doctor, you need HIM. I know how close you are! And what an Oedipus fuck-up he is," Bella said, with narrowing eyes.

"What, so that you-you can inject him w-w-with g-god-knows what th-that is," Patricia said, eye-pointing at the coffee table.

"You just get him to come over here, or I won't hesitate to slide this inside you," Bella said, flicking the tip of the blade with the fat of her thumb.

Bella sat on the arm of Patricia's chair, poking the knife to her waist. Patricia's neck wrinkled as she inhaled heavily.

"You spawned the devil, mother dear! So I don't give a damn about killing you," Bella said, whilst scrolling through the contact list on Patricia's iPhone.

Bella dabbed the one listed as, my boy, and thrust the mobile into Patricia clammy hand.

"If you wanna live, you had better make this work!"

CHAPTER 17

London's financial district, home of the Bank of England and The Stock Exchange, had received extra security provision since the 9-11 attacks on The World Trade Center. But aside from a patrol car rolling through the area three times a day, it had only amounted to additional CCTV coverage, albeit of every square metre of its interlocking streets.

Protection was reassessed following the 7-7 London terrorist attacks of 2005, when safety was enhanced considerably. Undercover operatives patrolled anonymously by car and on foot, twenty-four-seven. Technical advances in entry-exit systems had facilitated the immediate isolating of any 'alien' individual. Security across the capital's economic quarter and its financiers was now watertight.

The entire area, where historically the Romans had founded Londinium, was monitored every minute of every day. The FD was a recognised cobra-red target area. Anyone working in the district had a matrix ID lanyard, with chipped facial recognition, verified upon entry into the zone, via the mapping centre.

The square-mile, from the outer perimeter to its central point, with sky monitor tracking drones, was proudly referred to as the UK's, 'Fort-Knox.' It fell within the same risk level security banding as the capitals other 'major-threat,' buildings coded, BP, HoP and 10DS.

All deliveries, cleaning operatives and even interviewees were 'code 4' authorised. Individuals were screened well in advance of their stepping one foot inside the epi-centre of the UK's wealth pumping heart.

Pierre Lebouf's company HQ, occupied a central suite of offices in Cromwell House, on Lombard street; London's equivalent to Wall Street. It was an area steeped historically, and synonymously with the slave trade. The financial institutions here had insured the vessels that ferried over 3 million African people across the Atlantic Ocean. Fortunes were coined here, by heinous networks of individuals all linked to the Banks.

"None of that nonsense matters to me, Johan. I have new partners lining up to be involved on this one. I need a decision by five, or I'll pass it on," Pierre said.

He spoke with a laissez-faire arrogance that was laced with threat. Leaning back hard in his leather-bound recliner, Lebouf set his legs down slowly, crossing at the centre of his crescent desk.

"The Hunt starts in less than ten days, Johan. You'll be out of the game if I haven't heard from you by close of business. Your place will be vacated and the FundsTracker net will be reopened," Pierre said.

He exuded a confidence that seduced many a wealthy investor to place their unconditional trust, and funds with him. Lebouf's legitimate brokerage shielded his private venture, a ponzi-scheme that had given him wealth beyond measure.

"I just need more time. I've got three that have signed and the other guy is trans-atlantic as we speak. C'mon Pierre, you know I'm good for it," Johan pleaded.

The timing of the knock on Lebouf's office door was unfortunate and audible to his caller that he had engaged on speaker-phone.

"Come," Pierre demanded.

A folded note was passed to him that he opened noisily.

"Could you ask them to hold for me. Thank you." Pierre said, waving his assistant dismissively out of his office.

"Johan, I now have a blue-chip investor on hold. I cannot extend beyond five p-m. You either act as guarantor for your 'missing link,' and transfer me the funds. Or, you lose this opportunity," he said, slamming the phone down.

The note read;

'Your mother has phoned three times in the last twenty minutes and has requested that you call her - she has repeatedly stressed it is most urgent'

Pierre screwed and tossed it to the floor and jabbed at his iPhone.

"Hello Pierre," her voice sounded frail.

"Mother dear, do you remember what I've always told you about 'not calling,' at the busiest time of my day, unless it's 'life or death,'" Pierre said curtly, in tightly restrained frustration.

"I-I know darling but I do need your help urgently. I've had a fall and twisted my ankle, you see. I can't move!" she pleaded. "Could you come over?"

"Why haven't you called the concierge? That's what they're there for mother," he said, his frustration softening.

"Yes, yes I know but I'm not decent you see. I tripped stepping from the bath and, I-I can't stand up. I just couldn't ask them to come up, and find me like this," she said, breathing heavily.

"Can't you reach your robe, or a towel," he said.

She started sobbing softly. "Please Pierre, I need you."

"Yes, yes, ok, ok," he said, trying to calm himself more than her.

"I wouldn't ask if I wasn't desperate, darling," she said, before whimpering.

"I think I might have broken it,"

"Then we're going to need an ambulance, aren't we?" he replied.

There was a moment of silence between them, before she came back sharply.

"No, no, please don't call an ambulance, Pierre. I couldn't bear the embarrassment," she said. "Maybe later, once I'm dressed," she added, softly.

"Ok-ok, I'm on my way over. I should be with you in twenty minutes."

CHAPTER 18

"And there it is! Oedipus strikes again," Bella announced, easing the blade from Patricia Lebouf's ribcage.

Bella had tried and failed on a number of occasions to gain entry to Pierre Lebouf's office block; it was impenetrable. They had doubled-down on security. There had to be another way to get to him. After a little research and some 'life-habit' observational stalking, the key became clear: his mother.

"Mother's and son's; what is that all about!" Bella said, tittering as she stood over Patricia Lebouf, who suddenly looked very pale.

Pierre's only weakness, his achilles heel, was his dear old mum. With a landmark birthday approaching and easy access to Patricia's Facebook account, everything had fallen seamlessly into place. Some heavy duty tape squealed as it was wrapped around her chest, pinning her arms to her side.

"Please, just speak to Pierre, he's very fair you know. I'm sure you can sort all this out with him," she added.

"Very fair! You literally have no idea, do you," Bella said, headshaking. "I can't say I'll ever understand mother's and their infallible, precious sons!"

Bella laughed, louder this time as she kneeled down and strapped Patricia's ankles together.

"But, I've done what you ask, why can't you just leave me now?" Patricia said, with pleading eyes. "If this is something to do with that trial, he was acquitted, you know. Found innocent of all charges, he was," she added, with a high-pitched, pride.

Bella looked at Patricia square in the eye.

"It's just too damning, demeaning, for you to accept that your child could do something so evil. It's a biological refusal to even entertain the idea of any bad in your son," Bella said.

Bella peeled a length of strapping and ripped it from its coil.

"Look, I understand that you're upset about something he's done, but he can make it right, you know. I brought him up to understand right from wrong," Patricia pleaded.

"Accept it or not Mrs Lebouf, the world is going to know the truth. Pierre, your depraved son, is a barbaric sociopath that trafficks and abuses young women," Bella said, whilst peeling more tape.

"He's a very wealthy businessman, I'm sure he can.."

Bella thrust the thick strip of tape across Patricia's mouth, jolting her head back as she did.

"I know you are a deeply religious woman," Bella said, flattening the tape across her cheeks, to either ear. "And this has been an unholy mess for you.." she added, picking up the syringe from the coffee table.

Patricia shook her head, her watery eyes widening in panicked flicker.

"But I can assure you that he will pay for his ungodly crimes. For the monstrously vile atrocities he has committed." Bella said. "Now this is going to make you feel a little drowsy and imobile."

Bella grabbed Patricia's forearm and rolled-up the sleeve of her pink silk blouse, plunging the needle into the top of her arm. She squeezed the plunger hard through its barrel, syringing propofol into her bloodstream, instantly slowing her brain and nervous system. Within seconds her eyes rolled over white and her head flopped lifelessly to one side; she would remain unconscious for some time.

'A little too much maybe!' Bella mused.

CHAPTER 19

"Good evening Mr Lebouf," a young girl said politely.

She wore the standard concierge light grey trouser-suit, with a shiny name badge on her breast pocket; *Polly Brown*.

"We do apologise, sir, but the underground carpark is unavailable at present. Unfortunately we've had a burst pipe," she said.

Pierre Lebouf sat finger-tapping his steering wheel and revving the supercharged engine of his Jaguar F-type, having just pulled into the layby of Cavendish House.

"Could we possibly ask that you park around the corner there," Polly said, pointing directly ahead and then arching the back of her hand at ninety degrees. "It's just before the bus-stop. A turning on the right there, into Fengate terrace."

The fingers of Lebouf's left hand wrapped tightly around the wheel. "This is most inconvenient!" he said, glaring at the girl.

"We do have residents' approval to park vehicles there in the interim," she blurted, seeing the frustration in his narrowing eyes.

"Yes, yes," he said impatiently, his elbow disappearing inside as he sped off, making a hard right after fifty metres.

The girl followed hastily on foot, turning into the quiet cul-de-sac of Fengate terrace. Lebouf was halfway down the road, finishing parallel parking his Jaguar. She jogged within twenty metres as he stepped out of the low-slung sports car.

"Mister Lebouf," she yelled, puffing as she approached. "I do apologise, I neglected to give you this," she added, waving a postcard sized green card.

"What is it?" Lebouf snapped.

"It's a parking permit. Could you please pop it on the passenger side of your dashboard," she said, passing him the card that was emblazoned with the word, 'Resident.' "Thank you, so much, sir."

Lebouf snatched it, and flung open the passenger door. Ducking inside, he leaned in and threw the card on the windscreen. At that moment something dug sharply into the small of his back.

"Get in the fucking car, shithead," Bella whispered aggressively.

"What the fuck!" Lebouf squealed, wincing against the tip of the blade that had pierced his flesh.

With the palm of her hand, Bella shoved him hard, propelling him toward the driver's seat. The point of the knife swiftly reacquainting itself with his back.

"Get behind the wheel," she said, as she slid in behind him.

He half-hurdled the central armrest to distance from the knife, as she slammed the door behind her.

"Buckle-up and get this thing started," she said, poking the tip of the blade into his midriff.

"That fucking thing is actually cutting into me, you stupid bitch," he complained, as he turned and tried to grab her wrist.

Bella swivelled away, swinging back with her other hand that now clutched a stanley knife. In an instant the triangular blade rested on Lebouf's Adam's apple.

"Fuckin-well sit back, or your life's over right here and now!" she said.

Bella poked the other knife a little deeper into his side. Lebouf gingerly lifted his palms to the air, between pain-filled pants.

"I'm gonna slit your scrawny little throat. I'm happy to finish it here! This'll slice clean through, if you don't do as I fuckin well tell you," she said, grinning at his compliance.

Blood spotted the flank of his pale blue shirt, between his hip and rib cage. Bella returned the stanley knife to her jacket pocket and slid out a mobile phone.

"You see this," she said, flashing the image from the iPhone in front of him. "Mummy's dead in thirty minutes unless you do as I say. So don't try anything like that again. Hard for you to accept, Lebouf; but *I'm in charge.*"

"What the hell do you want from me," Lebouf said, behind a laboured wheezed.

"You'll see. Now drive," Bella ordered.

The engine hummed into life and he swerved from the curb.

"Is this about money? If you give me your account number, I'll transfer…"

His words were halted by panted excruciating pain, as the steel tip eased deeper into his flank, widening the wound. A glistening claret seeped, blotting further, his crisp shirt.

"I don't want to hear from you," she said, enjoying his every grimace. "It's very simple, Lebouf; follow my directions and mummy lives. Got it!"

Eighteen minutes later the Jaguar was parked off a side road, near the rear entrance to Silver Mews terrace. They exited the car as one, and walked quickly the cobblestoned alleyway. With the knife digging at his spine, Lebouf took keys as instructed, opened the padlocked gate, followed by the backdoor to the Victorian-terraced house.

"Sit there and strap these cable-ties around your ankles and wrists," Bella ordered, as they entered the property, through the kitchen door.

Lebouf sat on the plastic moulded chair and did as instructed. Behind him, with the knife at his shoulder blade, Bella leaned in and yanked hard, tightening the loose cable-tie cords. Lebouf's ankles slammed together, followed by his wrists as the ties snapped tight.

"Release my mother, and I can agree to whatever it is that you actually want," he said, with a tone of uncertainty.

Bella beamed as she laid the knife on the table and rounded the chair, to face him.

"I'm really not an unreasonable man. I'm sure I can offer redress for whatever your complaint is," he said. "Tell me please, what is it that I have done to offend you so?"

Bella shook her head, her face slowly filling with gleaming smile. She picked to release the end of a large reel of silver duct tape.

"You narcissistic bastard. You have absolutely no idea who I am or what you have done, do you? Your arrogance is truly breathtaking," Bella said.

Bella stuck tape firmly to his left cheek, before wrapping it three-times around his head. She eased it away from a nostril and then patted it, securing it flat across his mouth. His eyes bulged as she laughed a cackly chortle. A hint of rising hysteria echoed the bare kitchen walls.

Peeling again at the tape she strapped it around his chest, pinning his arms from the elbows up, as he wriggled furiously in protest. She tipped back the plastic chair onto its rear legs, dragging Lebouf from the kitchen into the dimly lit hall. A Tiffany lamp sat on the dust-filled floor, extending an eerie, long-shadowed reflection as the chair scraped into the dark, wood-panelled space.

Stopping, she delved into his trouser pocket, removing a 'PL' embossed gold keyring.

"Now let's get that laptop of yours and dispose of that vulgar car, shall we," she said, jangling the small bundle of keys in front of his face.

His bulging angry eyes, now blood-filling as capillaries burst.

"Of course, sorry, do forgive me. Let's get you settled in first, shall we," Bella said, with a wonky grin.

Pressing her palm against the panelled wall, *click-clack,* a single panel sprung open. Turning the chair to line it up opposite the opening, Bella shoved it forward, juddering him into the blackness.

She thrust her hands on his shoulders, pushing hard and tipping the chair-bound Lebouf deeper inside. He disappeared, tumbling face first, amidst hefty thuds as he rebounded the steep steps beyond. *Click-clack,* the doorway closed, instantly disappearing and seamlessly rejoining the wood panelled hallway.

Bella slipped silently out of the rear door of the house, padlocking the backyard gate, before exiting from the cobblestone alley. She stepped back onto the cold streets of East London and clicked to open Lebouf's car. It flashed twice, giving an obedient *chirp-chirp.* She opened the boot, removed his briefcase and laptop, laying them on the passenger seat.

Bella settled in behind the wheel of the F-type Jaguar and pressed the start button. It hummed softly into life as the white leather seat instantly warmed her rear. It had the chemical smell of a new car that she hadn't noticed before.

Bella hadn't driven for some time. Adjusting the mirror and tucking her seat to the wheel, she gripped the thick, pimple-rimmed steering wheel. Thumb-pinching the red button of the gear shaft, she slid it slowly from *P* to *D* and pulled away.

Glancing up at her reflection she beamed, a honeydew smile; she was going to enjoy this.

CHAPTER 20

PRESENT DAY

"Mrs Lebouf, is it okay if we ask you a few questions about your son, Pierre?" Tom Broad said softly as he stepped into her hospital sideroom.

Patricia Lebouf nodded gently, hoisting herself to a more upright position in her bed. The two detectives strode across the off-white linoleum. DI Neil Turvey was quick to skirt the bed, plump a crumpled flat pillow and prop it longways behind her.

Tom scrapped a chair to her bedside and Neil perched on the seat opposite and took out his pocket book, whilst clicking the top of his pen.

Patricia Lebouf had been in the private room of the Hatfield wing of St. Martin's hospital, for a week now. The suite was filled with the scent of fresh cut flowers, which adorned the side table and cupboards. Well-wishing cards were dotted between colour-laden vases.

"I have spoken to your officer's a number of times already," she said, her voice a little hoarse. "Would one of you mind?" she added, pointing at a large jug of purple-coloured liquid.

"No problem," Neil said, bouncing to his feet. "We do of course have your account of your assailant. We're more interested in talking about Pierre." he said, whilst pouring the drink into a bevelled glass tumbler and handing it to her.

Tom nodded with a pulled smile at his colleague before continuing.

"Yes, Pierre's car has been discovered on waste ground near an industrial estate in Chapeltown, Leeds," Tom explained. "Do you know of any connection he might have had to that area?"

"None whatsoever," she snapped back. "But he will be so pleased you've found his car. It's his pride and joy."

"Yes, err, unfortunately it's been burned-out," Tom said.

"Burned-out! How dreadful.. Why on earth would she want to go and do that," Patricia said, head-shaking.

"She?" Neil quizzed.

"Yes, the girl who assaulted me," she said sharply. "I thought you said you had the details!"

"Sorry yes, yes," Tom interjected. "Young blonde female, slim build, average height, brown eyes."

"She pretended to be my school friend, Margaret Cooper. Made herself look a lot older, with a wig and a face mask thingy." Patricia said, wheezing a little as she spoke.

"Yes, we have reviewed the CCTV from the foyer of Cavendish House, but as you say, she was heavily disguised," Neil said

Tom pressed on, "Patricia, we've heard from Pierre's business associates, and it seems considerable sums of money have disappeared from his private account. Would Pierre have kept his laptop or banking documents with him, or in his car?"

"I don't know about all that. He usually carries a shoulder bag across his chest.. I assume that would be from his work," Patricia said, sipping her juice. "But it's about that bloody trial, not his work! '*You spawned the Devil,*' that's what she yelled at me."

"We are considering all possibilities here, including that it might be a group of people that want to harm the three of them. It's not just Pierre. You will have heard about Mr Jackson and we're currently trying to track down Mr Darcy," Neil said.

Tom shuffled forward in his seat, "Pierre's business associates, Patricia. They have reason to believe that his finances have been breached. They report that significant funds have been taken from his offshore accounts. So it seems plausible that there might be a financial motivation at play here."

"Well yes, as I say, he always had his laptop with him. He carried everywhere in his leather satchel," she said. A concerned expression etching deeper into her features. "But what about finding him; have you got anywhere with that? It's been a week now!"

"His vehicle tracking system was one of the most advanced we have seen, so we have a record of its every movement, from the moment it left Cavendish House. We have a location in Plaistow, East London where it stops for a short while before heading north, ending in Chapeltown," Neil said, offering to top up her drink.

"Well I can't think of any connection Pierre might have with East London either, before you ask. Ghastly place! It's always been full of criminals," she said, with an eye-roll at Tom. "That Yorkshire town you mentioned, does ring a bell, the more I think about it," she mused.

"You might recall it because of Peter Sutcliffe. It was one of his old stomping grounds," Neil said, interrupting her thoughts.

"Peter, who?" she said, turning open-faced to Neil.

"Sutcliffe, Peter Sutcliffe. The Yorkshire Ripper. Some of his murders were committed in Chapeltown," Neil explained. "Could be coincidental, or it might be significant."

"Significant, how?" Patricia shot back, fixing a glare at Neil.

"We're not entirely sure at the moment," Tom said. "It's just another line of inquiry."

"Well I'm not sure how on earth you can suggest there might be a link with my Pierre and a serial killer," she said, in a puffy breath.

"It's just very odd, more than chance," Neil said. "Why leave it there? It seems symbolic, given the nature of what Pierre was accused of. It's as if they are saying something.."

"Saying *what,* exactly," Patricia said, raising her voice. "I don't appreciate what you are.."

"I do apologise, Patricia," Tom interrupted. "We didn't come here to upset you," he added, throwing a stern glance across the bed at his colleague. "We really appreciate your time and assistance. If you do think of anything else, this is my direct-line."

Tom stood up, placing a small white card on the bedside table, and cocked his head at Neil.

"Yes, thanks for your help. I hope you're well enough to get back home soon," Neil said, flashing her a thin-lipped smile as he got to his feet.

The detectives left the hospital. Halfway across the car park, Tom Broad received a call and tapped his iPhone to speakerphone.

"Go ahead, Spence. We're just leaving St Martins now."

"We've completed door-to-door on the streets where the car was parked for eighteen minutes in Plaistow, guv. Unfortunately, nobody can recall seeing the Jaguar. It's only the end house, err.., number 35, Silver Mews terrace, that we haven't had any response from."

"You can't say we've *completed* door-to-door if there's still another house to go to, Spence," Neil said, sporting a childlike smirk.

With an arched eyebrow at his number two, Tom said, "Find out who lives there and when they might be back in residence, would you Spence?"

"Yes we did make enquiries, guv. Apparently it's a very senior citizen who lives there; keeps herself to herself. She may be deaf as she doesn't respond to neighbours, who only get the occasional wave. One guy said that she doesn't answer the door after dark," Spencer said.

"Ok, well let's try her again tomorrow when it's light. A flash car like that, parked there for nearly twenty minutes. Somebody must have noticed!" Tom said.

"Where I'm from, they'd have had the wheels off in two!" Neil said, with a wink.

"What about CCTV?" Tom said, lifting his index finger at Neil.

"It was seen turning into the neighbourhood off the main trunk road, but the street where it's recorded as stationary has a black-spot. There's no coverage there, guv," Spencer said.

"Anything from the footage in Leeds, where it was torched?" Tom said, in a hopeful change in tone.

"It was parked-up on waste ground, so there weren't any cameras in the area. Funny thing though, guv," Spencer said. "Yorkshire Police have confirmed that the Jag was parked on the exact same patch of land where they discovered the first victim of the Ripper."

"That has to be significant," Tom said.

"I would definitely say so, boss. It was also the point at which the marches started and finished in the late '70's," Spencer said.

"Marches, what marches?" Neil said, with a wrinkled brow.

"Thousands of women marched in protest against the police curfew on them. The detectives in charge of the Ripper case had said that no woman should be out alone at night! There was countrywide anger," Spencer snapped back at Neil. "West Yorkshire Police were seen to be blaming women."

"Send me what you have on that will you please, Spence," Tom said.

"There are some really interesting national press articles from that time. So similar to the demonstrations that we had at the Old Bailey trial recently. All these years later and nothing's changed for women."

"Yeah-yeah, here she goes. Would you like me to chain you to some railings, Spence!" Neil said, eye rolling at Tom. "This is hardly 1970's England!"

"Please just ignore him, Spence," Tom said.

"Yep, that's a given, guv," Spencer said.

"And just ping me everything that you've got there over, will you," Tom said.

"On it as we speak, guv," she said.

"Good work, Spence," Tom said, concluding the call with a slow shake of his head at his number two.

PART III — TAKEN

CHAPTER 21
TWO YEARS EARLIER

"Hello," she whispered, her voice weak, shaky.

"My God, finally, she calls!" Bella said, with a heavy exhale. "Where yous been, girl?" she added, adopting their old Uni language.

"Err, sorry. Iye-Iye, I've been busy," she said. "I'm so pleased to hear your voice, Bel," she added softly.

"God you sound like you're about to burst out crying," Bella said. "What's happening babe, not boyfriend trouble again?"

A snivelling filled Bella's ears.

"Jesus, this ain't good. I'm coming to see you, Baby. What's your address.."

"No. No. You mustn't come here," she blurted, sobbing softly.

"Baby, I have to help you, you're my best friend," Bella said, insistently.

There was no response, only a deepening whimper, a stop-start sobbing that she fought to control. Breathing heavily between each fear-gripped sob, desperate to gain composure.

"Just tell me where you are and I'll come get you?" Bella said, feeling her own bottom lip now tremble, her eyes welling.

"It's too dangerous, Bel.," she whispered.

There was a fear-filled pause between them, an unnerving silence.

"It's man-trouble again, isn't it? You have to get away, to leave," Bella said, trying to be strong for her friend. "If he's laid a finger on you, I swear.."

"Th-they know everything.. they'll kill.."

"They, what!.. who's they? What do you mean.."

"I have to go now.." There was trepidation in her rising pitch, in her every trembled word.

"Oh no you don't. You're not leaving this call until I know you're safe," Bella said.

"I, I will get in trouble if I don't.." she blubbered, before a piercing, pain-filled shriek.

Bella jerked the phone from her ear, such was her friend's scream, before the line went dead. Stood bolt upright, she redialled the number. Rigid in shock she dialled it again, and again, as a tear escaped her watering eyes.

Wiping the sleeve of her hoodie across her cheeks, she rifled a chest of drawers before finally locating a small brown pocket address book. Bella dabbed carefully at her iPhone.

"Hello, Sadie?" was the instant response.

"Hi, Mrs Barlow. No, it's Bella, Bella Maxwell. How are you?" she said.

"Oh hello Bella. Sorry, my love, I was hoping it was Sadie calling," Mrs Barlow said.

"I'm sorry to call so late and unexpectedly, but I'm really worried about Sadie," Bella said. "I finally got to speak to her, and then the line got cut off. She sounded in trouble, scared."

"We're as worried as you are Bella. She's picked another wrong-un, I'm sorry to say. We've had a big falling out about it and she sided with him of course.

She told us not to get involved. So I can't be of much help, I'm afraid," Mrs Barlow said.

"I need an address if you have one please, Mrs B," Bella said.

"Now that, I can help you with. But please bear in mind that she wouldn't thank me for it," Mrs Barlow said, as she made her way into her dining room.

"Yes, that's not a problem; I didn't get it from you!" Bella said.

"Ahh, here we go.., 52 Lockwood Road, East Barnsted," Mrs Barlow said, before reading the postcode and confirming her mobile number. "She never answers the phone though. We haven't heard from her for weeks now."

"I'm going to try and find out what's been going on. Thanks for your help, Mrs B," Bella said.

"Well it's been nice to hear from you again, Bella. Perhaps we can.."

"Yes, we will have to have a proper catch-up soon," Bella interrupted, and hung up.

She swiped at her iPhone screen, tapping East Barnsted into Google Maps. She zoomed in on Lockwood Road, before switching it to street view. She held the phone a little closer as she swished along the Victorian terrace, checking door numbers as she did. There it was, a faded number plate '52', hung at 45 degrees on the virtually paint-stripped, pale blue door. The shabby-looking mid-terrace townhouse looked in serious need of attention.

It reminded Bella of their student digs, that she and her bestie, Sadie 'Baby' Barlow had shared when at Manchester University together. Her nickname had stuck from the first day Bella met her and was struck by her friend's angelic face. Her plump cherub-cheeks and the cutest spray of faded freckles bridging her nose. Sadie looked so much younger than everyone else at Uni.

Bella changed quickly, grabbing car keys and coat off the hook and leaving via the back door.

CHAPTER 22

"How the fuck did you get hold of that!" he bellowed, explosive in anger. "And who the hell were you talking to?" he added, in a splutter of spittle, firing down on Sadie's head.

Her chin instantly pinned to her chest, before his fingers slid her jawline as his hand fisted tightly around her throat. Sadie's feet lifted from the attic floor, as he hauled her up the damp-stained wall.

"So, you found your phone did you!" he snarled. "Well you ain't gonna be using that again!"

Sadie's face purpled before he flung her across the room with a sweeping thrust of his arm; like a baseball pitcher. She crumpled to the floor in a heap, gasping for air. He smashed the phone to the floorboards beside her, splitting it into pieces. She flinched and crawled to the wardrobe, cowering beside it.

The low ceiling above her was alcoved with a single skylight on one side, the size of a narrow tea-tray. Rain water had black-spotted the space around it, rotting the floor below it, where a seeping mould spread across its darkening boards. The walls of the little room were clouded in fungi, mushrooming from a mossy epi-centre in one corner.

The mould spores were so dense in places that she could almost see it breathing. It seeped, destroying all in its path, having long since peeled the nursery's pink wallpaper that had once depicted Disney Princesses. Faded shreds lay in the shadows of the walls amidst the deepening dust.

"There'll be no food for you tonight!" he sneered at her.

He strode slowly over to where she sat, curled up, with knees to her chest. A rusted metal z-bed sat along the far wall with makeshift bedpan beneath it. The stench of urine remained dominant of the stools that lay within it. It hadn't been cleaned out for days now.

"You're out of here next week, so you'd better shape up. I want a decent price. Clean yourself up," he snarled, throwing a plastic bag at her feet.

"I'll be back for pictures in an hour," he said, whilst digging in the waist pockets of his tan corduroy jacket. "Get some of this on you, and make it look good," he added, flinging tubes of cosmetics at her.

She shuddered as they clattered against the wardrobe, dropping at her discoloured feet. Sadie sat shivering in her underwear, curled in a ball. Her face remained in her knees, buried beneath a mass of dishevelled brown hair that almost covered her body. The wooden door thudded to a close before a hefty clank of metal as the chubb key turned its lock, ker-clunk.

Sadie Barlow unfurled herself, crawling from the small pine wardrobe and picking at the shattered pieces of her phone. She had only just discovered it the last time she had been allowed out of the room, and hid it beneath a rot-softened floorboard.

The tortuous weeks that she had spent in that room would soon be over, and yet Sadie knew, from the deep-voiced conversation she had overheard, that far worse was to come. Tears flowed effortlessly from her bushbaby eyes, flooding her rosy cheeks. On hands and knees she crawled the creaking boards to curl on the narrow bed, shuddering as she pulled the crochet blanket to her chin.

Her screams, strangled by fear, remained lodged in her throat. She whimpered like a wounded animal, defeated and awaiting its inevitable fate.

CHAPTER 23

MANCHESTER, ENGLAND

Posters of Zoe filled either side of the shallow bay window of their front room. Age-faded, they had been there for as long as anyone in the street could remember. It had been two years, but it felt like a lifetime. The grief of their loss had served to elongate time, and the Garrett family had lived each day in a constant state of distress.

And the time before that, when they were complete as a family, was all but a fading memory, a flicker through the photo album on her birthday. A day when candles would be planted and lit on Zoe's favourite, cream topped sponge. A cake that would never be eaten. Their loss was too great, their heartache forever raw, existing each day amidst the faintest whisper of hope.

Sara Garrett looked long and hard into the circular mirror that sat on her dressing table. In truth it was only a small chest of drawers, alongside which a pink cushioned stool sat. Greying Manchester skies provided only muted light that barely filtered the netted bedroom window; probably a blessing she thought.

No amount of expensive creams were going to smooth the lines that now ploughed her once soft complexion. Her pain-stained chestnut eyes peered back, propped by reddened sagging folds that only sunglasses could disguise. Sara was forty today. She felt, and looked, sixty.

Michael Garrett ripped one of the posters from the glass, and picked off the yellowing paper's tape-stuck edges. He screwed it all tightly, tossing it to the floor. A gut-churning pang of guilt rushed to his chest. A bull-like blast of air gushed his nostrils as he peeled gently at the second poster, working loose the sellotape from its corners. He removed it carefully as one, laying it across his lap as he slumped to the sofa.

MISSING: Zoe Garrett (16) it read above her picture. Appeal fundraising information, and contact numbers crammed the bottom of the poster.

Michael stared solemnly at his girl. It haunted him now, that media-branded image, her youthful energy and innocence that looked back up at him. From her excitable cheeky smile he could hear the giggle that followed. He had a way of making her laugh, even when she was at her grumpiest, which had become more often than not. But Mike still heard it every day. In the moments that he wrestled to fitful sleep, to the instant he awoke. In the early days, he thought she was back, there in the house.

The photo was taken on their family trip to Blackpool for Zoe and Sara's joint birthday. Zo was insistent that she was seeing friends on the actual day, so the weekend before her sixteenth they went away to celebrate. It would be the last time that he would see that smile.

The poster was all wrong, and Mike had said so from the start. It looked like something from the wild west; 'Wanted.' And the photo wasn't right; they needed Zoe's normal, grouchy expression. Her whole face changed when she smiled, it lifted and softened. Zoe looked beautiful, but they needed to find her. They had to show people what she would actually look like; she wouldn't be smiling.

They'd argued about it, of course. Sara won, as she had done about everything in the last two years. She wanted the public onside, sympathetic and motivated to look, to search and to pray for her little girl. She needed the world to love Zoe as she did.

Having been served with divorce papers yesterday, Mike had hardly slept, but was ready to resume battle. He had spent the night cooped-up in the box room. The mattress was lumpy and worn; bought years ago, when they had toddlers in the house.

"What are you doing?" Sara said, as calmly as she could. "Get them back up!"

Mike, broken from his daze, folded the poster across and laid it on the coffee table in front of him.

"They're coming down today. I don't care what you say, we're moving on. We have to, for the sake of us!" he said, surprising himself at how assertive he sounded. "It's been two years, we have to start living again, Sara."

"I don't care about us anymore Mike," Sara said, with hands on hips. "It's over between us."

"Look, we've gotta sort things out," Mike said, taking Zoe's poster over to the sideboard and slipping it in the top draw. "It's not good for you, me or Jack. We have to find a way through this, together."

He lifted a wooden framed photo of the four of them from the mantle. Jack was already taller than his dad in the picture, taken just before he had left for Uni, three years ago.

"Look at us babe, we're still a family," Mike said, waving the photograph.

"Jack's not here anymore and without Zo there's nothing left. I'm sorry Mike, but it's over," Sara said, easing sunshades from her spray-stiffened, immovable hair.

"I won't accept that, Sara," he said, following her into the hall. "Let's just sit down and talk about it."

"We've done all the talking, Mike. Besides, I have to be somewhere right now," she said.

The loss of their daughter had been catastrophic to the couple - it had broken them. They both loved her desperately. She was both a daddy's and mummy's girl. With an older protective brother Jack, Zo had it all and was at the centre of their universe, the heartbeat of the family. She had been the glue that had held them together, through good times and bad.

"You look good by the way, nice outfit," Mike said, just noticing that Sara was wearing her purple dress, the figure hugging one that she hadn't worn for ages.

Surprised and a little confused as to why his wife was so well dressed today, a surge of anger pulsed through him. The thought that she was visiting her solicitor jumped out, him having just been served with divorce papers.

"Going anywhere nice?" he pressed softly, submerging his annoyance.

"Yes, I'm having lunch with Tricia and Anna," she said, whilst squeezing her heel into a black stiletto. "You do know it's my birthday, Mike?"

"Of course! I've got a little something for you, but I wanted to give you tonight," he said, inwardly cursing his absentmindedness. "I was hoping we might go out and discuss things over dinner. I've booked us a table at Venitos."

He could surely get a late booking on a Tuesday. Sara eyed him for a moment, with a shake of her head and one-sided smile. His hands slid deep into the pockets of his jeans; he was lying.

"Bullshit you did, Mike," Sara said, unlatching the front door. "By the way, it's my fortieth, in case you didn't know!" she said, slamming the door behind her.

In bereavement the pair had become isolated, drifting into a darker emptiness that lay in wait. For Zoe's brother Jack, Uni provided much needed distraction and solace from the deepening depression that had consumed home. Whereas Mike became detached and insular in mourning her loss, Sara had simply refused to accept it. Zoe would never be dead, until it was proven so.

The police had been active in their initial efforts to trace her, but with every passing day it seemed less and less was being done. Early hot leads were quickly extinguished and new lines of enquiry, one-by-one insensitively labelled as dead ends. Despite ongoing appeals thereafter, nothing new emerged as months turned to years.

At one stage a connection to the so-called TikTokTrio case was considered. A Premier League footballer, celebrity DJ, and billionaire financier, had been accused of the abduction and murder of teenage girls. Three teenagers were found to have been taken from coastal resorts around England, in not dissimilar circumstances to Zoe's disappearance.

The three men were questioned extensively, denying any knowledge of Zoe Garrett or her whereabouts. They had since been tried, and acquitted of all charges.

CHAPTER 24

EAST BARNSTED

'What a shit-hole, baby,' Bella Maxwell thought to herself, staring across at 52 Lockwood Road. 'You can't be living here, surely.'

She had knocked on the door and yelled through the hole in the front door that doubled as a letterbox, without response. It seemed that nobody was home so, reclining a little in her car seat, Bella decided to sit and wait.

Sadie 'Baby' Barlow was her best friend, and had been since the moment they met, and buddied-up, on that first day at Manchester University. They both later shared that they'd felt an instant connection, an indefinable likability. It went deeper than their shared traits and sense of humour (and passion for practical jokes). They were inseparable. A look between them across a lecture hall was conversational; they had an almost telepathic understanding.

Sadie, being the youngest girl at Uni and still with childlike, chubby-cheeks, was nicknamed 'Baby'. Sadie and Bella both studied Law and thrived. The high-flyers of their year, they would micromanage mock trials, thrashing out legal technicalities. Their skills in evidence collation and presentation earned recognition of esteemed lecturers.

Socially they would mix with others, but always ended evenings together, recounting that night's drunken male advances, over a large Hawaiian pizza. Both had engaged in short-term relationships with guys. But from the nightclub gropers to the dark street stalkers, they held little regard for men.

Both girls came from a siblingless, single-parent upbringing. Grand-parent in Bella's case, having lost her mother, aged four she had endured extensive periods of poverty. For both, bullying was a daily occurrence, primarily as a result of their dishevelled appearance. Uniforms were rarely washed, and both recalled unkempt, clumpy long hair. Despite hardship, their academic brilliance would not be suppressed.

It was at Manchester University that the pair truly blossomed. And with bursary allowance, they had money for the first time. Shopping was finally a thing, a pleasure regularly paired with hair and nail salon visits. The ugly ducklings of childhood transformed into beautiful swans, embracing the calmer waters of adulthood.

East Barnsted was an impoverished inner-city borough, notorious only for poverty and petty crime; the two linking hand-in-hand. Lockwood Road appeared almost derelict. If it hadn't been for the curtain twitcher at 48, Bella might have driven straight through it, believing she had been given the wrong address.

The parallel rows of red brick terraced houses had no frontage, the front doors opening directly onto a narrow pavement. Nobody answered Bella's knocking at number 52, which had more than its share of tall weeds, sprouting between broken paving slabs. They all but covered the lower half of its paint-faded door. The ground floor window was boarded-up and the one directly above it had been smashed, leaving an ice-braking effect splintering from its centre. She knocked again, but there was no response.

Bella parked on the opposite side of the road and sat tight. She craned her neck, noticing a glint-like reflection in the fading light. Unlike the others, the rooftop of number 52 had a narrow pane of glass where a velux-type skylight had been fitted. The roof held a frosty-whiteness, in contrast to the red tiles of its neighbours.

For hours, nothing moved in the street, its silence was deafening, until it was broken by the shrill squeals of territorial cats that bolted Bella upright from semi-slumber. At 01:00 am she fastened her seatbelt and bounced her phone onto the passenger seat. It appeared nobody was coming home tonight. Before turning the key in the ignition, she peeled to release a mint from its cylindrical foil.

At that moment the door of 52 opened and was replaced by a man that stepped over the foliage that greeted him, turned and pulled the door to. The street lamp a few doors further up offered little until he passed directly beneath it.

An average looking middle aged white man, wearing tan chinos and a corduroy jacket with patches on the elbows, strode purposefully on. With a crown thinning patch catching the light, the man held a respectable, professor-esque appearance. Bella's eyebrows remained arched; he was clearly someone at odds with this place. Why hadn't he answered the door earlier, and where he was going at this time of night?

"Excuse me, sir?" Bella said, from across the street, bounding from her car. "I knocked on your door earlier.."

He paused mid-stride, half-turned towards her, statuesque for an instant, before tucking his brown satchel tightly under his arm.

"I wonder if you can help me. I'm looking for my friend," she said, puffing as she got within a few metres of the gentleman, who looked even more studious closeup.

The man adjusted his glasses, pinching the frame and wiggling them closer to his eyes, as if to examine her.

"I'm sorry, but I have absolutely no idea what you are talking about," he said, dismissively.

"You just came from number 52.."

"Yes, yes I live there," he snapped.

"I was given to understand that my friend lived there with her boyfriend.."

"Your understanding is wrong," he said, scratching the bridge of his nose before marching away.

"But could she be renting a room, or.." Bella said, falling behind him.

"I think I would be aware of that, don't you!" he replied, lengthening his stride as he approached the end of the street.

"Could she have lived there before you?" Bella's question was ignored. "How long have you been living there?" she shouted, as the man hurried on, disappearing around the corner.

Bella jogged and caught him up, grabbing at his left elbow. He flinched, yanking it to his chest.

"Excuse me, young lady!" he said, turning and berating her. "I repeat I have no idea what you're talking about. Kindly leave me alone, or I will call the police and have you arrested for harassment."

"Call the police!" she said, with widening eyes. "Harassment! What harassment?"

Bella stood shaking her head, as he again scurried away.

"I'm only trying to find my friend. She was living at number 52, possibly before you, dickhead!"

Bella turned and strode back to her car, regretting having approached the man, rather than follow him. He seemed very odd, jumpy and was definitely out of place in an area like this.

Bella started the engine, slid the heating bar toward the red banner, and cupped her hands in front of the slatted vent whilst peering over at number 52. Why hadn't the 'professor' answered the door earlier, and where was he going at this time of night?

The chilling thought that Sadie could be inside the property flickered in her mind. She bit gently at her plump bottom lip, then killed the engine. She bound over to the door, knocking hard. Calling her name and banging harder prompted some curtain tugging at 48, as Bella stepped back.

The professor hardly looked like the kidnapping sort. It was probably a case of Bella taking down the wrong address. She checked at time: 01:38. She would go and see Mrs Barlow in the morning and get the correct one, it was too late to call now.

CHAPTER 25

BLACKPOOL – ABDUCTION OF ZOE GARRETT

His nostrils flared and eyes widened, feasting at the grill plate, where fresh-cut white sliced onions sizzled. A side-eyed glance wasn't enough, he slowed to savour the aroma, from the meat-filled griddle.

"You fancy one, Zo?" Mike Garrett said, inviting his daughter, with a nod toward the *BurgerDreams* food bar. A small caravan, the shape of a hamburger and similarly painted, with a yellow stripe running across its middle.

Walking the entire length of the pleasure beach had certainly sharpened Mike's appetite. Sara and Jack had decided to brave the big-dipper, or at least its queue. The bigger rollers weren't their thing, so Mike and Zoe had time on their side. It usually ended up like this, with Zoe and her Dad strolling around, taking in the sights. The previous summer they'd spent a few days at Eurodisney. They had enjoyed it more watching the street parades, rather than standing in the neverending queues. The entertainment, and characters came to them.

"I'd rather have a doughnut, Dad," Zoe said, tugging at the crook of his immovable arm, as he drew to a stop.

The sweet treats were all the way back near the entrance, and not in the same league as the thick sausages that were browning nicely in front of Mike. Besides, he was already standing in the short line to the van.

"This'll fill you up much better than a doughnut, sweetie," Mike said, stroking her soft hair with his plump fingers.

"Ahh, come on Dad, it smells greasy, and there's no veggie option," Zoe complained, being the part-time vegetarian that she was. She tugged at his elbow a little harder.

"Look, here's a fiver. You go get your doughnut and something to drink," Mike said, peeling a note from his rapidly thinning wad. "Then meet me on one of those benches," he added, pointing at a crowded area of picnic-style benches, all of which appeared taken.

"Thanks, Dad," Zoe said, sparkly-eyed as she pocketed the money. She blew him a kiss and scampered off, her waist-long hair swishing behind her.

"Don't be long.. and I want change!" he said, with a beaming smile at the back of her bouncing head. He turned to review the menu board; now, *'chilli, or cheese dog'* he thought. He decided, both.

Zoe Garrett dodged through the throng of building crowds, finding her way back to the theme park's entrance. The music was loud here, all 80's songs booming out. They had noticed the fresh ring-doughnut stand, enjoying its sweet waft earlier, whilst waiting to get into the park. *'Great positioning,'* Dad had remarked.

'They get you as soon as you arrive, and then again when you're leaving. And, it's right by the gift shop,' Dad said, eye-pointing, whilst shoulder-rocking along to Madness. He was right of course, in Zoe's eyes, Dad always was.

A fresh-faced young guy in an Ellesse grey hoodie stood between the doughnut and coffee stands with an arm around a huge Winnie the Pooh. Zoe had spotted a row of Pooh-bears, and Tiggers on the Hook-a-duck stall earlier.

"Hiya," he mouthed, above the sound of Madonna demanding everyone, *'Get into the groove.'*

The young lad smiled over at her, resting his chin playfully on Winnie's head. He looked about her age, maybe older, wearing cool gear and white AirForce trainers. Waving the bear's paw, he beckoned her over, Zoe beamed back. There were quite a few people in the queue ahead of her.

"Hey, that's a cute bear," Zoe said, stepping from the line.

"I know, I just won him," he said, smoothing down the bear's red waistcoat. "But, he's yours, if you'll have him?" he added, doe-eyed.

"Aww really, that's so sweet, but I couldn't," Zoe said, wide-eyed. "Although Winnie is one of my all time faves!"

"Then you *gotta take him!*" the boy said, wiping the bear's paw across its eye. "He'll be upset if you don't," he said, flashing a perfect white smile.

"Well, only if you're sure," Zoe said, beaming. "Thank you so much. It's actually my birthday in a few days."

"Congrats, that's all the more reason. Here.. he's yours," he said, holding Winnie out.

He held Zoe's excited gaze, her youthful innocence, as he took a step back between the two stalls, bobbing Pooh bear in front of her. She reached out, slipping her hands around its tubby belly. At that moment his hands clasped her forearms, tugging her body hard toward him.

In an instant his arm was around her waist, his hand across her mouth, spinning and dragging her to the rear of the stalls. Behind him, a white van sat whirring, its side-sliding door gaping an inner blackness. Zoe, with eyes bulging and legs thrashing, was hauled inside to the *shhhstt* of the door as it zipped across. It was the only sound, she was gone in seconds.

The vehicle crept slowly away via a staff access point, unnoticed and muted by the boisterous sounds of the fairground. Minutes later, and after the last bite of his double hot-dog, Mike Garrett was meerkat-like in his scanning of the funfair. But Zoe wasn't there, and little did he know, he wouldn't see her again.

Sara could tell as she approached her husband that something was very wrong. Her face instantly etched with worry, and with every passing minute a deepening pain clamped her chest as a rising panic consumed her. It was incomprehensible and overwhelming, and a moment from which Sara, and the Garrett family would never recover.

CHAPTER 26

"So, we move her tonight?" the man on the phone said, abruptly.

"I just wasn't sure that you could do it that quickly," he whispered.

With the command of an Army Major, the man boomed, "It's not fuckin' rocket science. Location discovered; we close it down!"

"Yes of course, sorry," he said, softly.

"I'll ping you the number for the clean-team. Contact them now and get her moved to the transfer house near Heathrow, and await clearance. What's the name again?" the man said.

"Err, erm, it's Jade," he said, fumbling in his pocket. "No-no, sorry that's not right. Here we are, yes it's Sadie. Sadie Barlow," he replied, his cheeks reddening, as he checked his shoulder.

He stuffed her passport back inside the inner pocket of his corduroy jacket.

"Fine, let the cleaners in and get it to the safe house. There's another one down there already, so this could work out quite well," he paused, rustling papers. "Hang on a second, mate."

He heard him briefly in discussion with someone in the background "Yeah, we've got that sixteen year old Zoe Garrett that we picked up in Blackpool. Could we get them both on the same flight."

After some incoherent mumbling he was back, "Right-yes, get yours down there as soon as pal.."

"And-err, when do I get paid?" he half-interrupted. "I mean I've been holding her for a long time for you guys," he added, softening his tone.

"And you've had regular customers, at full prostitute rates," the man snapped back.

"Yes, yes I know, and the extra cash has been useful, but that's not what I did it for. And, it's not what the advert offered," he said, with a breathy exhale. "I'm sorry but I'm not some sort of pimp. I'm a University lecturer for Christ's sake!" he said, balling his fists.

"Look, just calm down. We have explained all this before. There has to be a holding period. You can't just fly them out of the country. We have to await clearance, to get papers in order, and cut any ties before we shift them. Patience, my friend," the man said.

"But when exactly do I receive the body stock payment you promise? I didn't do it for a few quid here and there!" he said, his tone hardening with every word.

"Look, you've had your fun with her too, mate. So don't start all this, 'woe-is-me' bollocks. We do see everything you know!" the man said.

"What - you've been watching the house?" he exclaimed, squealing slightly.

"Every fuckin' room mate. What do you think we do? Every location we have is pre-wired," the man said, proudly. "So yes, we know exactly how many times you've dipped your wick, Professor fuckalot!"

"Look, I just want to know when I'll get the fifty-k that was agreed," he said, whispering now.

"Same as we've said from day one; once it's through passport control at the other end, the money is transferred to you. Now you're wasting my time and risking a potentially breached location. So, get to work," the man ordered.

"Okay I'll.." he said, peering at his iPhone screen; the call had been disconnected.

He threw a limp smile and nod at the glassy-eyed woman, elbow-propped behind the counter of the 24/7 internet cafe. An icy blast bit as he exited, clattering the door shut behind him. His cell phone bleeped.

As he strode the desolate, moonlit street he dabbed his mobile, opening a text that displayed a new contact icon. He poked it and was instantly connected to the 'clean-team.'

CHAPTER 27

It was a cosy little house and yet an uncomfortable undercurrent hung heavy inside. There always was, whenever Bella visited, and *he* was there. Despite his obvious resentment of their house guest's presence, Lesley Barlow was desperate to please, to be hospitable.

"Sorry Bella, but it's the only address I have for her. Sadie did text it to me. Look.," Lesley said, flashing her phone screen in front of Bella.

52 Lockwood Road, East Barnsted

He tutted loudly from the other end of their dining-through-living room, whilst sitting in his armchair, mansplaying and glaring over, observing their every move.

"Well, this is the man who walked out of that house," Bella said, sharing an image with Lesley. "Do you recognise him?"

"Gosh, no. He's not Sadie's type at all," she said, behind a worried expression. "He's a lot older. He looks very well-to-do, doesn't he."

"Well unfortunately, he wasn't very helpful."

"Maybe she's renting a room from him," Lesley said.

"He said not. But I think he was hiding something, definitely lying!" Bella declared.

"Lying.. are you sure, Bella?" Lesley said. There was a slight tremble in her voice.

"There was lots of face touching, and an awkwardness about him," Bella said, circling the highly polished dining table.

"But why would he lie about that? He looks like a respectable gentleman."

"I'm not sure yet, but something wasn't right. The place looks derelict, completely run down," Bella said, shaking her head.

Lesley's partner, Roger, chuckled loud enough to be heard. "Tha'd suit her down'tut ground then, wun't it!" he said.

He remained slumped in his high winged armchair at the far end of their narrow living room, fixing his gaze to the wall-mounted television screen in front of him.

Bella ignored the interruption, turning back to Lesley, who's shoulders had slumped a little more. She looked considerably older than Bella remembered her. Lesley was always the same in front of her male partners, timid and on edge; like a mouse cornered by a tomcat.

"Look, it's been almost five weeks now, something doesn't add up. I'm going to go back there and see if I can get a look inside. I think Sadie's got herself into some kind of trouble!" Bella said.

"Well it wun't be first time, would it!" he chortled.

Bella slid on her jacket, slipping her iPhone into her pocket. Stopping at the living room door, she nodded reassuringly at Lesley. Her crumpled face stared helplessly back. She mustered a limp, pink-cheeked grin whilst fiddling with the newspapers that lay on the dining room table.

"She can't just disappear, and we all sit around doing nothing. We have to do something to help her," Bella said, in his direction, before marching down the hallway.

He grunted something indecipherable amidst some dismissive huffing.

Lesley scurried out of the living room after Bella.

"It was good to see you again, Mrs B. I'll let you know if I find out anything," Bella said, half-turned at the front door.

"Yes, you too, Bella. Do take care, won't you.," Lesley said, as the door slammed.

CHAPTER 28

52 LOCKWOOD ROAD, EAST BARNSTED

It was just past nine am when Bella pulled up and turned her engine off, parking in almost the exact same spot as the night before, opposite number 52. The same curtain from two doors down twitched as it had the previous evening.

Outside the property, a white van was parked, with its rear doors wide. The front door of the house was open and Bella could see a staircase to the left, off the entrance. She jumped out and crossed the road quickly. As she approached the doorway, she heard male voices inside, coming from upstairs.

Bella slipped inside, into the narrow hall. She was immediately hit by the stench of decay that seemed to surround her from the bare walls. It smelt stale, mouldy more fungi-based than food. Deep voices were arguing immediately above her, whilst shuffling something heavy across the floorboards.

Bella crept silently through the tapering corridor into a galley kitchen at the back of the house. It had been cleared of furniture and the cupboard doors hung open; every shelf was bare. Suddenly there was a plank groaning movement on the stairway. Bella eased the kitchen door to within an inch of closed, peering one-eyed through the gap.

Two thickset men struggled to manoeuvre the tight turn at the end of the flight of stairs, with arms hooked to either end of a huge bed. Expletives boomed from the man at the rear as he stumbled in missing the penultimate step. Re-establishing his hold, the two exited the house with their load.

Bella glided back through the hallway and bounded softly the stairs. At the top, a creaky floor-boarded corridor, had three open doors coming off it. Glancing in each, they were as below, stripped bare, leaving dingy dust-floating rooms in their wake. At the far end there was a part-banistered narrow flight of steps that led up to an attic door above.

The voices were back inside the house. Bella double-stepped, scaling the stairs, squeaking the final step at the faded green door at the top. She slowly turned the round metal handle. It was locked.

"Final check mate. You take upstairs and I'll do down here."

Laboured footsteps creaked the stairs.

'Shit, shit, shit' Bella spread flat to the door. There was nowhere to go, she twisted again at the door knob. There was thudding from below as the large man stomped the rooms, clattering wardrobe doors open and closed.

Bella slunk to her knees, her back pinned hard against the pale green door. She could see his shadow at the foot of the bannister now. She quivered as a booming voice echoed up from the ground floor.

"Are you done up there? I've already sealed the clink-room, mate."

A huge sausage-fingered hand smothered the ball-shaped turnall of the bannister post.

"You sure pal?"

"Yeah, I've got the key here mate," he said, impatiently.

"Ok, let's get going," he said, his fleshy hand disappearing. "Have you ordered the burn yet?" he quizzed, as he clattered downstairs.

The voices disappeared into the street with a clink of metal turning in its lock, followed by a hefty slam of the front door. The house fell silent. Bella blew heavily as she made her way downstairs. She searched, desperate for something to prise open the green 'clink-room' door, but each of the ground floor rooms were bare.

The boxy paper-peeling front room had been completely stripped of furnishings and light fittings. Discoloured rectangles bore evidence of the many pictures that once hung from the walls. Wires dangled from the ceiling and walls to either side of a black grated fireplace. The earthy stench hit Bella again, as her eyes trailed to the darkest corner of the room. A mushrooming growth clung high above skirting boards. Its stem-spiked spores rippled from the chill draught that had breezed in behind her.

Had this place ever been a home? Bella shuddered at the thought as she entered the back room. Here an open fireplace sat in ruin amidst crumbling stonework. Any stove it had once held had been carelessly removed. Bella grabbed the largest piece of broken brickwork and headed upstairs.

On her sixth swing of the brick, the round door handle buckled, collapsing from the frame. Bella poked a finger inside the fitting fiddling relentlessly, she wiggled the mechanism, twisted it hard, achieving a click. Ramming her shoulder into the flaking paintwork, the door burst open as she staggered three steps inside.

It reminded her a little of the attic space at her Grandfather's house, only this was worse, a lot worse. For a start it made her eyes sting. As with the other rooms it had been completely stripped. But unlike the rest of the house, here the pungency of human bodily odours were ripe.

Bella pinched tightly her nostrils as she scanned the room. Fingerprints were smeared across the glass skylight above. In desperation of fresh air herself,

Bella pushed and pulled at its handle but to no avail; it had been sealed shut. The ceiling around it was damp and there was a relentless dripping from its frame on one side.

Bella stood headshaking, aghast at the mould-ridden space. Could Sadie really have been here? Her mind was racing, her eyes welling. She shuddered hard against the icy cold that gripped the attic. Was it possible that this was all a mistake; Sadie had simply given her mum the wrong address?

But Sadie had sounded so distressed and was no longer contactable. It didn't make sense, or did it? Had she found yet another controlling, violent boyfriend?

There was a darker, less time-faded patch on the wall, from where a poster might have been stuck. Alongside it was a larger discoloured rectangular area, possibly the shape of a small wardrobe or large chest. At its foot there were some scratched markings near the floor, where a skirting board had previously run.

Bella flinched, as a mouse squeezed from a gap, barely a marker pen in thickness, scurrying across the room. 'On your way my friend,' Bella said to the little grey creature that disappeared into an invisible hole on the opposite wall. Mouldy patches ran the length of the walls, seeping from jagged cracks in the plasterboard and climbing to merge with the fungi-laden ceiling.

Dropping to her hands and knees, Bella took a closer look at the markings. The boards were damp here, and warm against the chill of the room. She instinctively cupped her nose as the foul stench of faeces hit her; like a slap across her face. Her eyes watered in protection of the stinging fetor.

Blinkingly, she refocused on the scratches. There was nothing to indicate when they had been made, but they appeared to be count marks; gates of five. Four downward lines, with a single mark slashed across them, counting five days. It had another gate alongside it and then another further along and another.

There were six gates and another three thicker lines, much darker and finger-painted, in red. Bella gingerly sniffed her hand that had rested on the floor, head-cocking; it was urine. She threw her nose into the crook of her elbow and leaned in again, adding the markings; thirty three.

A feeling of dread hit the pit of her stomach. Sadie had been uncontactable for thirty three days now. Bella poked her fingertip onto the last line, swiping across it. It smudged easily; it was fresh. Her complexion whitened as thick bile hit the back of her throat.

Sadie, her best friend, had been imprisoned here. Bella lurched to her feet, her stomach-turned as she doubled over and threw up.

PART IV – HUNTED

CHAPTER 29

ISLE OF EL–MARNEY, INDIAN OCEAN – PRESENT DAY

Bella, with her heart still pounding from her near vertical waterfall descent, crouched behind a patch of large-leafed bushes. She was now fifty metres away from Roman Darcy's private island retreat, the infamous Villa Asri. According to Pascal, locals say it means beautiful; a beauty that brings pleasure to the eye and a calm to the senses.

It was lit by garish laser beams that swept its walls, before funnelling skywards. The high-powered lights encircled the entire property that was set in isolation, nestled between majestic cliffs to either side. The dazzling lights had led the way. Bella's map reading session with Pascal hadn't been necessary.

A loudening hunting group had shocked Bella, fearing she had been spotted upon landing on the tropical island. But its boisterous participants and noisy hounds had suddenly distanced, heading off in the opposite direction, tracking goodness knows what.

A gunshot had sent her heart racing, as she sped ever faster to where she hunched now, scanning the white-walled buildings before her. She jerked her hand from the tree beside her as an extraordinarily large, furry caterpillar mounted her thumb. Bella lowered the zip of her windbreaker, flicking sweat beads that were pooling at her collarbone.

The complex was impressive, set over three floors. Its white walls were speckled with cone-shaped lamps; like Olympic torches. In the star-lit night the retreat's swimming pool glimmered, like a sheet of glass.

Bella dabbed her sleeves on her temples and sat on the thick grass, loosening her rucksack. Despite the late hour, it seemed eerily quiet, there were no signs of life. The large ground floor windows were tinted and those above had dark shutters pulled across. The upper terrace displayed a lengthy vine-woven Pergola. Blossom festooned the entire structure, tiny white flowers sprinkled like confetti at a church wedding.

There was a faint rustling behind her. Bella ducked, sliding something from the bag and tucking it inside her leggings. The thrashing was closer, she dropped flat to the ground.

Mumbled, croaky voices in a foreign tongue were nearby. Bella rolled slowly three times, squeezing beneath the lower branches of a thorny bush. Something rustled, before cawing from the bushes, as the sound of boots stomping undergrowth loudened. Bella reached out, finger-pinching the strap of her rucksack that still lay on the open grass, easing it toward her.

"Samba-leasi!"

Bella squealed as a thick-soled boot stamped down hard on her wrist.

"Samba-leasi!" the man repeated, louder this time. "Samba-leasi, Isconcho est-atil!"

A huge man appeared beside the bush, leaning down, hauling Bella to her feet, as the other man released his boot from her wrist. It bore an imprint of triangles that ran into her reddening forearm. Bella clutched it for a moment before it was grabbed and twisted to her shoulder blades. Pinning both arms high up her back, Bella shrieked, wincing as a sharp pain shot through her arm, jerking a tear from her eye.

"Get the hell off of me!" she demanded.

"Samba-leasi. Samba-.."

"Yeah, yeah, yeah; Samba-fuckin-leasi," Bella said, before another keen twinge.

"Samba-leasi," he said again, more excitable this time.

"I have no idea what that means, knucklehead!" Bella bellowed.

She flung herself forward at the waist, wriggling to escape their grasp, but the man tightened his grip as they marched her from the thicket, toward the villa complex. Bella squinted as they approached and she was bundled through the gate. Another man appeared with a swish from behind tinted double glass doors.

"Ahh visitors, how delightful!" the stocky man declared, shuffling over to meet them.

He interlocked his chubby fingers across his button-strained shirt. His piggy eyes flickered excitedly.

"Roman will be pleased, we could do with more staff," he said, winking at the men that stood either side of Bella, proudly presenting their find. "What's your name then, and what business have you, being here?"

The man's underbite was so pronounced that when he stopped speaking his bottom lip rested at the tip of his nose.

"Look, I'm with the British press, with permission to interview Roman Darcy," Bella said.

"Well I'm not sure about that," he muttered, whilst inspecting the rucksack the men had handed him. "But we'll soon find out exactly who you are, and more importantly who knows you're here. Chain her up," he said nonchalantly.

The pot-bellied man peeled green notes from a wad and stuffed them into the palm of the tall, army booted guard. "Well done Claud. This one has potential."

"I said, I am here to see Roman Darcy. I have police authority to be here," Bella said.

"Now, I very much doubt that!" he said, chortling. "Take her to the holding bay."

The men marched Bella off, toward the far side of the complex.

"Are you listening to me, shortarse! And what the hell is the holding bay?"

"Oh, you'll soon find out, and you will get to meet Roman in due course, my dear," he said, with a grin that rounded his nose. "We'll get a good look at you first."

"What the hell are you talking about?" Bella shouted, peering back at the plump little man.

Humming to himself he waddled back through the building's central sliding doors with Bella's rucksack swinging at his side.

CHAPTER 30

SILVER MEWS TERRACE, PLAISTOW, EAST LONDON

"Spooky old street this one guv, feels like summat outta Oliver Twist," Neil Turvey offered his observation, in his pitchy scouse drawl.

"Hardly," Tom Broad said, dismissing his number two's comment. "It's rather more upmarket than that, I'd say."

Headshaking Neil said, "Yeah-no, I'm talking about the posh bit, near the end of the movie. Yoos no's, when Oliver gets taken in by the rich-uns. He wakes up and they's all singing in the street."

"Yes, thank you Turvs! I know the part you mean.."

"Who will buy this beautiful mornin', who will buy this beautiful day.."

"YES, yes, thanks Neil! We don't need a singalong right now. Just get the bloody door open, will you!" Tom barked.

The two coppers stood on the doorstep of number 35 Silver Mews Terrace, the registered address of Charles Maxwell. It was the only residence that had failed to respond to police enquiries. Pierre Lebouf's Jaguar had been parked on a nearby sideroad on the night of his disappearance.

More significantly, data from Lebouf's KeyTrak device now revealed that a signal had pinged directly from this property. His car's keyfob had been fitted with a security button, which when depressed activated an alert, registering the owner's location.

Tom Broad stood to one side of the wide stone steps, whilst Neil swung smoothly the door-ram from ninety degrees. Its squared end-plate smashed heartily into the front door, just below its brass handle, rocking it an inch from its frame.

"Losing your touch Turvs!" Tom mocked.

"It even takes the experts a couple..," Neil puffed, as he swung back the door-ram again. "Of swings," he added, with a big grin.

The gloomy hallway creaked into view beyond the now hinge-swinging door. Charles Maxwell, the elderly owner of the house had been registered deceased some years ago.

"After you guv," Neil said, with a delicate queen-like wave and bow.

"Did you bring the torches?" Tom said.

"Err, no boss.. I brought the rammer!"

"Spence.. Spence. Can you bring us up a couple of torches please?" Tom called down.

DI Spencer stood alongside the squad car, seemingly guarding it. In typically efficient fashion she bound the three bowed steps with flashlights, offering her further assistance.

"Stay by the car and chase up any family connections to Charles Maxwell. Somebody's been in here, it's hardly derelict," Tom said.

"How do you know that boss?" Spencer said, peering into the desolate hall.

"No pile of mail. No webbing or dust-laden floor," he replied, pointing at the parquet flooring.

"Yeah basic coppering that, Spence," Neil said, winking at Tom.

"But the obvious sign of course, is..?" Tom said, widened his eyes at Neil.

"Err, that'd be the-err. What do you think, Spence? Come on I'll let you 'ave that one, girl," Neil said.

Tom snapped back, head shaking, "The light coming from the top of the stairs!"

The DI's heads rose as one, glaring up at the glow that illuminated the stairs and upper floor landing. Like dominos, crisp shadows from the bannister's spindles led down to the oval carving on the newel post, at the foot of the staircase.

"Shall we go in," Tom said, under-the-breath tutting.

They flicked the torches up to full beam and entered the stale smelling, oak-panelled hallway. It carried the look and feel of an outdated horror movie.

"After you guv, you're the Bram Stoker fan," Neil eye-rolled. "Besides, I forgot my crucifix!"

CHAPTER 31

Roman Darcy's popeye-like, tattooed forearms pimpled. He shook the contents of Bella's rucksack onto his desk.

"Can you sort that fucking thing out!" he bellowed, jabbing his finger at a large wall unit. He slid a lime green jacket over his vest.

"Sure, what temperature, Ro?" Joel said, waddling over to the box protruding from the wall.

"Anything but, fucking freezing!" Roman snapped.

The tubby man tapped at the number panel that chirped back at him. The large silver unit mounted high on the far wall whirred to a stop.

"Well there's fuck-all in here," Roman barked, pawing through the contents of Bella Maxwell's rucksack.

A hoodie, beanie, some waterproof trousers along with a water bottle and energy bars lay strewn in front of him. He dug inside the front zipped pouch and tossed a small pen-knife, clattering across the desktop. With a final one-handed shake a packet of gum landed in front of him.

"So who the fuck is she!" Roman shouted, flinging the gum at Joel before tossing the bag to the floor.

"We're not sure yet Ro, so I've put her in the holding bay," Joel said, picking up the gum and slipping it in his pocket. "She says she's press," he added.

"What, some media outlet, checking up on me again?" Roman snarled.

"Possibly. We found this handwritten note on her," Joel said, struggling to open a tightly folded piece of paper. "Ah, here we are, yes. She had details of your next three sets; dates, times and locations."

'Moonbay rave, Pink shell beach, and Warm water cove.'

Joel added, "This would suggest that she might just be chasing a story." He grinned at his boss, pleased with his finding.

"So why have you stuck her anywhere near the pits? You've just handed her a story, right there!" Roman said, snarling as he rounded the desk. "We'll have to get rid now, you idiot."

"We intercepted a boat earlier, so we possibly have her courier, and I've got Claude tracing back over her trail," Joel said efficiently, facing-off a stern glare. "W-Would you like me to bring her to you?"

Roman stroked the back of his bald head and interlocked his thick fingers around it.

"No, I haven't got time for this. I'm more concerned with the finances at the moment," Roman said. "Lebouf's payments still haven't come through. Fuck knows where he's disappeared too!"

"Yes, Ro on that, I managed to speak to Lebouf's mother, Patricia. She confirmed what she told the police; Pierre was kidnapped by a young female. Part of some 'women's rights' group, she believes," Joel said, scrolling his phone.

"Well it's cut our fucking cash flow," Roman said, adding, "We're gonna need final payments from the live-hunt participants in the next twenty-four hours."

"Not a problem Ro. They're arriving tomorrow and they'll expect that as we're only two days from the hunt now," Joel said, gurning at his boss.

"Anything more on Jamal?" Roman said, planting his butt on the edge of the desk that rocked a little.

"Only what the police have released; Jackson was murdered, and his body parts scattered across the Cheveley estate in east London," Joel said. "Possibly female activists again, Ro," he added.

"Nah. Jamal was a shit-for-brains footballer. He was already hated by half the population, then he put that nazi-loving shit on his socials. Fuckin twat," Roman said.

"Still, it seemed a bit gruesome, kinda personal, Ro," Joel said, his piggy eyes blinking.

"Well it's either that, or gangland-shit. I've been to that estate, it's riddled with knife wielding lowlife wanting to make a name for themselves," Roman said, now pacing the room.

"But with Pierre missing and Jackson dead, it's all a bit worrying," Joel said, perching on the edge of a Sherlock chair.

"I told them to get the hell out of the UK after the trial. The place is fucked," Roman said, poking a finger into Joel's soft chest. "All a bit worrying, my arse!"

"So you think we're safe enough here, Ro?" Joel said, softly.

A beam shot across Roman's cheeks.

"Safe. In the middle of the Indian Ocean, I'd fucking well think so, wouldn't you. Besides, I don't think you'd actually ever be a target, Joel," Roman said, releasing a belly laugh.

He wrapped an arm around his employee's shoulders, lifting him to his feet.

"Yeah, I suppose you're right. We should relax a little more," Joel said.

"Too fuckin right," Roman said, slipping his jacket off and throwing it on the armchair. "Talking of which, I will see our new arrival. Maybe break her down a little, find out the score," Roman said, with a widening smirk.

"You want me to bring her over?" Joel said, with a rising excitement.

"Yeah, clean her up and take her to my suite," Roman said.

"Yes, will do boss," Joel said, rubbing his hands.

"And you can send that northern troublemaker over later. That feisty young-un you mentioned," Roman said, his smile filling his square jaw.

"Oh, yes I will, yes. I'll sit in if you don't mind," Joel said, wiping a little saliva from the corner of his mouth. "Garrett, Zoe Garrett."

"Err, no fuckin names, Joel. Let's just stick with their numbers, shall we." Roman said, as the crease in his forehead furrowed.

"Actually, err-sorry, boss but she is only just eighteen. She's really good stock, we should get a decent sell-on. Maybe one of the Italian girls, Ro?" Joel said, with half a grin.

"Thank you, Joel, but I think I'll have my fill first, if you don't mind!" Roman said, glaring at his assistant.

"Of course, yes, sure thing, sorry Ro. I'll get that sorted," Joel said, eye-twitching as he fumbled with the door handle.

CHAPTER 32

"I think she's away at the mo, honey. I haven't seen her for a while," Peter said, as he strode jauntily towards the police officer.

DI Spencer was leaning back against the squad car, with hands tucked inside her equipment packed police vest.

"And you are?" Spencer said, butt-pushing to stand upright from the car.

"Peter Johansson, at your service," he said, with a cheeky grin, offering a limp-wristed finger-shake that Spencer ignored.

"Do you know the occupier of this property, sir? I assume you've already been interviewed if you live on this street," she said, tugging an unwilling pocketbook from her breast pocket.

"I'm at number 39, renting a room at the Maudsley's. Ron and Maureen mentioned they'd had a visit from the boys in blue the other day. Unfortunately I was out that day, hun," Peter said, gesturing across the road. "Hate to miss any drama, sweetie!" he added, with pursed lips, that shaped a heart.

Spencer eyebrows pushed into her brow as she clicked the top of her biro and flipped the cover of her pad.

"Could you tell me who lives here, sir?" she said coldly.

"Arabella Maxwell, Bella that is. She's not around much, she's at the boyfriend's mostly. So it's just her and grandad, now whatshisname. Gosh you've got me there!" he said, with a wrist flopping at ninety degrees.

"Charles. That's it, Charlie Maxwell. Anyways don't see much of him. Can't remember the last time I saw the old fella. But he must be quite old now, so you know, TV dinners and early to bed, I'd say," Peter said, resting the back of his hand high on his hip.

"Do you have any idea where we might find Miss Maxwell, sir," Spencer said.

"Bella's always a bit vague about where she's at, but usually at Carl's, I'd say. That's the BF. If she's not travelling for work, that is. Busy girl our Bel, a top lawyer you know. Now *that* she doesn't mind talking about. She was on that big sex trafficking case last year, I got chapter and verse," he said, excitedly. "I still can't believe they let those three guys off. Bella was not a happy bunny. Mind you, that football guy Jamal, ooohh, what a dish!" he added, open mouthed.

"Carl..?" Spencer said sharply, whilst smiling inside.

"Turner. Carl Turner. She's never introduced me but I'm sure he's hench. With a catch like Bella he'd have to be, wouldn't he," Peter said, with a wink. "Not sure where he lives though, flat in the smoke somewhere. I know he works for the local council over Cheveley way, I think," Peter said, with index finger peeling back his lower lip.

"It would be helpful if we could take a full statement from you?" Spencer said.

"Of course, yes. Happy to be interrogated by a policeman anytime. Will I need to be stripsearched?" he said, with head cocked and lips pursed.

"Thank you, that won't be necessary, Mr Johansson," Spencer said, dipping her head.

"Oh, what a shame!" Peter said, adopting an emoji-like sad face.

"Could I just ask," Spencer continued. "You've mentioned the Grandfather,

Charles Maxwell. But Bella's parents, do you know where we might find them?" she said, with pen hovering a fresh page.

"They both died, I'm sad to say, when Bella was very young, the poor kitten," Peter said, wide-eyed. "I remember she said her Dad had the big C, and Mum took her own life. Mental health issues, she'd suffered for years apparently."

"Thank you very much for your assistance, you've been most helpful. If I could take a phone number, we'll arrange a time to take a formal statement from you," she said, with a sweet smile.

DI Spencer took his details before tucking her notebook back into her police vest and bounding the steps of 35 Silver Mews terrace to consult with her colleagues. Peter Johansson bounced cheerfully off down the street with a shopping bag swinging from his elbow.

CHAPTER 33

The expansive space gleamed from its shiny tiled floor and high white walls. Only one of which was interrupted by a canvas depicting Rome with the Colosseum at its heart.

"I know you!" Roman Darcy boomed, the moment she was dragged by an elbow into his private suite.

In the far corner a sunken floor led to a cinema-style area around which semicircular, two-tiered seating curved. The screen flicked between pornographic images.

Bella wriggled hard, twisting away from the little man's grip from behind her.

"Can you get the fuck off of me!" she said, yanking her elbow free of his grasp.

Darcy raised his bulging forearm, finger-waving his assistant to stand back. Bella stood, rubbing her wrist as she scanned the palacios space. Joel shuffled off and stood in front of an arched entrance to the bedroom suite.

"Now I've had paps sniffing around before but I can't recall any hiding out and stalking me on my private island!" Darcy said. "Let's get a closer look at you shall we, I'm sure I recognise you from somewhere."

Darcy strode over, examining the girl's petite features, her huge blue eyes. His colossal face inches from hers, breathing heavily through flared nostrils, like a raging bull. She sneered up at him. His smirking eyes narrowed, enjoying her rising discomfort as she recoiled.

"Christ, you stink" Bella said, burying her face into her shoulder.

"Yeah, our Chef's a little heavy-handed with the garlic," Darcy said, with a face full of grin. "Now do tell me, have we met?"

"Only in my nightmares," Bella snapped back, instantly regretting her words.

"Now I have to warn you, I don't take lightly to insults," Darcy said, balling his fist.

Behind Joel the double doors to a bedroom were open. A meek looking girl was perched on the edge of an enormous wrought iron bed. Her head hung from bony shoulders like low-hanging fruit. An elaborate animal motif was carved into the oversized headboard that dominated the back wall.

"Look, Mr Darcy, can we just start again here. I've already told your goffer here," Bella said, glancing over at the short guy. "I'm just a journalist, looking for an interview, that's all."

"You were at the Court hearings?" Darcy said, rounding her to stand face-on.

"Yes, that's what I'm saying to you. I was part of the presscore assigned to the TikTokTrio case," she said. "I'm looking to get an exclusive; your side of the story. You were vilified by nearly all media outlets, and yet you were found innocent."

"Too fucking right, I was," Darcy said, with eyebrows joining his single-creased brow.

Darcy's fish-foul breath cut easily through the overly beeswaxed sideboard that she noticed Joel was now half sat on. Bella momentarily caught eyes with the girl, who remained sitting, slump-shouldered with head dipped. There was an air of foreboding in her fretful demeanour that hung like a noose from a rafter over her head.

Joel sneered at Bella, before stepping into the bedroom suite to clasp the gold doorknobs. Aligning the double doors, he pulled them too with a hefty clunk.

"So you wanna take my side of the story, do you?" Darcy said, pacing the room. "It's about time someone did!"

The furnishings all around her were ostentatious, statement led. They omitted the stench of vulgarity, of ill-gotten gains. The hide of a Tiger, with white fanged head still growling its final fury, lay in monstrous warning at the entrance to the bedroom. Darcy's lackey stood in ankle buckled sandals on its hind leg, fiddling with his iPhone.

"Of course, absolutely, why not," Bella said, still scanning the space.

Darcy settled to land on the arm of one of the two purple velvet couches that wheezed its displeasure. The soft knock at the suite's door required repetition.

"Come!" Darcy boomed.

"Dinner tray, Mr D-Darcy," another scantily-clad girl said softly, as she entered the room.

She moved quickly, swivelling the silver tray from her shoulder and setting down a plate that held a towering speared burger, on the coffee table. The young girl's juddering smile at her employer was belied by a nervous giggle as she placed a side plate alongside it. She flashed a twitchy grin at Bella as she paced back past her, headed for the exit. Fresh-faced, she could only be late teens and yet her forehead furrowed deeper than that of a woman of sixty.

"Wait!" Darcy spluttered, with a mouthful of food.

Halfway through the doorway, she spun instantly, tucking the tray under her arm.

"Yes sir, Mr D-Darcy?" she said sweetly.

"You can take this through to the bedroom," he said, with specks still flying from his mouth.

An unerring moment of silence filled the room as the girl hurried back over to replace the plates onto her silver tray. As she bent over Darcy's hand slid around her waist. She froze. A redness plumed from her neck, like paint drops in water.

"Just a second," he said, finger-pinching a handful of chips.

The girl remained statuesque, whilst he fed the food into his mouth, before releasing his clasp on her.

"You can wait in there with the other girl," he said, his head tilting in the direction of the bedroom.

Smiling anxiously, she hurried away, fleeting a glance at Bella, her wide eyes filled with trepidation. Her nerve-shredded unease at Darcy's volatility was palpable.

"And don't eat my chips," Darcy added, grinning at Bella.

Joel pushed open one of the bedroom doors, before closing it behind the girl.

"What do you want to do about our uninvited guest here, Ro?" Joel pressed.

Darcy strolled the sparkling tiles, his flip-flops squeaking at every pounded step. He stared hard at Bella, his single crease forehead ploughed the length of it, splitting his face from his skull. His dark eyes arrowed as he clamped his index finger and thumb to his square jaw.

"What media outlet?" he barked.

"S-sorry what, what?" Bella said, clutching her bruised wrist.

"Which outlet are you from?" he demanded.

"CNN UK," she replied, matching his tone.

"Based where," he countered.

"Canary Wharf."

"Where am I from?"

"Bristol, moving to London at fourteen and Ibiza at eighteen."

"Seventeen, actually! When's my birthday?"

"May 16th."

Darcy's shorts were thread-tested by his thick thighs as he strode the room. He hooked a fat thumb inside the shoulder strap of his vest.

"Ok, so what's your angle?" he said.

"Know the man, before the verdict," Bella said, eyeing him unblinkingly.

He stomped over to slouch on the sofa, leaving one leg dangling its low-rolled armrest.

"But they had the verdict; innocent of all charges!"

"Fixed. Corrupt. That was the outcry. If you won fairly, why the need to run away without the usual Court steps vitriol?"

"Run, fucking *run*! I didn't run," Darcy snarled, sitting upright.

"Sorry. Not my view, but public.," Bella said, softening the allegation.

"I don't give a shit about people's views. They don't know me!"

"Yes, I get that, it's just that people want to understand what happened out here, to all those girls," Bella said, pausing on seeing Darcy's darkening expression. "Who *do you think* was behind it?" she added.

"If you heard the evidence, in court, like you say you did, you'll know that we were cleared of any wrongdoing, that's all anyone needs to understand." Darcy stood, with a peacock-like puffed chest, "Listen, I just work over here. I'm an entertainer, a showman!"

"Look, I'm sorry Mr Darcy, it's been a long trip. I shouldn't have arrived without notice, but you've been extremely difficult to trackdown," Bella said. "Could I use your loo?" she added.

Darcy getsured with a nonchalant flick of his fingers at a door behind her. Bella disappeared into the restroom, clanking it locked.

"I knew I recognised that face from the trial, but she looked different," Darcy mumbled to himself whilst pacing the room with one hand on his baldness. "Maybe her hair, clothes."

There was an impatient knocking on the suite's door that Joel attended to.

"Claude's just found this in the grass where she was hiding," Joel said, passing Darcy a six-inch sheathed blade. "Now, why would a press officer carry a knife!" he added, eye twitching.

Darcy strode across the room, easing the shiny steel a few inches from its cover, before ramming it back and tossing it clattering to the floor beside the rug.

"That's it..! Fuck me, it's the hair. It was longer, and brunette and she had one of those lawyer's wigs on!" he said, with narrowing eyes.

A vein at Darcy's temple knotted and pulsed a royal blue.

"All that press association stuff; it's bollocks! She was a Barrister, for the prosecution!" Darcy said softly, with teeth flashing. "Is she on her own out here?"

"Err., yep, she booked into the GranPlaza alone and only spoke to one guy, who was her boat ride over here," Joel said, checking his iPhone. "Should we put her to work, Ro?" he added, his beady eyes flickering.

"Ab-so-fuckin-lootly, we will. What a crafty bitch," Darcy mused, excitedly. "Now then, Host, Hoare or Hunt?"

"She's sprained her wrist under Claude's size nines earlier, so hosting's out and she's the sort that would bite your prick off, so I wouldn't think Hoare would work. Although she's a pretty thing, Ro, we could just sell her on?" an animated Joel said.

"Too old, and besides I don't want any comeback. Stick her in pit one with the other runners. Let's just get rid, as soon as," Darcy ordered, as they both turned to face the bathroom door.

"Aside from Pierre not coming, everything's in hand for the Hunt," Joel said, adding, "I have managed to sell another place, so we're back up to capacity."

"Good, just make sure our guests are all well catered for," Darcy said.

"Would you like me to deal with this one, Ro. While you, eat?" Joel said, eye-nodding his boss in the direction of the bedroom.

"Yeah, good idea. Dinner time, I think," Darcy said, winking at Joel whilst peeling his vest from his barrel-chest and sliding off his flip flops.

Darcy disappeared into the bedroom, clunking the door closed behind him, leaving Joel standing outside the bathroom.

CHAPTER 34

DI Turvey checked the last of the kitchen cupboards, declaring, "There ain't nobody living here, guv. Not unless they live off cockroach soup! They don't have a bean in here."

"Yeah, it's all very strange. There's nothing in the wardrobes and chests upstairs either. Who lives like this," Tom Broad rhetorically quizzed as he joined Neil in the galley kitchen at the rear of the house.

"The invisible man guv?" Neil jibed, to a muted eye-arching response.

"Boss.. boss?" DI Spencer shouted, from the front door, stepping into the hallway.

"We're through here, Spence," Tom yelled back.

"I've just had some useful intel from a friend of the woman that lives here. It's a, Bella Maxwell, who resides at the house with her grandfather, Charles Maxwell..," Spencer said enthusiastically.

"That ain't likely given the state of this gaff, Spence," Neil said, interrupting.

"Well he did say she spends a lot of time at her boyfriend's. He-is-err., one Carl Turner, boss," Spencer said, flicking at her notes.

"Good work, let's track him down then and see if we can find Miss Maxwell. Do some preliminaries on her, will you Spence," Tom said.

"Yep, already on that.." Spencer said.

"Not sure where that leaves us with the mysterious Grandad, guv?" Neil said, butting-in.

"Yes, that is odd. Let's do some trace work from government registers, work and pension trails," Tom said, sighing. "He certainly isn't living here anymore."

"Boss, on Maxwell.." Spencer said, with pen waving.

"If he's *living* at all, guv?" Neil said, with widening eyes.

"Alright Turvs, let's not go Columbo on this. We keep our focus on the task in hand; locating Pierre Lebouf. Why was his car parked outside this property and his key fob registered as being within these walls," Tom said firmly.

"On that, boss.." Spencer said, before she was interrupted again.

"That name rings a bell you know guv, Bella Maxwell. Like she's been involved with the police or something legal," Neil said.

Spencer followed the detectives as they strode into the hallway. "Yes, that's my point, sir," she said, trailing the two men.

Tom paused, with hand aloft, prompting the other two to stop.

"Hang on a second, Spence," Tom said, his fingers disappearing into his thick dark hair. "Do you know you're right, Turvs. What's Maxwell's connection with Lebouf? His Lawyer, maybe."

"Yes, according to the neighbour..," Spencer said softly, before being overridden.

"Possibly acted for all three of them, guv; the TikTokTrio," Neil said, whilst tapping at his iPhone.

"Wait a minute," Tom said, leaning against the wall. There was a faint *click* from the panel he leant against. "Wasn't there a *Maxwell* on the team that prosecuted them?"

"That's what I..," Spencer said.

"Gotcha. I remember seeing her at the trial, a bit of a looker!" Neil bellowed, spinning his phone screen at his colleagues. "That's her!"

In a horse-haired wig and black cloak, the angelic face of Bella Maxwell smiled back at them.

"Brilliant, well done, Turvs," Tom said, with a firm nod at his number two. Adding, "I believe we have our prime suspect," as he pushed away from the wall, *clack*.

Tom marched off, barking instructions at Spencer, to establish the whereabouts of Arabella Maxwell. Behind them a single oak panel swung silently open, as the three officers disappeared outside. Oblivious, they pushed high the police tape as they exited the Victorian terrace, scuttling down its stone steps.

CHAPTER 35

The metal casing resembled a drain cover, only twice as wide and thick. It clanked angrily back down into its cast iron frame as Bella descended, stepping from the last of the steps that protruded from the wall. She stared defiantly up through the grille at the sneering faces that had escorted her there.

"Oi, Samba-leasi boy. Warn Darcy that he'll have the local police force on his doorstep at first light," she yelled.

The men mumbled thick-tongued words under cupped hands, elbowing each other and prompting laughter that hung, before disappearing with them. It was pitch black in the space behind her. From the illuminated building above, a chimney of light cut through the grille, casting narrow rectangles to the floor at her feet.

Bella had been dragged from Darcy's suite to the back of the property along an asphalt pathway. It ran between a storage area and some large air-expelling metal units, where the stench of garlic and onions plumed in steamy spirals into the night sky.

Bella clambered the six rung ladder, poking her fingers through the solid iron grille plate, pushing hard skyward. Against her grunted efforts, it sat tight, immovable, rooted in its frame. Through it she could only see huge satellite receivers, housed on the roof of the complex. Beyond that was the shadowy vegetation-clad cliff that she had scaled earlier. An imposing, monstrous sight with jutted peaks clawing at the inky skies.

Bella's throaty screams for *help* were fruitless, drifting emptily into the star-filled sky. She descended slowly back into the hole to the intense heat at its base. She laid her palm on the laddered wall, lifting it quickly from its burning surface; like a bare-foot step, on sun scorched sands.

In the darkness of the area beyond the shaft's light it felt cooler. Bella ducked, lurching to stagger deeper into the cave-like space. It was appreciably more comfortable with each step. Half-hunched, she waited for her eyesight to adjust, eyeing the glimmer of a gravelly path. But the blackness was all consuming.

With fingers stretched, she fumbled to locate the sidewall of the cave. She shrieked as her hand brushed hair, a skull., sending her scampering back to the shaft of light. With hand clenched around a rung of the ladder, as if a life-raft, she peered anxiously back into the hole.

"What the hell is that! Is somebody else down here?" she shouted, squinting hard to follow her voice into the darkness.

CHAPTER 36

"*Shh* please, Mademoiselle, keep quiet," a husky female voice murmured.

Bella's cheeks puffed in relief - she was not alone in that hell-hole. She gazed into the dark space that was slowly revealing itself. Along the wall of the cave, the end of a narrow bench-like beam came into view.

"Who are you.. and why are you here?" Bella said, lowering her tone, embarrassed by her scream.

"*Pas de questions.* They is watching, always," the girl mumbled.

Bella squinted deeper into the murky dimness that crept slowly from its dusty floor. Bony feet and spindly calves emerged before scrawny white thighs joined them in ghostly apparition. The still faceless woman sat stiffly, as long-fingered hands came slowly into focus.

"Can you show yourself please, Mademoiselle?" Bella whispered back.

The girl inched painfully to the end of the bench, into the light that filtered from the grill above them. Long dark hair half covered her sunken pasty face as she came eerily into view. Sticklike arms hung from her vested shoulders, her hips jutting high of no-longer white knickers.

"What happened to you?" Bella said softly, in grimace. "Quel est ton nom?" she added quickly.

"My name is Monique, and please, English is fine," she said, crossing a stick-thin bare leg over the other.

"I'm Bella, and we've gotta get out of here, Monique," Bella said, noticing that the young French girl's feet were bruised and toes were black.

"There is no chance of escaping this place," Monique said, easing thick tangled locks from glossy eyes, the colour of chestnuts.

"There has to be, Monique. There's always a way out," Bella said.

"Not from this.. how do you say, *enfer..*?"

"Hell," Bella said.

"*Exactement*; welcome to Hell! *Economise ta force* for the Hunt. You will need it," Monique said croakily.

"Hunt, what do you mean, 'the hunt'? They put a stop to that after the massacre here. They can't have started that again, the police are monitoring them, surely to God?" Bella said, dropping to her haunches alongside Monique.

"We will all die here, like the others before us, Bella," Monique said, her voice husky with dryness.

"Look, I met with the survivors, I know what happened on this island. We had the men in custody and were told their whole operation had been shut down!" Bella said, staring into the girl's defeated face. She held the same deadened expression that Bella had seen before.

Monique slid back into the darkness. Bella cradled her head as she ducked, stepping cautiously deeper into the cave.

Bella, careful in sitting alongside her, squinted to refocus on Monique. "We have to find a way out of this, Monique."

"I say no more," Monique mumbled, curling a slender finger to her blistered lips. Her head dropped to her chest, a single glistening tear falling to her cracked lips. Her matted hair flopped, curtaining her face.

Bella leaned back against the coolness of the rocky wall, it felt moist. She blew heavily, its soft echo rebounding deep inside the cave. Opposite her, another narrow bench was now visible, similarly fixed into the rock wall.

Bella suddenly sat bolt upright, squinting hard as milky-white legs ghostily appeared on the bench opposite. Blinking harder into the mistiness, more stick thin calves and thighs, flickered into vision; as if emerging from a steamy sauna.

Bella squinted intensely into the abyss, horrified at the emerging outline of a gaunt-looking girl further along, and then another and another. All sat motionless and silent, perched on the seemingly endless bench, in this, waiting room of death.

"What the hell!" Bella said, lurching to her feet.

In turning to the Monique, the shape of a shorter, younger girl sitting beside her emerged from the foggy dimness, and alongside her, there was another.

"Christ Almighty, how many girls are down here!" Bella bellowed, her shout echoing back louder.

CHAPTER 37

"My God, man," the Chambers Clerk said, forcefully. "I said she took the verdict badly. NOT that she wanted to kill the accused. We are all professionals here!"

"Sir, I'd appreciate it if you could adjust your tone," DI Neil Turvey requested politely.

"We all took it badly for Christ's sake, it was many months' work!" he spouted on regardless.

"But, Miss Maxwell, she met with the victims, heard their stories. It would have impacted her more personally?" Neil pressed.

"Bella, like all of us, put her heart and soul into trying to secure a conviction. Jackson will be no loss to civilised society and Lebouf, well," he exhaled heavily. "To be honest, I hope you never find him, the sadistic bastard."

"Sir, I understand.."

"If you're looking into anything it should be the verdict, the Jury, corruption. The Judge, certainly misled in parts," he added, under his breath. "That's where criminality might lie."

"You say, Maxwell's on holiday now?"

"Yes, and more than entitled to it," he said. "Works bloody hard does Bella. So what of it?"

"It's just that we've spoken to her boyfriend, Carl Turner, who informs us that she's currently working overseas, on Chambers' business," Neil said, with a raised eyebrowed.

The chief clerk stood, headcocked, with his bottom lip folded out.

"What she chooses to tell her other half is strictly her business, and of no concern of ours. But no, she isn't currently engaged on any work commitments of ours."

"There's no possibility that you could be mistaken about that, sir? Or that Miss Maxwell might be working for another set of Chambers, freelance?" Neil said, with pen poised.

"I'm Head of Chambers here, so no, I'm not mistaken about that," he snapped. "And for your records, she is retained under an exclusivity contract. Bella is tied to us contractually, unlike the relationship with her boyfriend, you understand?"

"Thank you sir, I do," Neil said, with an eye-roll. "If she does get in touch, please do let us know." Neil clicked a crisp white card onto the desk.

"I think I've given you more than enough of my time, don't you officer? Good afternoon," he said, tossing the card into his desk drawer.

CHAPTER 38

MARYLEBONE HEIGHTS (2 HOURS EARLIER)

The stench of urine stemming from the stairwell, carried to the door of the flat. Tom Broad rattled his knuckles against the paint-flaking door, before noticing the black buttoned doorbell that sat to one side. He poked it and stepped back to stand alongside his smirking DI, Neil Turvey. They waited as a shadowy figure grew ever larger in the door's frosted window panel.

"Can I help you?" a floppy haired man asked, through the gap that the security chain allowed.

"Good morning sir, Mr Turner?" Tom said.

"Yep, Carl Turner, that's me."

"I'm DCI Broad and this is my colleague DI Turvey. We're hoping you might be able to assist us in establishing the whereabouts of someone we urgently need to speak to," Tom said, side-glancing at a head poking from the doorway of the neighbouring flat. "Could we possibly step inside for a moment?"

"Sure, no problem. Apologies for the peejays - it's my day off," he said, stifling a yawn.

Carl Turner pushed the door closed before scratching its chain across and widening it. He shuffled half behind it to allow the officer in. "Is this about last night?" he said, belt-tying his dressing gown

"Last night, sir?" Tom replied, with arching eyebrows.

"Err, yeah all that shouting and bottle smashing in the alley round the back?" he said, before releasing a jaw-clicking sigh. "Thought it might be another stabbing, or sumut?"

"No-no, sir," Tom said, headshaking. "We're trying to trace the whereabouts of a Miss Bella Maxwell. We understand that she's a friend of yours?"

"My girlfriend, yeah, that's right. What do you want with Bella?" he said, open-faced.

"When did you last see Miss Maxwell, Carl?" DI Turvey said.

"Couple of nights ago. Why?"

"Do you happen to know where she is now, sir?" Tom pressed.

"Err, yeah she's away with some work thingy. Some overseas conference, or sumut," he said, ruffling his blonde curls clear of his eyes.

"Whereabouts is the work thing, Carl?" Neil said, whilst strolling around the small living room, stopping at a photo frame on the window sill.

"Maldives, I think she said. Why?" Carl said, yanking the picture from Neil's hand.

"Do you know where.." Neil said, before being cut off.

"Now look, can you please tell me what this is about?" Carl said, carefully replacing the photo frame. "Bella's a lawyer for christ's sake, certainly no law breaker!"

"Sorry sir, it's just that Miss Maxwell may be able to assist us with our enquiries into a missing person. I'm sure she, as you suggest, hasn't done anything wrong," Tom said, softly.

"Good looking girl you've got there, Carl," Neil said, nodding at the photograph.

"Yeah, I know that. Thanks!" Carl said.

"Could you possibly confirm her hotel and flight details for us please, sir?" Tom said.

"Yeah sure. She wrote it down for me somewhere, but strictly for emergencies she said, she's gonna be busy all week with seminars and whatnot," Carl mumbled, disappearing into the back bedroom.

"Does she live here with you full time, Carl?" Neil called after him.

"Yeah mostly," he yelled back.

"Only we also have an address for her at a, Silver Mews terrace, in Plaistow," Neil said, flicking at his notebook.

There was no reply as the two coppers scanned the living room. Tom, headshaking, mouthed 'slow down' to his partner.

"Here you go," Carl said, pleased with his find, passing a crumpled piece of paper to Tom.

"That's Bella's hotel details and her mobile. But as I said, she's gonna be mad busy this week so didn't want calls," Carl said, before muffling a yawn.

"Thanks, you've been most helpful, sir," Tom said, with a nod.

"No problem. Anything else I can help you with," Carl said to Tom.

"Err, Silver Mews terrace?" Neil blurted, with a head shake.

"It's her Grandad's place. Bella stays there sometimes," Carl said, looking at Tom.

"That's great. We'll be in touch if we need anything else from you, sir," Tom said, eye-nodding Neil toward the front door.

As the officer's reached the end of the corridor Neil half-turned back. "You on the Council are you, Carl?"

"Yeah, why do you ask?" Carl said, standing at the entrance to the living room.

"Sorry pal, just me being nosey. I noticed the lanyard there," Neil said, pointing at a rucksack hanging from a run of three hooks in the gloomy hallway. A local authority staffpass was tied to it.

"Don't cover the Cleveley estate do you, sir?" Tom said.

"Yeah, we maintain that area," Carl said, propping an elbow on the door frame.

"Nasty business over there the other night," Tom said.

"Tell me about it, I'm the supervisor of those blocks! We've had to hold off all works and even cancel refuse collections over there," Carl said, enthusiastically. "Don't suppose you guys know when we can expect clearance?"

"Just as soon as we've eliminated *everyone* who had access to the refuge area," Neil said, with a long face.

"Well, Council-wise, it's just me and the deputy. That's it. We did tell you guys that. It's left open to residents on weekdays and locked overnight by us," Carl said.

"We know it was locked by the killer after the murder. So there was a breach in your security somewhere," Neil said, pointedly.

"I doubt that mate! My key never leaves my possession," Carl said, pushing past Neil and pulling a keyring chubb from his bag.

"Anyone else have access to your bag?" Neil pressed.

"Look, it's either on my back, or by my side until I get home. Then it's hanging up here," Carl said, looping the bag back on its hook.

"That's good to know, thank you sir," Tom said, turning the front door latch.

"Don't mind me asking, but how long have you known Miss Maxwell?" Neil said.

"Coming up, two years now," Carl said, proudly.

"But what do you actually know about her.. do you trust her?" Neil said.

"Yes *I do*, and I think you had better leave now," Carl said, crossing his arms.

"I just hate the thought of people being used," Neil said.

Carl grabbed the latch from Tom and pulled the door to his chest. Neil met Tom's knowing nod and the coppers exited the flat.

CHAPTER 39

ISLE OF EL-MARNEY (TWO YEARS EARLIER)

Sadie Barlow's cotton shirt stuck to her skin and was covered in widening patches of perspiration. Her face was a sheen of sweat as her blindfold was removed. Blowing hard, she cleared salty drips from the tip of her nose that disappeared instantly into the searing blaze.

Releasing her wrist straps she was shoved from the truck, blinking in the blinding sunlight. Sadie shaded her eyes with her hand, before it was snatched and pinned to her side, with an aggressive shout, 'Samba-leasi.' The younger girl that they shoved alongside her was a picture of distress.

At least they were no longer alone. Sadie lifted the corners of her mouth into her cheeks as best she could, in a reassuring glance at the girl. But her tear-stained face only trembled. She looked so young, fifteen maybe. Hopefully she'd only recently been captured, and hadn't endured the terrors of these violent sex-traffickers. The last few weeks had felt like years.

'We'll be okay,' Sadie mouthed, despite knowing that they wouldn't. The two women were shuffled forward, stumbling in ankle chains. They ducked at the sudden caw screeching overhead, to the bellied-laughed amusement of their guards.

Yellow tipped, red-winged Macaws, fluttered in flight before feather-rustling into land. Their emerald breasted plumage puffed proudly as claws settled, clasping the curly branches of nearby bushes. The men marched them on, shoving the girls towards the back of a white walled building. As they turned the corner of the hotel-like complex, they stood them up straight, released their grip and stepped back.

Rowan Darcy sat sprawled in a huge oval-cushioned lounger, his flip-flopped feet facing them. The thick-set man eased slowly from his slouch, sliding his raybans to the peak of his knuckle-toed bald head.

"Now then, what do we have this time?"

A majestic still-watered pool shimmered behind him. To his side, under a large rubber-leafed tree, a short man in breast-pocketed shirt and ill-fitting shorts, stood tapping an iPad.

"Two from the UK, Ro," he said, scrolling his screen. "Zoe Garrett, sixteen years old. Origin Manchester, picked-up at a funfair in Blackpool - 3 days ago."

"Looks good," Darcy said, now perched on the edge of his sunbed. "And..?" he added, scowling at the other girl.

"Ahh-yes, this is the one we had to hold for a while, a dark web response," the little man said, flicking at his pad. "Here we are, yes. Sadie Barlow, twenty five. OG Cambridge, PU at a club in East Barnsted - 35 days."

"East where?" Darcy said, as he strode over to inspect the girls.

"East Barnsted, it's a town somewhere in the midlands, Ro," Joel, his assistant said, squinting across at the women.

"A shit-hole like Brum, is it?" Darcy said, addressing the woman directly.

"I-I d-don't actually, c-come from there," Sadie said.

"Iyy-Iyy-Iyy," Darcy said, mockingly. "What's the story on this one, Joel?"

"Barlow was a private pick-up, some ex-tutor of hers. Clubbing night, Rohypnol snatch, I believe," Joel said, swiping his iPad. "We've paid him half so far, Ro."

"Well, it looks like we need our money back; fuckin twenty five!" Darcy said. "I thought we agreed under twenty," he barked.

Joel swiped quickly at his iPad. "Yes, she is a bit older but the report says she-err.., here we are; 'Looks young, baby-face, freckled cheeks'. Or, she could be one for the hunt, Ro? We did say they didn't have to be young for that," he added with an eye-twitch.

"I suppose the hunters won't care too much," Darcy said, standing directly in front of Sadie.

Sadie's body jerked violently as Darcy's huge hands ripped her shirt apart.

"Nice assets though," Darcy said, smirking as he groped her bare breasts.

"Pl-please don't, please," Sadie said softly, stumbling backwards.

"Stand the fuck up, straight," Darcy demanded, with one hand raised to the side her head.

"Pl-please, I-I-I," Sadie whimpered, with tears filling her eyes.

"Iye Iye Iye, fuckin what," Darcy boomed, slapping her hard across her cheek.

Sadie shrieked, sending wing-flustering birds to the skies amidst shrill cawing. Her head slumped, her face a capillary-rashing red from the skull-jerking blow.

"Remember the reduced rates on damaged goods, Ro," Joel said, waggling his pen limply in the air.

"Yeah, pick on someone your own size, dickhead," Zoe said.

"Oh, my oh my.. what have we here then?" Darcy said, turning slowly to his left.

He strode over to Zoe, towering over her and took a heaped handful of her top. She squirmed, barely wrapping her palms around his forearm, as he lifted her.

"Well, well, well. You left the engine running on this one, guys," Darcy said, grinning at the two guards, who flashed pearly-white smiles at their boss. He raised his clenched fist.

"Remember those trade-in values, Ro," Joel said. "And she's a youngun. They'll be bidding for her, big time," he added, cupping a chubby hand to his dripping brow.

Darcy lowered her to the ground, slowly releasing his grip on her tee.

"Yeah, yeah, fuckin trade-in values!" Darcy said, mimicking his assistant. "They still need breaking in, don't they!" he snarled.

"Let's just spin the dial on this one then, shall we. Get the old chick on the next hunt," Darcy said, and walked over to the nearby wall.

He stood beside a sundial-like construction that was fixed to the side of the building. It was split into three segments and had a spinning arrow fixed at its centre. Each section had an elaborate image set within it. One depicting a knife crossed with a rifle in the shape of an X. A second pictured a tray with a wine glass. The third resembled the Kappa emblem, with two female figures with their legs apart.

Joel emerged from the large-leafed tree, squinting into the brilliant light. "You will work hard whilst you are here, and if you survive long enough, you will be sold on," he announced.

"Host, Hoare, or Hunt.. any preference gobby?" Darcy said, scowling at Zoe.

With arms crossed, Zoe sneered at him, indifferent to her impending fate. Darcy grabbed the arrowhead, and flicked his wrist. The arrowhead raced around the dial, squeaking as it passed between the segments. The pointer slowed, wobbling past the drinks tray and entering the gun and knife section, before clicking wearily on to a stop.

"Hoare! Lovely. Pit number three for you, and I'll be seeing you later," Darcy said, air-kissing towards Zoe. "Get her cleaned up a bit first will you guys. Oh and stick the oldun in pit one with the other runners."

The guards instantly clamped the girls at their elbows and shuffled them away. Darcy pulled his cell from the side pocket of his khaki shorts and slid his shades to the bridge of his nose.

"Ro, I need to talk to you about security. There's a few issues that need to be dealt with," Joel said, retreating to the shade of the tree.

Darcy pinned the phone to his ear, mouthing, 'you deal,' and dismissively finger-flicking his assistant away.

"Jamal, it's me. We got some fresh meat in buddy. Are you coming over at the weekend?" Darcy said excitedly, before releasing a burst of laughter. "That's your fourth fuckin' red this season!"

He settled back onto his white cushioned lounger. A girl in swimwear appeared at his side, placing an ice filled glass on the box table beside him.

"Oh, by the way, Pierre's arriving tonight with some Texan high-flyer, serious player he reckons. Apparently our stetson'ed friend is keen to meet our sporting superstar. Fuck knows why!" he added, with another bellyroar.

CHAPTER 40

PRESENT DAY – PRINCESS MARGARET HOSPITAL

Bernadette Bateman's room was filled with a colourful array of fresh cut flowers filling nearly every inch of surface space and a fair amount of the floor. Dozens of well-wishing cards squeezed between vases.

"How's an old gal like this manage to get a private room?" Tom Broad whispered, with a pinched expression.

The police officers peered between the open slatted blinds into her room. Two nurses sat either side of Bernadette chatting and laughing. One filled her drink glass and unwrapped a fresh straw, whilst the other read to her from a selection of cards and letters.

"Never mind the room guv," DI Neil Turvey said. "How come she's so bleedin popular! It's like the Buck-house forecourt after Lady Di!"

"Well let's see what the People's Princess has got to say about her grandson, that she supposedly forgot she had.." Tom said, knuckle-tapping on the glass and entering.

The nurses sprung to their feet, turning sharply toward the intruders; like soldiers at a checkpoint.

"Is it fair to say that Mrs Bateman is finally able to speak with us?" Tom said, with his head tilted and open-faced.

"Well, err. I don't know about that, just yet," one nurse said, instantly inheriting a concerned frown. "Bernie, what do you think?"

"We have seen you all having a good laugh together," Neil said, peering around a nurse at Mrs Bateman.

"I should be okay for a few minutes, officers," Bernie said croakily. "It's all just been such a shock."

The nurses bustled out of the room, with the taller one stressing they would be back to check on her in, 'five minutes, no longer', and that, 'she mustn't be overly pressured.' Neil nodded along as he closed the door behind them.

"I'll get straight to the point then, Mrs Bateman," Tom said, squealing his chair legs to the end of her bed. "Could you confirm to us what your relationship is to the deceased, Jamal Jackson?"

"He's my grandson," she replied softly, slipping a thick slice of orange into her mouth.

"And you didn't recall that fact when you agreed to become a Juror at Jamal's trial?" Neil snapped, with a rising eyebrow.

She turned her head slowly to eye Neil who was standing on the other side of her bed. A trail of juice trickled down her chin. Tom tugged a reluctant tissue from its box on the chest of drawers beside him, handing it to the pensioner.

"Well they never actually asked me about JJ," she said, smiling sweetly at Tom.

"Look, let's not get pedantic about this Mrs Bateman, you should have declared your relationship with Jamal to the Judge," Neil said. "You should not have been on that Jury."

"Well I wasn't exactly sure of what I was supposed to.."

"Say that, 'he was a family member' for Christ's sake," Neil interjected.

The old woman laid her palm on her chest. Tom shot a teeth-flashing glare at Neil.

"Listen, Mrs Bateman, we're not here about that. It was a mistake, by you, by the Court, whatever," Tom said, wide-eyed. "The fact is that Jamal has been murdered and we need your help to find out who might have done this."

The pensioner took some deep breaths and a sip of water, as Neil settled in the seat opposite Tom. The coppers shared a glance as Neil flipped open his pocketbook, slipping the pencil from its spine.

"Jamal was my only grandson. I didn't see him for the first ten years of his life because of his father. He was a wrong-un, beating up on my daughter and after a time on Jamal too. I saw him off eventually, but his momma wasn't coping and got into some bad company," she said, with a soft tutting.

"Alcohol, drugs and petty crime became my daughter's daily life. And that child woulda followed her down that same pathway to hell. It was no place for Jamal, so I took the boy in," she continued, with a slow shake of her head.

Tom topped up Mrs Bateman's drink, turning the straw towards her and securing the glass in her hand.

"Long story, short," she declared. "I raised the child, boy to man. I gave him the chance to grow, to be the man he wanted to be."

Neil's scoffing was met swiftly by Tom's brow-shelving stare. "Please, do go on Bernie," he said.

"Well you know success followed, the boy done good. His talent brought him money, but with it the curse of fame. That's where your answer lies," she said, her head easing back into her cushion.

"Jamal never wanted trouble, but when you're famous, it finds you. That's what that whole trial business was about; envy. They're all jealous you see, I saw it on my estate. Jamal, he looked after me, paying for some home improvements, but people don't like it," she said.

"So someone from the Cheveley estate decapitated Jamal because you got a new kitchen. Come on!" Neil said, with a lip-lifting sneer.

"DI Turvey!" Tom barked.

"Ok, my apologies, Mrs Bateman," Neil said, flipping a page of his notepad. "How about you tell us about Jamal's business associates, Lebouf and Darcy?" Neil said.

"Neil, leave it," Tom said.

"Time's up, officers," she said, reaching for the red cord dangling beside her headboard.

Mrs Bateman started coughing and holding her chest just as a nurse appeared at the door.

"Gentlemen, I think that's enough for today, thank you," she said, with stiffening features.

"Thank you for your time, Mrs Bateman," Tom said, nodding politely.

"Yes, that's it from us you'll be pleased to know," Neil said. "The perjury issue will be dealt with by the CPS, who are considering your prosecution, and a retrial." he added with a cheek-pulled grin.

The coppers strode the fresh bleached corridors toward the exit doors.

"Look, she doesn't have a scoobydoo about her precious grandson," Neil said. "Even less of an idea about who wanted him dead."

"Probably right there, but I'll tell you what.," Tom said. "It was bloody clever getting on that jury, but to convince them all to turn-in not guilty verdicts. Wow!"

"Yep, you've gotta hand it to the old girl, that was some feat!" Neil said.

PART V – VERDICT

CHAPTER 41

SIX MONTHS EARLIER – THE OLD BAILEY

Desks covered with crisp white tablecloths had been pushed along the back wall, opposite the shuttered windows. An impressive oak table filled the central area, with twelve high-backed chairs surrounding it. The seat at the head, nearest to the Jury room's entrance, was reserved for the appointed Foreman, Mr Lyons. Miss Donovan, his nominated deputy, sat facing him, with the other ten members of the Jury on the seats between them.

Mr Lyons had suggested that everyone change seat each day to hear differing opinions on the evidence that has been presented. Lyons referenced pre-arranged seating plans ruining many a dinner party for him, when stuck with the same awful bore all night. The reality was that most jurors chose who they wanted to sit next to and had remained there since week one. Juror number nine, Bernadette (Bernie) Bateman settled on the seat next to the foreman.

The twelve would vote each day, within minutes of being retired (usually around four o'clock), without deliberation between them. The foreman wanted a 'straw poll', an instant verdict on that day's evidence; people's 'gut reaction,' as he referred to it. He was meticulous in his note-taking, recording each member's comments. Lyons was in many ways the perfect foreman, committing with gusto to the role.

The group almost entirely sang from the same hymn sheet; the TikTokTrio were guilty. The evidence was overwhelming. Yes, there were circumstantial issues, countering witness accounts and the DNA profiling had potentially been compromised. But the Defendant's expert's submissions on skin and fibre transference were regarded as 'flaky' at best. His report was picked to pieces, raising more than the odd eyebrow of incredulity from the Judge.

Despite the seriousness of their predicament and heinous crimes of which they stood accused, the defendants exuded an unerring arrogance. They sat with casual demeanour, sneering at the prosecution benches, often interrupting submissions, to the gavel thudding Judge's protestations. The thick-set man, Roman Darcy, was removed from the dock on many occasions, to spend the afternoon in a holding cell.

"Members of the Jury.. I'm pleased to finally say that you may now retire to consider your verdict."

The Judge's words were greeted with hushed cheer from the public gallery, at the long awaited conclusion of all evidence and final summations.

"Please bear in mind the directives I have given you throughout the trial; You are not permitted to discuss matters outside of your body of jurors and deliberations should be confined to the jury room," the Judge said, with a solemn nod at the foreman.

Mrs Bateman was nudged twice before stirring from her slumber, to allow the top pew of jurors to depart the courtroom. Deputy Chair, Miss Donovan and her colleagues shared some smiling eye-rolls. The group quickly settled into the familiar surroundings of the jury room where sharp rays lit the back wall, glinting off the silver tea urn.

"You okay Bernie?" Miss Donovan said, as the pensioner slid heavily into her seat, plonking her oversized handbag on the table. "Looked like you dropped off in there."

"I'm fine, thank you dear," Mrs Bateman said, smiling sweetly up at the young woman. "Just listening with my eyes closed," she whispered, with a wink.

"You must be good at that by now!" another juror chuckled, placing a hand on Bernie's shoulder.

"You leave her be, she's done great to get through this," Miss Donovan said. "We all have!"

"She knows I'm only joking, don't you Bern," the juror said. "I reckon we're friends for life after this aren't we."

Mrs Bateman, with head half turned tapped his hand, winking up at him. "You've all been so kind, but I'm afraid it has taken it out of me. Would anyone mind if I were to sneak off for a little afternoon nap?" she said softly.

Others circled their elderly, fellow-juror, with saucered white cups in hands, each adopting a soppy grin. One waved over at Mr Lyons the Foreman, who was in deep conversation with the court clerk.

"Err, Mr Foreman, is it ok if our Bernie slips away?" Miss Donovan said.

"Absolutely not! All deliberations must involve all of you from now on," the Clerk to the Court interjected.

"Sorry Bernie, but it gets a bit strict from here on," Mr Lyons said, with his bottom lip poking out.

"I'm just so tired," she whispered, looking up at Miss Donovan with watery eyes.

"Surely we can all agree to retire this afternoon, and start afresh in the morning?" Miss Donovan said, arm-folding at the court clerk.

"Well the Judge needs a unanimous verdict, and in my experience that can take some time," the clerk said, twisting one end of his curly moustache.

"We've just heard some hefty closing submissions in there. I'm sure it would help us all if we could sleep on it!" Miss Donovan argued to those around her.

There was mumbled agreement across stern faces as jurors' eyes cast in the direction of the stocky court clerk, who stood finger-twisting his necktie; Oliver Hardy-like. Mr Lyons cocked his head, open-faced at the clerk.

"Well, I suppose, as long as you're all in agreement with that," he said, disappointedly. "It goes against my recommendation, of course, and you've had the court directive on evidence pollution."

"Good-good, then that's agreed," Mr Lyons declared. "I, for one, could do with some fresh air after that courtroom. It was stifling in there!"

Mrs Bateman got to her feet, clasped Miss Donovan's arm and whispered in her ear, before rustling in her bag.

"Guys... guys. Before you head off, Mrs B would like to say a few words," Miss Donovan said.

"Thank you dear, you're such a sweetheart," Mrs Bateman said softly, with a familiar twinkle in her eyes.

"I feel," she said, peering around the room. "As if I have made friends for life here. You've all been so kind," she added, to much ahhing and kiss-blowing. "Don't get me started," she continued, tugging a tissue from the sleeve of her cardigan and dabbing it in the corner of her eye.

Mr Lyons placed a plastic cup of water in front of the pensioner.

"Thank you dear," she said, pulling a stack of white envelopes from her handbag. "I'm not good at speeches.. only good with pots and pans, my Cyril used to say! So, I've written a card for each of you to take home," she said, looking at the smile-filled faces she had come to know so well. "I hope you believe every word I say inside, and know how strongly I feel."

"We love you, Bernie," one Juror shouted, much to the amusement of the group.

"That's very kind of you, Bernie," Mr Lyons said. "I'm sure I speak for everyone, when I say, we have all become very fond of you too."

Miss Donovan, stood alongside Mrs Bateman's handing out the envelopes as each named recipient filed out of the room, leaving the foreman and court clerk, who was waiting to lock up.

"Ah-ah-ah!" Mrs Bateman tutted at Mr Lyons as he poked the tip of his finger into the flap of his envelope. "Not till you get home, Mr Foreman."

"Oh, all right Bernie, you little tease," he said, holding the door as the old lady shuffled out with Miss Donovan.

The Court Clerk paced the room, tidying away cups and tucking chairs into the table and laying out notepads. He glanced back admiring his work, before pulling the heavy door too and locking it behind him.

He hadn't noticed the envelope perched in its wire holder at the centre of the boardroom table. The court sealed verdict card was already signed inside.

Despite the fact that the Jury's deliberations weren't due to start until the following morning, their unanimous verdict was already confirmed. The foreman and his deputy's forged signatures were inked below the defendants' names that aligned with the words, Not Guilty.

CHAPTER 42

Beads of perspiration trickled from the brow of Lucy Donovan as the pathway got steeper. She slowed while exiting the leafy copse, leaving behind birdsong as she jogged on towards the summit of Muswell Hill.

Amy Winehouse filled her ears as she squinted-in the vast expanse of straw-like parched fields below her, as she rounded the crest. The slopes were dotted with sunbathers that had found their preferred vantage on the undulating elevation. The city's skyline was crisp in focus against the cloudless, brilliance of the day.

Yet another buzzing notification interrupted Amy's invitation to 'Valerie' to come on over. The bench ahead was vacant and Lucy sat and unzipped her running belt, easing her iPhone from it. 'What could be so urgent,' she cursed.

Sweat bulbs trickled from Lucy's steeping eyebrows. The Jury4Justice WhatsApp group was flashing 45 messages. 'We've got the afternoon off guys!' she muttered.

Muting her playlist, Lucy dabbed the group's scales of justice icon and squinted into the screen, cupping her hand over it to read;

"Tell me this isn't only happening to me... you all opened your letter from Mrs B?"

"Yep I got one too.. I don't understand it!"

"You got the red powder?"

"Yeah, I can't wash it off! But it's the tracker I'm worried about"

"Wtf"

"Tracker?"

"Bottom corner of the card.. Circular thingy between the cardboard"

"Shit yeah, about the size of a five pence piece?"

"You got it"

"You seen the message? I'm assuming they're all the same"

"Here's mine.. (attached)"

Lucy zoomed in on the attachment; reading the message on the greeting card under her breath;

'It's been good getting to know so much about you and your loved ones.

I'm glad we have all agreed on a verdict of **Innocent**.

Keep in touch and do stay safe, Mrs B.'

The same handwritten note was inside everyone's card, under a large typed message; 'Congratulations, it's over!'

Lucy shuddered, as two cyclists whizzed past her, panting heavily. The beauty of the day was lost as she read on;

"Forget that, sinister as it is! Has anyone else got a visitor outside their house"

"Err, I live in a flat on the sixth floor, thank you Charles!"

"Sorry Mo, no offence"

"None taken, but if there is anyone I aint seeing them from up here, Lol"

"Shit. I got one"

"Yep me too"

"Unless hells angels have moved in next door I think mines perched on the wall opposite my apartment block"

"Shit.. There is a biker guy looking up here"

"Don't panic - seems like we've all got them"

"OMG what we gonna do about this"

"Obviously vote innocent and live to tell the tale"

"We can't just do that after all these weeks of evidence"

"Yeah lets be honest - they're guilty as sin"

"You're not picking up on the gravity of our situation here. This is scary!"

"We just have to stick together. They can't just intimidate us like this"

"What say you, Mr. Foreman, Miss D??"

"Well, my not-so-friendly guy just knocked on and shoved a parcel in my hand."

"My dude's just standing there like he's guarding the place. What'd he say to you Mr Lyons?"

"Nothing. Not a word. He just delivered a sealed box the size of a child's shoebox, with a business card attached - see below"

Lucy tapped and scrolled, enlarging the picture. She shuffled along to the end of the bench, as a young couple lingered in front of her before taking a seat. Cupping a damp hand over the image, she squinted closer. A powder pink card with elegant calligraphy read;

TTT - Tea Time Treats

A gift for you and your family

p.s…We don't do porridge!

"Jesus… all that for a box of bloody muffins!"

"Maybe it's a gift from the Court service for our time"

"Wake up guys.. TTT.. ring any bells!"

"Fuck me, my biker chaps knocking on"

"Shit that could be a bomb inside that box Mr L"

"Someone's at my door"

"Don't answer it. Shit there here now too"

"Fuck me, that's some aggressive banging"

"Call the police"

"DO NOT do that. They obviously know everything about us.. Where we live, our family!"

"My kid ain't back from school yet!"

"They'll know if we go to the police"

"Are we answering them or waiting for doors to fall in"

"My chaps being rather persistent too"

"Let's just take the box!"

Lucy Donovan jumped, her heart missing a beat at the roar of a motorcycle engine crackling immediately behind her. The couple alongside her upped and strode away. The driver sat straddling his seat as he swung a black rucksack from his back.

"I don't think motorcycles are allowed up here," Lucy said, placing an authoritative hand on her hip.

With tinted visor down, the shiny helmeted driver remained wordless as he dug into his bag. Lucy stepped back onto the pedestrian pathway, spun and began jogging away.

She glanced over her shoulder as she plugged in her airpods. The biker pinned the rucksack to his back and revved his engine. Lucy increased her pace swiftly to a sprint as she peeled off the track and onto the grassy slope. Lengthening her stride further, she bounded towards the park gates at the foot of the hill.

Having been released early by the Court, Lucy had decided to make the most of it. She'd thrown her bag, with the envelope from Mrs Bateman inside, on the kitchen table. Donning her favourite gymware, she headed straight out.

Blowing heavily, she unzipped her turtleneck lycra collar and descended the lower slope to within twenty metres of the gates when a coldness took her. The black-clad motorcyclist was there, waiting at the entrance, beneath its iron archway. She turned sharply heading for the exit further down. Hearing a piston roaring start up, she sped to a sprint.

At the east gateway the motorcycle closed, before she veered off, hurtling back up the field leaving a scorching tyre skid of the fat wheeled bike behind her. It wouldn't come over parkland covered in sunbathers. Angry engine growling continued as it sat on the perimeter pathway as Lucy headed toward the southside exit.

Just call the police, Lucy! But a call might endanger her fellow jurors, who'd all received suspicious parcels and threats referencing their families. The three men on trial were extremely violent and exceptionally wealthy; a dangerous concoction!

She slowed to a jog, peering back. The motorcycle had gone, disappeared, amidst the traffic beyond the perimeter fencing. Lucy about-turned, powering back to the now vacant gate.

What if's filled Lucy's head as she cornered the exit and scuttled across the traffic filled road, to a prolonged horn blast of an irate driver. Flicking a middle finger high above her head, she pounded the pavement, weaving through meandering tourists and dodging the pushchairs.

Her heartbeat leapt at the familiar thrusting roar of a motorbike. A glance over her shoulder confirmed it. The black helmeted driver was back, weaving speedway-like between cars.

Lucy took the next left, bolting down Juniper Street, crossing and darting into the alleyway at the rear of Ealing mews, before cornering a sharp right into Percival terrace. The engine hum softened at each bollard-ended alley. But still it prevailed, with increasingly angry splats at each laboured exit.

From Percival she scampered the narrow stone steps onto Churchill Way, racing on. The long Victorian terrace tapered toward a footpath at its end. A bike would struggle with the steps and the concrete posts might block its route. Ahead were houses to either side, she was fuzzy-minded at whether to chance door-knocking.

If no one is in; you waste time, you're trapped. If they are; you put them in danger.

Lucy jumped at the blast of pistons, sleeve-wiping her face as she darted between properties. She shot beneath an archway, tearing between walled backyards at their rear. She scampered a maze of alleyways, zig-zagging, before exiting onto Chalk Pit road.

Lucy recognised the redbrick buildings ahead and charged down the centre of the road, cornering right at the Duke of York. She jogged to a walk as she reached the crossroads at Cromwell and Varsity. Stopping at the steps of the blue lamped building, she doubled-over panting at her knees just as the revving returned.

At the top of the road, the motorcyclist sat, near the Public house, motionless in defeat. Lucy flung her middle-finger high and bounded the steps of the police station.

"I need your help. I can't tell you who I am or why I'm here, or I'll endanger others," Lucy blustered, her mind was racing. What was in the boxes her co-jurors had been given? "I've been chased by a guy on a motorcycle!"

"You're not making much sense, sweetheart," the desk Sergeant said, with a slow head-shake.

"He's still outside!" she blurted. If they agreed to a not guilty verdict this would all go away. If they didn't, they might be killed. "I, we need protection!"

"Now can I take your name, my dear?" he added, with a thin grin.

"No, I told you I can't tell you my name, I'm the only one that hasn't been caught!" Lucy said, staring at the white shirted officer.

"Well you're nice and safe now, sweety. So let's start with your name, shall we?" he said, leaning over his desk and winking at her.

"Shit, you're not going to help me, are you?" Lucy said, shakily.

"That is what we are here for, Miss," he said, with an eye-roll.

"Look, can you protect me or not!" Lucy demanded.

"Yes, of course I can, honey. But we will need to take down your particulars first," he added, smirking at the officer behind him.

Lucy viciously zipped her top to her chin and crossed her arms. "Can I see your supervising officer?" she snapped, feeling her pulse rising.

"Not without good reason you can't, no," he said, beaming smugly.

"What do I need to do to be kept safe for twenty-four hours," she said, with narrowing eyes.

"Well now, safe from what exactly, my sweet?" he said, glancing over his shoulder with a soft chortle.

"Look, can I just stay here while I work this out?" Lucy said, with a slight thump on the counter.

"Now why would a nice young girl like you want to go into one of our grubby old cells," he said, beaming at her.

"Please, I just need protection, while I make some calls," Lucy said, fist-clenching.

"I think I'm starting to understand you, darlin'" he said, with a slow nod. *"Had a row with the boyfriend, have you?"*

Lucy Donovan swung her white knuckled fist, cracking cleanly the bridge of the desk Sargents nose. Three minutes later she settled onto the end of a bed in an eight by six windowless cell.

In registering the assault, Miss Donovan was automatically dismissed from the Jury, being the subject of criminal charges. In her absence, the Jury's not-guilty verdict was accepted by the trial Judge.

PART VI – CAPTIVE

CHAPTER 43

PRESENT DAY.. EL−MARNEY

The thunderous grumble of rock dragging across rock shook Bella from her semi-conscious state. Despite the discomfort of her seated position, she had drifted in fitful slumber.

A crescent-shaped shard of brightness from deeper inside their dungeon slowly lit the concrete floor. Sparkling dust filled the widening void as the huge rumbling rock crept ever further from its wall.

"Jesus, what is this, Indiana Jones!" Bella said, taking in her new surroundings.

An unsettling eeriness gripped the cave as it inched to reveal an ever-lengthening row of bare feet opposite Bella. The grumbling loudened as the sharp beam intensified into squint-filled eyes, turning from its glare.

One, two, three.. Six girls sat on the bench opposite, all pencil thin with angular features. Bella leaned forward to count her side; another six. Twelve girls imprisoned down here, in the bowels of this remote Island. Pascal was right, despite their trial, they were doing it again.

As the huge stone rolled a final turn, it unveiled an arched opening in the rockface, with a floodlit expanse beyond. Their cellar-like cave was now aglow and its scent of bodily odours less harsh. Anguished faces flickered nervously between one another, as a shadow grew larger in the jagged archway, blackening the hard floor.

"Samba-leasi, samba-leasi!" Shouts boomed into the cave as a muscular-framed man ducked inside, clearing the arched entrance.

"Oh god, samba-fucking-leasi boy's back!" Bella said, releasing a snigger from the pasty-faced blonde girl on the opposite bench.

Bella beamed over at the doe-eyed girl with thick hair that trailed to her waist. She met her with a sad smile before dipping her head. Monique, the French girl beside Bella, bounced a finger to her blistered lips. The girls looked hauntingly thin with sunken eyes set in drawn, pained expressions. They all wore the same mottled green top and matching shorts, like Army fatigues.

"Samba-leasi, ontario et-vous!" the man barked, more insistent now.

As one, the women lurched to their feet, shuffling in the direction of the guard. The pigtailed ginger girl at the front squealed, stumbling to the ground as her ankle rolled beneath her. Accepting the hand of the woman behind her, she rose quickly, wincing and hobbling on through the archway. The large guy and another man stood to either side.

It was dazzlingly bright and airy in the space ahead. The rockface had wires running its sides and strip-lighting above. A queue began forming at some butler-style sinks that were fixed around a central stone column.

The girls plunged their hands into the deep terrines of water, slurping desperately and splashing its coolness over their faces. Bella, still blinking-in the brightness, scooped to sip a handful of water, keeping one eye on the guards. Behind them the muscle-flexed men rolled back the weighty rock, re-sealing their sweat-filled dungeon.

"Samba-leasi, samba-leasi!" the shorter guy turned and squealed.

"Yes, thank you, Leesee boy," Bella said. "Does anyone actually know what the hell that means?" she added, looking at the girls who rushed to finish their ablutions.

191

"I think it just means move-on," the little blonde girl said, with a sweet smile. She'd tucked her thick blonde locks behind her ears, her face glistening. Her long hair dripped relentlessly, dampening her shorts.

"Guess we'd better do that then," Bella said, with a wink.

The group rounded a corner at the far end that Bella hadn't noticed was there. Beyond it they trudged a narrowing jagged corridor, running twenty metres or so, towards another brightly lit area. Here, central stone pillars had mirrors fixed to its sides with metal troughs below. The troughs were filled with a mass of shiny objects.

"It's make-up!" Bella said, with a burst of laughter. "You want us to put some lippy and slap on for you?" she added, staring back at the two men.

The taller guard was still crouched in negotiating his exit from the shallow corridor. The little guy stomped over, grabbing Bella's elbow and shoving her toward the trough.

"Whoaa, easy tiger," Bella said, twisting to pull clear of his grip.

"You are making up now," he said, pointing at the pile of makeup.

"Why are we making up now?" she asked, with palms wide.

"Samba-leasi!" the tall guy bellowed as he approached, sliding a blade from a holster that flopped at the side of his shorts.

"You'd better do as he says," the little blonde girl whispered, pointing at a six inch scar across her abdomen. "He will use it," she added, before reaching into the trough of cosmetics.

The other women were already busily daubing make-up onto their faces, whilst trying to catch a reflection of themselves in the smeared mirrors. The men spoke angrily with vowel-filled words as they strode to the opposite end of the cave. A curved stone stairway disappeared upwards. The tall guard sat half-perched on a stool beside the steps speaking into a crackly walkie-talkie.

"We use make-up for hunt, Bella. Like in war movies," Monique said. "You know, Braveheart, is warpaint, no?" she added, seeing Bella headcocking.

Monique smeared blue eyeshadow across half her face, whilst Blondie painted two thick lines of lipstick across her cheeks and nose.

"Christ, are we really going to war!" Bella said. "The local Polizia were putting a stop to this. Darcy's supposed to be being monitored!"

"Samba-leasi," the shorter man said. "Number ones," he added, finger curling at the nearest woman.

The ginger girl, who now looked very different, hobbled over to the man, who grabbed her wrist and spun her around.

"Bit touchy-feely that one," Bella said, to the blonde girl who stood next to her. "He needs teaching some manners."

The tall guard took a canister of some sort and rattled it as he waved it across the girls back. He shook it again, this time moving it up and down her legs. Turning her again, revealed the number '1' spray painted across her back and thigh. He rattled the canister again before applying the number to her midriff.

"Number twos, samba-leasi," he said, with an impatient finger beckoning another girl.

"What's all this about?" Bella whispered to Monique. "Some sort of auction?"

"No, that's only for rouge. We are verte, greens; the hunt," she said, her lower lip drooping.

"Red's?" Bella quizzed, as they watched number three being sprayed.

The baby-faced blonde girl said softly, "The Red's are for prostitution.. to be sold." She looked too young and innocent to even know the word.

"You must have done the selection wheel; Hoare, Host or Hunt?" Monique whispered, her eyebrows arching in symmetry.

"I guess I missed that bit!" Bella said, eye rolling. "So what happens on this hunt.. what are we actually hunting for?"

"We don't hunt anything, Bella," Monique said, with a sorrow filled expression.

Blondie's dainty fingers slid to interlock with Bella's. "We are the hunted ones!" she said, with Bambi-eyes staring up at Bella.

CHAPTER 44

"Settle down now guys!" Tom Broad barked. "Gather around, grab a seat," he added, beckoning the officers at the back of the room forward.

Neil Turvey shuffled clear of a strong waft of cologne before shouldering between a couple of burly officer's in conversation, ducking to land at a table near the front. He slid into a moulded plastic chair alongside DI Spencer, winking his delight at securing a prime seat. She remained with hand raised, like an overly enthusiastic primary school kid.

"In a minute, Spence," Tom said, waving an open palm dismissively in her direction.

He rattled at a small white pot, struggling to remove its lid, before shaking pills into his cupped hand. He head-jerked them back, waterless.

"Sir, I've got some good feedback from.." Spencer persisted.

"Not yet!" Tom snapped.

Her familiar drift of Dior encircled Neil as her arm dropped.

"Let's get to it now, shall we chaps," Tom said, glaring at two coppers standing at the coffee dispenser chatting loudly.

"*We have a person of interest.* One, Arabella Maxwell, 'Bella' as she's known," Tom said. "Now Lebouf's car was data-logged outside her address and his key fob registered a *bleep* from inside the property."

On the board behind him, enlarged picture of Maxwell was pinned above photographs of three men. Maxwell, with brunette shiny hair flowing over her shoulders, sported a white silk blouse beneath black barristers gown. She beamed, seemingly challenging all in the room.

"Maxwell's boyfriend, Carl Turner, tells us that she's abroad at a work-based event." Tom said, with his index finger on the smiling image behind him. "Her employer advises that she is currently on annual leave; there is no work event."

"Neil?" Tom said, nodding at his number two and stepping to one side. He stood with elbow propped on a filing cabinet.

"Thanks boss," Neil said, standing front and centre. "Bella Maxwell was part of the legal team that prosecuted the TikTokTrio, devoting a year of her life to the case. The trial ended in failure for Maxwell, with these men walking free!"

"Biggest miscarriage of justice, *ever.*" DI Spencer mumbled.

Neil pointed at the police photographs. Pierre Lebouf, dark-suited, with familiar conceited grin, was central to Jamal Jackson on his right, whose picture had a red cross through it. The distinctive bulldog-featured, shaven-headed Roman Darcy was pictured to his left.

"Jamal Jackson was murdered on the Cheveley estate, his body cut-up and decapitated," Neil continued, to a raised eyebrow from Tom. "We know that Maxwell's boyfriend, Carl Turner, works for the council and has keys to the waste disposal area; the scene of Jackson's murder."

Spencer scribbled frantically on her notepad and turned it to face Neil.

"Lebouf was abducted from outside his mother's apartment in West London. An unknown female accessed the building by deception, luring Lebouf there," Neil continued, head-shaking at Spencer. "His car was stolen, and later discovered in Chapeltown, Yorkshire, burnt out..."

"The exact location of the Yorkshire Ripper's alleged first victim," Spencer shouted.

"Alleged?" Tom said, his elbow still propped on the cabinet, with head now resting in hand.

"There were a number of unsolved murder's before Chapeltown that bore the Ripper's MO. But Sutcliffe was never charged," Spencer said.

"Yes, thank you Spence!" Neil said loudly. "The point that I was trying to make is that the car made just the one stop, here, before heading north," he said, pointing at a picture of a quaint looking Victorian terrace.

"That registered owner of the property is a Charles Maxwell, Bella's grandfather," Neil continued. "She flits between there and her boyfriend's place."

Tom strolled over to the whiteboard, as Neil stepped to one side.

"So, Miss Maxwell evidently has involvement in the abduction of Lebouf. And, had access to the murder site of Jackson," Tom said. "She was described as 'mortified,' at the Jury's verdict."

Neil waved his hand. "Maxwell is reported to have said; '*I don't accept that verdict. Something has to be done about this*,'" he said, flipping his pocket book.

"That's just a heat of the moment rant," Spencer said, head shaking. "We've all been there."

"This was her tirade directed at the Judge! It's from the stenographer's record," Neil said, with a pulled grin. "Maxwell was the only person who spoke with the survivors; *the tender dead*, as they were labelled. It became personal," he added, turning to Tom.

"The tender dead?" Tom said, with bottom lip rolling out.

"That's what they became known as," Spencer said. "The sole survivors from the massacre on that Island. The three girls were discovered in a disused well. They'd thrown themselves down..."

"*Yes*, thank you, Spence," Neil interjected. "We've established Maxwell as our 'person of interest,' so there's no need to go into all that."

"Just discussing motive, Neil!" Spencer said, reacquainting her rear with the seat.

Neil screwed his face at her before clicking the laser pointer into life. A red dot appeared on the white board.

"Ok, so where is she now?" Neil said, directing the light to a map. "If follows that she's after the third guy, Roman Darcy. And this.. is his last known whereabouts," he added.

He swept the dot across a map that detailed a chain of islands speckling the Indian Ocean.

"This is an image from Google Earth of one of the more remote islands; Isle of El Marney. Set between these two rocky outcrops, is his impressive resort," Neil said, circling the laser dot. "Unfortunately it's that isolated that we've been unable to contact Darcy, but Spence has left messages via his various social media accounts. Spence?" Neil said.

"Thanks Neil," Spencer said, getting to her feet. "I haven't managed to make contact with Darcy yet. But BA have just confirmed that Maxwell boarded a flight to Jakarta two days ago.." she said, flashing a side-glance at Tom.

"Clearly she's going after him then, guv. Darcy's going to need protection given what happened to Jackson and Lebouf," Neil said, eyeballing Tom.

"*Err..* if I might finish," Spencer said, finger-wagging. "I have carried out a deep dive into Darcy's current affairs, which were, up until a few days ago, heavily interlinked with Lebouf."

"Interlinked?" Tom said, head cocking.

"There was a daily transfer of '*investment returns*'; huge sums. These funded a business called '*Big Game X*.' We managed to access the site via Lebouf's personal log-in and passwords that his mother provided," Spencer said.

Pages from bank statements filled the whiteboard behind her, evidencing the regularity and size of financial transactions between the two men.

"I think we're going off at a tangent here, boss. It's Maxwell we're after!" Neil said, head-shaking. "The legality, or otherwise, of individuals signing up to some Safari shoot at fifty-k a pop is irrelevant to us."

"No-no, let's hear this. Spence, go on," Tom said, flashing a frown at Neil.

"Well it looks like Darcy and Lebouf are up to their old tricks, sir. An increasing number of girls that have been registered as missing."

"Missing persons will be on that, guv. It's not our remit!" Neil said, with a heavy exhale.

"But surely we need to.." Spencer said.

"As a British citizen we need to offer Mr Darcy police protection, and apprehend Maxwell!" Neil said, stepping across her.

"Yes, I think you're right, Neil," Tom said.

"But sir, if I could just finish," Spencer said, flush at the cheeks. "This isn't the usual, lion hunting experience, sir."

She stepped to position herself alongside Neil. Tom nodded impatiently at her.

"They're offering something different. It's a dark web space, so it's heavily encrypted. They require a hundred thousand dollars before allowing access to locational details."

"A little beyond our police budget, Spence!" Neil said, with a mocking smirk.

"Look, what are you suggesting is going on, Spence?" Tom said.

Spencer said. "They've resumed their sex trafficking operation. Twenty two young women have been abducted from the UK in the last six months. The TikTokTrio are clearly back in business and they've ventured into another area."

"It's a trade in women for sex, Spence," Neil said, flashing her a wonky smile. "What's new?"

"I'm not sure, but the mega-rich always drive the newest craze, sell the latest fetish," Spencer said, to a shrill wolf whistling at the back of the room.

"Alright, that's enough!" Tom said, with a palm raised. "Neil, Spence, my office please. I've got the psychologist coming in shortly, so we can discuss this with him. Everyone else, your briefs are on the team email."

The noise levels went from nought to sixty in seconds as the meeting disbanded.

"*Sir*, can I just add," Spencer shouted, across the chatter-filled room. "I think interviews with Lebouf's associates should be a priority. A member of his staff has been calling about significant funds that have gone missing.."

Her words evaporated amidst the fast dispersing officers.

"And, Maxwell, *Guv*," Spencer said, chasing Tom toward the exit. "We need to get the full picture before we go after her?"

CHAPTER 45

"What's your name, hun?" Bella said, cupping the blonde girl's hand.

"Zoe., I'm Zoe," she said, with the sweetest of smiles. "My friend's used to call me Zo."

"Well listen Zo, I'm Bella and you and I are gonna stick together and get through whatever it is they've got planned for us up there," Bella said, with a confident wink. "How long have you been here?"

"I'm not sure, but the French lady, Monique, came just after me. She marks off the months. Last count was twenty three, I think," she whispered.

"Jezz, that can't be right Zo. You've been here for nearly two years?" Bella said, with a furrowing brow. "But we had the bastards in custody. The authorities here said they had shut down their operation and searched the entire island.

"But they took us to a different island, before the Police came. Makam-Raja it's called," Zoe mouthed softly, as the shorter man shouted something in their direction. "We were shipped over there."

"But they said they'd investigated neighbouring islands. InterPol were *assured* that there were only three survivors." Bella mumbled, head shaking.

On seeing a sadness swamp Zoe's eyes, Bella said, "I met with one of the girls, you know?"

Zoe's face instantly lit, "You met the wishing well warriors? They're legends. We heard that they broke bones throwing themselves down that well to survive!"

"They broke more than just limbs, Zo," Bella said, turning Zoe to face the far wall. "So who's been running all this whilst the TikTokTrio were under lock and key?"

"I dunno, but it's bigger than just them, Bel," Zoe whispered.

The guards continued spray-painting numbers onto the women; like branding cattle.

"Number nines. Numbers nines," the shorter guard hollered, pointing at a dishevelled-looking girl with scraggly hair. Clumps of it were missing where her scalp shone through.

Her clothing sagged from her stick-thin frame. Her top hung loose from her collarbones, her shorts flapped around skinny legs. Her movement was stilted and awkward, pigeon-like.

"Who is that girl?" Bella turned to whisper in Zoe's ear.

"That's Gloria, she's an icon. Italian, I think. She's been here the longest. She actually managed to hide out down here, in the cave. They thought she'd escaped!" Zoe said, hand-cupping a giggle.

Zoe stepped with Bella a little further away from the group.

"Gloria's been disciplined harder than most. She's gone full circle; started as a host, then hoare, until she got too thin for their liking, so now she's on the hunt. A lot of those selected for the Hunt are rejected reds," Zoe said, with a shrug. "They expanded the *Hunt* to the other island because of the number of guests they have."

"Wait, Zoe. So how many of you were transferred to this other island?"

"Around twenty of us, but they split us up. We came back here, but Sadie and the others were kept on Makam-Raja and they started doing hunts over there.

It's smaller and more isolated," Zoe said with a sad smile. "But it's a really beautiful place, Bella."

"Wait, did you say, *Sadie?*" Bella whispered loudly, pimples prickling her forearms.

"Yeah, Sadie, we came over together. Nobody knows about Makam-Raja, everyone thinks it's uninhabited," Zoe murmured. "The locals believe it's sacred land that cannot be touched, so they won't go near it!"

Bella said, wide-eyed. "What's Sadie's surname, Zoe?"

"Numbers twelves!" the thickset man barked at them.

The other girls were already lined up in order, all now brightly numbered, with faces painted. Zoe peeled away from Bella, trudging towards the men.

"Zoe, please.. What's her surname?" Bella said, her head spinning.

Zoe half-turned with a shrug, before standing with arms aloft in front of the guard, who rattled his can of spray paint.

"What does she look like, Zoe?" Bella said.

"Brown hair," Zoe whispered, stroking her own. "Round smiley face, brown eyes. About your age and height," she added, finger pointing at Bella.

Bella shuddered, digging fingers into her scalp. A deep swell of anger hit the pit of her stomach. The tall man shoved Zoe towards the line of numbered girls and beckoned Bella over.

"Samba-leasi!"

The short guy grabbed Bella by the arm, tussling with her and turning her around. With a gormless toothy grin, he rattled a can of yellow labelled paint, marking her '*13*'.

"Special prize," he said, teeth-gleaming at his mate. "Iz unluckies for you, no!"

The men belly-laughed, enjoying some mutual bicep jabbing as Bella joined the other women.

Zoe looked up at Bella's watery eyes, "Did you know her?"

"It sounds like my Sadie, but I can't be sure," Bella said, placing a hand on Zoe's shoulder. "Is there anything else you could tell me about her?"

"She talked about University a lot. I remember that because she went to Manchester, where I'm from," Zoe said, smiling, adding, "And she had a cute load of freckles across her nose."

Bella dropped to her knees, holding her face. "Oh god, no!" she mumbled, cupping her mouth. "Shit, it's her.. That's my Sadie."

The tall guard bellowed something into his walkie-talkie to an equally loud, crackly response.

"Sadie Barlow is my best friend," Bella said, whilst struggling to stand. "Where is she now Zo?"

"We were hosting together until the transfer to Makam-Raja," Zoe said, helping Bella to her feet. "Gloria overheard them saying they're charging *a hundred thousand to hunt there,*" Zoe added, whispering the last bit.

The men stood shouting at each other, before the tall man resumed his conversation into the walkie-talkie.

"So, Sadie could still be on Raja?"

"I doubt it, it's just used by the hunting parties," Zoe said, with a downturned mouth. "Girls don't ever come back from a Hunt, Bella," Zoe said, lip-biting.

"I have to try and find her, to get over there," Bella said, as a tear jerked, dripping to the ground. "Can you help me?"

Zoe said. "Well, Makam-Raja's the little island nearest.."

"..nearest to this one. It means, 'the king's tomb'," Bella said, tugging the sleeve of her tee to wipe her face.

"You know all about it then, Bel," Zoe said, her eyes widening.

"Yep, I had a history lesson from my tour guide on the way over here!" Bella said, winking at her young friend. "Apparently, many centuries ago, *it was the King's last resting place, and legend has it that his many Queen's were left on the island to grieve for the remainder of their lives,*" Bella recited, recalling Pascal's lecture.

"Wow, you've really done your homework," Zoe said, beaming up at her.

The group started shuffling forward, approaching the bottom step. Sharp shards of light pierced the air, dust particles spiralled down from the warmer air above. The first of the girls began trudging their ascent of the steep stone stairwell.

"Sadie could be hiding there.. if she escaped the hunters?" Bella said, her bottom lip rolling.

"But they've got knives and guns, Bella. We hear them shooting," Zoe said softly, before plodding the first steps.

From the brilliant brightness above the same rectangular shadowed shaping filled the floor at the foot of the stairwell, as it had in the first cave.

The big guy with a terminator-like monobrow leaned over, whispering in Bella's ear, "Samba-leasi!" He beamed a yellow-toothed grin and shoved her hard between the shoulder blades, sending her stumbling to the bottom step.

CHAPTER 46

Tom Broad's office was tight. Metal chair legs clanked as Neil Turvey passed the usual door-holding chair to the Criminal Profiler, Jeremy Forsythe.

"Could I just run my findings by you on the Ripper theory, guv?" DI Spencer asked, already settled on the seat opposite Tom.

Tom slurped heartily from his football mug, replacing it sloppily on the corner of his desk. He reclined in his cushioned seat, interlocking his fingers behind his head.

"Yes., but first things first," Tom said. "Let's prioritise getting Maxwell into custody shall we."

"The Ripper, you say," Forsythe said softly, half-turning to the female detective. "Yorkshire, or Jack?"

"Sutcliffe," Spencer said, nodding at the elderly psychologist. "There's a pattern emerging that suggests we might have a copycat."

"I'm not sure that's prioritising, Spencer," Neil said, with a Roger Moore-like eyebrow.

"Please, if you wouldn't mind.. do indulge me," Forsythe said, sliding his tortoiseshell glasses to the tip of his nose. "I studied the case at the time and wrote a thesis," he added, with a little grin at Tom.

"And a bestseller, professor!" Tom said, beaming at him.

"Indeed, yes, A Mind To Kill did sell rather well, but please do go on," Jeremy said.

"Well, we know that Lebouf's car was discovered in Chapeltown, Leeds," she said.

"Yes, I noticed that from your report. It struck me as more than a little coincidental," Jeremy said, turning to face the young DI.

"Since the trial, crime records have revealed a spike in murders of men across the country. Bodies have been discovered across Leeds and Bradford and today I received confirmation that another man, a building site foreman from London, was found in Huddersfield," Spencer said, flicking at her pocketbook.

"Probably a job for our friend's up't north then," Neil said, with a wink at Tom.

"He had no connection to that area, he was a Londoner, born and bred. His skull had caved in following blunt instrument force to the back of his head," Spence said, head shaking at Neil. "Besides that, there's evidence that he was moved post-mortem."

"Where exactly were these bodies found, detective?" Jeremy said, with a little saliva trickling the corner of his mouth.

Spencer passed Forsythe her notebook, peeling it back at a neatly listed page of addresses. Tom topped up his mug from a coffee jug sitting on the filing cabinet behind him.

"This is quite remarkable. These are the precise locations where the Ripper left his victims," Jeremy said, folding over the page. "How exactly were they presented?" he added quickly.

"Presented?" Spencer said, pursing her lips.

"Yes, how were they found; injuries, body position., were they posed?" he pushed.

"All fairly similar really," Spencer said, retrieving her pad. "Mostly blunt trauma to the head, clothes removed, or pulled down. Yorkshire police initially felt they might be sex crimes, but there was no evidence of intercourse, bodily fluid or interference," she added, tucking a face-trailing hair behind her ear.

"If I'm not mistaken these are mirrored-crimes, not copycat killings," Jeremy said, squeaking his elbow-patched arms on the desk.

"Mirrored, how-so?" Tom said, leaning forward.

"They would appear to be, eye-for-an-eye murders; male for female," Jeremy said, with a crinkling brow.

"But these other murder's aren't our concern, Prof," Neil said, grimacing. "Guv, we only have Lebouf's car that was coincidentally found up there!"

"Yes, these other victims, Spence. Is there any link to our girl, Maxwell?" Tom said.

"Well, they're all men from the Capital, like her," Spencer said, flashing through pages of notes. "One guy., err., a bricklayer that they found in Manchester…"

"Manchester! We're getting sidetracked here, guv," Neil interrupted. "That's not even Yorkshire Ripper territory!"

"Ahh now," Jeremy said, cutting across him softly. "Sutcliffe did commit a murder in Manchester. One night after driving his parents back to their home in Bingley. And if I'm correct in my mimicking theory, then the body of this man was discovered in an allot…"

"Allotment, correct!" Spencer said, in harmony with the elderly professor.

The room fell silent, suspended in thought for a moment.

"The point that I was just trying to make," Spencer said, breaking the silence. "Was that the victim, the brickie, was working on a building site near the law chambers where Maxwell worked. I've checked the timeline, sir. She would have walked past him every day."

"Jesus wept!" Neil said, with a puff of his cheeks. "Are we seriously surmising that Maxwell, a slip of a lass, has gone on a one-woman killing spree. Murdering men in revenge for the crimes of the Yorkshire Ripper, decades ago?"

Jeremy Forsythe's eyes narrowed, peering over the top of his glasses as Neil.

"There may be a lot more to this that we realise, Neil," Tom said, then looking squarely at Jeremy. "But we're not suggesting that Maxwell's behind all of this, surely?"

The professor poked his glasses to the bridge of his nose and stroked his chin with his stubby fingers.

"I'll say it for you Prof.. It's doubtful that Maxwell was involved in any of these random crimes. It would have been impossible for her to have single-handedly done this," Neil said, flashing a smirk at Spencer. "Oh, and don't call him Shirley!" he added, with a wink at Tom.

"But she's not alone," Spencer said. "Did you not hear the cry of female voices over the summer? Christ, they were marching across every city!"

"Oh, here we go, the women's right's speech, again!" Neil said, crossing his arms.

"Do you know, you're actually part of the problem!" Spencer snapped.

"Enough!" Tom barked

"Yep, you're right sir, enough!" Spencer said, getting to her feet. "That was their slogan, their movement, which I have to declare, I support," she added, grabbing her chair before it toppled. "I'm happy to be removed from this investigation."

"Remove you from the force, you mean," Neil whispered loudly, eye-rolling at Tom.

"That's uncalled for, Neil," Tom said.

"No seriously, boss. Is she actually saying she supports crimes committed by these feminist movements?" Neil said.

"Oh, just fuck off, Turvey!" Spencer barked, grabbing the door. "You're a dinosaur, you don't have a scooby doo."

CHAPTER 47

Bella Maxwell bound up the curved stone stairway, catching Zoe and clasping her forearm.

"Where did you say you were from Zo, Manchester?" Bella said.

"Yeah, I'm from Manc, but I was snatched at a fairground in.."

"Blackpool!" Bella said. "You were last seen near the entrance, by the coffee and doughnut stand!" she added quickly.

"Oh my god, someone saw me," Zoe squealed. "Don't speak to strangers, my Dad always said. One stupid mistake!"

Zoe's face dropped, her bottom lip quivering, staring down at the uneven steps.

"The boy that grabbed me was standing between two stalls. He had a winnie-the-pooh bear and waved me over. I'll never forget it," Zoe said, welling up.

"The owner of the coffee shack remembered seeing you, he thought you were queue jumping," Bella said, stroking her arm. "You were, 'there one minute and then disappeared into thin air,' he told the police."

Zoe spilled over with tears splattering the grey step. The tall, sinewy guy barked an echo-filled, 'samba-leasi,' as he came up behind them on the spiral staircase. They continued the climb, with steadying hands pawing the crumbly rock-face.

"Oh my goodness, Zo," Bella said suddenly. "I met your mum!"

"What," Zoe said, turning to face her. "When, how, what did she… what did she."

Zoe cried, falling into Bella's arms, soaking her chest. A large hand shoved Bella's back, jolting them both. They struggled on upwards.

"She came to Chambers to meet our legal team," Bella said, in a hushed tone. "She was convinced that the TikTokTrio were involved in your abduction."

Bella gripped Zoe's shuddering shoulders as they trudged on.

"She was desperate to find you, she loves you so much, Zo. I could hear it in every word she said," Bella said, whispering into her ear.

Zoe wailed, a harrowing echoing cry. She flopped with head in hands to the step, her tears splashing it's hard surface. The familiar deep hollered words of the guard below them was accompanied by a fist, thumping into Bella's spine.

"Fucking well Samba-leasi off, you steriod-fueled fuckwit," Bella shouted, turning to shove his pectoral-pumped chest.

But he grabbed her wrist in one motion, twisting it hard into the small of her back.

"Yous fookings samba-leasi, now!" he said, his rancid breath billowing her face.

"Let's go Zoe, don't worry we'll be okay," Bella puffed between winces. "I'll look after you, I promise?"

Zoe got to her feet and trudged on, with Bella frogmarched up the remaining steps behind her.

CHAPTER 48

"Now just stop right there, Neil," Tom said, interrupting his number two. "Spencer has carried out some exceptional investigative work on this," he added, staring unblinkingly at DI Turvey.

The door had just about held onto its hinges following the noisy exit of DI Spencer.

"I agree," Jeremy Forsythe said, with a little nod. "Certainly some lateral thinking is important here. We need to consider the bigger picture."

"Quite! And Spencer has been badgering us about this, for a while now," Tom said, finger-wagging at Neil.

"She does seem highly motivated, I must say," Jeremy said, dipping his head to peer over his spectacles at Neil.

"Aside from her research into Darcy's business ventures, on the darkweb, Spence has reviewed records of women abducted across Europe, and all unsolved cases here. And now established a potential link to these murders in the North," Tom said, with a heavy sigh.

"Yeah but, potential, guv, we don't know.."

"None of that has been considered by anyone else here!" Tom said, cutting across Neil.

"The Ripper theory is feasible," Jeremy said softly, cleaning his thick framed spectacles. "The pinpoint accuracy of deposition sites is beyond coincidence."

"The work by Spence here is commendable," Tom said, glaring at Neil.

Neil shifted uncomfortably between buttock cheeks, with a grimace. He poured from a silver teapot on the desk, filling two cups and sliding the saucered one to the Psychologist.

"Yeah, but what she was saying about supporting the 'Enough' movement, that's not on!" Neil said. "If they're responsible for crimes," he added, his hands unfolding on the desk.

"Spencer understands their sentiments and shares their belief that there was a miscarriage of justice. Christ, we all thought that, didn't we!" Tom said, with shuttered face. "She's not condoning murder."

"Sounded like she was signing up.." Neil sniped.

"That's bollocks Turvey and you know it," Tom snapped

"Yeah, but all that feminist stuff…"

"Go and get Spence back in here," Tom said, talking across him. "And you can apologise to her whilst you're at it."

Neil slunk to his feet and left the office. Tom threw an apologetic eye-roll at Jeremy, who gave a nonchalant shrug before dunking his biscuit. He seemed to be enjoying the show.

"Office politics, I'm afraid Jeremy, apologies for that," Tom said, rattling at the packet of biscuits.

"Not at all. At my age, you've seen it all before," Jeremy said. "Tensions of the relationship kind, I would suggest," he added, behind a thin grin.

"Really? Well I hope not. Never a good idea when working together," Tom said, leaning back with fingers interlocking behind his head. "Shit, you might be right, there has been some previous."

"It can sometimes engender an overt competitiveness," Jeremy said. "She certainly seems focussed, a credit to your team, Tom."

Tom sat, head-scratching. "Excuse me for a moment, Jeremy."

Stepping from his office, Tom intercepted the arrival of DI's Turvey and Spencer in the corridor. Overseeing Neil's apology, he ushered Spencer into the office, holding Neil back.

"Turvey, I want records of missing UK girls from the last three years. All unresolved cases of 15 to 25 year olds," Tom said firmly.

"Boss, I can allocate that.," Neil said, with a shrug.

"No, I want you on it," Tom ordered. "Cross reference each one; you're looking for any connection to Maxwell. Check schooling, university, family or neighbourhood links. I want any association flagged."

"But the crimes unit..," Neil mumbled.

"Whilst you're at it, we need historic crime reports from the 'Ripper' murders that Spencer identified. And I want a spreadsheet on the murdered men, where they lived, worked; full profiling!" Tom barked. "Again, I want any link to Maxwell."

"That's a lot of database research.," Neil said limply.

"Well, you better get to it then," Tom said, with a hardened stare. "We need some good old fashioned coppering on this. You've seen a good example of it from Spencer," he added, with a curled thumb on his shoulder.

"S-sir, with respect, what about Darcy? He still needs warning and police protection," Neil said. "Maxwell has travelled out there with clear intent.

Shouldn't we be getting over there?"

"Yes, I'm aware of that," Tom said. "I'll be taking Spencer with me."

Neil's wordless mouth gaped, like a scream mask.

"No need to iron that Hawaiian shirt of yours," Tom said, as Neil slowly turned. "Oh, can you ask Tina to organise the next available flights for us.. there's a good man," Tom said, tapping his shoulder.

Tom clunked loudly his office door behind him as Neil trudged down the corridor.

"Thanks for that, sir," Spencer said, fleeting Tom a wide-eyed smile.

CHAPTER 49

"Roman.. Roman?" Joel said, furtively scanning the suite. "Our guests have arrived."

He crept gingerly into Darcy's bedroom as a hostess rushed out, brushing past him.

"Ro., are you ready for them?"

There was only silence as he peered around the expansive bedroom. Joel approached the bathroom door with his index finger cocked and rising. He dropped it at the sudden gush of water, stepping back to perch on the end of the purple chaise. Seconds later the door swung wide and Roman Darcy filled its frame.

"What the fuck, Joel. Do you ever knock!" he boomed.

"Sorry Ro, I did try knocking," Joel said. "Are you feeling okay, boss?"

"Yep. Good to go," Roman said, flinging his cream bathrobe to the floor.

Joel turned sharply, averting his gaze from his employer's naked form. Smirking, Roman stood with hands planted on his buttocks and hips thrust in the direction of Joel.

"It's-err just that you looked a little peaky and.. we're running a little late," Joel said, nodding at the digital clock sitting by the bed. The large rectangular box on the cabinet displayed 09:54. "Most of the hunting group are in the courtyard, and I've asked Claude to assemble the runners in the dome. We've got thirteen now, with that new arrival."

Roman said as he strode over to the slatted white wardrobes, swishing them open. "Good, any sign of Tex yet?" He clanked at the hangers, releasing a flamingo patterned shirt and slipped it over his shoulders.

"Not yet, but shouldn't we get things started? It's just Tex and some guy that took Pierre's spot.." Joel said.

"Shit, I do look a bit off colour," Roman said, leaning into the wall mirror. "What the fuck," he added, wiping a film of dampness from his forehead.

"Here," Joel said, handing Roman a towel. "The guest's, Ro?"

"They can wait," Roman said, digging in his chest drawer. "Let's build the excitement a little, shall we."

Joel watched as Darcy bent over, his shirttail no longer skimming his buttocks.

"I could parade the girls and get the betting started, if you like?" Joel said.

"Good idea," Roman said, tugging on some cock-hugging boxer shorts and wriggling into his chinos. "Pass me my watch," he said, whilst mopping his brow again.

"Here you go," Joel said, adding, "Can I get you some water or something, Ro?"

"No, you can fuck off and let me have my breakfast," he said, flumping into a wide rimmed whicker chair.

A platter laden with toast and eggs lay on a circular table with cafetiere and a jug of juice. Joel shuffled out of Darcy's suite, to meet and escort the latest arrivals to the Dome.

CHAPTER 50

"I'm going to keep this brief, Tom," the Chief Superintendent said, leaning forward and planting his elbows on the desk.

Breaking eye contact, Tom peered over the Chief's shoulder at a building crowd of protestors, journalists and TV crews, cramming Scotland Yard's forecourt.

"Sir?" Tom said, deciding to remain standing.

"Someone within the service has leaked to the press!" he said, with a deepening frown. "They have the name, *Maxwell.*"

A large white banner was being unfurled by activists, who were now gathering in numbers on the opposite side of the road. The Chief fixed Tom with an authoritative glare, balling his hands.

"This investigation is our number one priority," he said.

"I understand, sir." Tom said, with head bowed.

Media headlines had trailed the suspect's name, *Maxwell.* Linking her to both the murder of Premier League footballer, Jamal Jackson and the mysterious disappearance of city financier Pierre Lebouf.

"Lebouf is an internationally acclaimed figure. He has significant business and political links here," the chief said.

"I, I'm not sure I follow, sir?" Tom said, squinting to read the placards in the street below.

"He's a crucial part of the square mile, and to put it mildly; we've had a market wobble," he said, face crumpling.

Tom shuffled forward with eyebrows raised, "Chief?"

"There are considerable economic consequences to his disappearance. It's had an impact. You know.. on investments, pensions, savings!"

"Surely, that's of no concern to us, sir?" Tom said, his bottom lip folding outward.

"It is when the press pack smells a scoop and *the PM's demanding answers!*" the Chief snarled, waving his iPhone at Tom. "Lebouf can't just disappear, you must have some idea where he is?"

"Well, we do have his car and last location.."

"And this suspect, Maxwell, she's absconded?" he added, uncrumpling his face.

"Not fled, exactly," Tom said, with fingertips on the edge of the desk. "We believe she's gone after Roman Darcy, the third member of the TikTokTrio, sir."

"Let's leave the gimmicky names to the redtops shall we," he said, reclining into his high backed seat. "*Why are they* referred to as that, out of interest?"

"It's their social media pull, with Jackson being a footballer and Darcy an influencer.."

"A *what..?*"

"An *Influencer*, sir, it's social media jargon. Let's just say, he's popular, with millions of followers; as a musician, and successful deejay," Tom said. "Even Lebouf went viral selling his 'life-start' funding packages to students."

"The word 'viral' should be kept relevant only to disease, and as for influencer!" he said, shaking his head. "Now, what evidence do you have on Maxwell for the Jackson murder?"

"In addition to her having key access to the murder site on the Cheveley estate, we also now have a confirmed DNA match," Tom said, laying his iPhone on the desk.

"Ahh, marvellous!" The Chief glanced at the image on the screen; a multi-lined graph, marked, '99% *match*' at the bottom.

"Only received in the last hour, sir. It places Maxwell inside the apartment of Bernadette Bateman, where Jackson's head was discovered, in the fridge," Tom said, repocketing his phone.

"And this, Mrs Bateman, was a relative?"

"Yes sir, Jamal Jackson's grandmother. And, you might recall, juror number nine at his trial!" Tom said, with an eye-flicker.

"Yes, quite how she slipped through the court system to sit on a four week trial of her own grandson, I'll never know!"

"Six weeks, actually sir," Tom said, tugging his notebook from his trouser pocket.

"Background checks established that Bateman fled from her abusive husband in the Caribbean; becoming one of the Windrush generation. She was heavily pregnant and went into labour on the voyage," Tom said, glancing at the Chief's stony face.

He continued apace. "She was penniless, so with the onboard medic's assistance the baby was taken by the British authorities for adoption. Bernadette Batemen disembarked, disappearing with the mass of new arrivals into the Capital. Years later she tracked down the medic on the dockside, and discovered the whereabouts of her adopted baby girl."

"Jamal Jackson's birth mother?" the Chief said.

"Exactly, sir. Quite a resourceful woman, Bateman!" Tom said, with a beam that was instantly dissolved by the frosty expression opposite.

"Let's get to it shall we Tom, where are we now?" the Chief said, checking his left wrist.

"We've been unable to contact Darcy on his private island, although understandably he's not the greatest fan of the police. So I'm booked to fly to Indonesia tonight, where we know from flight logs, Maxwell currently is," Tom said, flicking through his notebook.

"Any idea what the score is with this guy, Darcy. What's he up to over there?" the Chief said.

"We've got Winkman on a deep dive to infiltrate his network. Potentially there's criminality there, possibly some form of trafficking. So far Winks hasn't been able to get beyond a certain level of their encrypted framework."

"Well it's hardly the Pentagon, surely?" the Chief said, interlacing his fingers.

Tom said, into a hard stare, "He'll keep at it, sir."

"And what about Lebouf, anything else there?" the Chief said, his elbows digging into the desk.

"Bizarre, but absolutely nothing sir," Tom said, with lips pulled to his teeth. "Lebouf's mother's description of her assailant matches Maxwell - height, age and build."

"No photofit?"

"She was disguised as an elderly woman in the apartment block's foyer, sir,"

Tom said.

"But the camera outside the building, where Lebouf pulled up in his Jaguar?" the Chief pressed.

"She was uniformed as concierge, with the camera behind her. Chauffeur-style hat and a staff overcoat with collars up. CCTV offered us nothing, sir," Tom said, open-faced.

The Chief dismissed a flashing light on his intercom system.

"We have recovered his car's track-box that records the vehicle stopping just once, a stone's throw from Maxwell's house before it was abandoned and burnt-out, up in Yorkshire," Tom said.

"Well he's clearly not flown with Maxwell to Indonesia. So dead or alive, Lebouf's either at the house.."

"..Already searched her property in East London, sir," Tom interrupted.

"*Or*, somewhere in Yorkshire," the Chief finished his sentence. "We do have additional manpower available to you, Tom," he said, cracking his knuckles.

Tom nodded, peering at the window. A banner flapped high above the protestors heads, that read, '*Justice for the Dead*'.

"How many have you got flying over there with you?" the Chief said, with an eye-rolling glance over his shoulder.

"Err, just myself and DI Spencer," Tom said.

He clocked a placard further down the pavement emblazoned, '*Justice now - The Maxwell Way*'.

"Surely you need more support than that?" the Chief said. "Darcy remains a British citizen, under a threat to life notice. We must be seen to be acting properly here," he added.

A distant chanting could now be heard, on the ninth floor.

"With respect sir, I don't think we should be going in all guns blazing.." Tom said.

"And *Spencer*, why Spencer. She's very young, still green," he barked. "Take Turvey with you, he's one for the future."

"Turvey, err. I've had some issues.."

"Issues, what issues?" the Chief said, tilting back in his chair.

"Well err, nothing major, sir."

"*Good*, well that's decided then, take Turvey," the Chief concluded.

Tom pulled a grin, "I-err, just think he's maybe a little.. a bit too lighthearted, jokey."

"Nothing wrong with a bit of banter, Tom. Besides this will re-establish his focus."

"But sir, I'm really not sure," Tom said, knuckle-leaning on the desk.

"Look Tom, I need to speak to Turvey anyway, so I'll have a word. Anchor his attention a little," the Chief said, eye-pointing at the door. "Have a good flight, and keep me posted."

"Will do, sir," Tom said, tapping the desk, before spinning away.

CHAPTER 51

The luxury resort's inner courtyard was a cacophony of excited voices, punctuated by raucous laughter, drowning out the natural sounds of the island. Native tongues of every continent rose into the crystal clear sky. The earlier haze of dawn had shed, replaced by piercing rays.

Waist-twisting young women weaved effortlessly between the affluent men. Their boisterous chatter softened into muttered jest as their blue bikinied hosts arrived with refreshments. Shiny silver salvers swivelled down from their shoulders to rest on their hips.

The men spluttered greedily between bites and quaff's from tall fluted glasses. The swelter sharpened squints of the few without shade, stood nearest to the thick glass dome that sat centrally in the pavior square.

"The sound of the hunt!" Joel shouted.

An ancient horn trumpeted, in calling them to order; Lord of the Flies, conch-like, in its control. The rambling raucousness hushened, falling into silence at the haunting, siren-like blare. He stood beaming, his piggy eyes flickering across the courtyard at his honoured guests.

"This horn was first used in 1534, on the downs of the English countryside," Joel said, with widening eyes.

He blew heartily into the conical instrument, releasing a lengthy wail into the glassy skies.

"The need to hunt is inbred, Neanderthal-like, it remains a part of us," Joel said, with a crooked smile.

Stepping from his two-step platform, he waddled over to the wall on his right.

"In medieval times, Foxes were referred to as Beasts, that were hunted for pest control," he said, with a nose-hugging grin at his attentive audience.

Tugging at a gold braided rope, a small red curtain drew across, unveiling a portrait of a pasty-faced youth. Wearing a silver-buttoned scarlet jacket, the long nosed boy sneered arrogantly, his head cocked to one side.

The image seemed outdated, carrying more than a hint of a classist past. A painting that in polite society was best forgotten, hidden in some dark corner of a stately home.

"But it wasn't until 1753 that it became a sport, thanks to the great Hugo Meynell. Hugo, at just eighteen began breeding his dogs for speed, stamina and smell."

"We don't need a fucking history lesson!" one man hollered.

Joel marched back, remounting the platform, with horn in hand. The top of his thinning head poked clear of his wall-shadowed stand, sparkling in the brilliant light. He turned and blew long and hard as the eerie blast reverberated around the glass dome.

"Get on with it man!" a voice boomed from the back of the courtyard.

"Just-Just a little context for you all," Joel said, fumbling to lay the horn down and grab his clipboard.

"We've not paid shit loads of money for this bollocks!" a croaky voice shouted. "Where the hell's Darcy?" he added.

"Err, R-Roman will be with us shortly," Joel said, with glistening palms aloft. "More refreshments, anyone?"

An eruption of grumbling spewed from the frown-faced men as Joel waved aggressively at the women that huddled beside the entrance to the restaurant.

"Don't think you can palm us off with booze. We've all paid a fortune for this Hunt experience, and that's what we expect!" one man bellowed, to some supportive cheers.

"Ok-ok. We shall start the hunt shortly but I will need to explain the rules," Joel shouted above the rising din.

"Fuck me, we all got the email, we know how it's gonna work," boomed the croaky voice. "Just get on with it!"

"Right-right, yes, I will, I will," Joel said, dabbing his thinning hairline with a pink handkerchief. "B-betting first though, please gentlemen," he pleaded.

The group's mumbling dampened slightly and Joel seized the moment.

"The runners will shortly appear from the centre of the dome. Each is numbered, for target and identification purposes. Their odds have been calculated on the basis of age and condition, similar to horse racing," Joel said, to muttered approval. "Betting sheets are being handed out now."

Joel beckoned three girls from the building behind him. "The jackpot winner will be the last runner found alive, with pay-outs on each-way bets, on the final three standing."

"Or crawling!" a man from the middle of the group yelled, to jeers and a shrill whistle.

"What about the animals?" one guy shouted.

"Animals will be released tomorrow on all runners surviving day one. They can be tracked by those on the platinum package," Joel said. "There is still time to upgrade if you haven't already done so," he added enthusiastically.

"And its a fucking good watch, I can tell you!" a peaky looking Roman Darcy boomed, from the sweeping balcony above them.

Cheers rose as faces looked skywards, to a chanted crescendo, 'Roman, Roman'. Darcy was only missing robe and wreath, as his hand raised Cesar-like, hushing the cries of adulation.

"My good friends, countrymen and all that bollocks!" Darcy said, beaming. "I don't need one up the arse from you lot. I just need your wedge, so place your fucking bets and wager them high. Joel, bring out the runners!" he added, pointing at the thick glass dome.

Heads turned sharply with eyes fixing on the aztec-carved totem pole, standing proud at the centre of the sandy-floored dome. A steadily widening hole appeared at its foot, as a metal grille plate scraped slowly across the dusty surface.

A breath-held silence gripped the courtyard in anticipation of the runner's entrance from the bowels of the island. The colosseum-like atmosphere building with every inched movement of the weighty cover.

CHAPTER 52

"Zipady-doo-dah, zipody-ayy," Turvey sang softly into DI Spencer's ear.

She jolted from her seat, in the front row of the Boeing 747.

"What the hell are you doing here?" she said, with head-turned, in whispered snarl.

"Lovely to see you too, Spence. DI Turvey reporting for duty," he said, beaming and saluting.

The front three rows had been cleared for use by the Police, in order to discuss matters in relative privacy. The toilets and exit points at the front of the plane had been sectioned off.

"Where's the boss?" Neil said, still cheshire cat like.

"In there," she said, nodding forward. "You know what he's like, pre-flight!"

"Yep," he said, settling into a seat in the opposite run of three. "Just hope he's not going to delay our take off. Commercial flight full of holidaymakers and all!" he said, with a wink.

Neil tightened his belt strap before clicking the buckle into its holster. Spencer, sporting sarcastic grin, unceremoniously tossed a neatly bound report into his lap. The cubicle door ahead of them clicked.

Tom appeared, tucking his polo shirt into his chinos, "Ahh Turvs, you made it then."

"Never in doubt guv, thanks for the late call-up. I knew you loved me really," Neil said, pursing his lips.

"What the hell are you wearing," Tom said, with widening palms.

"Just blending in, boss," Neil said, pinching the collars of his Toucan print shirt. "You do realise that one of us needs to go undercover."

"Not like that, you don't!" Spencer said, slow headshaking.

"And, I won't be needing that," Neil said, throwing the police report back to Spencer.

"This is the latest investigation analysis we have, boss," Spencer said, waving the report at Tom, before smirking across at Neil.

"And this, is the up to the minute intel, we have," Neil said, digging an A5 booklet from the satchel at his feet. "It's come straight from Winks, in comms, guv. It has everything we need on Maxwell and the very latest on Darcy's dark-web operation."

The attention of fellow passengers appeared to have been pricked. Tom gestured for Spencer to take the next seat across, splitting his colleagues further.

"All right, let's start as we mean to go on shall we. I'm in no mood for another Punch and Judy show from you two!" Tom said, standing between the two rows of seats. "We have to work together on this."

"Now then, the latest, what have you got there, Turvs?" Tom said, with his hand out.

"I'm happy to brief you guys on this?" Neil said, laying the spine of the book in his boss's palm.

"Ok, but keep it down," Tom said, as a, 'cabin crew, seats for takeoff,' announcement came across the tannoy.

"Techy shit aside, Winks uncovered a '*Black Cavern*' anomaly, that he dived through to shadow a private forum called, '*fresh meat*,'" Neil said, in a hushed tone that sharpened his Liverpudlian accent.

"And this is without the technical jargon, is it!" Spencer said, with a lopsided smile.

"Spence," Tom said, half-turned. "I expect better from you. Go on Turvs."

"Basically this '*forum*' is some kinda exclusive club for magnates, the mega rich. Tax-dodging moguls and their shity offspring, you know the sort," Neil continued excitedly.

"We're not here on behalf of the Inland Revenue, Neil," Spence said, as Tom's finger appeared in front of her.

"They're not just Brits. This is the world wide web, Spence! The majority of members are Yanks," Neil said.

"Ok yes, we're not the IRS either," Tom said, with a glance over his shoulder. "Cut to it Turvs, the plane lands in 15 hours!"

"Sorry boss," Neil said, puffing his cheeks. "These people are part of a larger network, they're just the tip of the Iceberg!"

Tom's face creased more than usual.

"For every Forum member, and Winks recorded seventeen of them, each has active tracking trailers," he said, pausing on seeing Tom's widening eyes. "'Sponsors', they call themselves."

"So you're saying..?" Spence said.

"The Forum members are merely Bots, sorry Robots, guv. They act as a shield for their Billionaire sponsors, from right across the globe. Winks estimates there are around thirty silo-encrypted accounts behind each member! So we calculate there are.."

"*Five hundred and ten,* members," Tom interjected. "But *what* exactly is Darcy doing?"

The airhostess waved from the galley at Tom, mouthing, *seatbelt.* He nodded back, fumbling with the buckle.

"They've taken their operation to a whole new level. *The Ultimate Hunt* is what they're calling it. They bought another Island where they keep animals," Neil said.

"Are you talking, Beagles and bugles, like a fox hunt?" Spencer said.

"They got permission for the importation of lions, leopards, and tigers! Winks discovered the animal registration document - page near the back, boss," Neil said, pointing at the booklet on Tom's lap. "They've even got a Polar Bear down there!" he added, with eyebrows aloft.

"Big game hunting isn't new. Some American doctor was vilified a few years back after paying thousands to hunt lions in Africa," Spencer said, matter-of-factly.

"Spencer, my dear friend, it's not game hunting, the animals hunt *humans*! The abducted women, to be precise. The Black Cavern exchange network is advertising it as the supreme killing experience; human versus beast'.

"What the hell!" Spence said, with mouth dropping, she grabbed the report from Tom's lap.

"I take it this has been forwarded to the local police?" Tom said.

"Yeah, we've sent them everything we found. 'Disinterested', isn't quite the word," Neil said.

"It's happening over the next few days, and they've already got.." Spencer said, page-flicking. "Twenty nine people signed up for it!"

"Thirty, actually!" Neil said, with a wide smile. "Winks managed to get me registered in time."

"You have got to be kidding me!" Tom said, with a Rooster-like cock of his neck.

"Nope, why do you think the Chief called me in?" Neil said, blowing his fingernails and rubbing them on his chest. "My undercover training is complete!" he added with a wink.

Tom, head-scratching, said, "How'd we get funding for that?"

"Now, here's the clever bit. Winks managed to fool their banking system that we'd transferred the deposit; Police comms access; unbelievable!"

"That is going to be incredibly dangerous," Spence said, passing the booklet back to Tom.

"Aww, and here's me thinking you didn't care!" Neil said, blowing her a kiss.

"Seriously Turvs, you don't need to do this," Tom said sternly. "We don't even have a plan in place. We're on foreign soil, with a brief to apprehend Maxwell and protect Darcy, as a British national. Not to investigate his criminal business practices!"

Spencer said, glaring at Neil. "We should just get the local police to investigate."

"There *is* a plan, guv. One which won't blow my cover and deals with the second part of our operation over here," Neil said.

"Ok, well let's hear it once we're up in the skies," Tom said, double-checking the buckle of his seatbelt.

"Err, we're actually already up, sir," Spencer said, beaming.

"Very smooth take-off, wasn't it guv," Neil said, with a smile fit to burst.

"Jesus, are you sure," Tom said, peering over Spencer's shoulder at the sky-filled oval window.

The sound of jangling bottles in front of them was interrupted by a very loud tannoy announcement regarding refreshments.

"Well I certainly thank you for the distraction, Turvs. I didn't feel a thing!" Tom said, shoulder-rustling into his seat.

"Any drinks please, officer's?" the stewardess said.

"Why not!" Neil said, enthusiastically, planting his head on the headrest.

"We have cold beer, sir?" the hostess said, displaying one of the bottles from her trolley.

"You read my mind," Neil said with a nod.

There was some soft tutting and head shaking opposite.

"Oh, come on, '*last requests*' and all that!" Neil said, to Spencer's furrowed brow.

CHAPTER 53

The breath-sapping heat intensified with each laboured step up the circular stairwell. A piercing brightness lit the way, with ever sharper shards whitening the rock walls. The chain of frail bodies trudged achingly upwards, to the echoed barks of their jailers.

"Halts.. Halts," was the cry from the shorter guard at the top.

"Halt!" Bella said, half-turned to Claude, the other guard that had her forearm clamped to her back. "Your Nazi leader taught you that one, did he?"

Claude twisted her wrist a little harder, lifting it between her shoulder blades. A squealed wince was all he was getting. A voice boomed from his hip-clipped walkie-talkie, as he flung Bella to the step. Zoe and the women above them had each stopped and slumped to sit on their step.

The clanking of weighty metal clattered downward. The steel edges of a grille cover above them, scraped across the lip of its seat, widening a opening. Its clanging reverberating belltower-like down the spiral stairwell, filling their echo-chamber. As it fell silent a blinding glare illuminated their rocky staircase in all of its jagged ugliness.

"Samba-leasi," Claude bellowed, and the girls hauled themselves to their feet.

They continued the climb, their hands clawing the walls. Glistening, angular faces of fear, trailing unruly hair, squinted up into the brightness above them. Zoe glanced her shoulder at her new friend, mustering only an enigmatic smile. Bella beamed back, winking in reassurance.

From the top step, the guard stepped to a small platformed area, directly below the sunlit opening. He guzzled heartily from a water canister, his sweat sheened baldness glistened as waves of shimmering heat floated down. Unclipping his holster he stood with dagger in hand beside the top step. Spirals of dust danced amidst the dazzling brightness around him.

He impatiently ushered the girls toward a five runged rope ladder that hung loosely beside him. It was hooked to the lip of the sun-lit opening above them. Relentless streams flowed from his temples as he waved the knife, pointing up, at the intense light overhead. Unsteadily, one-by-one the skeletal girls hauled themselves to disappear into the melting pot of brightness.

The girl ahead of Zoe, marked 'eleven' pleaded with cupped hands for some water. Her face, a picture of desperation, her limbs trembling. His manner instantly soured, amidst ear-shattering demand as his knife jabbed at her waist. Clasping slowly each rung she hauled herself up, elbow-hooking each step before crawling into the sunlight above.

Zoe pulled herself up with relative ease with the rope ladder swinging wildly below her, as she disappeared into the burning glow.

"I don't suppose we get a knife too, do we?" Bella said, smiling at the shorter guard.

She felt the hand of Claude on her shoulder, as she reached for the ladder. "Samba-leasi, thurr-teen," he said, with a snigger. His smirk revealing a gap between his front teeth.

Bella met his smile, whilst launching a mule-kick behind her, crashing her heel hard into his crotch. It sent him backwards, tumbling into the rock wall. She instinctively hip-swivelled, avoiding the short guard's knife lunge, before thundering the arch of her foot high into his testes, folding him in two.

His knife fell, clattering to the ground between them. He stumbled to grab her, as she dived to the floor, scooping the blade and spinning. In an instant he was there, towering over her, but with the blade pointed at him, he backed up slowly.

Claude staggered up behind her, his arms arched, sumo wrestler-like, just as she spun. Pirouetting, she showered his face in a gravelly mix, whilst slashing his chest. In an animal-like grunting he stood, clawing at his eyes. Balling her fist tight, she unleashed a white knuckled uppercut, jerking his head back and dropping the giant to his knees.

The other guy closed on her, his huge hands outstretched, but Bella didn't hesitate, darting between them. She thrust the knife like an Olympic fencer, its tip slicing easily between ribs, as a ruby backspray sprinkled her face. Air-gasping he collapsed, thudding to the floor, just as Claude stumbled to his feet. His enormous frame, filling the tight space.

"Back the fuck off, big boy!" Bella barked, with one hand on the ladder and dagger pointed at him.

Bella bound the ladder in seconds, scrambling out onto the hot sandy surface above. The other women shuffled clear, as she spun, holding the knife at the hole. The bulging whites of Claude's eyes peered up at her, his beefy hand curling a rung of the ladder.

"Help me pull this thing over," Bella said, her fingers slipping between the gaps in the chunky metal grille plate.

Zoe clutched the other side and tried to haul the weighty cover towards the hole, but it sat fast in the sand.

"Help us!" Bella shouted at the zombie-like girls. They stood staring at her, as if observing an alien being. "Do it, now. Help us!" she bellowed again.

Two, then three and a forth girls dropped to their knees. Then a fifth and sixth joined them, and the grille plate slowly moved, gravel crunching, over the surface. Wide-eyed Claude stared up at Bella, who fashioned a fingertip farewell wave.

With a final heave, the cover scraped over its metal frame, clunking into place. Bella scrambled to her feet to the muffled sound of applause that filtered into the dome-like structure they were now in.

"Where the hell are we?" Bella said, squinting at the glass cage that surrounded them.

PART VII – INFANCY

CHAPTER 54

BELLA — AGED FOUR

She pushed her cheek flat to the windowpane, feeling each rain splotch as it splattered hard against it. Out there, beyond the row of houses with their chimneys standing proud, there was only blackness. But it was somewhere that Bella would rather be. She tucked her hair behind her ear and pressed it harder against the cold glass.

But the pattering couldn't hide it, the shrill sound cut right through. It worsened with every moment; the seconds like minutes, each minute like an hour. Bella peeled her face from the window with elbows-high, cupping her ears to drown it out. The screams pierced through, rebounding up from the wood panelled hallway below. Relentless cries for mercy, before the haunting howls from each pain-soaked blow. Her tiny body screwed in turmoil, her knees curling to her chest. Tears wet the pillow as she buried her face. But still it was there, the tortuous sound, now met by the thud-thud of her pounding heart.

And then, it was gone, replaced by an uneasy quiet. Bella screwed her eyes tight, whispering in prayer from tear-drenched lips. Her peeking eyes listened closer, as a soft whimpering pricked her ears; the pitch of a scolded dog.

Uncurling from her bed, with teddy scooped to her chin she stepped into the foreboding silence. With widening eyes, she padded barefoot along the floorboards wincing at each shallow creak. An eeriness lay beyond the door, where a cold stillness gripped the house.

The tall walls of the landing filled with sharp shadows from below. The Tiffany lamp's glow reflected high the ornaments around it. There was nothing now, not a sound from down there, as she peered between each of the bannister's spindles.

"M-m-mummy."

Her voice was shaky and broken, she barely recognised it. Bella swallowed hard.

"Mummy, are you there?"

Her soft words barely passed the top step. She trembled, staring down the long wooden staircase. The shadows were unmoved, sinister in their darkness. Nothing stirred.

Her tiny toes curled at the squeaked warning of the third step down. Her body froze in breaking the silence. She crouched with teddy, Mrs Muggles clasped tight, its limbs flopping from her damp palms. With fingers barely curling the handrail, she peeked through the spindles, down there. Beyond the doorway, in there, in the kitchen, where her nightmares always took her.

It was always from there, where the sounds came from. The puffed-snort of him, like an earth-hoofing bull, before the crashing of furniture, and the shrill screams of her mother.

Bella trembled against the chill of the rickety house; her threadbare pyjamas no defence to the winter's night. But at the foot of the stairwell, a calmness came and sat with her, in the quiet. The gentle tick-tocking of the Grandfather clock, hypnotic with its golden pendulum's rhythmic sway. She stared at the lamp's pretty pink tassels, hanging low from the folded cloth shade.

A clash of metal, like falling symbols from a drum kit jolted fear back into

Bella. She blinked eyelid bulbing tears and blew gently from parting lips. A slither of yellow framed the door where the scary sounds lived.

Bella stepped soundlessly over and stood beside the little lamp, her protector in the darkness. She gently kissed Mrs Muggles, releasing her to sit safe beneath its orangey glow. Bella turned to face that door, where the noises came from, the cries of agony, that froze her in fear.

Lower lip blowing to clear flyaway hair, she eased the door open, peering around it. She leaned in, and the light sheened her plump cheeks.

Bella's scream was ear-piercing, burying the shouts that greeted her.

"GET OUT! Get the hell out of here," her grandfather barked.

She spun around in an instant. Wide-eyed and trembling, the sight of her mummy laying there flooded her. Her tiny feet pounding at the bare wood floor, thumping ever harder at each step that she climbed, before scampering into her bedroom and slamming the door.

Bella dived beneath her duvet tucking her knees tight to her tummy. The gruesome image filled her every thought as she wailed. Bella screamed out her heartache, until his words filtered in.

"Bella. Bella dear," his gravelly voice was different now. Tender, soft. "I've got a friend of yours here Bella; can he come and play?"

Mrs Muggles, her teddy.

"Look who's come to see you Bella," his voice was close by.

She froze rigid to the slump of the mattress.

"It's Mr Muggly, your teddy bear, Bella."

Bella's face hardened, her brow dipping low.

"Your Mummy's going to be alright, Bella," he said softly. He was over her now, whispering his words. "Don't you want to give Mr Muggly a little cuddle, sweetie."

The bed squeaked as it arched, she could feel him beside her, leaning over. Silent now, her sobs were gone.

"Mummy's had a little accident, that's all honeycup." His arm arched her bed. "She's going to be fine. She's asked me to bring your teddy up and a bedtime drink."

"Go away!" she yelled.

"Oh, come now Bella, there's a lovely glass of milk here for you." His hand gripped the duvet.

"You don't want Mr Muggly to be lonely do you?"

"It's Mrs Muggles!" Bella shouted. "Not Mr Muggly!"

"I'm sorry Bella, that's what I meant. Of course it is, it's Mrs Muggles. Now you and your teddy need to be brave, because mummy's got to go away for a little while. A nice doctor's going to look after her."

He peeled the bottom corner of the duvet. Bella's watery blue eyes, half shrouded by hair, peered out.

"Now I need you to drink this up and have a really good sleep. It's going to be me and you for a while now, my gorgeous little girl."

The crumpled face of her Grandfather smirked, with his crooked, crocodile smile.

CHAPTER 55

BELLA – AGED SEVEN

Charles Maxwell was Master of his empire, a boundary-pushing genius; a scion of the financial world. But, like Icarus, he had flown too close to the sun. The highly successful financier had fallen unceremoniously and rapidly from grace.

He sat, as he always did at this time of day, in his sun-faded armchair beside the sash window. Gargoyle-eyed, he gawked down at the child-filled street. His hands traced ever-quicker the smooth pine that shone through the thready armrests.

"I-i-is there anything to eat?" Bella said, to the back of his chalky-white scalp.

She stood at the parlour door. A brightness flooded the high-ceilinged room that she wasn't allowed to enter.

"What!" he snapped. Turning sharply, his narrowing eyes glared, piercing the space between them.

"The c-cupboard is em-empty. P-please can I have s-some money?" Bella said softly, to her ashen-faced grandfather.

Her oversized greying school shirt hung loosely about her skirted thighs. Its fingertip-skimming sleeves, dirty and frayed.

"What the hell do you think you're doing, coming in here!" he snarled. A plume of spittal sparkled across the room. "How dare you set one foot in here!"

"Iya, I-I just wanted to get something t-to eat," Bella said, as goosebumps prickled her forearms. "T-to help you with the shopping," she added quickly.

The aged man lurched on an armrest before staggering to his feet.

"How dare you come in here and disturb me. I'll give you something to think about, never mind eat."

The old man stumbled, catching his knee as he rounded the chair in grimace. His rocking shadow broke the dust twirling sunbeams that permeated the front room. His psoriasis-like skin now revealed in all its red blotchy ugliness.

"Iy-I didn't mean t-t-to.." Bella said, stepping back to half disappear behind the dark wood door.

"STAY WHERE YOU ARE!"

She froze as the scaly-faced man trudged towards her. Averting her eyes from the odious sight she fixed on the Barn Owl that sat plinthed on the wall. The reek from his whiskey-kissed mouth reached her before his scouring-pad hand clasped her neck.

Bella squealed, blurting 'sorry' as his bony fingers combed into her tangle-filled locks, dragging her out into the hallway. Her neck jerked sharply as he yanked harder at her tousled mane, his screwed-face towered over her.

"You'll spend the next week in the attic, my girl," he spewed.

His rancid dreg-drained breath flooded her, as she choked, spluttering for air.

With his grip slipping, Bella spun away with a feather-light skip, before his hefty boot clipped her ankle. She skidded on the parquet floor, clattering into the wall, click-clack.

A wall panel parted from the others, revealing a recess behind it. He pounced, slamming it back flush to the panelling. But Bella had seen it.

Yanking her by the wrist to the stairwell, he dragged her up the stairs and across the landing. Key jangling, he unlocked the little door at the end. Ragdoll-like he tossed her inside and slammed the door closed, re-jangling at its lock.

Bella sobbed as she climbed the narrow stairs to the little room above, where webbing decorated the ceiling and roaches scurried its floor. On the discoloured mattress she sat with knees tucked to her chest, staring at the sky-filled window. Her view to the heavens, where her mummy lived now.

She felt somehow closer to her up here, where the stars shone brightest. She never saw her again, after that night, but the memory burnt deep. Of how she lay in that widening pool of red, with an arm stretched towards her. She wore the pink beaded bracelet that Bella had made her, at nursery, that day. Its heart-shaped beads spelt, mummy.

Older now, Bella just knew, they were lies that Grandad told her. All those promises, unkept.

'She's 'unwell' but will get better.. She'll be back with us soon.'

Mummy was gone forever. Of that, Bella was sure.

CHAPTER 56

BELLA – AGED 14

Despite her tender years, Bella knew the truth of what happened that night. Her mother's beautiful face speckled bolognese-red, her contorted body strewn across the linoleum. Defeated eyes blinking the blood and hurt, aching to muster a wide-eyed smile, desperate to reassure her screaming child. 'It's okay, baby.'

Young Bella clutched onto that last image of her, branding it into her heart. And as the years passed the pain was different. A growing inferno of hurt, a building rage from deep inside. She had remained captive, in that cold empty house, confined hostage-like in his squalor.

Bella's salvation was schooling and the respite it brought from the hateful man, she called Grandfather. The local comprehensive provided her nourishment of both body and mind that she devoured with gusto. She channelled her anger, excelling in sports where it was easily released. She captained the hockey and netball teams and was crowned freestyle swimming champion at the nationals.

"Have some more soup, grandfather," Bella said, already ladeling the steaming white broth into his rim-cracked bowl.

"No more, Iye-Iye, I said no," he snapped.

His translucent-skinned hand shook his wrath, as the spoon slipped his grasp, clattering to the floor. Bella dumped the hot pan back on the stove, high-shelved the salt cellar and tossed the empty soup can in the garbage. The old man coughed, spluttering flem to the sleeve of his thick-knit cardigan.

Charles Maxwell had been unwell for months now. Physically, his deterioration had been stark, whilst his mental decline had been slower. Of late, his sentences were stammered and forgetfulness now matched his dizziness, both seemingly the price of ageing. His appearance was that of a ninety year old, masking the man of many years younger.

His motor skills were obsolete. Rapid muscular weakening had restricted his venturing from the house and had seen him defeated by the stairs. The urine stained mattress from the attic now lay in the parlour, with a makeshift bedpan at its side.

Charles once held a place at the top table of the city's elite financiers. In a pitiful fall from grace, the cufflink flashing high-flyer of a decade earlier was an irrelevant, ill-tempered halfwit today.

Maxwell's downfall was the tutoring of the up-and-coming messiah, his prodigy, Pierre Lebouf. Until the Apprentice took his crown, becoming the new, big thing.

Lebouf knew far too much about 'old-man Maxwell' and it was easy to take him down. From a portfolio littered with rule-bending criminality, to his own-goal personal vices, including a penchant for underage girls.

Lebouf catalogued a wealth of evidence against his superior, burying the former money master under a mountain of corruption charges. Commercial litigation was the softer option against the damning footage Lebouf retained, recording Charles Maxwell's sexual transgressions.

It signalled the end for his elder, the hedge-fund guru. Seamlessly replaced by his younger charge, the slippery futures-fixer, Pierre Lebouf. The graphic footage ensured Maxwell's compliance and swift departure and proclamation of his pupil's worth; the king is dead, long live the king.

All litigation was ceased and Maxwell's incarceration averted, following his counterthreat; the filing of rape allegations against Lebouf. Maxwell's daughter Selina, pregnant at fifteen with Bella, had reported the incident that occurred at Lebouf's nightclub.

"Have you transferred me the money yet? I'll pick up your prescription once you do," Bella said to her pasty-faced grandfather.

From the moment Maxwell introduced Selina to Lebouf he had retained an unhealthy interest in her. On her birthday Lebouf invited her to CityCatz, a gentleman's club that he owned in Knightsbridge. It was there that Selina alleged she was gang raped by Lebouf and his associates.

"Only p-pick up my m-medicine," he said, with a gravely croak. Spluttering to add, "Do you h-hear me!"

Grandfather barked his angry orders. But he looked different now, his eyes set deep in a cement-grey shade of sickness. They were weaker, almost pleading. He wiped his mouth on a stained cuff, rolling it across his angular, stubbly chin. A choky cough erupted as he slid his bank card from his pocket. His rope-raw hand clasped Bella's wrist as she took it.

"I m-mean it, I'll be ch-checking the account. G-get straight back here once you-you've g-got it!" he said, wheezing his exertion.

"Of course," Bella said, smiling. "Relax grandad, drink your tea."

CHAPTER 57

15 YEARS EARLIER – CITYCATZ NIGHTCLUB

"This is where we wanna be Selina, red-carpet skippers," she said, giggling.

"You're not wrong when it's like that outside, hun," Selina replied with a shiver.

Her forearms were pimpled and she shoulder-shuddered off the chill, stepping into the warming foyer.

"Come on, Pierre said he's buying, didn't he," she said, butt swinging as she heel-clacked up the marble stairway.

"Wait up, will ya," Selina said, getting her hand stamped.

Still quivering from the arctic blast on the West London street, Selina Maxwell chased her bestie up the flight of stairs. Beaming at the thrill of their queue-jumping exploits, she felt a rising excitement at what lay beyond the famed CityCatz sweeping staircase.

Weighty gold-leafed double doors were hauled apart to a cacophony of inaudible chatter, drowned by the heavy DandB. The subtle shared wink of the penguin-clad doormen was missed by Selina's pal who, with arms aloft, swayed into the deafening beat. Shuttering strobe lights flitted across a sea of bobbing heads as Selina alighted the final step. Her friend disappeared into the throng that rippled, wave-like as one.

"Miss Maxwell?" the doorman said, leaning to speak into the side of her face.

"Yes, that's me," she said, with a honeydew-smile.

"Mr Lebouf has asked that I escort you to the VIP suite," he said, with a widening grin. He had a hard chiselled face that suited his job.

"Yeah sure, that'd be great. I'll just get my friend," Selina said, eye-scanning the expansive dance floor.

"We can bring her along in a little while. Looks like she wants to dance first," he said, into her silver hooped ear.

"Yeah, me too," Selina said, walking on, into the floorthudding club.

"Err, miss," he said, gently clasping her bare arm.

She turned sharply, dropping her smile, tugging her elbow clear of his hand.

"Sorry miss, but Mr Lebouf doesn't like to be kept waiting and you wouldn't want me getting into trouble now, would you," he said, with another toothy beam.

"Can't we at least get a drink first," Selina said, arm-crossing and wrapping her fingers around her soft caramel, bottle-tanned arms.

His fellow door-buddy chuckled, "Believe me Miss, he'll have plenty of drinks waiting for you up there!"

"But my friend.."

"Trust me Miss, I will find her and bring her along shortly. Now I understand you have a complimentary pass to the VIP lounge, so please have the courtesy to meet your host," he said, offering his arm.

"Well ok, if you insist," Selina said.

She slipped her hand into the crook of the doorman's arm. He strode forward, hand-easing clubbers from his path, to a spiral metal staircase on the far side of the venue. He unclipped to release a heavy rope-chain from across the handrail.

The clacking of Selina's heels on the metal rungs was inaudible above the thudding beat that softened as she exited at the top. Through a door marked *Private* lay a plush lounge area of soft cushioned booths surrounding a half-mooned bar. The suite was completely empty aside from the tall boy in an oversized white shirt standing behind the bar-stooled counter.

"Cool, I love it!" Selina squealed in her escort's ear. "Will you go get my friend now, pleeese?"

He nodded with a thin grin, ushering Selina to the end stool, the purple one of the three low-backed velvet seats. The others two were red and gold; all three gleamed with silver button-down edgings.

The doorman leaned over the counter, his shirt buttons scraping the marble as he whispered in the skinny barman's ear. The boy nodded his understanding and spun around, putting a tumbler in hand.

"Champagne would be great, thanks," Selina yelled across, with a cheeky grin. "I am eighteen, you know. Got my ID here if you need it."

"That's ok," the doorman said, pushing her card-clutching glossy fingernails away. "The house cocktail is for Mr Lebouf's special guests."

"Ok, sounds good," Selina said. "Don't forget one for my friend."

"Mr Lebouf will be with you shortly," he said, turning away with iPhone slapped to his square-jaw.

"CityCatz cocktail, madam," the skinny guy said, placing a salt rimmed crystal tumbler on a tinted glass coaster.

"Sweet," Selina said, with a wide-eyed beam. She clasped the icy drink, picking the lime wedge from its rim. "Not seen one with leaves in it before!"

"It's mint," the barman said. "Enhances the flavour," he added with a subtle wink.

Selina face-shuddered at its bitterness.

"It takes a few sips to adjust. Try sucking the lime," he said.

"Err, I'd rather not ta," she said, with another judder. "You got any cider?"

The guy looked sheepish, turning away smartly and checking the optics behind him.

"I was only asking!"

"*Cider!* Come come Selina, this is a classy establishment. You don't want to insult me do you?" Pierre Lebouf said, tutting as he moseyed up behind her. He slipped his hand over her spaghetti strapped shoulder.

"Oh, hi Pierre," she said, feeling flush and re-clasping the weighty tumbler. "Sorry, I-I'm just not used to the taste I suppose."

"Well you drink that up like a good girl," he said, smirking as he slid a finger under her strap. "Now I promised your father I'd give you a tour of the club, and, maybe you could do a ten minute set for us?"

"Wow, that would be fantastic!" Selina said.

"He said you were a big music fan," Lebouf said.

She beamed, sipping at the cocktail, saying, "How about some rap?"

"I'm sure that would go down very well. Knock that back and we can get to it," Lebouf said, running his hand down her back. "We've got a celebrity guest tonight."

Selina jerked her head back, downing the drink.

"That's it, now let me show you my office first," he said, sliding his palm to her waist in a seamless caress.

"Goshhh, that's strong stuff that Pierre," she said, half-slipping from the stool.

"Let me help," he said, wrapping an arm around her as she stumbled forward.

Selina's weight shifted suddenly, her foot sliding from under her. Her heel snapped as her ankle rolled, but she was silent. Lebouf folded his arms tight around her hips, dragging her through a door behind the bar. The barman looked away, continuing his duties, polishing already gleaming glasses.

A softer, almost soothing thudding met them on the other side of the reinforced fire door, where Lebouf's office was situated. He lay Selina, semi-conscious on the two-seater sofa. Selina's body was limp and immobile, her voice-box muted, but her eyes bulged in panic.

Lebouf looked down at her, sniggering and pulled his iPhone from his jacket.

"I've got Charles Maxwell's daughter, Selina. You wanna take-away or eat-in?" he said, behind a smirk.

He tutted, tapping his finger on the tip of her nose.

"Sure, rear entrance at o-two hundred, I'll text you the key-code and a photo. She's a hotty, just your type," he said, leering at her. "My guy will take her home afterwards, just message me when you're done."

Lebouf posed Selina on the couch, shuffling her short dress up over her hips and tugging the shoulder straps below her elbows. He clicked away at his phone before exiting the building via the rear fire escape. Resetting the alarm code before driving off in his Jaguar.

Twelve hours later, Selina shot bolt upright in her bed at the sudden shooting pain in her rectum. She was naked. The drowsiness was instantly gone at the weird sensation, as another sharp stabbing spasm took her breath. Her hand dived beneath her duvet, cupping her vagina. Selina's blurry eyes jerked tears as she stared in horror at her blood soaked fingers.

Selina Maxwell had been gang-raped by a group of wealthy business associates of Pierre Lebouf; The Hymenites. Depraved, deviant monsters, who's fetish was the defilement of young girls.

Selina's baby, Arabella, *'the bastard child'* as her grandfather referred to her, was born nine months later.

Arabella *'Bella'* Maxwell would never know the identity of her father, a rapist. Four years later, the death of her mother Selina was compounded by Bella's care being passed to her grandfather, Charles Maxwell, a paedophile.

PART VIII – BROKEN

CHAPTER 58

PREPARATION FOR TRIAL

Haversham House and Gardens was a former treasure of the National Trust. A prestigious mansion of yesteryear, holding both majesty and historic poignance, to which thousands would flock each year.

An estate that had been passed with title bestowed inheritance through generations, enjoying huge swathes of countryside where cattle would roam. From its tightly trimmed lawns and shapely hedgerows, to the ornamental walled garden, it exuded opulence. Its sweeping driveway and wide gravelled courtyard provided more than a hint of grandiosity from times gone by.

But following the mental health crisis and National Health Service collapse, it became (along with others), a government commandeered property. The house was the giveaway, now with treacherous white plastic windows, a mismatch to its still ivy-clad facade. Its deep-grained oak door and central brass knocker, replaced by glass panelled doorway with silver-plated buzzer, in hideous contrast.

"*Haversham House*, how can I help?"

"Hi, yes it's Bella Maxwell, for Doctor Thornton."

The buzzer groaned its reluctant hum in acceptance of the visitor. Bella shoved hard, releasing the door from its catch. Inside, a freestanding shiny-topped reception desk stood shameless to the grandeur around it. Sat centrally, it appeared woefully out of place in the high vaulted hallway with a sweeping staircase arching the wall behind it.

"Miss Maxwell, take the left hand corridor through the double doors and turn right, and follow it to the end," the stony faced receptionist directed, with wrist bent gesticulation. "Please wait in the Orangery, Doctor Thornton will meet you," she added, with a bland grin.

Bella mirrored the expression as she marched by, with satchel clutched to her side. The echoes of the vast hall disappeared behind the heavy double doors as she strode the corridor. The white walls dazzled a starkness in sharp contrast to the aged oak floor that still creaked its history.

Room doors dotted the passageway, each displayed gold plated signage that bore names with follow-on letters, boasting their importance. *Doctor* this, *Professor* that, before the *Manager* and *Chief Executive's* offices at the far end. Bella took a right where the Library room faced her and the creaking floor was muted by thick pile carpeting.

At the end of the corridor a young woman, with head dipped, tottered in Bella's direction. The girl's shoulders rocked pendulum-like as she ambled on, until half peering up she clocked Bella and turned abruptly.

"Are you ok there?" Bella said, quickening her pace.

The girl's arms instantly pinned to her side, and she turned to face the wall. Her incoherent muttering got louder as Bella approached. The girl was shaking as her mutter loudened into a stammer of jumbled words, then numbers, '*six two four, six two four, six two..*'

"Can I get someone to help you?"

With vein-bulging eyes her body trembled as she released an ear-piercing shriek. The balls of her hands thudded into her temples, before her spindly fingers clawed, raking her hair. She screamed in distress.

"It's ok Tamara, she's just a friend, dear. Just a friend," a large woman bellowed, stepping from the glass doors behind Bella. "Breath with me Tamara, *1-2-3, breathe, 1-2-3 breathe..*"

The girl's incoherent stammering returned, merged with a low humming. The buxom lady pinched the sides of the little black box that was clipped to the lapel of her bright pink jacket.

"Mary, could you attend to Tamara please. Orangery corridor, thank you," she barked into the device.

Back-sliding the wall, the girl dropped to the floor, pulling her knees to her chest. Her eyes remained fixed on the lady as her hum-like mumbling softened.

"Ah, now then you must be Miss Maxwell. Do please come through, my dear," the lady boomed with a huge smile. "I'm Jane Thornton."

"Hi, is-err, is she going to be ok?"

"Yes yes, she might need a little time, but she'll be fine."

"I'm so sorry if I, I startled her."

"Not at all. It's my fault, running a tad late I'm afraid. Besides, there is the theory of exposure therapy, amongst our commision," she said, widening one of the glass doors. "Do come through."

"That was, *Tamara*, did you say. Tamara Bowman?" Bella said.

"Yes, that's Tamara. One of the three survivors that I believe you are acting for?"

Bella, statuesque for a moment, stared vacantly back through the double doors, watching as a plastic aproned woman scuttled down the corridor to attend to Tamara.

"Miss Maxwell, if you would.." Jane said, with an arm aloft.

"Please, call me, Bella."

"Of course yes, Bella."

Jane ushered Bella into the high ceilinged, orangery. It overlooked a huge expanse of manicured gardens with brightly flowered, scalloped borders.

"I thought we might sit in the comfy seats, and discuss your requirements," Jane said.

"Great, thanks Jane," Bella said, placing her bag on the hardwood floor beside a plump cushioned armchair. "Is that usual? ..Tamara I mean, the way she was just now."

"Unfortunately, yes," Jane Thornton said, sitting in the centre of a three-seater settee opposite.

The floor to ceiling shelving behind her was stacked with some heavy-duty looking books. A pile of manilla files sat on a table between them.

"When I spoke to your colleague I did explain that two of the girls aren't in any condition to speak about what happened," Jane said, whilst pinching again at her lapel. "So it's only Marcie that you'll *hopefully* be able to talk to.."

"Yes Ms Thornton," came a robotic voice.

"Ahh yes, tea and biscuits in the Orangery please. Or would you rather coffee, Bella?" Jane said.

"Tea's fine, thanks."

"Yes, two for tea thank you," Jane said with a rosy cheeked smile at Bella. "Now, where was I?"

"Two of the women are struggling to communicate.," Bella said, sliding a notepad from her satchel.

"Yes, I am afraid it's completely out of the question at present. We are still having to heavily medicate the girl's to get them through the day," Jane said with a shake of her soft-permed head. "Still.. it's early days!" she beamed.

"I don't mind sitting quietly with the girls, for them to familiarise themselves with me. If it's a stranger-danger, kind of thing?" Bella said, with widening eyes.

"No-no, absolutely not. Now I was very clear about this with your supervisor. It's just far too soon, my dear."

"I appreciate it might be difficult, but I do need to at least see them. If only for a short while, to observe.."

"*Observe!* This is not a zoo," Jane snapped, with the sternness of a sergeant major. Jane's soft features somehow stiffened, as Bella shuffled forward to sit upright.

"*Tamara* suffered a catastrophic brian injury after hitting her head on the stone wall of the well that she jumped down. She understands very little of what is said to her.."

"Yes, I'm aware of the circumstan.."

"*Jasmine* was mute on arrival, and remains catatonic. It would be far too traumatic to introduce her to anyone at this stage. It would set us back from the tentative progress that we have made," Jane said, crossing her legs.

"And, *are you* making progress, or had a breakthrough? I mean, has there been any improvement *at all,* since their arrival here?" Bella asked, uncapping a biro.

"We are doing *everything* we possibly can do for these girls!" Jane said, arm-folding.

"I didn't mean to imply.."

"Twenty-four hour care and attention from all of our ancillary staff.." Jane puffed.

"No criticism of your work here was intend.."

"Daily visits from professional services, psychiatrists, psychologists, specialists with expertise in human trauma, you name it! We've had them morning, noon and night!" Jane said, her eyes watering.

"Please, *MISS THORNTON*, Jane please," Bella said, with her hand raised. "My apologies. I understand, I do. I accept what you say; *you're the experts*."

Jane dabbed a tissue in the corners of her eyes and sighed heavily. "It's just been so difficult being with the girls, seeing their families everyday, living in grief. Hearing what their children were like before all this, you know.."

"I'm sure they very much appreciate the way the girls are being cared for."

"W-we do our best, we really do, you know. It's not easy, but we won't ever give up on them," Jane said, shakily.

"I would very much like to see Marcie, if that is possible please Jane," Bella said, hoping to move on. "I understand that you have her file for me?"

Jane puffed gently, leaning across the oversized coffee table and tugged a two-inch file from the stack of papers. Checking its label she set it to one side, before peeling a second hefty manilla folder and flopping it on top of that one. Clasping the bottom file, white-labelled '*Marcie Stone*', she slid it across the table.

"These are Marcie's papers. I've printed each of the girls' records off here for you here. We can't let you have access to our IT system, but everything we have on the three of them is in these folders," Jane said softly.

She sat back dabbing again at her eye. Bella took the file and spun it around.

"I understand, thank you," Bella said, fleeting a sweet smile. "We're on the same side here Jane, you know that, I hope."

"Yes, I know," Jane sighed. "I'm sorry for the outburst, it's just.. well it's been tough, seeing these precious girls. You just can't imagine the horrors they must have gone through!"

"I'm sure," Bella mumbled, already focussed on the inside of Marcie Stone's file. "These pictures, this one opposite Marcie's?"

She half-turned the inside cover of the folder towards Jane. Two photographs were pinned to it. One of Marcie Stone, cadaverous in appearance, ashen and drawn with pained expression. Her gaunt hollowed cheeks and dark, downturned eyes bore witness to the trauma of her captivity.

"Yes, I'm sorry to say that's Marcie," Jane said, with a little shake of her head. "It was taken within an hour of her rescue from the island. They'd only just pulled them from the well," she added, cocking her head to peer at the dead-eyed image.

"No-no, sorry Jane. We have that one at the office," Bella said, turning the file the full 180 to face Jane. She poked her fingertip on the glossy photograph that was paperclipped next to Marcie's picture. "I meant this one?"

Jane slid her clear-framed glasses from the breast pocket of her blazer. Slipping them on, she pulled the file across the table to examine the image. The picture was of a young woman of around eighteen, with shiny chestnut hair tucked neatly behind tiny ears, accentuating her high cheekbones and radiant smile.

"Ahh yes, sorry I haven't seen the photos for a while, they don't show on our computer record for some reason. Probably weren't uploaded property," Jane said, with an eye-roll.

The girl in the picture had a model-like glow. A Cara Delevingne lookalike, beaming an almost laughing wide smile.

"These are our B and A snaps," Jane declared. "It can sometimes help with therapy, to remind them.."

"*B and A*?" Bella quizzed.

"Sorry yes; '*Before and After*'. We retain images of what the girls looked like before their abduction and after their rescue. That's Marcie on the day before she was kidnapped. She was only sixteen," Jane said, finger-tapping the shiny photograph.

Bella snatched the file, swivelling it around. She took a sharp intake of breath, her eyes flicking between the images, mumbling, 'what the hell did they do to you'.

CHAPTER 59

"Marcie… or Marcia?" Bella whispered, half-turning from the door.

"It's Marcie, her dad was a big Peanuts fan," Jane returned in a hushed tone.

Bella's eyes narrowed, her nose wrinkled.

"The cartoon?" Jane said. "You know, with Charlie Brown and that dog, err.."

"Snoopy!" Bella said, with a nod, before turning to face the door that was labelled, 'Buttercup Suite.'

"Yes, that's it! Marcie was the clever one, always had her head in a book," Jane beamed. "It's all in the file, we took so much background. Anything to prompt a positive memory. Anyway, dad got to name Marcie and mum named her twin brother, Michael."

"Ahh, ok thanks. I'll take it from here if you like?" Bella said, refocusing on the muted yellow door.

"That's not going to happen, my dear. Marcie might be the only one that is able to communicate, but it's not a given that she'll speak to you. It's all about trust," Jane said, with a head shake.

Jane's chin connected without definition to her neck, a fleshy flap wobbling when she spoke and more so when her head shook.

"Sorry, yes I just hoped to make a connection without taking up any more of your time."

"We'll just see how we go first, shall we," Jane said sternly. "We have to make sure Marcie's in a good place to meet someone new. Let me introduce you."

She knocked softly on the solid wood door and eased it open slowly, brushing over a thick pile, cream carpet. Hoovering had left neat lines across it, like freshly mown lawn.

"Marcie, Marcie my sweet," Jane almost sang her name.

At the far end of the room, half hidden behind a large single bed, Marcie was sitting on the floor, leaning against the bed. Only her thin-haired head and bony shoulders could be seen. The palm of Jane's hand hovered in front of Bella's stomach, as she mouthed, 'wait here'.

"Marcie, it's only me. It's Janey, my sweet," Jane said softly.

Jane crossed the room toward the patio door on the back wall and perched on the tubular arm of an armchair near the end of Marcie's bed.

"I've brought a friendly face to meet you sweetie."

Marcie's head began to rock slightly, in time with a hollow moaning.

"It's ok now Marcie. Her name is Bella. She's with us; a friend."

Marcie nostrils flared with breathy puffs as her rocking increased. The panting, throaty sound became steadily louder.

"It's ok Marcie. Remember what we do; One, two, three, puff, puff, puff," Jane said, in a quiet order. "With me now Marcie; one, two, three, puff, puff, puff. And again Marcie, come along now; one, two, three, puff, puff, puff. And again... good girl"

After a few minutes Marcie's whimpering lessened and her motion slowed to. "Well done, well done you," Jane beamed as she beckoned Bella over.

"Hiya Marcie, I'm Bella. I'm here to find out about what happened to you. To all of you, on that island."

Jane pushed a finger to her lips and directed Bella to the patio door, to face Marcie. She sat hunched, with knees clamped to her chest. One hand gently stroked the carpet, her bony fingers disappearing into the pile. Either side of her were the same semi-circular patterns; like angel-wings in the snow.

"Now Marcie, this is Bella. She's here, to help," Jane said, in another sweeping change in tone. Like a Headmistress now, scolding a naughty pupil.

"Hi," Bella whispered, half waving a hand.

"I need you to be strong now Marcie and help Bella. You can stay there and Bella's going to sit here in the safe seat, ok," Jane said. "I'm going to be standing right here alongside her," Jane added, pointing at the floor.

As Jane stood up, Marcie blinked over, in a fleeting squinted glance at Bella. Her hollow, vacant eyes peeking at the intruder.

"I, I, I d-d-don't w-a-want.." Marcie's voice was frail, broken, like an upset toddler.

Marcie had stopped her carpet stroking and her skinny arms were wrapped around her knees, atop of which her chin now perched. Cocking her head she fixed an empty gaze on Bella, who settled into the chair, offering Marcie a soft smile.

"I really am here to help, Marcie. I want to help you get through this," Bella said. With a smile adding, "I need to understand what happened back there. On the Island?"

Marcie's face dived between her kneecaps with hands across the back of her head. Bella looked up at Jane in a grimace.

"It's ok Marcie, nobody is ever going to hurt you again. You're safe here, remember," Jane said. "Bella is going to be visiting us regularly to get to know you. She's a really clever lady. Bella's going to make sure those nasty men stay in prison. So we need to help her, don't we sweetie?"

Marcie peered over, eyeing the stranger behind the crook of her elbow. Bella leaned over, laying a chocolate bar on the end of the bed.

"This is for you Marcie, I hope you like it. It's my favourite," Bella said softly.

Marcie stretched a long arm, grabbing the candy. She sat gazing at the brightly wrapped chocolate bar. "I l-like this one too," Marcie whispered, with a broken smile.

Jane and Bella exchanged a nodded beam.

CHAPTER 60

It was at six forty-five on a Sunday evening in November that Marcie Stone arrived at *Dreams and Screams*, a skate rink and bowling alley combo. Dad, wanting to get back and catch the end of the football, had dropped her off a little early.

It was Marcie's sixteenth birthday and she was meeting her three closest friends. Bowling was booked for seven and a table was reserved at Dreams Diner at eight. They had admission tickets to the ice rink from nine. Dad was stern in his reminder that mum would be picking her up at ten thirty sharp, firing warning that Marcie be ready and waiting.

Sadly, Marcie would never set one foot inside the entertainment venue.

Bella's approach had worked and a level of trust had been established. Over the first few meetings Bella spoke only about her own life, before hearing a single word from Marcie. She became a little more relaxed and open with every visit. Marcie would be in her pyjamas stretched out on her bed, happily sipping a milkshake.

CCTV had recorded her Dad's car park drop-off and Marcie scampering up the five steps to the venue's entrance. She stood with one hand around the door's silver pole handle, waving back at her Dad. His Volvo departed the parking bay at 18:47. Marcie then turned, looking across her shoulder, momentarily distracted as she stood by the door. She appeared to be engaged in conversation, and by her casual demeanour and smile they were possibly known to her.

The bowling alley's entrance doors were never pushed by Marcie, who instead skirted the perimeter of the building towards an unidentified youth. Their interaction was picked up by a security camera from an adjacent property. His dark hoody shielded his face, until momentarily glancing up when passing her a large cuddly toy of some sort.

The boy appeared to be of a similar age and height; white, male, wearing a blue 'NY' baseball cap under his hood. At 18:55 Marcie disappeared abruptly from view into a side passage between buildings that fell beyond the camera angle. That much was already known by police and prosecution. There were stark similarities to the kidnapping of Zoe Garrett, from a funfair in Blackpool. Including one eye witness account of a *'shifty-looking'* boy lurking on the periphery of the fairground.

After Bella's fourth visit Marcie openly described the circumstances of her abduction. She explained that a young, pretty-faced boy had called her over. He was carrying a gift that he bought for his girlfriend, explaining that they had had a big argument and split up. He seemed cool, so she chatted whilst waiting for her friends to arrive.

"At first I-I thought I recognised him from school, but they all wear similar stuff," Marcie said, sliding a cushion over her lap. "The way he talked about his girlfriend and how upset he was; he was so sweet. I remember he was blonde with a nice smile," she added, with half a grin tugging unsuccessfully at her lips.

Out of the blue he passed her the teddy bear, a Winnie-the-Pooh. As she reached out to take it, he grabbed her wrists, yanking her into the alley. She remembered opening her mouth to scream, but it was like, 'nothing came out'.

She recalled being bundled into a large white van with a side sliding door that zipped shut behind her. Marcie was sure that the young guy didn't get in. She never saw him again, but his face remained imprinted on her mind.

A thickset man inside the van pulled a cloth-like bag over her head, tugging it tight to her neck. He pinned her to the floor of the van as it sped away. Marcie remembered hearing some engine revving and feeling lots of jerky movements as she bounced around on the metal floor.

"It was like they didn't know how to drive, or the driver kept hitting things. After that I felt this burning, sickly taste in my throat, before I you-know, passed out," Marcie said, as a single tear rolled down her cheek.

Bella had managed to build Marcie's confidence. The two young women had fashioned a closeness, a friendship, with Bella arriving each week with milkshakes. Marcie was talking a little more each time as previously blocked memories filtered back.

"When I first arrived on the Island I thought it was beautiful," Marcie said. "You just heard this heavenly birdsong everywhere, and the whole place was so bright and colourful, I mean the flowers, the sky, the trees. And the scent was so pure and fresh, like the best perfume ever," she said, grinning.

Bella had pushed Marcie a little too hard about the girls she had travelled with to the Island. It had been heartbreaking to lose them, having become so close. Their DNA was established from burnt bone fragments. Marcie began body-rocking and it was clear she wasn't ready to discuss what had happened to them. But she was able to describe life on the Island and how they arrived there, by boat.

"The three of us were walked across the golden sand. It felt so warm and soft and the sea! You could see right through it, Bella, to the fish."

Marcie had been held captive for a day short of two years, surviving the final day massacre by leaping down an ancient disused well. The bodies of other girls had cushioned her landing, saving her life. Prior to that, Marcie, with many others, had spent two days being hunted by the VIP guests visiting the resort.

By chance a local fisherman had come ashore and stumbled upon a severed limb. Shocked by his discovery, he took it to the local Politzia on the mainland. It took another five days before they authorised a search team to investigate.

"Because I was younger than most I was lucky and worked in the resort centre. First on 'clean and serve', that was the easiest. Then as a hostess," she said, with a darkness shadowing her eyes.

"When you're young they want you for.. you-you know. If you're older they're not bothered if you die; you can be part of the next hunt."

Bella said, softly. "What can you tell me about the hunt, Marcie?"

A teardrop plopped from Marcie's eye. "It-it's just what they d-did. You know for the VIP's," she said, her head dipping.

"How often was there a hunt?"

"I-I-I don't know.. mainly in the summer, I think. During the rainy season it was only a few times." she said, half-smiling at Bella. "Sometimes they needed extras, to add to the older girls. I managed to hide, ducking down at the back during roll-calls."

"What happened to the girls on the hunt... what did they tell you about them, Marcie?" Bella said.

Marcie drew her knees to her chest and turned away. "Nobody ever came back from the hunt, B-Bella. No-one."

Bella opened an envelope telling Marcie that she was going to show her a picture. She laid the photograph at the foot of her bed.

"Did this man go on the hunt? Do you recognise him, Marcie?"

Marcie began rocking from side to side and humming, with a rising intensity.

"He can't hurt you now, Marcie. Do you know his name?"

Marcie began clawing her head with fingernails digging at her scalp. Bella yanked the emergency cord at the side of the bed as Marcie started wailing and shaking in distress.

"Ok let's put that picture away."

Stuffing the photograph of Roman Darcy into her bag, Bella wrapped an arm around the young girl's shoulders.

CHAPTER 61

Jane Thornton's familiar heel clacking waddle down the corridors of Haversham House, and the floral scent that wafted behind her was somehow comforting. She was the rock that saved her patients' from the shipwreck of their lives. Always there for them, positive and smiling. She offered a lifebuoy for them to cling to.

Jane was a bizarrely reassuring blend of both Mother Teresa and Margaret Thatcher. Mixing the deft, caring touch of the Saintly Nun, with the stern, authoritative nature of the Iron Lady. Jane was ferociously protective of her ward; their rehabilitation was everything to her.

"Last visit today," Bella chirped, as Jane approached her.

Bella signed into the red Haversham crested visitor book, for her twenty fourth and final time.

"No, surely not," Jane complained.

"Yep, I'm afraid so Jane. The trial starts on Monday!"

"Gosh, that's crept up on us, hasn't it," Jane said, with a cheery grin lifting her rosy cheeks. "I do hope it's not the last time you'll be visiting Marcie though. She'll want to keep seeing you, my dear."

"Yes of course," Bella said, laying the pen in the central crease. "It's funny but I feel like Marcie and I.. we've become good friends."

"That's because you have, my lovely. Marcie's recovery owes an awful lot to you dear. You've been her salvation!"

"Well, I'm not sure about that," Bella said, pinking a little.

"Well I jolly well am!" Jane said, whilst flipping the book closed. "She's going to need you going forward too, you know, after the trial."

"Well, I'm hoping that'll be ok with Chambers. But I'm not sure they will agree; professional distance and all that.."

"Knicker's to all that balderdash. You're coming back and that's an order!" Jane said, finger-wagging. "Err, Mary could we have tea for three in the buttercup suite please."

"Actually just two, thanks Mary," Bella said, pointing at a drink carton with pink straw poking from her handbag. "It's strawberry. A little treat for Marcie, as it's my final session.."

"Now I don't want any mention of that in front of Marcie. Not after all the progress she's made. She's aware that you're not going to be around for a while because of the trial, but after that, let's keep it open, shall we?"

"Obviously I would like to report back to Marcie, after the verdict."

"Yes, she needs to hear that from you Bella," Jane said, looping her hand through the crook of Bella's elbow. "You just make sure you get those three monsters put behind bars, for a very long time!"

"Oh I'm sure we will Jane," Bella said, smiling at her as they strolled down the long white corridor. "The evidence against them is overwhelming. They'll be going to prison for the rest of their lives, I'm positive about that."

"Good, good. Now we've had a camera set up in the library, which we have reserved for you all morning. So there's no rush," Jane said, easing one side of double doors open. "I can't believe you've managed to get her this far. And agreeing to do this, after where we started!"

"I know, she's so much stronger now," Bella said, beaming. "I've been over it a few times already and it's all written down. She can leave any parts out that she's not comfortable with. The bigger problem was getting the Judge to allow it. Impact statements are generally only allowed from relatives. Needless to say the defence put up one hell of a fight!"

"Well, they can't seriously expect her to stand up in court in front of those, those beastly beings, after what they did.." Jane puffed.

"I quite agree!" Bella said, nodding. "And they wonder why so many rape cases are withdrawn. With some trumped-up Barrister waiting to intimidate anyone who's brave enough to take the stand. It's not enough that she has to live with the nightmare, she then gets humiliated and torn to shreds by some upper-class, silver-spooned Etonian, showing off in front of his sniggering rapist client. It makes my blood boil."

"Yes, I see that," Jane said, with a chubby knuckle poised below the 'Buttercup Suite' sign. "Although I do quite agree; the law is an ass, as they say," she whispered.

"Marcie, it's Jane, and I've got Bella with me my darling," Jane said softly.

"Come in, come in."

CHAPTER 62

"M-my. My name is Mm-Marcie. M-Marcie Stone," she said quietly.

Marcie looked unsure, her face a picture of uncertainty, an anxiety flitting her eyes. Her vocal cords almost locked, as she stared over at Bella. She smiled back, nodding reassuringly, mouthing, 'breathe' whilst tapping the top of her chest, 'one, two, three'.

Taking sips of water and deep breaths, Marcie continued slowly.

"I was kidnapped on my sixteenth birthday. I have been shown photographs of the three Defendant's, labelled court exhibits 1, 2 and 3."

Her words were met with an air-pumping fist from a beaming Bella, standing behind the camera's tripod stand.

"I can confirm that I recognise the men as, Roman Darcy, Pierre Lebouf and Jamal Jackson. All three were involved in my abduction, and subsequent r- rape and torture. I was held against my will by them on a remote Island for two years," Marcie said, with a puff of her cheeks.

Bella's smiling eyes watered. 'You've got this,' she mouthed. Marcie nodded, turned the page of her pink notebook and continued.

The recording of Marcie Stone's victim statement ran for seven minutes and twenty two seconds. Almost the exact same time it took from her Father's dropping her outside the bowling alley, to her disappearance behind the venue. She was rescued two years later from a remote island in the Indian Ocean. Marcie was discovered at the base of a dry-well. Under torch light crumpled movement revealed her, and two other girls, lying amidst a mass of decomposing human remains.

Aside from the Court recording, Bella had taped transcripts from her many hours with Marcie. A blow-by-blow account, recording the gruesome nature of her daily existence on the island. This disturbing chronicle would remain burned into Bella's conscience. A deep bond of respect and loyalty grew with every word Marcie recounted from those dark times.

A steadfast commitment to justice pulsed in Bella's every thought. She was unflinching in her dedication to the downfall of these monsters. The loathsome barbarians that had destroyed the lives of so many girls; dismembered and discarded like waste. Her fragile psychologically imprisoned friend, Marcie, was the only survivor able to tell their tale.

Marcie's arrival on the island had coincided with that of the latest VIP. The fluster of the transport guard offloading the girls meant they were thrown unassigned into the holding pit, for later job assignment. Security and transport staff were at 'all hands' in preparation for the 'Hunt'. It meant that Marcie had spent her first day on the tropical island, unattended and unshackled below ground.

Marcie explained how there was a web of underground tunnels that led from each 'Pit' to the 'Dome'. A huge glass structure where the girls were paraded, like horses at a racecourse. There were three pits, each housing girl's from their allotted role; hoare, host or hunt.

On that first day Marcie explored the cave in the dimness, attempting to find an escape route. There was none. But what she did find was a girl that lay hidden down there, wedged into a crack in the rock wall. She hid where the passage was at its blackest, at the midpoint between larger caverns. Marcie stumbled right on past her at first. Her fingers even went across the girl as she fumbled along the rocky wall, toward the light.

"Ciao amico," came a thick whisper.

Marcie remembered screaming as she spun around, stumbling to the ground. It's echo seemed to bounce back louder from the chamber ahead; she thought it was someone else. A soft grin tickled her cheeks as she recalled the shrill of her own shocked scream. As she staggered to her feet, her eyesight adjusted, refocusing on the jagged wall.

The skeletal frame of Gloria slowly emerged from a splintered crack in the rock. It was almost a made-to-measure fracture in the rockface, a crevasse with custom fit bends for her limbs. As she slid out, and into bone juddering movement toward Marcie she backed away; fearful, and yet mesmerised. Gloria reminded her of the fighting skeletons from Jason and the Argonauts.

"Ciao, amico.. friend yes," Gloria said, croakily.

Once the shock of Gloria's misshapen form subsided, Marcie almost enjoyed testing her spoken Italian. Language's were a subject where she had excelled at school. It was the only moment of excitement she recalled, before hearing the tales that Gloria recited under foreign tongue.

"Benvenuto all'inferno!"

'Welcome to.., 'Hell'?" Marcie said.

"Si si," Gloria said. "Sono mostri.. Monsters, yes!" she added, her eyes spinning in hollow sockets.

Marcie remembered how Gloria told her about the 'Hunt.' She explained that any girl that proved difficult, or that was unwilling to serve and pleasure, was selected for it.

Their captors' motto, displayed in four languages in signage across the compound and repeatedly barked at Pit-counts was: 'Obey or face the hunt of death.' Gloria offered Marcie no crumb of comfort, or hope of escape. Tunnels from the metal grille covered pit shafts, leading only to the Dome.

Gloria had been held captive the longest, often escaping to hide out in the woods, before dog-sniffing search teams found her. After her last 'incident' she was flung into the Pit, destined for the hunt. She explained, with a pinched smirk, that she had fled her allotted guest's suite having bitten down hard across the shaft of his penis, completely severing it.

"Scricchiolio," Gloria said, to a shrug from Bella. "Err, in Francese, they say, Le-crunch!" she beamed. It was the only glint of happiness Marcie ever saw in her eyes.

Gloria had crunched through it like a stick of celery before tossing it out the window and making her escape. Still spitting blood and sinew, she had sprinted across the main courtyard before Claude, a man-mountain of a guard, caught her. Moments later, Roman Darcy appeared on the circular balcony of his villa suite, which overlooked the entire site.

Gloria was tied to a totem pole that stood centrally inside the Dome, where later that night she was beaten by Darcy to within a hair's breadth of her life. He ordered an assembly to bear witness to Gloria's brutal punishment, heightening his exhilaration in the adrenaline-fuelled assault.

Gloria's jawbone was shattered and her ribcage collapsed under an endless barrage of blows, each joyfully inflicted. At one point he turned, peeling his sweat-laden shirt, his bulging shoulders like a raging bull. Darcy flashed a crooked smile at his horror-struck audience. Only Claude, in toothy white grin, shared his amusement.

"They're like dogs, the harder you kick 'em the more obedient they become," Gloria heard him say to Carl, his tubby assistant, who had brought him water, mid-beating.

The bandaged, wheelchair-bound VIP rolled across the gravel at first light to observe Gloria's battered body. Its wheels squeaked ominously in the dusty silence as it bounced the gritty surface to the totem pole. She remained unconscious as he hawked, firing a flemy splutter to her bloodsoaked face.

At Darcy's invitation, the cockless man agreed to return to the resort some months later to hunt Gloria, rather than put a bullet in her head there and then. His helicopter flew him away moments later with his manhood in an ice-packed cooler beside him.

"Domani" Gloria had said, with haunting eyes staring right through her.

"Tomorrow?" Marcie said, in a pitchy squeal, "The hunt is tomorrow?"

Pushing her knuckle-knotted, twiggy finger to cracked lips, Gloria slid back into the hairline crack in the rockwall. Contorting in an acute angular motion her bony shoulders and hips disappeared. Her broken body vanished in the shadowy recess.

CHAPTER 63

From her mock exams, taken the week before her abduction, Marcie secured a grade 9 in Art. She had used her skill to draw the most amazing map of the underground network of tunnels that ran beneath Darcy's resort on the Isle of El-Marney.

The Indonesian archipelago had formed from a volcanic eruption centuries earlier. The close proximity of coastal tectonic plates accounted for the staggering height of the Islands peaks, and formation of a myriad of hollow channels beneath them. The chain of isles were outstandingly beautiful, a natural wonder; an explorers paradise and conservationists treasure. That was, until islands were privately purchased by Pierre Lebouf.

In the comfort of the plush library at Haversham Hall, Marcie spent many hours sketching the most incredible images from her previously blocked recollections of the island. Her spooky, ever darkening shading of the intricate web of tunnels prompting many-a shoulder shudder, but she pressed on, undeterred.

Bella's research established that Darcy, funded by Lebouf, had set up a marketplace catering for the latest fad. African big game shoots had all but faded out, given public damnation of the 'sport'. Their dark web advertising revealed a voracious appetite for a new, fetish-led game. An entirely different recreation, 'A Human Hunt' to the death.

After successful launch events, a premium category was created to cope with increased demand, where the hunter could stalk at night; The Moonlight Hunt. Bella discovered it, beyond an soft encrypted mole-hill, being sold as;

'The ultimate hunting experience! In darkness the thrill of chasing 'prey' through the forest is intensified, senses sharpened. Every twig snap crisper, each brush of the bush amplified. The sight of 'flesh' flashing between trees, more exhilarating'

"The first few months was mainly just fetching and carrying, cooking and cleaning, menial tasks. We would work all day and late into the night serving drinks," Marcie said, between noisy sips of her fast emptying shake carton.

"After the last guest returned to their suite we would be taken to the Pit and sleep until first light. Claude would bark us into life and march us back to the resort to do pretty much the same duties again."

Marcie hadn't really appreciated how lucky she was at that stage. But when three new girls arrived, her 'easy life' was over. The new arrivals replaced her and two others who were hosed-down in the inner-courtyard and sent to Pit 2 to, 'dress and make good' as Claude put it.

"Having been paraded inside the Dome for selection, we were each assigned a guest and escorted at knife point to their suite. We were expected to be compliant to their particular demands," Marcie said, straw-slurping her empty drink.

On that first night Marcie stood beside the door, in the suite of a flabby bellied man. He was sitting with arms propped behind him on the end of his bed. He was naked. Marcie would only say that she had fought off his advances, kicking him hard between his legs.

"Claude slapped me so hard that I lost a tooth, but I still lay in the pit relieved," Marcie said, welling up. "I thought they'd put me back on host duty after that."

Bella took her drink carton and passed her a tissue.

"But the next night it was the same room and that same fat man. He slapped me twice across my face, so I said I'd do what he wanted," she said, dabbing at her eyelids.

"Oh Marcie, I'm so sorry," Bella said, tugging at the tissue box.

"But, I was only pretending, playing along, Bella. I leaned over him, and gouged his eyes with my thumbs," Marcie said, with a sad smile.

"Well good for you, hun," Bella said. "What happened after that?" Marcie fell into Bella's arms.

Claude broke Marcie's jaw that night before he flung her down the pit, breaking her ankle in the fall. She was put to work in the kitchens for a while after that, until her injuries healed. Then one night Marcie was taken to the resort's penthouse suite.

The details of what occurred were too painful for Marcie to vocalise. She remained traumatised by the horrific encounter. But over their next three sessions she managed to write down some of what happened;

Roman Darcy was waiting for her, stood glaring in a disturbing silence, enjoying her unease. Marcie fought him from the moment he laid a hand on her, thrashing with everything she had. But it wasn't enough. Clasping a fistful of hair he jerked her head back, almost snapping her neck as he snorted into her face. Darcy dragged her to his bed and flung her across it.

Marcie spat and screamed as he shuffled astride her, pinning her legs and clasping her wrists in one hand above her head. Darcy's strength was overwhelming. Marcie was frantic in wriggled struggle, like a fly stuck-fast in a web. He smirked, wordless as a single crease in his baldness deepened.

The venom of Marcie's fight evaporated into defeated cries as Darcy raped her. She screamed the agony of his every thrust, burying her tear soaked face from him.

After that, Marcie was assigned to a room and different men each night. Emotionless, she would stare vacantly at the ceiling, tracing the shadows that fluttered from the drapes as they billowed gently in the warm breeze. Lifeless, her body would rock in time with their motion, until they left.

In the early days tears would roll her cheeks, but after a while they dried up. When ordered to perform oral sex, she would think of her good friend Gloria's tale of 'Le-crunch', which always made her giggle.

CHAPTER 64

When the girls first arrived, the gated entrance to Haversham Hall had seen paparazzi hugging its walls, clamouring for a snap of them; the survivors. Bella would often drive away from there in a trance-like state, acutely affected by Marcie's daily recollections.

But it was only on her penultimate visit that Marcie had finally opened up about her final days on the island. Bella had taken her through the police report and witness statements.

Darcy's security boats had been increasingly aggressive in shepherding many a-fisherman and tourboat away from its coastline. The police had sided with the land owners, warning local traders to avoid the area. But the lure of a spectacular catch or sighting of a dolphin, often spotted circling El-Marney, was too tempting.

From police records, a local fisherman had ventured ashore to basket fruit, to add to his aquatic haul. Paoulo had stumbled across human remains whilst trekking inland. Panicked at the distant sound of gunshot, he tripped, releasing a severed head, rolling from the undergrowth. Its snow white face bore the pristine aire of youth, a childlike innocence. Grabbing the wrist of a crudely hacked forearm that lay nearby, Paoulo ran.

An hour later, he stood in front of the commisionaire of Politiz, slapping the severed arm on his desk; action had to be taken. The resultant search of the Island revealed the gruesome extent of a massacre. The unholy slaughter was graphically recorded by a catalogue of photographs. Body parts were strewn across the island, in what appeared to be merciless, frenzied attacks.

From its sloping wooded hillsides to the sandy coves the once beautiful island was a bloodbath, spotted with human remains. Unidentifiable dismembered limbs, scattered like bovine cuts, as if awaiting release of Lions.

At dust filled clearings, blood darkened trails evidenced final, despairing moments. The landscape was re-fashioned with molehill-like heaps of fleshy mass; the forest glade, peppered bolognese-red.

The search took days, with additional manpower drawn from local volunteers. At dawn a flotilla of boats would channel to the island from the mainland, ferrying back under darkening skies with their ungodly loads.

It wasn't until day three, as dusk submitted to an indigo sky that a piercing cry rang out. A young cadet, with a voice not yet broken, shrieked his gruesome discovery. A boy in his late teens, and an even younger cadet had been tasked to check again the northern tip of the island, and a ramshackle hut that was there. With torch light scanning quickly through the shack, they radioed it in, 'all-clear: empty', and marched on.

The pair took a different trail away from the wood cabin, a shortcut to basecamp. They traipsed an overgrown shingle pathway that weaved a course to the beaches below. Only the sound of waves lapping the feet of the rocky cliff face beneath them, joined their steady descent.

At halfway down, the starlight captured something oddly different, inland of their hilly path. It stood distinct from the mass of vegetation that swamped their tangled route. A sheen from a stony structure glinted back.

The lead cadet, ever inquisitive, thigh-brushed the dense thicket to what sat at the end of a narrow clearing. His young companion torch-beamed the spinney, sending the cadet's shadowy movements high into the surrounding trees.

After some heavy crunched tread with arms aloft, his elbow-swinging quickened, as the brush tapered. His narrowing shadows knitted to merge as one in the murkiness ahead. A dampness was here, the still air filled with an odour distinct from that of the forest.

The shallow stone structure seemed out of place in an area where nature alone thrived. On approach, the wall's circular shaping became apparent, rounding either side of a thick wooden post. Opposite, another chunky timber strut protruded, although but-a fraction of its twin, snapped jagged to a stump.

A Well, of some sort, where the island's aboriginal tribes once drew freshwater from the subsoil. Or more likely simply used it cistern-like, in collecting rainwater. A lush emerald-green clasped most of its stonework, in an ivy-clad smothering embrace.

As the young cadet closed, the now familiar hum of insect winged excitement was paired with the head-jerking stench of decaying flesh. With his flappy shirt sleeves cupping his face, he clicked his torch into yellowy brilliance.

With a hand to the post he peered inside, panning the light to the foot of the well. Its mossy stone walls cylindered a leafy wetness to some distance below. The macabre sight at its base bounced back to greet him. A mass of interwoven limbs, lifeless contorted bodies heaped in a tangled rotting pile.

The mutilated carnage spewed from the depths of hell. A dumping ground to conceal evil, or a death jump to avoid capture. An intensifying hum filled the shaft in a whirring echo; like a caged motorcycle rider. Rancid warm air billowed the tunnel, its putrid stench swamping him. His stinging eyes scanned the misshapen, bloodied remains.

His heart jumped, thudding his chest, at the slightest of movement. Squeezing up between carcasses, a rodent crawled the fleshy mound, pausing to feast upon torn facial tissue. He turned away sharply, with his fly-swarmed torchlight, before lurching in convulsion to vomit at his feet.

His fresh-faced colleague arrived at his side, sporting a wrinkly-nose grimace and unbuttoning his sleeves. Side-stepping his friend, he took a look for himself. Seconds later came his shriek, rebounding the tree canopy and sending nested birds to the skies, in a cacophony of noise.

"Hidup, hidup, mereka hidup!"

"Alive, alive, they're alive!" Bella read from the search team's report, smiling softly at Marcie, who sat with her chin resting on her kneecaps.

Marcie, with tear-stained face shuddered, a deep shiver from her core. Bella flopped the file onto the side table and laid a blanket and her arm around Marcie's shoulders. Although still thin, she was far less frail than when Bella had first met her.

"Could you tell me a little about how you got to end up down there, Marcie. Do you remember what happened?"

Releasing a heavy sigh, she turned to meet her friend's reassuring smile and nodded slowly. Bella tugged twice at the tissue box before tapping the voice record button on her iPhone.

PART IX — VALOUR

CHAPTER 65

EL-MARNEY – NOW

Roman Darcy's suite was literally a breath of fresh air. Its coolness swept over Bella as beads of sweat burst from her hairline. Trickling streams rounded her cheeks to drip from her chin, splashing the shiny tiles.

"Any chance of a glass of water?" Bella said, in a throaty rasp.

Darcy's laughter was both raucous and mocking, genuine in its amusement at the request.

"Funny is it? You, treating women this way!" Bella said, defiant with her hands on hips.

She stood with shoulders back firing a loathing smirk. Darcy towered over her, his face reddening.

"We know who you are, Maxwell, and you will suffer badly for fucking up the start of our game," Darcy said, with spittal flying.

Darcy's chubby little assistant, Joel, sat in a carver chair on the far wall, disinterested, attentive only to his iPhone.

"You're dying, Darcy," Bella announced, with a broadening grin that slowly parted her lips.

"What the fuck are you on about, bitch?" he barked, in a gravelly croak.

Darcy's brow-line ploughed as he eyed here. His mouth fixed in a snarl, his flaring nostrils snorted as he stepped a little closed. He was enormous, shadowing her with his bull-like rounded shoulders. His chest ballooned under his buttoned Hawaiian shirt.

"I'm talking about you. You must be feeling it; sweaty palms, blotching skin, a hoarsening of the throat. I can see it. Look at your face, you're puce," Bella said, beaming up at him. "It's over, Darcy!"

Now it was Bella laughing, mimicking his taunt, staring fearlessly at his blotchy-face.

"Did you really think you could escape justice, after what you've done," Bella said, with smiling eyes. "For what you did to those girls.."

The ferocity of Darcy's strike across her face was such that it lifted her clean off the floor. There was an audible crack. Dazed and shaken, she lay half propped up between the wall and hard floor. Joel offered barely a cursory glance from his phone.

"K-k-kill m-me, why d-don't you," Bella puffed, between laboured breaths. "B-but if I die, you'll die!"

The kick to her abdomen lifted her from the tiles; her midriff punted like a rugby ball at conversion. He towered over her petiteness, seemingly itching for more.

"You mess with my operation, you die, bitch," he said, spittle firing from his blue-lips.

"W-wake up you f-fuckin m-moron!" Bella spluttered. "Kill me and you'll never know what I've given you."

He paused mid-backlift, slowly lowering it to the floor.

"What the fuck are you saying, Maxwell?" Darcy said, hauling her to her feet in one fist-filled motion, ripping her tee.

Bella panted, wincing out the pain. "You're s-slowly dying, Darcy. You will be dead within the next twenty four hours."

He shifted her like a ragdoll to one side whilst peering into the wall mirror. "I've got some jungle fever, so fuckin what. I ain't dying, bitch," he bellowed into her face.

Darcy's huge features blurred in front of her as his hand clasped her throat, squeezing it. He slapped her cheek, jerking her head to one side.

"You better start saying your prayers, bitch," he said, finger-clamping her face to face his. "I'm gonna mess you up, then pass you around. And anything left, I'll feed to my dogs."

His breath was rancid and thick. Bella spluttered it away as his grip tightened around her throat.

"We got any of those Necro-sorts in the group, Joel?" he said, with head half-cocked to his shoulder.

Joel snapped his head up, "Necrophiliacs? Yes, we do indeed, Ro."

"Good. Then I might as well finish you off now," Darcy said, slamming and pinning Bella to the wall by her neck.

Bella's face whitened, her eyes bulging as she gasped despairingly at the thinning air. Darcy tossed her to the floor and turned away, striding to the fireplace on the opposite wall. From above its carved mahogany mantelpiece, he pulled and unsheathed a twin-bladed hunting knife.

Bella lay struggling to breathe, clasping at her throat, desperate to open its airway.

"It might be worth making an example of her, Ro," Joel said softly, his head-dipped, submissively.

"What the hell are you on about?" Darcy snarled.

"Well, she did get some of the other girls to help her, in the Dome. And she does have something of a building following on the socials; more than the usual 'MeToo' stuff," Joel said, flashing his iPhone in Darcy's direction.

"It's all the same old feminist bollocks!" Darcy sniped, admiring his knife.

"I know Claude would appreciate seeing her suffer a little more, considering what she did to Manu!" Joel said quickly.

"Manu. Who the fuck's Manu?" Darcy barked.

"He's our Pit-man. He runs security in the Pit, Ro," Joel said.

"Well he's done a pretty shitty job of it, ain't he," Darcy said, picking a dried blood splat from the knife.

"Y-you know, wh-who I-I am," Bella said, hauling herself to sit upright against the wall.

"Ah, it speaks," Darcy said, grinning across the room at Bella.

"I was on the prosecution team. You s-saw me every day in Court," she said, gingerly twisting and clutching her ribcage. "Don't you think we found out everything about you three deviants?"

"Watch your mouth, bitch," Darcy said, approaching her.

"You're going to, *ahh-ahh,* have to help me," Bella puffed. "Help me, explain this to your master, Gonzo," she added, peering at Joel between Darcy's legs. "This muppet just ain't getting it,"

Bella winced to half-stand, still clasping her middle. "We had a-access to your medical records, twat-face," Bella said. "I know about the nasal spray you take every night, to aid your sinusitis!"

295

Joel disappeared suddenly, darting noisily into the bathroom, amidst a clanking of items hitting porcelain.

"Who gives a fuck!" Darcy said, lurching at Bella and re-establishing his grip on her throat.

"Iy-yah, I-yah g-g-got tuew-yt," Bella wheezed.

"I can't hear you," Darcy said, with a crooked smile that mirrored the crease across his forehead.

"Pois-pois, Iy-yah poisssun," Bella squealed as her pupils disappeared, leaving white.

Darcy lifted the knife, resting its point high on her cheekbone, just below her eye.

"Cool eyes," Darcy said as sky blue briefly reappeared. "Big uns too! I might feed them to Rolf," he added, with a snigger.

"She got to it, Ro!" Joel yelled, stumbling back into the room.

"What?" Darcy said, headcocked.

"It's been tampered with!" Joel said, waving a little white tube, pinned between his thumb and index finger. "Take a look," Joel said, passing the nasal spray to Darcy.

Darcy flung Bella to the floor and strode over to him. "Where?" he barked, staring at the small bottle-shaped container. "I can't see fuck-all. There ain't no pinpricks."

"Look at the bottom of it, there's dirt across the base," Joel said, pointing up at it.

"Well I could have done that!" Darcy snapped, with a face full of anger.

"But we found her hiding in the bushes, Roman. She wasn't strip searched and we let her use the bathroom, remember?" Joel said, reaching for the little pot.

"Fuck, that's bollocks, there ain't no spiking point!" Darcy hollered, shoving Joel, stumbling backwards. He wiped the bottom of the bottle and squeezed the spray repeatedly, watching the solution puddle on the coffee table.

"Just maybe I put it in the same way it comes out," Bella said, still rubbing her neck. "Just a hunch!"

"And it's true what she said about having your medical records," Joel said, straightening the collar of his short sleeved shirt. "They had it from our disclosure to the prosecution, it was a legal requirement, Ro."

"Well it looks alright, smells the same," Darcy said, sneering at the liquid.

"That's because it's colourless, odourless and tasteless, you dimwit," Bella said. "Have a lick, why don't you, it'll speed things up!"

"What the hell did you put in here, bitch?" Darcy boomed, snarling over at her.

"There is a cure," Bella splurted, as Darcy marched toward her. "I have the antidote," she added quickly.

"We'll you'd better start talking," Darcy said, his eyes flaring.

"You kill me. You die," Bella blurted, as he reached for her throat. "Do you get it; *If I die, you die.*"

"You tell me what's in this fucking thing, right now," Darcy said, flinging the spay at her feet.

"It's a drug called Thallium," Bella said, sidestepping him, to look at Joel.

"Th-al-lium!" she mouthed slowly. "Get on your google, Gonzo!"

"Call the quack Joel, get him over here now! Send the chopper," Darcy ordered.

"There's no time for that Darcy," Bella said, with a grin tickling her lips. "I've already checked; there's no supply of the antidote, this side of the Alps. I have the only one!"

"So what stops me beating it out of you.. I'll take your fucking eye out, right now," Darcy said, his knife rising from his side.

"Yeah you kill me if you like! But do that and you'll die a slow agonising death, so my work is done," Bella snarled into his face.

Darcy wiped a thick sheen of sweat from his head with the back of his hand. "Get me some water!" he coughed.

"She's right Ro, it's some form of debilitating toxicant," Joel said, staring at his iPhone.

"I'm the only one that has access to a vial of the antidote," Bella said, wincing and clutching her stomach.

"The antitoxin is only available in the US," Joel said. "Sorry.." he muttered, swiping frantically at his phone, adding, "or some European cities. We wouldn't get it here in 24 hours, Roman!"

"Oh fucking clever, bitch," Darcy spluttered. "So what is it that you want for this, vial?"

Bella grinned through her pain, "You can start by putting that thing down!"

"So what.. you want money?" Darcy said, flinging the hunting knife to the sofa.

"Now, are we ready to discuss this properly?" Bella said, stepping away from him.

"Just name your fuckin price, Maxwell," Darcy snarled.

"Tut-tut, that's no way to do business!" Bella said, grimacing in straightening fully. "And do you seriously think I came here for money!"

"You aint stopping my business here! I fucking well know that," Darcy said, squaring up to her.

"Well let's look at the facts, shall we?" Bella said, whilst dusting herself down. "The clock is ticking. Every vein in your body is slowly being infected."

"Fuck you, bitch," Darcy said, spitting flem to the floor. "Ok, so what, you have a friend or someone over here, you want to get out?"

"You'll soon be coughing blood," Bella said, strolling between the two men. "The poison is steadily taking over every muscle in your body. Look at your blotchy face!"

"Water, I said," Darcy barked at Joel, before coughing into the crook of his arm.

"So who is it you want to save?" Darcy said, examining the spittle speckled on his sleeve. "I'll let your mate go, now where's the fucking antidote!"

"Oh, I think we can do a bit better than that, don't you, Gonzo?" Bella said, to the chubby little man, who continued head down, pouring water into a glass.

"Don't fuckin push it," Darcy croaked, before swigging from the glass.

"It says here that it became an effective murder weapon, that was known as.," Joel said, thumb swiping. "Known as 'Inheritance Powder', people fed it to elderly relatives. They also used it in prisons to kill rats!"

"How very apt, I came here to destroy vermin," Bella said, with narrowing eyes, sneering at Darcy.

"Alright Joel, I get the fuckin' picture. Name your fuckin price then, Maxwell?" Darcy said.

"That's more like it," Bella said, with a widening smile. "Now then, your life Darcy.. what would you do to save it?"

PART X — RETRIBUTION

CHAPTER 66

"His name's Pascal. He was a witness at Darcy's trial, and he's a friend of Maxwell," SIO Tom Broad explained, having just slammed down the hotel telephone. "We're meeting him in the hotel lobby in ten minutes," he added, checking his watch.

DI Spencer was perched on a stool beside a narrow desk near the patio doors. DI Neil Turvey in a flamboyant shirt and shorts was stretched out across the double bed with hands cupped to the back of his head. Tom paced the white tiled hotel room.

"He's agreed to show us where he dropped Maxwell off, on El-Marzey, and explain what her plan was. Apparently he was due to meet her at the same spot twenty four hours later. She never showed up. The guy's completely panicked!" Tom said.

"You mean, El-Marney, guv, the island where..?" Neil said, with a developing frown.

"It's the island where the bodies were found, where Darcy's been resident for the last few years," Spencer said, flinging a booklet across the room to land on Neil's lap.

"Ahh, El-Mar-ney, yeah I knew that!" Tom said.

Neil elbow-propped, unfolding a map across the peachy bed cover. A colourful picture of the curved peninsular with dotted islands arching it, nearly covering the double bed.

"What time's your pick-up, Turvs?" Tom said, again glancing at his wrist.

"Five minutes ago! And they call this a VIP service," Neil said. "Apparently I'm the last to arrive and have already missed the 'bidding process', whatever that means!"

"Be careful over there Neil. This isn't your average undercover op," Tom said, rolling his sleeves to the elbow.

A heavy double knock at the door saw Neil swing his legs ninety degrees and spring from the bed. He slung a loose rucksack across his shoulder and with a head-tilting wink, blew a kiss at DI Spencer.

"Good luck buddy," Tom said, passing Neil a small black box. "Keep us posted on this thing, when you can."

Neil nodded, tucked the device into his trouser pocket and shook his boss's hand. "See you on the other side," he whispered.

"Good evening sir, Mister Blake is it?" an official sounding voice said on the other side of the door. Their footsteps and voices faded behind the clunk of the hefty door.

"He's a liability, Tom. And what's that all about, calling himself, 'Mr Blake'?" Spence said.

"Well he couldn't use his own name, and we've banned him from using 'Bond,'" Tom explained with an eye roll.

The whirring of a lawn mower engine merged with garbled conversation near the patio window, prompting Spencer to her feet. She swished the heavy drapes across and clicked on the bedside lamp.

"Look, I know Neil's a cocky so-and-so but it may actually be useful to have him on the inside. To see exactly what Darcy and his cronies get up to over there!" Tom said.

He stood staring at the spectacular mural on the pastel blue wall opposite the bed. It detailed the great array of island's that peppered the coastline off the mainland. Each island was named in fancy calligraphy, with darker shaded land reflecting a steep mountain range.

"Impressive, aren't they, Tom," Spencer said softly, stepping behind him.

"Apparently this little island here, Mak-am-ra-ja," he said, pointing at the smallest isle. "Is the one Darcy and Lebouf have bought recently."

"Beautiful, I'm sure," she whispered. "But I meant these."

Spence turned him around slowly by the shoulders. She was topless. His gaze rose slowly to meet hers, as she slid her fingers through his thick dark hair.

"Spence, I don't think this is a good idea. We have to meet with Pascal in, in," Tom said, with pleading, puppy-dog eyes.

"Oh, I think we have time," she purred, tilting her head with a lip-parting smile.

She kissed him softly whilst unfastening her pencil skirt and wiggling her hips. It dropped to the floor. Stepping over it, she wrapped her arms around his neck.

"I am a married man, you know," he said, gingerly placing his hands on her bare hips.

"Aww, how sweet," she teased, pouting.

She ran her long fingers through his shiny hair, combing it back from his face and kissed him gently with an open mouth.

"I mean, we only just got here, and we.. we need to.."

"Hush now," she whispered, her fingers sliding to his crotch. "I know you want this too."

She kissed him tenderly, her soft tongue entering his mouth as Tom's hands slid from her waist, caressing her silken skin, his fingers splaying her white-thonged buttocks.

Tom scooped her up, carrying and laying her on the bed, where he shuffled his pants to his ankles.

CHAPTER 67

Dulcet chatter drifted across the reception lounge from the hotel's busy main bar. Its double doors were pinned back, allowing drinks-laden waiting staff to pass easily between the two seating areas.

"Mister De-Lu-zio, is it?" Tom said, struggling with pronunciation.

Tom and Spencer joined the slim, middle aged man sitting at the table, half-hidden behind an impressive display of tropical plants. He rose from behind the circular table, offering his hand. A silvery grey colour was dominant in his thinning hairline, which was swept back from his brow.

"Please, it's Pascal. Call me Pascal," he said, greeting the British Police officers with a warm smile.

"My apologies for our late arrival Pascal," Tom said. "Err, this is DI Spencer and I'm the Senior Investigating Officer, Tom Broad. We spoke briefly on the telephone earlier. Do you mind if we record our conversation?"

"No, not at all, of course. Very pleased to meet you both," Pascal said. "As I said to you, I cannot speak with the authorities here, so I contacted the Police in London. I was relieved to hear that you were already heading over."

A light footed waiter appeared from nowhere and stood wordlessly beside their table. He noted their order for refreshments with a polite nod, before disappearing. Tom tapped and placed his iPhone in the middle of the table.

"Now I appreciate that Miss Maxwell is a friend of yours, Pascal, but I must remind you that she is wanted for questioning in the UK in connection with the murder of Jamal Jackson, and the disappearance of Pierre Lebouf," Tom said, whilst they all settled into their cushioned seats.

"I know nothing of this, 'murder or disappear' but Miss Maxwell needs your help," Pascal said. "The Menjana, the polisi here, is corrupt and offers no-help. How you say, they are-err, 'in the pocket' of Darcy. He buys their cooperation, their silence. He employs all the workers on the Islands, so to most, Darcy is their hero."

"And Roman Darcy, is he on the island, El-err-Marney, right now?" Tom said.

"Yes, yes, he is always there," Pascal fired back. "Look, Bella.. Miss Maxwell, she is in trouble, I am sure."

"When did you last see her, Pascal?" Spencer said, leaning over the glass coffee table.

"The night before last. I take her to El-Marney in a small boat and drop her on the Eastern tip, at a small cove below blackclaw cliff. I agreed to meet her there twenty four hours later. I waited for many hours until Darcy's patrol boat spotted me and chased me off again.."

"Again, you say?" Spence interrupted.

"Yes, they see me when I drop her and start shooting at my boat. This is why I know Bella is in trouble, they must have seen me dropping her there. If she was captured then she would be thrown in the Pit with the others," Pascal said, with increasing speed.

"But what was her intention.." Tom said, before being cut across.

"Wait, what do you mean captured and thrown into a.. 'Pit' you say?" Spence said, tucking hair behind her ear. "And, who was shooting at your boat?"

"You do not understand," Pascal said, with a deepening exasperation. His deep tanned face crickled. "They own the island, it is a private land. Darcy and Lebouf run it as their 'Leisure resort' for rich clients. They have kidnapped girls from all over the world there, to entertain men."

"But Pascal, hang on a minute here," Tom said, with palms raised. "Their operation was shut down. Those men were arrested and stood trial for those offences."

"Yes, but you let them out! How do you say in the UK; 'the law is an ass'!" Pascal said, his eyes bulging. "You think they're going to do a desk job now?"

Spencer eye-rolled an, 'I told you so' smirk at Tom Broad. "We had suspected as much about Darcy but hadn't received any intelligence," she said.

"I'm sorry to hear about any illegal activities, if that is the case. But can you confirm what Miss Maxwell told you of her plans in coming here?" Tom said, whilst digging to release his notepad from his buttoned breast-pocket. "And what has she said to you about Jackson and Lebouf?"

Spencer surreptitiously shook her head at Tom. Pascal got to his feet, sneered with a tongue-clacking tut at the officers, sliding the thick strap of his bag across his chest.

"You think I came here to help you, to arrest Bella, when it's her life that's in danger!" Pascal snarled.

"Please Pascal, I know she's your friend but we do need to establish the facts. She simply can't be allowed to take the law into her own hands," Tom said. "Roman Darcy's life could be in danger."

"You talk about facts. I'll give you the facts.," Pascal said breathily, attracting the rubber-necked attention of an elderly couple on a nearby table.

"Pascal, I'm sorry," Tom whispered loudly. "Please just sit back down," he added, glancing over his shoulder.

"Bella is the only one in danger!" Pascal said, with a rising fury. "She is the only one brave enough to try and stop these men; these monsters. There are girls imprisoned over there!" He jabbed a pointed finger at Tom. "And you talk to me about facts."

"Pascal, please calm down," Tom uttered under his breath, with head dropped.

"You only seek the facts that you need; to arrest Bella. To allow these men to carry on doing what the hell they like!" Pascal said, with a sneer welded to his face.

"Listen, we were not aware that they were back to their old tricks," Tom said, in a hushed tone.

"Old tricks! You talk about the facts that you need to arrest Bella. But it's just, 'old-tricks' with Darcy!" Pascal said, head-shaking.

"Look, Maxwell has come here with dangerous intent. Darcy is clearly in some jeopardy," Tom said, folding his notebook and clipping the pen to its spine.

"Screw-you, arsehole!" Pascal said, scraping his chair noisily to one side.

"Please Pascal, can we just talk about this," Tom said, before lip-biting while watching him march across the cool atrium.

"I think he's got the UK confused with the US," Spencer said, while smiling up at the young tray-holding waiter who had arrived silently back at their table.

The two officers sat in silence as he threw down three hotel motif coasters and delivered two ice filled tumblers. He poured from, then placed, the bevelled glass bottles alongside each one. Theatrically, he presented a long stemmed glass in front of Spencer, before nodding at the officers and disappearing without a sound.

"Old tricks? My god Tom!" Spence said, with a little head-shake. Her fingers parted in lifting her chilled wine. "I thought I was with Turvey for a minute there!"

"So did I," Tom said, eye-pointing at her drink.

CHAPTER 68

"You are very late, Mister Blake," the speedboat driver shouted over his shoulder.

The engine revving increased dramatically as the boat swerved right to battle the pounding waves head on. The local chap, seemingly enjoying himself, beamed back at Neil.

Neil, half-crouched behind him, braced himself and slipped his shades back into his top pocket. He grinned at the guy, "Better late than never!"

Steering one-handed, the stocky little man clunked the gear stick up a notch. "You are missing the bidding for the girls," he yelled.

Neil's fingers squeezed a little tighter around the pole fixed to the back of the driverseat and widened his stance. "The bidding, you say?" Neil said.

"Betting on who you think will win," he replied to Neil's blank face. "You know, choose a girl - your runner?" he added, with an eye-twitch.

"Ahh, yes of course," Neil said, dropping to his haunches.

"I'm sure they saved you one, yeah!" the little man shouted enthusiastically.

The boat swerved hard right again, cutting a wave in half and jolting Neil backwards. He stumbled, falling to slump across the white leather bench that encircled the back of the speedboat. He grabbed the railing that ran along the side of the boat.

"How much longer?" Neil bellowed, reacquainting his feet with the deck.

"I'll get you there in time for the hunt, you no worries," he said, flashing Neil a buck-toothed smile.

Neil regretted his inflight meal, a lamb bhuna, as his inners churned again. The little boat thrashed on through the waves that broke high on the vessel's side, spraying clean across it. A salty wetness rhythmically showered Neil as his head began to spin. His complexion shaded a minty green, as he fought a rising urge to hurl up his stomach contents.

"Only five more minute, Mister Blake," the driver said, giggling excitedly.

"Good, good," Neil said, whilst scanning the deck for the water bottle that he had a moment ago.

"You relax now Mister Blake, El-Marney just over there," the driver said, in a pithy squeal. He pointed at a jutted speck of brown that broke the seascape, piercing the horizon.

'Thank fuck for that' Neil mumbled, with a pulled grin at his chauffeur.

CHAPTER 69

"Well, you certainly messed that up!" Spencer said, with a little headshake.

She drained her wine, placing the elegant glass almost on its coaster. Tom shuffled to the edge of his seat, flashing a cold grin at the plump, tight-permed woman that was staring over at them.

"Look, we need to be straight with people, Spence," he whispered. "We're here to investigate the murder of Jamal Jackson and disappearance of Pierre Lebouf. We have to recognise that Roman Darcy is in danger now that Maxwell's on his island, El-Ma-nery."

"*El-Marney,*" Spencer said.

"Exactly yes, El-Marney. We have to warn him," Tom said, again, feeling eyes on him.

Spencer pinched her watch face saying, "Pascal dropped Maxwell there 36 hours ago, so I think Darcy already knows she's there."

"Not necessarily, she may still be lying low," Tom said. "Either way, we know that she's stranded over there, so we have them both on the same island."

Tom half turned, to look up as the portly woman sidled up alongside him.

"Don't mind my intrusion, but I couldn't help overhearing you talking about Darcy," she said with a distinctive east London accent.

"Err, sorry miss, but this is a private conv.."

"I assume you're British police officers and that they've sent over to protect that scumbag," she said, propping a folded palm on her hip. "Only that guy

313

doesn't need any sort of help from you. He's the one that needs to be arrested!"

"I'm sorry miss, but we are not in any position.."

"It's Miss Maxwell that you should be helping. As far as we can see, she's trying to deal with these lowlifes single handedly. Ain't that right Howard," she said, maintaining her hard stare at Tom.

Her meekly nodding husband, half hidden behind her, sported an embarrassed smirk.

"We do get the newspapers out here you know, and my niece is still missing. Jemima came through here on a trekking holiday, coming-up two years ago now. Not that you lot have a clue about what happened to her!" she said, with a rising bluster. "Sure as hell Darcy had something to do with it."

"Miss, I really don't think this is the time or.."

"Excuse me, Mrs Houghton, but this is an area for private conversation of our guests," a blazered man said, suddenly appearing. "You must come with me please." A shiny gold badge on the breast pocket of his purple blazer read *Manager.*

"Well, okay, but you look out for Miss Maxwell, mister," she said, pointing at Tom.

The Manager squeezed his hand through the crook of her elbow, turning her around slowly.

"Maxwell has done more than any of your lot. I followed every day of that trial, those three men should never have been released!" she said, turning from their table.

She walked off slowly alongside the hotel manager, muttering her complaints. He nodded along, waving over at one of the table attendants. Howard mosied along behind them, clutching his wifes oversized handbag.

"She's right you know, Tom," Spencer said.

"Look, we need to stick to our brief," Tom said.

"So what do you propose we do now?"

"Hang on a sec," Tom whispered, eye rolling as a boyish-looking waiter nearing their table.

"Err, another white wine and, err, what are you having Tom?" Spencer asked.

The young waiter, sporting a charming smile, scribbled on a notepad that lay on his silver tray. Tom shook his head and the boy disappeared with a white toothed beam.

Wall lights flickered into life, Mexican Wave-like, around the entire reception lounge. A thudding double beep vibrated Tom's iPhone from the centre of the table.

"It's Neil - he's landed and is being escorted to the resort centre now," Tom said.

"That's good news," Spencer said. "And.. what else did he say?" she asked between a hiccup.

"Only his usual banter, that you don't need to hear!" Tom said.

"Tell me," Spence said, leaning in with narrowing eyes.

"He just said, 'Apparently, they're saving a couple of girls for me'. You know what he's like, he thinks it's Carry on Camping over there!" Tom said, with an eyebrow raised.

"Twat!"

"Exactly!" Tom said, jumping to his feet. "Look, I'm going to speak to the local Chief of Police. Find out what they know about what goes on, on this Isle of El-Marcy."

"*El-Marney*," Spencer said, with a soft smile.

"Can you call in to HQ and see where we're at on the whereabouts of Pierre Lebouf," Tom said, trousering his iPhone. "Oh, and speak to the psychologist, Forsythe, see what he's got on Darcy, and this '*ultimate killing experience*' business."

Spencer slid her mobile and pocketbook from her handbag, clicking the top of her pen.

"And Spence, do it back in the room, please," Tom said. "Let's try and keep everything professional and *discreet*, shall we?"

"Of course, yes, you're right. Are you coming back with me?" Spencer said, staring up at him.

"No. I'll get a cab to the local police station. I'm told it's only ten minutes from here. I'll give you a call once I've spoken to them," Tom said.

Tom strode away, just as the smiley, light footed waiter appeared with a sparkling glass at the centre of his round tray. She took the drink with a grateful nod at the young man.

Tom stood at reception ordering a taxi, as Spencer meandered off with her wine in hand, back to her hotel room. She was followed at a discreet distance by the young waiter.

By the time Spence reached the door of her suite she felt quite woozy, and had veered unsteadily from the footpath several times. She had dropped her glass in the bushes before staggering on to her door, leaning against it whilst digging a keycard from her bag.

As Spencer stumbled through the doorway a slim arm slid swiftly around her waist, squeezing it tight, like a Boa constricting its prey.

"I'll help you, Miss."

"I-yer, izz-err ow-kay," she stammered, her mouth dry, her lips barely able to part.

"You are a little drunk, no?" he said, lifting her from her feet.

He was remarkably strong for someone so small, carrying her inside and heel-clipping the door behind him. Her vision now blurred at the edges, her pupils fixed centre in narrowing focus as he laid her across the bed. Spencer's limbs felt numb; they no longer had movement.

"I have another one for you," the man announced exuberantly, almost singing the words into a little phone that he angled to his ear.

Spencer heard the hiss of net curtains, swishing along their pole, before the heavy drag of drapes being drawn. She dry-blinked, registering a hazy light that had been clicked on.

"You say you need more, I get them!" he said, with a childlike creepy giggle.

The man began rummaging the contents of Spencer's bag that lay strewn alongside her on the bed.

"I-izz, po-po-l-izz," Spence slurred from one side of her mouth. Her head lifted just a fraction, before she lost consciousness.

"I want best price. Blonde, twenty years, afferletic build.. good body," he chimed excitedly into his tiny phone.

He yanked her arms up, flopping her forehead against him whilst he pulled off her top, dropping her unceremoniously back down.

"Okay, ten minute. It's room 251, the sunset suite," he said, before tucking the phone into his waistcoat, like a snooker player repocketing his chalk.

CHAPTER 70

"Damn, these fuckers get everywhere!" DI Neil Turvey said, slapping the back of his neck.

"You want some spray, Mister Blake?" the guide said, passing him a white can with a picture of a red insect emblazoned on it.

Turvey took the canister and sprayed liberally from his ankles up.

"Thanks, buddy," he said, handing it back. "How long is it until we get to the resort from here?"

"Oh, only twenty minutes, my friend," he said, with a toothy grin. "We cut up here from the beach path, through the forest. I'll take you past the old wishing well."

Jesus christ, what is it a tourist attraction now? Neil mused.

The young tour guide, who had driven Neil over by speedboat, hummed to himself whilst swinging his machete at any vegetation that had dared to stray across their pathway. It led them steeply from the little sandy cove where the boat now bobbed alongside its makeshift pontoon.

A shrill caw of exotic birds nesting filled the tree canopy overhead, as the intense heat of the day sank into the tropical island.

"We won't be able to walk these paths tomorrow, hey?" he said, flashing a goofy smile at Neil, the latest guest to the island.

"No, why's that?" Neil said, whilst arm-flapping to clear a soft buzzing from his face.

"Why? The *Hunt* starts tomorrow morning." he snapped back, wide eyed.

"Ahh, of course, yes. The Hunt! I'm looking forward to it!"

"Not normal hunting, no," he said, with a crackly laugh. "They release animals to catch girls this time!" he added, beaming over his shoulder.

What the actual, fuck, Neil offered a meek grin. "But we're not actually killing though," Neil asked. "It's some sort of game?"

The guide stopped in his tracks, turning to face his guest. "You pay for Hunt.. you are Mister Blake, yes?" he said, his head cocked, rooster-like. His machete, fixed at his side.

"Yes, of course I am! It's just my first trip here, and I wasn't sure how it all works," Neil said, with a rising authority. "You mentioned animals?" he added, trying to soften his guide's demeanour.

"They are only released on the survivors from first day of hunting, you see!" he said, his smile returning. "You didn't get the brochure and schedule?"

He swung his rucksack from his back and started digging into a side pocket. He passed Neil a pamphlet, before shuffling it back around his shoulders and continuing the climb. Merrily resuming his rhythmic hum and branch thrashing.

"Ahh yes, of course, I remember it now," Neil said. He shoved the schedule into his back pocket and hurried on after his guide. "Does anyone actually live on these other islands?"

"Yes, of course, Mister Blake," his escort replied, chuckling. "They each have fishing communities, except Makam-Raja. That is sacred ground, no one is allowed there."

"Ahh, now I recognise that name," Neil said, squinting at the fast widening vista behind him. *Your bosses have bought that one pal!*

The skin-clinging humidity increased as they scaled upwards at an ever-increasing gradient. Neil's forehead spotted in a salty gleam. Looking out as they cleared the taller vegetation the panorama that was unfolding appeared stolen from a fantasy movie; it was otherworldly.

"Wow. Some view, huh?" Neil puffed, catching up with his guide, who was singing softly and lashing away.

The entire eastern side of El-Marney's shoreline now traced out beneath them. Stretching from jagged cliffs on the northern tip, across the many cave-hugging inlets, to the gentler shelved slopes of the south. The coastline juddered like the lines of a heart monitor, with each spit of land carpeted in white sand.

Beyond its shore, the sea looked smooth and still, at odds with Neil's earlier experience. The vast expanse of glassy waters were a picture of glistening tranquillity, broken only by other islands. All unique in shape, each boasting a vivid green lushness. In an arched speckled chain, the archipelago from El-Marney stretched almost to the mainland.

"Who owns all these islands?" Neil said, turning to his guide.

But the little man was now chopping some way ahead at the denser foliage inland from their coastal trail.

"This pathway hasn't been used for some time, huh?" Neil shouted upwards.

"I'm taking you a shortcut because you are late, but not many come this way now, you see. It is taking longer than I'd hoped!" he shouted down to Neil.

The closest island had a soaring, shadowed clifface, jutting angrily from the seabed below it. The little Isle looked majestic, towering the still waters that foamed gently around it, framing its rocky shore. There was an eeriness about it, standing cold, without the green carpeted valleys of its siblings.

"What's that island called?" Neil yelled up, with an outstretched arm.

The little man swivelled with his machete pointing out. "That is Makam-Raja; The temple of Kings," he said, proudly.

"I think your boss, Mr Darcy owns that," Neil shouted.

"Nobody *owns Makam-Raja*, Mister Blake!" he said, waving his machete. "I told you that it is sacred land. It holds the tomb of the great warrior King, it must never be disturbed."

Neil swiped his glistening forehead and plodded on. The squawking of birds had been replaced by intermittent rustling in the undergrowth.

"The clearing is ahead now, Mister Blake," the guide called down. "You wanna see the ancient well, where they found the bodies of the girls?" he beamed.

"No, I've-err heard all about it, I don't need to see it, thanks. Let's just get to the resort shall we," Neil said, with a high-cheeked grin.

"Ok, it is still very smelly near the well. But Mr Darcy's dogs, they like coming here, no!" he said, with a broken laugh.

"Darcy has dogs?" Neil said.

"Yes, he uses them in the hunt and does not feed them for days before; Basil and Sybill," the short man said, with a titter. "You know of Fawlty Towers, Mister Blake?"

"Yes, of course; *Don't mention the war!*" Neil said, to the blank-faced man.

"There are still bones there, near the Well. The police didn't take everything away," he said, before turning to thrash the bracken at his waist.

"I thought Darcy might get shut down after that," Neil shouted, above the chopping. "After all, it was on *his island*?"

"But they didn't catch him, no," he said, sniggering. "Besides, the girls were '*of the devil*', they need to be taken," he added, with a finger tapping his temple.

"Of the devil?" Neil said, before fly-swatting again.

"Mister Darcy, he only takes devil-girls," he said, with an eye-twitch.

"But, *devil-girls*, come on!" Neil said, with a frown.

His guide backed up, stepping clear of the coarse fern and took a few strides down the slope towards Neil. "You *are* part of the *inner sanctum*, Mister Blake?" he said, his eyes bulging.

"Look, I've paid a lot of money to be here, my friend!" Neil said, finger-wagging.

"You know the password, Mister Blake?" he said in a sharp change of tone, with his machete loosely pointed at Neil.

Neil, shaking slightly with sweat beads streaming down to his neck, said, "*Heterodox.*"

The little man's crooked face softened, releasing a broad smile. He spun, marching ahead with the blade swinging at his side. Sparkling beads sprinkled the still air as Neil finger-swiped his glossy forehead.

"We can cut through here," he said, turning from his bush chopping. "It circles the well and lead out to the resort trail, by the river. Only ten minutes from there, Mister Blake, sir."

Neil nodded, poking his thumb up. *Thank Christ for that!*

CHAPTER 71

The gravelly road that the three wheeler took from the five star hotel to the Stacion du-Gardia could barely be described as a lane. Tom Broad felt every bump of its stony terrain whilst being bounced around in the back of the tuk-tuk-like vehicle.

His pained expression in back-clutching stagger from his ride was faded by the warmth of his greeting upon arrival at the local Police station.

"Mister Tom Broad!" Chief Massoon cried out from the side entrance to the law enforcement offices. "Come straight through my good friend. You my fellow Columbo, yeah!" he beamed.

Tom nodded politely at a young guy behind a glass-screened desk as he was ushered through the reception area. He gratefully took the beaker of water offered to him by another man who looked like the twin of the man at reception.

"Thank you for agreeing to meet with me, Chief Massoon," Tom said slowly, mindful of his pronunciation as they headed toward a room in the far corner of the open plan space.

"Please, it's Javeer," the Chief said, shoving his door to open a little wider. "And I call you, Starskey, or maybe Hutch, yeah?" he added, with a gravely Sid-James chortle.

"Tom is fine thanks, Javeer," Tom said, with a thin smile.

"Now, I am happy to help you if I can. Please take a seat," he said, with an arm around the British detective's shoulder, steering him into his cluttered little office.

"Chi-Chi, some tea please for our esteemed guest," Javeer shouted back through the doorway.

"I have another hotel pick-up to do, boss?" Chi-Chi said, appearing at the door.

"That can wait a little longer. Tea first, then you can go," Javeer said.

Tom cleared some papers from his chair, placed them on the desk and sat down, having first brushed the dust from his seat. "How's law and order been in these parts," he asked, with a smile.

"Oh, very good. Very quiet, you know. Small Islands, no trouble," Javeer said, scratching his chin with his forefinger and thumb. "No need for Popeye Doyle, yeah!" he added, followed by the same croaky cackle.

"Yes, I'm sure," Tom said, easing his notebook from his breast pocket.

"How about you, in England? You have many murders to solve, no?" Javeer asked, leaning across his paper-strewn desk.

"Yes, it's never quiet, I'm afraid," Tom said. "But, if we could get straight to it, Javeer?"

Javeer shuffled bundles of paperwork together, shoving them into a reluctant desk drawer. "Yes-yes, tell me why you came here, to our little paradise," Javeer said, beaming at Tom. "No holidays for you, Inspector Clouseau, huh?" he added with a throaty chuckle.

"It's about Mr Darcy, Roman Darcy. I assume you know of him?" Tom said, straightening up.

"Yes, of course, I know Roman. Everyone knows Mister D!" Javeer said.

"Then you'll know about the murders that took place on the island of El-Marzie, and that Darcy stood accused of these crimes?" Tom said, laying his palms on the desktop.

"El-Marney, you mean, Tom!" Javeer said, with a titter.

"Yes.. well following the trial, Darcy and his two acquaintances were acquitted. Are you aware of all this?" Tom said.

"But Mister D, he was never responsible for these killings, how you English say; Storm-in-teacup!" Javeer said, sniggering.

"It was a massacre of young women on this, El-marzee, an island owned by Darcy!" Tom said, staring stern-faced at the Chief. "There were only three survivors, Javeer."

"These ladies were all Mister D's staff, he nearly lost everything," Javeer said. "We believe it is the work of crazed tourists that take too many drugs, no!"

"Javeer, the girls were identified as having been kidnapped from countries across the globe."

"Not kidnapped, Tom, no! They come to work in paradise islands, they love it here," Javeer said, pointing at a faded poster on his wall, mapping the Archipelago. "How Kojak says it, 'Who loves ya, baby!'" he added, with a head-tilting wink.

Tom glared across the desk. "The girls were raped and tortured, they were held captive, Javeer! It's shocking that nobody has been imprisoned for these crimes."

"Yes, nasty business, some bad men that Roman had to dismiss. It was not good for tourism; two hotels went bust," Javeer said, leaning back in his oversized chair. "But as you say, Mister D was acquitted by the English court.

The best in the world, no, Mr Sherlock," he added with a tittering smirk.

"And since that trial Darcy's co-accused Jamal Jackson, has been murdered and Pierre Lebouf is missing," Tom snapped back, with fingers splaying the desk.

"I know these men, yes. Very sad, what happened. They too bring great prosperity to these shores," Javeer said, with shrugged expression.

"Look Javeer, let's cut to it here. Given what happened to his business partners, we believe Darcy is in danger. Our chief suspect, Arabella Maxwell, arrived here a few days ago. She was dropped off by boat at El-Marcie two nights ago," Tom said.

"Mr Darcy, he knows how to look after himself, he is fine, I'm sure," Javeer said.

"I have a legal commision from the UK to ensure Darcy's safety, with articles of extradition," Tom said, sliding folded papers from the side pocket of his cargos. "The UK needs your help here, Javeer," Tom said, in a sharpening tone, passing him the document.

"I'll level with you here, Tom," Javeer said, his tiny hands flattening the papers out on his desk. "We don't interfere with Roman and his work, he brings much wealth to locals. He is the number one employer."

"That order gives us the power to extradite.." Tom, finger pointing, started to explain.

"These papers have no authority here, Tom," Javeer shot back. "Besides, I know you don't want to help Roman, you want to arrest him, close him down again, Mister RoboCop!"

"Javeer, we just need your support in checking on Darcy's safety. A few men and a boat to take us over to El-Maarr.."

"NO. No, I won't do that!" Javeer said, crossing his arms. "He has important guests this weekend. If you want, I can call and check on him?" he added, with a little head-wobble.

"Yes, please do so, thank you," Tom said, with a wide-eyed nod at the corner of the desk.

"Okay, okay," Javeer said, grabbing his telephone handset and punching zero-one, then the speaker-phone symbol. He laid the receiver on the desk and sat back re-folding his stumpy arms. Tom slipped the document back into his trouser pocket and sipped at his beaker of water. Both men listened intently to the pitchy ringing, drrr-drrr-drrr. Drr-drr-..

"He's not there. I told you it's a busy time for Mister D," Javeer said, stretching to return the handset to its cradle.

"Hello, Javeer. It's Joel," came a whispered voice.

"Ahh, hello Joel. I have a British policeman here asking that I check everything is ok, with Roman?" Javeer said. "Has he been contacted by a girl name Maxwell?" he added, with an embarrassed tittering.

"Yes, she is here.." a muffled voice said before a thud, and the line went dead.

PART XI – VANISHED

CHAPTER 72

The vegetation was at its most dense here, with bracken standing beyond head height. It tumbled without resistance to his blade, stacking in huge swathes to either side.

The little man hacked away, clearing a pathway to the peak where the majesty of the island unveiled itself.

"Wow! That is incredible," Neil said, aghast at the wondrous vista.

Sparkling clear waters cascaded in glistening brilliance over smooth stones at the crown of a three-tiered waterfall. Blooms of every shade swept curtain-like from its rocky walls. The trundling waters babbled onward into a winding stream.

Tropical flowers festooned the lush greenery that carpeted the undulating landscape. Their beauty was magnified by the orange sunset in a kaleidoscope of colour filling the valley.

"You see, the Garden of Eden does exist, yes," the man said, sleeve-patting his brow.

"Indeed it does!" Neil mused, *But God couldn't stop evil seeping in.*

As they stood, two squawking parrots swooped low overhead, their wide-winged flaps breezed the ducking men as they swept majestically into the vale in a blaze of primary colours. It didn't seem possible for a hotel to be here, somewhere so serenely beautiful, where nature flourished.

"Lots of wildlife here!" Neil said. "Are we getting close now?"

"Only ten minutes from here, Mister Blake."

"I'm sure you said that ten minutes ago," Neil said.

The man ploughed on, snaking a route down to the river that lay glimmering below them. Within minutes they were at its bank where Neil dropped to one knee, splashing his face and neck. The guide stood watching him with the machete at his side.

"God, I needed that!" Neil said, glancing up at him. He scooped again at the refreshing clear waters, soaking to the crook of his forearms and sloshing his face again. "Okay to drink, do you think?"

"*No drink*, Mister Blake," he said, headshaking. "Investigation party, they say it is contaminated. Dead girl lay in it for many days."

"Jesus, you could have mentioned that before!" Neil said, bouncing to his feet.

The men continued along the towpath that meandered the river edge, before crossing it downstream where large stones sat proud of the water's surface. In the distance a faint bellowing echoed into the valley, an odd sounding cry.

"Sounds like a wolf?" Neil said, raising his eyebrows.

"Something is not right, Claude usually meets me here and takes the guests into the resort," the little man said. "Maybe he is busy with another guest. No problem, Mister Blake, I'll take you."

The two headed on toward an impressive copse of trees, boasting pink-leafed blooms the size of dinner plates. Their low hanging branches bore brightly coloured fruit.

"A little sustenance, maybe?" Neil said, pointing at the plump fruit drooping above them.

"That is *sasanam*, Mister Blake," the man said, with a wonky grin. "Is poison!"

Neil instantly released his hold on the branch. Its shake showered them confetti-like in budding white blossom. A sudden triple-layered howl took Neil's breath away as it echoed the trees around them.

"What the hell is that?"

His guide started tittering, "It's just Basil and Sybil, Mister Darcy's dogs."

"At the risk of sounding like a six-year-old.. are we nearly there yet?" Neil said, fixing a stern gaze on his guide.

Just as the little man raised his hand to indicate their direction of travel, Neil's iPhone buzzed, ruffling his Khaki shorts. He turned, stepping away and slapped it to his ear.

"Go ahead," Neil said, taking a few more steps back along the trodden path.

"We've been told that Maxwell was taken to the island by a friend, but the local Police won't help us, they're firmly up Darcy's arse," Tom said. "Seems he pays well, if you get my drift!"

"Yep, similar story here," Neil said, peeking back at his guide.

"Their Police Commandant phoned Darcy but only spoke briefly to his assistant, Joel. He confirmed that Maxwell was there, before the call was cut off," Tom said, adding, "How's it going over there?"

"Apart from being on the set of Fantasy Island, you mean," Neil whispered, scratching the back of his calf. "By all accounts it sounds like Darcy's carried on where he left off here; they've got girls and wealthy customers. The trial was merely an inconvenience!"

"Well according to the police chief here, the massacre over there was apparently the work of drug-crazed tourists!" Tom said.

"Oh no boss, my guy knows it was Darcy," Neil said, cupping his hand to his mouth. "But he's brainwashed the locals into believing it's for the greater-good, to rid us of devil women. It's like some sort of deranged cult!"

"*The greater good*! Christ Almighty, it's like we're on another planet over here," Tom said, striding into the coolness of the hotel atrium. "Well, just remember Turvs, it's an 'observe only' op. Don't intervene unless there's a risk to life," Tom said, nodding at the receptionist and mouthing '*two-five-one*'.

"It is an absolutely breathtaking place though, boss. I mean, if you ever pictured heaven.."

"All right, spare me the tourist jargon.. are you actually at the resort yet?"

"Not yet, would you believe, but I'm told we're only *TEN minutes* away!" Neil said softly, smiling back at his guide. "We had to take a longer route to avoid the *Well*, and my meet and greet guy, Claude, hasn't shown up."

"Is that irregular or suspicious, and what on earth's that noise?" Tom said.

"My chap doesn't seem too bothered about it," Neil said. "He's gonna take me in, and that's just Mr Darcy's dogs," he added matter-of-factly.

"Well they don't sound too friendly, Neil. I don't want you blindly walking into danger over there," Tom snapped. "By the way have you heard from Spence?"

"No, I thought she was with you. Have you tried the bar!" Neil quipped.

"I left her here to phone the shrink, Forsythe. He's done some research into Darcy's '*ultimate killing experience*', that you're attending. Apparently he's also got intel on the other guests that you're going to be mingling with," Tom said.

"Yeah, I could do with that as soon as.."

"Look, I've gotta dash," Tom said, adding, "We just need confirmation that Darcy is alive and well, and eyes-peeled for Maxwell."

"As soon as I get to the resort I will look out for our esteemed host," Neil murmured, turning back to his guide, who was standing waiting. "And if Darcy has got Maxwell, I'm sure he'd be delighted to hand her over."

"Let's hope it's as simple as that!" Tom said as he headed toward the hotel restaurant. "HQ now has access to ShareCom CCTV covering all mainland exit points here and the airport."

"The net is closing on her," Neil whispered, waving the short man on. "Leave it to me, boss," he added, dabbing the end call button.

The crazed barking boomed ever-louder, reverberating the trees, sending feather-flustered birds from their nests. The pitchy squeals of branch-swinging monkeys joined the rising cacophony, as they scrambled from the canopy. Neil stared up in awe at the loose-limbed animals.

"This is getting kinda like, Jurassic Park!" he said, to the chuckling little man, ahead of him.

CHAPTER 73

The elderly gentleman slumped heavily on the desktop at reception. Greeting him with a welcoming smile, the receptionist was swift in issuing his room card and offering iced water.

"*Jeremy?*" Tom said, in a tone he thought he'd lost to post-puberty.

Relieving his aching back, Jeremy Forsythe dropped his duffle bag to the marbled floor and tugged a large yellowing handkerchief out of his corduroy trousers. The Met's senior criminal psychologist turned whilst dabbing his brow.

"It *is* you!" Tom said, striding over. "I was literally just talking about you. What on earth are you doing over here?"

"Hello Tom," Jeremy said, offering a limp handshake. "Yes, a bit of a way to come, and rather hot!"

Tom, aware of some unwanted attention he had drawn, grabbed Jeremy's bag and ushered him towards the seating at the back of the foyer.

"I'm not sure, if you've been brought up to speed yet, Tom," Jeremy said, under a soft wheeze. "But things are heating up somewhat on this one. There's been something of an international fervour, shall we say."

"Wait, before you start," Tom said, with a hand raised. "Did you get a call from DI Spencer? Only she appears to be missing."

"No, I didn't, but then I have been travelling. Poor signal and all," Jeremy said. "Missing, you say? That is rather worrying, given what's been going on over here."

"Yes, indeed it is," Tom said, perching on a small sofa. "But you were saying, the latest?"

"The Chief Super wanted me here, he authorised my attendance last night. It seems something of a cult has been established on the islands here," Jeremy said, whilst removing his tweed jacket.

Seeing Jeremy's sweat laden shirt Tom waved over a waiter and ordered two icy drinks, and a pot of tea at the professor's insistence.

"You mean on El-Marnez?" Tom said.

The elderly expert loosened his necktie and slowly rolled the sleeves of his pale blue shirt that was a considerably darker shade in patches.

"*El-Marney*, Makam Raja, possibly others," Jeremy said, peering over his glasses. He unbuckled the side pocket of his rucksack and placed a notebook on the table.

"French intelligence informs us that a number of their nationals are still held on these islands. These girls remained captive even after the arrest of Jackson, Lebouf and Darcy," Jeremy said, sliding his tortoiseshell glasses to the bridge of his nose.

He opened his pad and licked his finger, flicking at the pages. Jeremy cleared a crackly cough from his throat before sipping from the ice crammed glass that had arrived promptly.

"It seems our French counterparts had an undercover operative infiltrate their operation following the massacre on El-Marney," Jeremy said softly.

"Something that we should have done!" Tom said.

"Quite," Jeremy said, leaning to rummage again in his rucksack. "The TikTokTrio's 'business' interests were simply held in abeyance, pending their release. French Police say they have verified images of girls as young as twelve being held there," Jeremy said.

"Spencer was right about all this.. these guys just carried on," Tom said. "Aided and abetted, I might add, by the local authorities here. I've just spoken to their head of Police; corrupt is too soft a word!" he added, shaking his head.

"It's a little worse than that, I'm afraid," Jeremy said, whilst pouring tea from a little silver pot. "They're very much part of the operation. The police here are not only protecting Darcy by providing security, they are actively kidnapping women and sending them to him. We have a whistle-blower."

"Bloody hell, it just gets worse!" Tom said, wide-eyed. "We're going to have to expose this and get government involvement to shut them down, and grant extradition orders."

"As I said, there's an international effort at hand, Tom. It's going to take time to pull everything together," Jeremy said, digging in his multi-pocketed rucksack. "But we do have an intercontinental sealed warrant, for the immediate arrest of Roman Darcy."

Jeremy passed a crumpled but official-looking document across the glass table. He moistened his index finger to clear twiggy grey eyelashes that were obscuring his vision.

"This should do the trick in sidestepping Jurisdictional nuances and officialdom!" Jeremy said, with smiling eyes peering over his thick framed glasses.

"But even with this, it ain't going to be easy!" Tom said, sipping at his fizzing glass. "We have a dossier on Darcy, he's something else.. aside from physically being quite a unit. At least we have Turvey over there, on the

338

island."

"You really mustn't underestimate this chap, Tom. He's quite the psychopath!" Jeremy said, retightening the strings of his duffel bag.

"Ok, let's have it then; what else have you got on him?" Tom said, checking his shoulders before leaning forward.

"Reviewing the prosecution files from the trial and the French intelligence was interesting. But coupling that with our access to their darkweb enterprises, proved fascinating," Jeremy said, tongue wetting his lower lips.

"Just the headlines please, Jeremy," Tom said, aware of the shrink's enjoyment of vocabulary.

"The barbarity with which Darcy is treating these women is beyond one's conscious imagination. It's inhumane. He's a sociopath at the farthest end of the scale," Jeremy said, crossing his legs. "Pent-up frustrations from his time on remand appear to have triggered an almost tribal savagery. Darcy's the most brutal of sadists that I've come across"

"Yeah but Jeremy, we already knew what he was like, and what they were getting up to.."

"*Before,* these men were engaged in the sex-slave trade; kidnapping and trafficking girls, selling them on," Jeremy interjected. "*Now,* they've changed the game. Girls are selected for their athleticism - to run! It's part of a new, fetish-driven perversion, a hunt to kill women, and their wealthy customers are flocking to it."

"Whoa, are we sure this French guy's got this right?"

"He's seen it first hand, Tom, and there's another weekend of hunting coming up!" Jeremy said, finishing his tea. "Humans crave evermore adventurous stimuli; it's always been within us. Think about the Christians in the Colosseum, in Rome. It's recorded that after a time the crowds dwindled, bored with watching Gladiators slaying each other. They sought something new, more exhilarating, increasingly savage; so they introduced animals."

"Wait, we're actually talking about wild animals here?"

"We are.. Darcy's been collecting them for years. Illegally imported, he has them shipped directly to the island where he keeps them in a small compound," Jeremy said.

"They should have thrown away the key when they had the lunatic," Tom said, with a hefty puff of his cheeks as he got to his feet.

"Darcy's childhood is interesting, and undoubtedly holds the key to his psychopathy," Jeremy said, flicking through his notes.

"As ever, Jeremy, I'm sure it does," Tom said, sidestepping the table. "But I have no burning desire, or the time, to understand his inner workings. Particularly when I have one detective that's disappeared without trace and another that's about to meet this madman!"

CHAPTER 74

The shards of light that pierced the wooded area widened as its trees tapered to the clearing beyond. As they strode clear of the treeline, meadowland lay ahead of them, sloping to some low-rise buildings in the near distance.

"Land-O-Hoy!..Is that civilization I see," Neil said, oozing sarcasm.

"Yes, Mister Blake, we are nearly at the resort now," his guide said. "It looks very quiet there."

The dog barking had faded to a scalded whimper. A silence fell about the two men as they marched on with renewed energy. They blazed a trail as they ankle-thrashed the open grassland. A deep hum of insects whirred overhead.

"At least that dog's piped down," Neil said, speeding up to stride alongside his guide. "Maybe it's finally been fed!"

Their boots swished noisily through the thick grass, sending crickets springing from their blades. The little man unclipped the walkie-talkie from his belt, thumb-tapping its side as it crackled into life.

"Hello Claude? Anybody available for a guest welcome, please?" he said, before tapping again. "Hello Claude, can you hear me?"

The resort came into sharper focus, gleaming in the fading brilliance of the day. Its facade of whitewashed walls, broken only by tinted patio doors. The complex formed a shallow pyramid over its three floors with a small belltower peaking at its centre. Below it, a balcony swept around the top floor suite. The glass doors on the ground floor reflected a dazzling burnt-orange sunset across the field. A soft grumbling reverberated from the terrace area.

"It is very strange, nobody being here, I don't understand what is happening, Mister Blake," the little man said, screwing his face. He resembled a grumpy bulldog.

"It's like an oasis in the desert!" Neil said, spotting a sparkling swimming pool behind the resort's boundary wall.

"You want a drink, Mister Blake?" the guide said, offering him a water canister.

Neil swigged heartily, nearly draining it before leaning forward to pour its remnants over the back of his neck. The little man continued tapping away at his device, yelling Claude every few paces, ever louder. They strolled through the open gate, noticing the walls had lines of electric fencing along the top of them. A long shiny tiled path led to the main entrance directly in front of them. The area to their right was a gardener's delight, whilst the other side was hard landscaped around the pool.

"Oh shiit, Oh shiit!" the little man said, instantly spellbound by the sight to his left.

"What, the fuck, is that!" Neil said, his eyes nearly removed from their lids.

On the terraced area beyond the pool, a huge black pelt rocked gently over the open-bodied remains of another animal. A breathy growl resonated the walls around it.

"That iz B-Basil.. or Sy-Sybil, Mister Blake," he stammered, with eyes fixed on the bloodsoaked scene.

They stood statuesque, mesmerised, listening in morbid fascination to the brutal sounds of flesh being ripped from bones. The savage scene, barely a stone's throw from them. Ragged and defleshed, the dog's limbs flopped lifeless as the predator feasted.

"I don't mean the fucking dog, Manuel!" Neil said, under a thick whisper.

Huge flexed paws slashed mercilessly again, opening the canine's guts with the ease of a child clawing wet sand. A deeper guttural rattle held the jaw-dropped men transfixed as its snout disappeared in a flash of white, into the Doberman's carcass.

"Th-that i-iz Y-Yogi, Mister. Yogi, he not supposed to be out of his cage. This is bad, very bad."

"No fucking kidding!" Neil whispered. "Quietly, let's get inside before it notices us."

The guide turned quickly, brushing an urn, one of many lining the path and sending it tumbling from its stand. Its clattering shatter drew the attention of the black bear, its huge head instantly lifted. It reared-up, releasing a gut-wrenching bellow.

"Jesus Christ!" Neil murmured. "Just take it slow, nice and steady to the building."

The bear roared, bouncing from the mutilated dog in one smooth bound. Table legs scraped and a chair toppled as it cleared its path to the men. Its shiny black pelt glistened as its shoulders rippled with every stride towards them.

"Run. Run for your life!" Neil yelled, sprinting for the doors to the building that were still a good tennis court's length away.

But the guide spun, darting the other way, back down the path, as if aware of a better escape route. Maybe hoping their splitting-up would aid his escape. Neil turned, blowing hard as he clasped the door handle, relieved to see that the animal had veered away.

"Where are you going?" he hollered. "There's nowhere to hide out there!"

Neil stood, watching as the bear pounded through the gateway and into the open field. It was closing fast on the guide, despite his legs almost blurring road-runner-like. But the bear's bounding motion across the grassy terrain was majestic, its speed was breathtaking. Within seconds it pounced, barrelling hard into his back, rolling with him like a bowling ball.

It straddled the flailing man, with a front claw clamping and piercing his fleshy neck. Neil watched helplessly, wincing as the animal buried the man's thrashing head into its jaws. It mauled furiously, ripping from side-to-side, tearing the man's face clean from his skull.

Neil shoved hard at the double doors, then tried yanking them forcefully toward him. There was barely a rattled movement, they were locked tight. Jesus Christ. He clattered a fist repeatedly on the doorframe, then hammered with both hands harder.

Peering through the tinted glass, the reception desk was vacant, there was not a soul in sight. The place looked pristine, immaculate, like a showhome ready for viewings. Still clasping the door handle, as if a lifebelt at sea, he spun, scanning all around him. The entire resort resembled the Marie Celeste.

He stepped back and lifted another Urn from its stand whilst casting more than a fleeting glance at the still mauling bear. Neil flung the vase two-handed at the glass door. It rebounded with a soft bump off the tempered glass, smashing in large fragments at his feet.

You've gotta be kidding me!

CHAPTER 75

"Screw you, Putin!"

"Abso-fuckin-lutely!" she said, pausing behind the middle-aged guy sitting at the cocktail bar, in the Airports VIP suite. "Somebody should have taken that guy out years ago."

The television screens here were all set to international news. A bedraggled war correspondent reported from the bombed streets of yet another besieged European city. Hard hatted and wearing an oversized padded vest, she updated CNN viewers on the dictator's latest conquest, all in the name of The Motherland.

"Sixty five people in that residential block, women and kids, for Christ's sake," he said, with a cursory glance to his shoulder.

She stepped to lean against the bar. He shuffled a half-turn on his stool for a closer look. "N-no survivors, they're saying," he added, struck by the attractive woman, staring up at the screen alongside him.

She clocked him, in the mirror-backed bar, eyeing her. "That's Hitler mark two, right there!" she said, as a picture of the Russian leader filled the screen.

The man, in his forties, was sporting a diamond encrusted wedding band. His gaze meandered her body as he dabbed a napkin at the corner of his mouth.

"I'm Josie, Josie Brown," she said, turning and offering her slender hand.

He almost went to kiss it, but instead shook it softly and introduced himself, offering to buy her a drink. She accepted, sliding into the leather barstool beside him and hooking her rucksack over its armrest.

"A vodka coke would be great, thanks Ted," she said, with a smile that lit her face. He fleeted a glance over her shapely thighs as she folded them towards him. She laid her fingers on his broad shoulder, squeezing it. "I have to say, it's great to finally meet a fellow American out here!"

He chuckled a little nervously. "Likewise, honey," he said, before turning to wave the bartender over and pulling a thick wallet from his jacket.

"Hmm.. southwest, I'd wager?" she mused, with index finger below her glossy-lipped pout.

He chortled, "You got me pegged there, honeybun. Texan, born and bred."

The bartender plonked two tumblers on coasters that he'd thrown down like a croupier, and placed a small bowl of olives between the crushed-iced drinks. She beamed a thank you nod at the barman and took a sip of her drink. The doorman was back at his post, attending to some new arrivals at the lounge's entrance door.

"Now how's about a pretty little thing like you, I'm guessing west coast?" he said, with an open-mouthed grin.

"Oh, state to state. Career chasing mostly, but I guess Kansas is still home. Regular little Dorothy at heart," she said, with a head-tilting wink.

"That's some impressive looking Stetson, you'ze got there. Matching your suit an'all," she said, noticing the huge rimmed grey hat sat on the next stool down. "Business trip I'm assuming?" she said, with widening eyes.

"Was supposed to be, but got cancelled late notice. I didn't even get a chance to see the sights," Ted said, slurping his drink.

"That's a darn shame, you missed one hell of a country, they got here. It's got all sorts going on," she said, stirring her drink and laying the cocktail stick on her bottom lip.

"Yeah, I heard the islands are awesome," he said, loosening the strings of his bolo tie.

"Well, get yourself comfy. I guess I'm gonna have to tell you all about it," she said, clinking her glass on his. "Looks like we're gonna have plenty enough time!" she added, eye-pointing at the departure screen, set above the optics. It was filled with red-flashing lines.

Ted slugged, draining his tumbler and waggled a finger at the bartender.

Thirty minutes earlier Bella Maxwell, having successfully cleared security check-in, paced through the crowded concourse. The airport departure monitors were filled with the red-flashing word, Delayed. There were just the two yellow-worded notices reading, Proceed to gate, both short haul destinations; Thailand and Papua.

"Hi, do you mind if I borrow your pen? Luggage labels!" Bella said, with a soft smile at the bookshop attendant.

She had repeated the biro request at the counters of several shops in the terminal and pocketed a marker pen from the clerk at security. Bella had also acquired scissors and a bottle of bleach from a service trolley that had been left unattended outside one of the washrooms.

Under a peaked cap and with her denim jacket high-collared, Bella now sat centrally in a long row of hard-backed seats, disappearing amidst the child-heavy families to either side. But more importantly from her vantage she could see the silver-plated double doors to the VIP lounge. One door had been pinned back by an officious looking man in a light grey suit and chauffeur style hat. He stood, scanning the concourse every few minutes with his clipboard in hand.

"Sorry love, he's just overtired," a middle-aged woman said, with a weary smile.

Bella nodded sweetly before dipping her face back into her crumpled paperback. The toddler's puffy-eyed mother hauled the screaming child to her knee and bent again to scoop his toy car. The father didn't flinch from his slumber on a seat three along.

Television monitors were fixed at thirty metre intervals, running the length of the concourse. All were muted with subtitles in Jawa rolling the bottom of each screen. A woman was reporting from Makassar, one of the mainland's busiest ports. Over her shoulder images of a large white yacht anchored off the coast, zoomed in and out of unsteady focus.

Another guest arrived at the VIP suite's doors, quickly followed by an elderly couple. The attendant greeted them with a pulled grin after a careful check of his clipboard, before stepping theatrically to one side with extended arm.

And there it was!

Flicking in symmetry the length of the multi-screened concourse, the face she didn't want to see; her own. The picture had been pulled from her employer's website, they took it on her first day there. Seeing it was forever scarred by the humiliation she had suffered only minutes earlier at the building site.

A blonde bob curled her cheeks, framing her face. Open-mouthed, almost in laughter, her sparkling smile lit-up the screens. It was unmistakably her. Bella hunched her shoulders and squeezed hard at the peak of her baseball cap.

A text-feed delay meant that Bella's picture had disappeared from the screen by the time her name, Arabella Maxwell, appeared below the live TV reporter. Bella recognised the Javanese words, 'Polisi menduga ingin' alongside her name; 'Police suspect wanted'. She tilted the tip of her hat to her nose.

The doorman hauled the VIP Suite doors together, disappearing behind them. Bella shouldered her rucksack and headed over, sidestepping the toy strewn floor. Clasping the steel-handled door, she eased it ajar, the coast was clear. Bella slipped inside the exclusive lounge.

Soft music drifted across a low-lit area to her right that boasted some sumptuous looking sofas, few of which were taken. Beyond that a red carpeted restaurant with white tablecloth seating was roped-off, Oscars-style. The potpourri laden glassware couldn't disguise the waft of garlic.

The doorman's clipboard lay on a glass-topped table beside her. Bella scanned the listing, flicked it from the front page and penned, 'J. Brown' at the bottom. Picture-signage indicated the restrooms were in the far corner of the suite. On her immediate left, tucked behind an impressive row of Yuccas was a swish-looking marble topped Bar.

A well dressed, man-mountain of a guy was sat on the middle one, of five barstools, at the mirrored bar. Gotcha! Bella stuffed her jacket and cap into the rucksack and headed over.

CHAPTER 76

"I'm telling you, there's not a soul here, it's like the Bermuda triangle!"

"They can't have just vanished! Maybe this hunt-thing has already started," Tom said.

"Boss, please listen to me, the only thing here is a very large bear that's roaming free! There's absolutely nobody else here; no Darcy, no Maxwell, no guests, staff, anyone!" Neil said, puffing as he marched the peachy corridors of the resort.

Neil had managed to gain access via a fire door to the kitchens at the rear of the property, slamming it closed behind him.

"Don't panic Turvs, we're coming to get you," Tom said, with eyes flicking back to the TV screen in the hotel foyer. "Darcy's hit the news over here, they've got crews at the harbour reporting something about his yacht that's anchored off the coast. God they love that guy."

"Jamal Jackson's something of a cult hero here too, probably all those football betting syndicates. They've got his signed framed picture everywhere," Neil said, pacing the hall.

"By the way, they know that Maxwell's our prime suspect, they've got her face plastered across the telly. Probably heard it from UK broadcasts," Tom said

"Well maybe she's on that boat," Neil said, striding yet another pot-plant dotted corridor.

"I'm heading to the old town harbour now, see what all the fuss is about,"

Tom said.

"Did I mention that there's a fucking huge bear on the loose over here, that's still chewing on my tour guide!" Neil said, opening another door to an empty bedroom. "You need to get a chopper over here boss, and bring guns!" He stepped cautiously into a larger suite, checking inside the swish-door wardrobes.

"I'm on it Neil. Just stay calm and search the building," Tom said, rolling his eyes at Jeremy Forsythe, sitting opposite.

"Weird thing is all the guest rooms still have all their stuff in them. Clothes, shoes, all their toiletries," Neil said, peering into the mirror-tiled wetroom.

"Like I said, the guests are probably just out exploring the Island," Tom said.

"Well, I ain't going back outside boss," Neil said, pounding the next corridor. "Not with Yogi still out there, and I ain't even met Basil yet!"

"Look, you're safe inside, Turvs. Just try and get as much evidence about their operation as you can. Laptops, phones, anything that you can pull from hard drives. Have you checked Darcy's office yet and the staff areas?" Tom said.

"There's a third floor, '*Private Apartment*' sign up ahead. I'll take a look, but I aint happy about hanging around here, it's bloody creepy. You've seen The Shining!" Neil said, bounding the shiny-tiled steps.

"I'm going to try the local cops again, hopefully they'll be more helpful if they hear Roman Darcy is missing," Tom said. "Have you heard from Spence by the way?"

"No, but I've been kinda busy!" Neil said, puffing as he hurdled the final steps.

"Yes, of course," Tom said, getting to his feet. "Look, let me make some calls and I'll get back to you as soon as."

"Please do, boss," Neil said, leaning against a door with a sign that read, *'Presidential Suite'*.

CHAPTER 77

FOUR HOURS EARLIER

Seven women had hurried wide-eyed from the resort, warily boarding the luxury Yacht. Incredibly, Roman Darcy had told them they could leave the island.

"*It's not enough!*" Bella snapped. "Grant the others their freedom, or you'll get nothing from me."

Darcy spluttered hard to clear his tightening throat, his deterioration had been swift. He sat slumped on his seat, his face a sickly concrete-grey.

"You've had this fuckin lot," Darcy said, waving vaguely in the direction of the skinny girls. "And that's enough!" he barked.

Bella paced the deck with a pained expression, staring at the fragile women. They looked fearful and broken, institutionalised by their captivity. Two of them wrapped their arms a little tighter around the youngest looking girl that had a blood soaked cloth wrapped around her wrist. They all wore matching outfits, shorts and vests in royal blue - the colour of Darcy's '*hosts*'.

"Your life's gotta be worth more than these few girls, Darcy," Bella snarled. "If you want that antidote, then I get the others. Or you *will die!*"

She tapped at the iPhone that she had snatched from Darcy's assistant, Joel. "There it is! The vial is waiting for you portside," Bella said, waving it at him. Her friend Pascal was on the screen, with the harbour behind him.

Pascal held a little glass bottle clamped between finger and thumb in front of his face. "Release the other girls and you'll live, Darcy," Bella said, now standing over him.

He slouched, floppy-limbed across the soft cushioned bench. Firing phlegm at her feet, he lurching to grab her, but she easily side-stepped his laboured move.

"It's pulsing your veins, filling your organs, weakening your every movement. It's like a boa-constrictor, tightening its grip with every breath you take, Darcy."

"You fu-fuck-ing bitch. You'll die for thh-isss," he slurred, with one hand grasping at the seating behind him. The acidic mucus burning the back of his throat, again coated his tongue. He spat hard, but couldn't shift it.

Bella leaned down, pointing into his face. "Like I told you, if I die, you die. Look at you, you're already halfway there. *Tick-tock*, your time's running out, Darcy!"

"Just do it, Roman," Joel pleaded, moving to stand alongside his boss, with laptop tucked under his arm. "We can start again with the syndicate."

"What the hell do you mean, syndicate?" Bella said, frowning at the tubby man.

"Ok, ha-have the b-bitches. Just do it, be-before I-I change mm-my..," Darcy said, in a hoarse croak. He clutched his throat, demanding, "Wa-water, war-ter!"

"Right, now open that fucking dome!" Bella barked at the sweaty little man. "You said you can control everything from that, so get to it."

Joel peeled open the laptop and perched himself on the end of the large table in the central area, between the stern sides. The women remained in huddled mass, boggle-eyed at Darcy.

"Ola, piscus, titana. Le giris a'la voyage," Joel yelled up at the Yacht's skipper. *"Pronto!"*

The captain shouted one word back before bounding down the gangway from the boat and sprinting the lengthy boardwalk.

"What'd you say to the boat driver?" Bella said.

"I told Nabrik to go and collect the girls and bring them here, quickly."

Joel tapped frantically at his laptop as Bella stepped behind him. The screen split into a number of CCTV-like boxes, each with a *HD* picture perfect image. Double-tapping on the image of the dome, it filled the screen.

Inside the sweltering glass globe the women lay listless on the gravely floor, two of them sat propped against the totem-pole. Their faces glistened in a colourful sheen of sweat; the warpaint having melted. Outside its thick wall the male guests remained, seated in a shady area to one side, with drinks in hand, chatting, laughing. Seemingly unaware of the cancellation of their *Hunt.*

"Get that fucking thing open, now!" Bella demanded. "They're dying in there, you moron."

"Yes-yes, I'm attending to it," Joel said, as a bead of sweat trickled quickly from his temple, disappearing into the folds of his chin.

He keyed a four-digit code into the laptop, before bouncing a fat finger on the enter button. The glass door moved, tilting just a fraction, changing its angle of reflection of the sun.

"Is that it!" Bella fumed. There was no reaction, or movement at all from the women who lay lifeless, dying inside the furnace-like dome. "Can they even see that it's open?"

"They see it," Joel said, pointing a chubby finger at the monitor. One of the girl's turned in the direction of the door. Propping herself on an elbow she nudged another and staggering to her feet. "Besides, it makes a loud click when it's released."

"I h-hope they're all fu-fukin dead," Darcy stammered, his lips bluish. "W-water, I s-said, water!" Joel jumped to his feet, stretching to grab his bottle from the table.

"Sit back down!" Bella boomed, snatching the bottle from him. She rolled it down the deck to the women at the back of the boat. "These girls need water," she barked, ordering Joel to find more from the kitchen below.

The girls inside the dome were slowly hauling themselves to their feet, the first of them pushed to swing the door open fully. The men were pointing, laughing as the girls reached the exit, their heads lifting to gasp at the soft breeze. One was crawling on her hands and knees, another tugged the arm of a girl that remained prone.

Darcy had passed out. "Oi, Gonzo," Bella bellowed down the stairs to the rooms below deck. "You need to radio the skipper, I want all the girls collected from the *other pit* too!"

"There aren't any others."

"Bullshit! The *reds*, I think you tossers call them. Release those girls, or this piece of shit dies, here and now!" Bella snarled, sneering at the chubby man staring up at her.

"Ok-ok, I'll remove the pit cover and inform Nabrik, but please let me get Roman some water!"

Bella nodded, before refocusing on the laptop. "These girls are dying on their feet, they're gonna need transport."

"There's a caged truck that Claude uses to move the animals," Joel said, appearing on deck. "It would get them here quicker?"

"Do it!" Bella snapped, muttering *Animals!* as she stared at the CCTV. Joel radioed Nabrik.

Moments later a truck bounced across the meadow near the front of the resort, disappearing to reappear in the next image at the dome. Nabrik jumped out, speaking with some of the men whilst opening the caged doors at the back of the truck and ushering the women towards it. One by one, the girls clambered aboard before the truck juddered off toward pit 3. When the battered cattle truck finally cornered onto the soft, white sanded beach, Bella was waiting.

Amazement-filled eyes beamed over at Bella, seeing her standing there unguarded, free. Some looked bewildered. Tears wet the eyes of Monique, who blew a kiss from the back of the truck. Alongside her, the legend, Gloria, imprisoned on the Isle for longer than all, and suffering more than any. She gently nodded her approval, mouthing, *Magnifica.*

Gingerly, the long line of girls trudged barefoot towards the sand-dusted pontoon, before boarding the Yacht. Young Zoe flung her arms around Bella with tears streaming as she jumped from the rear of the truck. Muffled chatter rose as they joined the girls in blue at the rear of the boat, gazing at the sight of their captor and master, Roman Darcy, lying unconscious. Wiping to dry Zoe's cheeks, Bella helped her, and the last of the girls onboard.

Bella ordered Joel below deck for water and any foodstuff on board whilst she peered again at his laptop, clicking at the resort screened images. The plush reception area looked eerily vacant. Two guests were wandering the corridors, returning to their rooms, fearing their fun-packed day had come to an abrupt end.

The kitchen was empty, with gleaming silver surfaces and sinks, it looked brand new. Another image swept the swimming pool and terrace to the front, panning the meadows beyond. Three men were sat in conversation under a yellow parasol beside the pool.

"That's all there is below, there's no more food or drink," Joel said, appearing beside her.

"What do these do?" Bella said, pointing at *house-shaped* icons in the toolbar. One with a *bell* inside it, the other a *key*.

"That's the alarm and locking system for the entire resort. Don't mess about with that," Joel said, his eye-twitching. "Can I have my laptop back now?"

"Absolutely not," Bella said, shoving Joel's hand away. "You wanna save your boss, then I suggest we get this boat moving!"

"Can I at least get Roman some water now?" Joel said.

Darcy had deteriorated, it sounded like he was gargling his own phlegm. Joel lifted his head to sit upright alongside him and tip water to his lips, before shouting orders up to Nabrik. The boat's engine roared into life as the yacht lurched immediately from the jetty in a foamy departure.

Bella poked the alarm button symbol that started flashing red and white. In the distance an intermittent blaring echoed the island, like an air raid siren. The CCTV showed people inside the resort buildings making their way out.

"Pascal, we're on our way," Bella said into the iPhone. "ETA twenty minutes, twenty-nine women on board. See you soon, my friend." The girls huddled as one at the stern passing the water bottles between them.

Bella joined the women, reassuring the youngest looking girl who sat clutching her wrist. Darcy's beady eyes sparked back to life, he remained slumped in silence eyeballing the girls that now packed the rear of his luxury cruiser. They inched a little tighter, feeling his gaze.

"How did you get this injury, Maize?" Bella said, to the petrified slip of a girl.

Maize whispered into Bella's ear, "I had to feed the animals, and h-his dog Basil bit me."

Bella returned to the table and tapped at the laptop. She clicked again through the live camera footage, enlarging the darker image from an area of the resort that she didn't recognise. As she zoomed in on the picture, silver-barred cages came sharply into focus. A large pen housed two Doberman's that lay passive near the back of their cage.

Finger-widening, a shot of a smaller enclosure came into view. Bella neck-jolted from the screen to glare in disbelief at Darcy. "Really? You sick bastard!" she said, angling the laptop to face him.

Head shaking slowly, Bella's finger hovered over the *house* icon in the toolbar. The one with an image of a *key* inside it.

CHAPTER 78

A flotilla of boats churned frothy lines in their wake, breaking the glassy waters as they sped toward the huge white cruiser. Fisherman's tugs and all manner of tourist craft chased a number of news reporter-filled speedboats. The Polisi emblazoned vessel trailed them in a Dunkirk-like race across the crystal seas.

In the distance long skinny arms swung from the high sided luxury Yacht, like the tassels of a lampshade. But they weren't the usual bikini-clad, sun-shaded girls associated with sumptuous cruisers found in these waters. These women were rake thin, with bony hips poking high of ill-fitting shorts. With shoulder blades resembling coat hangers, from which their filthy vests flapped.

An hour earlier, the grossly disfigured body of Roman Darcy was discovered washed up on the shore near the fishing village of Ohaj-am. The large man's torso was pin-cushion-like in the multiple stab wounds that punctured it.

Darcy's face was disfigured beyond recognition. His jawline had been slashed Joker-like to his ears, the blade had ripped through his cheeks. The size of the flap-gaping lacerations exacerbated by flesh nibbling creatures, of sea or shore.

Cavernous eye sockets stared hauntingly skyward, terrifying the local children that found him, afloat in the shallow sandy brine. Darcy's eyes had been speared from their sockets, like seafood forked from shells, his face now resembling a Halloween mask.

A news reporter's boat pulled up alongside the Yacht, shouting up at the girls in a foreign tongue. With camera rolling and a photographer clicking alongside him, the scribe repeated his question, louder to the blank-faced girls. They looked confused, dazed, squinting down at the bobbing boats.

The formal identification of Roman Darcy was already underway at the Capitals morgue. His ravaged body had been transported in a convoy of official vehicles akin to a celebrity's funeral. A local fisherman had seen to the removal of blue crab from the body's cavity and blanket wafted, clearing the hum of lava laying Carrion flies.

Early identification was confirmed by village residents that lined the beach area around his corpse. Darcy's familiar animal print open-chested shirt barely clung to his shoulders. It was the only clothing found on him. His manhood was missing, hacked deep from its root, leaving no trace of maleness.

"We know Darcy is gone, we can come aboard, please?" he shouted, in broken English, repeating it in pigeon French. "We talk about what happen to you, no?"

A piercing siren from the Police boat drowned his words, as it closed in. The smaller vessels steered away to either side of the patrol boat as it passed between them, like a shoal of a fish on a shark's arrival. It took another two blasts of the siren before the reporter's speedboat engine was re-ignited, pulling away slowly.

"You is all free, you are safe. He doesn't hurt you anymore. You can go home now, yes!" the same reporter shouted up at the bleary-eyed women.

The head of police, Chief Javeer Mayisoon, bounded the steps hanging from the side of the Yacht. At the top rail, with pistol in hand, he spun around, waving the gun at the reporter's boat with some choice words. He repeatedly bellowed across the Yacht's deck, that 'Misses Maxwell' show herself, whilst directing his officers to search the cruiser.

Mayisoon radioed orders to the Stacion du-Gardia that they close the borders and send a patrol unit to the airport. He demanded the blank-faced women tell him where Misses Maxwell was, angrily firing his gun over their heads. The young women huddled tight, saying nothing.

CHAPTER 79

The ladies restroom in the airport's Premium lounge was lavish. A deep shelved make-up counter ran across the length of the far wall. Weighty scalloped mirrors hung from gold-linked chains, above each of the five shell-rimmed cream basins. The floor to ceiling tiled space was perfumed with a scent of lavender.

Bella tipped into a bin the potpourri from its bowl that was sitting on a vanity table. She ran a little water into the bowl and locked herself into the disabled cubicle. Bella emptied her rucksack of the items she had picked up earlier. Wriggling, she removed her jeans, cutting them across at mid-thigh level before pouring the bleach liberally over them. She set them on the door's coat hook.

With the marker pen she quickly blackened her white trainers. Snapping the pen's plastic casing and that of the numerous biros she had acquired, Bella scissored to open their tubing. Squeezing hard, black ink oozed, instantly darkening the bowl of water.

Bella reversed her nylon white rucksack to black and stuffed her baseball cap inside. Leaning over the toilet she cut her hair, trimming it short to the sides and at the nape of her neck. Blonde hair filled the toilet bowl. Bella poured the inky mix over her head, massaging it into her now punkish style hair.

A sudden click-clacking of heels was joined by pithy dialect and laughter. Bella waited for the whir of hand dryers to fade and conversation distanced behind the washroom's closing door.

Bella unlatched the door and hooked her bleached shorts to a dryer that burst noisily into life. Ducking her head under another dryer, the whirring hot air dried her hair in seconds. Daubing her fingertips with soap from the dispenser, Bella spiked her dark hair high.

Slipping on her shorts and denim jacket, Bella swung the rucksack onto her back and vacated the restroom. As she crossed the lounge she saw Ted with the clipboarded Doorman alongside him at the bar. They were in deep conversation, barely flashing her a cursory glance as she strolled by. Bella looked back as she rounded the table at the exit door, the two men were headed toward the ladies' washroom.

Bella strode the concourse apace, arriving two minutes later at gate 22, where her flight to London Heathrow was ready for boarding. She merged swiftly into the fast building queue.

CHAPTER 80

Neil Turvey flopped back into the thickly cushioned La-z-boy recliner and scanned the room. On the wall in front of him was an impressive muriel of the Islands. El-Marney sat central in the Artipelago, its coastline boasting white sand beaches along its southern shores.

Neil fizzed open a can of cola that he'd taken from the mini-bar and glugged at it, savouring its sweetness. The suite was opulent despite being minimalist in decor. The bathroom was plush, with large tinted mirrors and finger-touch cabinets that disappeared behind them.

The open plan space included a dining area that was flooded with light from a bi-folding patio door. A darkwood twelve-seater dining table with high-backed carver chairs was surrounded by huge canvases, adorning the walls. They featured Darcy, with shotgun in hand, on Safari alongside some of Africa's finest animals, an elephant, giraffe and a rhino. Even one with a tusk flashing Hippo venturing from its mud pool.

In pride of place was a picture of Darcy with his hand buried in the mane of a Lion, that stood obediently beside him. It looked staged, fake. Neil bounced from the recliner to take a closer look. He squinted in the brilliance of the sunset that engulfed the room with an orangey glow.

Behind the bi-fold doors there was a balcony, and beyond that he could see the top of a dome-like structure. Intrigued, he swung open the bi-folds, stepping out onto a sweeping balcony. The glass dome stood in glimmering magnificence before him, set in a courtyard below.

Neil's jaw dropped in casting his gaze to its centre, and the sight of many panicked men, seemingly trapped inside it. Almost immediately every face was glaring helplessly up, waving with open arms, as Neil tugged his iPhone from his cargo pants. A number of the men appeared frenetic in panic, pointing at something outside of their glass prison, directly beneath the balcony. Neil leaned, stomach-bending over the shiny guard rail to gaze down.

"Fuck me!" he muttered. Answer the bloody phone, boss.

Two sandy-backed muscular beasts paced below him, where the dome curved near the windowed walls of the resort's restaurant. Brushing each other as they crossed, like sentries on guard, they strode ten paces, before turning 180. Their deepening growls, chillingly directed at those imprisoned inside.

The men crowded to the central pillar, shouting words, unheard. The big cats pounded on, pausing only for huge splaying paws to test again the hard glass surface. Neil fumbled with his phone, dabbing again, a damp finger at the call button.

One of the animals stopped, bounding from its hind-legs onto the domed structure, with slavering jaws widening against the glass. Its incisors and claws work their sharpness into the transparent surface to a shrill grating; like fingernails down a chalkboard. A thick trail of saliva sparkled over the glassy surface.

"Tom.. thank fuck for that," Neil said. "We're gonna need that chopper, and guns, sharpish!"

"What's happened, Neil?" Tom said, as deepening roars reverberated the courtyard. "What the hell is that?"

"I finally located the other guests, trouble is the local wildlife found them first," Neil said.

"Yeah, we know about the animals, Darcy's been importing them for a while," Tom said. "They're all kept under lock and key, and they've assured me that the bear you saw will head for the forest, away from the resort. It's their natural habitat."

"Well listen up boss, cos I'm telling you! The animals have taken over the asylum," Neil said, eye-swivelling below him. "It's us in the cages now!"

"What exactly are we talking about here, Neil?" Tom said.

"Lions, Tom. Lions!"

CHAPTER 81

Tom Broad sat alongside Jeremy Forsythe in a tight-walled room, finger-tapping his rising frustration. The windowless polizi room at the Stacion du-Gardia resembled more a holding cell than a waiting area.

"This is ridiculous," Tom said, getting to his feet. "We need some answers, and we need them now!" Some time had passed since the discovery of Roman Darcy's mutilated body.

Tom flanneled his brow on his elbow-rolled shirt sleeve. The shrill-voiced police officers' excitable interactions outside had faded in the last few minutes. Jeremy wafted his oversized handkerchief, mopping his face before clearing his stuffy nose.

"As I said Tom, this is only the tip of the iceberg," Jeremy said, slipping his spectacles to the tip of his nose. "The authorities here are going to be very busy; they have a lot to cover up!"

"UK interforce police have emailed. They're reporting another dead body that might be of interest," Tom said, passing his iPhone. "Young, male, found in the north of England."

"A Ripper site again?" Jeremy said, peering over his half-moon spectacles.

"Yep, and he was a southerner, before you ask," Tom said, pacing the room.

"Yes, I see that, 'London construction worker'.. 'found on open ground near Bradford'," Jeremy said softly, reading the report.

"Not exactly a builder this time," Tom said, turning mid-stride. "This guy was the gatekeeper at a works plant in central London, managing traffic in and out of the plot."

"The same construction site though," Jeremy said, stumbling slightly as he got to his feet. "That's the crucial point; Dove Engineering, just off The Strand! Where our girl, Arabella Maxwell walked past every day," he added, with a little smile wrinkling his cheeks.

"Jesus Jeremy, don't sound so pleased about it. It might sound like you admire the woman!" Tom said, with a heavy sigh, resuming his six-yard pacing.

"Well you have to agree it's a pretty remarkable feat if Maxwell has carried out all of this alone," Jeremy said, fastening the buckle of his satchel. "The report says that this guy had been dead for at least ten days, so like the others, Maxwell was still in the UK at that point."

"Are you ready to get out of here?" Tom released another shirt button and necked the dregs from his beaker of water and tossed it into the wire bin. "I don't think Chief Mayisoon is going to be seeing us any time soon." He slid his jacket from the chair and threw it over his shoulder. "With Darcy murdered, he's more concerned about catching Maxwell than we are."

"But what about DI Spencer, Tom, and what that reporter you spoke has said?" Jeremy said, looping his lengthy satchel strap over his head.

"We don't actually know that Spence's been abducted, but they have her details and I've stressed the urgency," Tom said, holding the door for his colleague. "He only suggested, she might have been shipped to one of the other islands, possibly Makimraza."

"Makam-Raja," Jeremy corrected with thistly eyebrows raised. "It would make sense, with Darcy's consortium having bought the island recently. Should we try and get over there?"

Tom eye-rolled as the aged professor shuffled past him. "Whilst I admire your enthusiasm, Jeremy, it would need to be searched by professionals," he said. "You did hear the latest from Turvey!"

"Yes, yes of course," Jeremy said, with a thin-lipped smile. "The other possibility is that Spencer was taken by another from their syndicate. In which case she might be being held on one of their boats off El-Marney. Certainly their Yachts should be searched."

The two strode through the unmanned reception. The open plan office behind it was now deserted and the Police Chief's room at the far end empty. "Jeez, did we miss the fire-drill!" Tom said.

They exited into dazzling sunlight via the car-lot that was similarly deserted. The many dust-coated vehicles that had filled it on their arrival were now gone.

"The only way we're going to get boats searched is with international pressure," Tom said, digging a card from his pocket. "It was UN intervention that got the girls picked up from Darcy's boat and taken to safe refuge, away from here."

"Have they established who the women are yet?" Jeremy said, shielding his eyes with a cupped palm.

"It's just like before Jeremy, they're completely broken, barely able to speak," Tom said, putting his phone to his ear. "But their pictures are already out there and being circulated globally. Thank goodness for social media and the press, reporters from across the world are arriving by the hour!"

"Taxi, sla-sla tromi, Ila, Stacion de-Gardia," Tom said. "Cee-cee, Polizia."

"It does have its good news stories then," Jeremy said, adding, "Social media," to Tom's widening eyes. "Although, they will be barely recognisable, I'm sure."

"They'll find the families of these girls," Tom said. "Maxwell might earn some brownie points with a Judge, if she played a part in their escape! Ten minutes, by the way. The taxi."

"Played a part, Tom? I'm sure she master-minded the whole thing." Jeremy peered over the rim of his spectacles at his cell phone before turning it to face Tom. "And there's a growing army of Maxwell supporters, she's started something of a revolution!"

"Yes, I saw that. Seems things are getting a little pensive back home," Tom said, nodding.

The image showed flags fluttering from world landmarks, Sydney Opera House, the Eiffel Tower, the Empire State building and London's Tower Bridge. They carried the same emblazoned message; FLM MaxwellLAW.

"FLM?" Jeremy said, scratching at his straw like eyebrows.

"It used to be text talk for Fun, Love, Money," Tom said. "But now it's the fastest growing social movement; Female Lives Matter!"

PART XII – EVASION

CHAPTER 82

The plane was far from full and Bella had stretched across a row of seats, sleeping for most of the journey. She woke up to notice that the stewardess had kindly laid a blanket over her. Even better, she had left a warm breakfast tray on the fold-down table.

Bella ate heartily from the heat-sealed pack of scrambled eggs and bacon, guzzling the pot of orange juice in one go. The Captain announced rather proudly that they had made good time, making up for the delays experienced at Jakarta airport, prior to takeoff. We would be arriving at London Heathrow in just under ten minutes, where the local time was 06:15 and the temperature, a rather chilly 3 degrees.

The elderly chap to Bella's right, nodded across at her. "I hope you appreciated the blanket?" he said, with an expectant grin.

"That was you?" Bella said. "Thank you, very kind."

"Always the gentleman," he said, with a wrinkly wink.

Bella offered a nod of gratitude, before striding the aisle to the toilet cubicles at the front of the plane, feeling the old man's eyes on her. She dabbed at the soap dispenser and re-spiked her side-flopping hair. Returning, she met his leer with slanted eyes and shuffled down to the window seat.

From the pocket of her shorts, Bella tugged to remove and count the wedge of dollars she had stolen from the American at the airport lounge. She flicked Ted's iPhone into life, tapping in the passcode she had seen him use. There was no signal yet. She flopped her head to the headrest, feeling again an unease at the gawk of the senior citizen.

Bella reset the time on the casio that she'd snatched at the Airport, it had been many hours since the demise of Darcy. Inwardly she smiled, the women would be safe now, their families getting the news that they had prayed for.

The thought of her bestie, Sadie Barlow, dead, killed at the hands of Darcy and his crew, hit Bella with a gut churning agony. A single tear trickled her cheek, settling for a moment at her petit bow before its saltiness rolled her top lip.

"You ok, my sweet?" he said, peering over.

Bella fleeted barely a grin, refocused on her oval window, where swathes of green fields were flashing between thinning clouds. Noisily a stewardess collected miniature spirit bottles from his tray. A widening smile crept across her face, recalling Darcy's desperation when she held his precious antidote.

Once anchored off the mainland, Pascal had boarded the Yacht with the supposed vial of medicine; his remedy. Darcy was lolling, clutching his middle in soft groan.

"Here it is, Darcy!" Bella had declared, waving it in front of his bloodshot eyes, before sending the little glass vial smashing to the deck.

Darcy had flopped from his seat, crawling over the glass sharded decking, his tongue lapping all around it.

"You fucking dumbass!" Bella said, standing over him. "It's water, just water. You really think I'd save an evil bastard like you!"

"B-i-t-ch, y-you fu-fu.." he stammered, elbow-propping to face her.

"Save your breath Darcy, it's over," Bella said, pulling together the corners of a tablecloth.

Bella clattered the selection of knives and kitchen implements onto the deck in front of the women, unflapping the cloth. The girls remained unmoved, staring at Darcy; the malicious mastermind behind their abduction and imprisonment.

At the crude suggestion of Darcy's Texan billionaire associate, like wild horses, they were *broken-in*. Most of them had been raped by Darcy. Insubordination was brutally *thrashed-out*, to achieve utter compliance. Defeated and spiritless, the girls were subservient, sexslaves, to be passed between his guests.

"You've got two choices," Bella shouted up at the boat's Skipper. "You wait for the authorities, who are already on their way and *you* become part of all this?" she confirmed, nodding at Pascal. "Or, you can jump ship, and swim to shore?"

Without hesitation or utterance, the Skipper flipped off his shoes and dived majestically into the sparkling waters. Gloria eyed the knives, sliding a thick handled carving knife from the pile.

Joel now stood alone on the top deck watching the ship's Captain swimming away, a horrified expression creased his chubby features. "Wh-what about me?" he said.

The girls gazed at Darcy, the monster that now lay flailing, like a fish out of water before them, the demonic beast responsible for their tortuous lives.

"I think these girls might want a piece of you too, Joel!" Bella said, turning to the women, some of whom were following Gloria's lead and selecting a knife.

A huge splash rebounded the sides of the yacht as Joel disappeared beneath the surface. He reappeared thrashing at the water, frantically swimming in the direction of the harbour.

Bella waved a USB stick at her friend, saying, "The authorities will catch up with him, he'll get life for his part in all this." Adding tearfully, "We got them, Pascal!"

"So, so proud of you, Bella," Pascal said, wrapping an arm around her shoulders.

"Hey, I'm just pleased you remembered my plan B," Bella said, wiping her cheek. "Now, let's get the hell out of here!"

The plane's landing at London Heathrow was as smooth as the Pilot's voice, announcing their arrival. Bella popped the overhead compartment and tugged down her rucksack.

"You need a hand with that, sweety?" the elderly man said, his coffee breath wafting over her.

"I'm fine, thank you," she replied without turning.

Bella stood in the crowded aisle, with the old man behind her for what seemed like an eternity, waiting for the exit doors to be opened. Bomber jacketed *security* men were positioned at either end of the plane, standing in pairs at the foot of the stairs that were finally in place.

"Please, you go first," Bella said, half-turned with a smile.

"No-no, ladies first., after you, sweetheart," he said, inching a little closer.

It was clear the dishevelled man hadn't had the most comfortable flight. The pungent reek of bodily odour outstripped the whiff of caffeine that fouled his breath. Bella's trudge toward the exit, and the refreshingly chilly air, was accompanied by several bumps from behind. His arm brushed her as he stretched to grab each headrest. Bella swung her rucksack clumsily to her shoulder, catching him unapologetically.

As they reached the cabin Bella struck up conversation with a stewardess, side-stepping into the galley area, allowing the odious pensioner to pass. Thanking her for the breakfast tray, she dived swiftly back into line behind him, as they alighted. He was laboured and shaky, clinging to the nearside handrail.

The security guard at the foot was waving people quickly on. Halfway down, the line stopped whilst the peak-capped guard examined the papers of two young women. As Bella neared the bottom, she ankle-clipped the elderly man, sending him tumbling head first, into the family three steps down. Amongst screeched expletives he landed amidst a heap of writhing bodies.

Bella bound the steps, blurring with the falling mass. The security guards jumped backward before stepping in to assist, tugging at the old guy before seeing that his foot faced the wrong way. In the screaming commotion Bella ducked under the staircase, waving frantically at the men who were unloading baggage from the hold on the opposite side of the plane.

"Get that wheelchair over there will you!" Bella shouted at the older of two luggage haulers.

The younger guy, in a backwards-turned baseball cap grabbed the wheelchair from the top of a pile of multicoloured suitcases. The other man took it, unfolding it in one smooth motion and wheeled it under the aircraft whilst Bella clambered aboard the baggage-relay vehicle. She slid on a Hi-Vis vest that she found on the dash and yelled at the young guy to join her.

"You ain't supposed to be in there, miss," he said, with an arm propped on the perspex door.

"Get in here, you idiot. Do you know who I am?" Bella barked. "I'm with the *Health and Safety Executive*. And aside from that appalling, *avoidable*, accident over there, you're not exactly compliant yourself," she added, eye-pointing at his head.

He snatched his football-logoed cap from his head, throwing it to the dashboard beside a clipboard, the front sheet of which read, *work rota*. He jumped behind the steering wheel.

"What's your name, boy?" Bella said, lifting the clipboard and its string dangling pen.

"It's err, Ben. B-Benjamin Thornton, miss," he said, flicking the hair from his brow.

"Then I suggest you demonstrate to me, Benjamin, that your vehicle operational skills are better than your presentation," Bella said. "Now, move!"

"We-err, hadn't quite finished loading, Miss," he said, fastening the velcro strap of his vest.

"Priorities boy. Priorities!" Bella snapped. "I assume you did your Health and Safety training before starting here, Benjamin?"

His silver-chained, open necked chest plumed a tomato-red, blossoming his neck. "Yeah, yes of course. S-sorry!" he said, yanking his safety belt across.

"Then let's go, I need to get this incident reported quickly. They're going to need an ambulance over there!" Bella said, with a little head shake. "I have a number of other significant breaches to attend to this morning. You can deal with *unloading of baggage* later!"

Benjamin checked all his mirrors before the vehicle hummed softly, gliding smoothly across the taxiway toward a large warehouse-like building below the main terminal. Bella explained to the young airport employee that a number of 'no-notice' inspections were being carried out across *LHR* today. She would need his staff pass to access the shopping concourse, where a number of unsafe duty-free storage issues had been flagged.

"I assume you haven't divulged key entry codes to anyone outside of BAA security personnel," Bella said, whilst inspecting the staff rota.

They marched from the baggage cartport slot, near the conveyor belts, towards the fire exit security door. A number of male staff, mostly idly slumped across luggage, eyed them. Ben's face was flour-white as she continued her interrogating as they walked. The men stared over in a mix of wrinkling brows and nudging elbows.

"I need you to show me exactly how you would exit this *supposedly* secure unit," Bella said sternly, with a tut-filled face.

As they strode by the staffroom she quizzed him about his background. Once stood beside the exit door, she received a question-mark gaze from a senior colleague, who had paused his suitcase slinging. Bella returned an unforgiving glare.

Benjamin tapped six digits into the keypad whilst she simultaneously flattened his staff pass to the touch screen box, as directed. The steel door buzzed loudly for a few seconds before clicking open to the chattering din on the other side.

Bella thanked Ben for his assistance, slipping the lanyard over his bowed head and positioning his staff pass centrally on his chest; as if presenting an under 10's football medal. She removed and folded her hi-vis vest, laying it across his outstretched arm.

She swung her rucksack to her shoulder whilst requesting confirmation of Benjamin Thornton's address for the record. Bella confirmed that he would be commended for his assistance today, and that she had noted his admirable personal qualities in caring for an elderly relative.

Bella disappeared behind the heavy security door to merge instantly amongst those filing from the arrivals corridors, integrating seamlessly into a bustling shopping area.

CHAPTER 83

"There's another seven or eight yachts, anchored off the east coast. It's like millionaires row around that little island," Neil Turvey said, peering down from the helicopter.

The chopper swivelled, tilting left and arching away toward the mainland.

"Which boat did they find Spence on?" Neil said, looking solemnly at his boss, sat opposite.

"We're still not sure who the yacht belongs to," Tom said, adjusting his headset and microphone prong. "They're checking the leasing records. Most of these luxury cruisers are hired by the week, fully crewed."

"Bring the fucking crews in then.. they must be in on it," Neil said, shaking his head. "They must have seen Spencer being dragged onboard, along with the other girl they found."

"*Girls!*" Tom said. "They found *three* girls chained-up in the engine room."

Below, the dense canopied forest hid the waterfall that cascaded to the flower-filled valley, where an armed search team tracked the black bear. Neil threw a frown-filled head shake at the paradise island of El-Marney as the chopper clattered noisily above. Lush greenery faded into shallow sloped white sand beaches, against which the turquoise waters barely rippled.

"So where have they taken Spence now?" Neil said, teary-eyed.

"She's being examined at the medical centre on the mainland and that evidence is being processed as a priority. I've got her booked on the first flight home after that," Tom said. "She'll be alright buddy, Spence is a tough cookie."

"Allright!" Neil said, with a puff of his cheeks. "This sort of thing stays forever, it aint ever gonna leave her. We need to nail these bastards!"

"I know, I know, and we will," Tom said. "You've been through a fair bit yourself down there, Turvs. Are you going to be okay?"

Neil had waited for over three hours, watching two hungry lions pacing the resort's inner courtyard, clawing furiously at the glass dome. Evermore agitated, the wide-jawed big cats had pierced its surface, fracturing the structure. He'd thrown foodstuffs pulled from the kitchens to distract them, before their attention returned to pounding at the splintering dome.

"I was fine once I saw that shooter's darts hitting the butts of those fucking lions!" Neil said, shuffling centrally on his bench. "But now I just wish they had eaten those low-life bastards. That glass was about to give, it had a crack the length of a giraffe's neck."

"They won't be going anywhere," Tom said, sliding his aviators from his head and looking out to sea, the mainland was closing fast. The pilot half turned, waving splayed fingers, shouting, '*three minuto*'. "They have them in Jakarta, where the military have taken over. The local police here were corrupt, on Darcy's payroll."

"You don't say!" Neil said with an eye-roll. "Seems like the whole fuckin' place was on his books, my guide certainly was!"

"Didn't deserve that though, Turvs," Tom said, with eyebrows rising over his shades. "They're still recovering body parts! That's how the search team is tracking the bear."

"No, fair enough, that was just brutal," Neil said, screwing his face. "What the hell were they doing with all these animals and girls, it's all just so fucked up!"

"Big game hunting wasn't enough for them," Tom said, tugging a note from the breast pocket of his shirt. "According to our shrink, Jeremy Forsythe, '*It's an irresistible desire to push the boundaries, find a new summit. Human's endless quest for evermore stimuli; a higher high*'."

Neil said, wonky-mouthed. "Bit odd that Forsythe, he gives me the creeps."

"Well that's what he told me earlier, over coffee!" Tom said, unfolding another page. "*It would have ignited a pleasure within the temporal lobe, releasing a dopamine rush to a virginal cortex.*"

"Jesus, all a bit deep, aint it?" Neil said, with a puff of his cheeks. "Why's Forsythe's actually over here?"

"This is big now, Turvs, not just back home, but internationally," Tom said. "We needed a profile-study character trail on Maxwell, to predict her next move."

Neil clasped the overhead rail. "Well I think Maxwell might have got it right about those three bastards; they should never have been let off. They got what was coming to them."

"You can't be saying that buddy," Tom said, open-faced. "Besides, Lebouf's still missing and it's not just the TikTokTrio, there are dead bodies turning up across the north of England!"

"But Maxwell's over here, unless she has an accomplice?" Neil said, with widening eyes.

"It's probable that she *was* in the UK when these other murders took place. And all of the victims have a tangible link to Maxwell," Tom said.

"She *is* still over here I take it, the borders have been closed; she can't get out?" Neil said.

"Yep, all road and rail border crossing points, seafaring ports and the airport are on high alert," Tom said, checking his watch. "Maxwell's cornered."

"Arresting her over here would be something of a coup, I can see the headlines now! I'm sensing a promotion might be in the offing, boss?" Neil said, with a wink.

Tom lifted his aviators from his eyes. "The next time Bella Maxwell sets foot in the UK, it'll be with *my handcuffs* on her wrists," he said, with a firm nod at his colleague.

CHAPTER 84

Her name filled the breaking news banners of television screens that dotted the restaurants in the airport. Pictures flashed between a dockside reporter on the mainland, to drone shots of the idyllic island of El-Marney and the many yachts moored off it.

Bella darted into the toilets. She had spent nearly half of the dollars she stole on a dark rollneck, jeggings and black bomber jacket. Changing swiftly, she flattened her spiky hair and tugged her baseball hat low. Stuffing her rucksack into the waste bin, she headed for the taxi rank.

Three men lounged around the bonnet of the first cab, one casting her a quizzical look. She swivelled and headed back inside, it was too risky to be locked inside a taxi. Bella strode toward the escalators below the sign, 'To Trains'.

The underground was comfortingly warm against the wintry chill, the carriage filling quickly with blank-faced people, nobody uttering a word. Bella stood, head-dipped, next to the doors as it thundered through the tunnels, before wheel-squealing excitedly back into the light. Slowing to a whirring halt, dozens more crammed to find space that didn't seem to be there.

A red top newspaper carried the headline, 'Darcy found dead' with a picture of the celebrity DJ, in familiar flamboyant shirt behind his decks with arms aloft. Images of Jamal Jackson and Pierre Lebouf featured lower down the page, alongside a larger one of herself. She leaned a little closer to the tabloid's tagline, 'Maxwell on the run. Lebouf still missing.'

Rattling deeper beneath the capital, the air seemed to thicken. Bella loosened the zipper on her jacket. The claustrophobic squeeze of bodies rocked in rhythmic motion as one, as the packed train wheezed on to the next station.

And, there it was, *again*.

Pressed hard against her left buttock, its shape unmistakable. No wallet or cellphone rammed in a trouser pocket could disguise it. She face-screwed at the cigarette reek as she twisted a quarter turn and shuffled, inching away. The grumbling groan quickened again, before wheels and tracks squealed their metallic differences, straining under their ever increasing load.

Within a minute, the blaring rush of light was back as the train whistled, racing from its tunnel. A blur of colour flashes the smeary windows as it whizzes to a stop. The woman was staring, the same one as before. At the inrush of commuters, Bella manoeuvred away, grabbing the handrail opposite, dipping her face to the shoe-filled floor.

A blackness took the carriage for a moment, before its lights flickered reluctantly back. Bella pulled away sharply from the hairy hand of another, brushing her's in the darkness. The lung-gasping swoosh of the double doors barely wafted a breeze. Few departed, yet many more packed in, shaping arms and legs to squeeze between others.

Aisles of luggage-laden travellers, now joined by bagged shoppers and shoulder-satchelled workers. Young and old, bumping and nudging, unapologetic in snaking between knee-tucking rows, resenting the intrusion. Faces of indifference, now a picture of disdain.

And there it was, *again*.

The same bitter tang of tobacco-ridden breath, a constant pressing at the curve of her rear. Bella shifted an inch, but it followed her there; there was nowhere to go, no room to escape it.

It lengthened and hardened as the train cornered and tilted. The mass of bodies swaying her way, then his. The ear-piercing screech of metal wasn't enough to disguise his exultant pant, that billowed her cheek.

Enough!

Bella spun one-eighty, her stomach pinned to his, her face in that of the pervert, who side-eyed away. There he was in all his glory, the cowardly sex-pest, seeking his pleasures down here among the sewer rats. Middle-aged scruffy man, taking his chance in the crowded darkness, to fondle young women, to masterbate. Having a power over them, down here, in this his squalid lair. The monstrous Morlock abusing another innocent Eloi.

She slid her hand down, loosening his trousers and grasping his manhood in a finger-wrapping grip. He turned slowly to face her with reddening cheeks and wobbly chin, he looked confused, unsure. *Shhh*, she mouthed with a tightening hold, as the black windows disappeared, flashing blindingly bright. The train shuddered to a halt and the double doors widened, releasing some from the hellride.

His cold dark eyes quivered in confusion, searching for answers in hers, that teased a slow wink. In tightening body-shuffle, passengers squeezed all around them, as she moved him toward the cool air. Sliding a hand to his lapel she held him there by the doorway, until the doors groaned back across.

With a soft smile she shoved him backwards, whilst maintaining a vice-like grip on his vein-pulsing penis. He stumbled just a half-step back, through the fast-narrowing gap. Blood oozed between her knuckles, coating her fingers, as her nails pierced his flesh. As he tried to pull away his trousers tumbled to his ankles.

She rebalanced him, tugging his cock hard back towards her; like a naughty dog on a leash. Elbow-wrapping the handrail she braced, resisting his desperate arm-thrashing. Stretching his penis to meet the closing doors, they clamped right across his fast shrinking dick. The buffers, not registering an obstacle, trapped it fast at its stem.

"This groping shit ends now, arsehole," Bella shouted through the windowed door. "*Enough!*"

Bella slid the scissors from her pocket, presenting them at the window to the puce-faced man. He pleaded for his release, waving frantically at the far end of the train. But the tube started rolling, as he shuffled alongside it, skipping ballet-style at first, before lateral bounded steps. The skips of a Sunday league linesman, trying to keep up with play.

Bella scissored the gristly shaft, its blades hacking it near halfway through before the engine's whirr deafened and he tripped in flesh-ripped release. He collapsed, writhing on the platform, clutching the bloodied stump of his manhood.

As Bella stepped away, the man's reddened helmet remained stuck midway up the carriage door. It looked like an overripe strawberry. After a few seconds it plopped unceremoniously to the floor in a trail of blue veins; like a gymnast's flailing ribbons.

Amidst gasps and muttered expletives, wide smiles beamed from behind a sea of iPhones. Some spun swiftly back to the window, sniggering at the dickless man, until the tunnel blocked their amusement.

And as their laughter faded and chatter softened, one woman started clapping, slowly at first. Bella peered cautiously from the floor to face her fellow travellers. Amongst shared nods, others joined the applause. One guy stood to offer his seat. Nearly all were clapping now, some cheering from further down the carriage.

One young woman with shiny hair and caramel tan stood in the aisle and continued filming. Professional looking, in a cashmere ankle length coat, she clasped the handrail above her head and called out.

"Are you Bella Maxwell?"

CHAPTER 85

"Cancel that beer, will you. Just two coffees here and one for the guy in front of us, thanks love," Tom Broad said, passing the airhostess his plastic.

Tom threw a stern nod at Neil Turvey, who was peering back at him through the gap between seats. Jeremy Forythe unfolded his table, placing a little brown book alongside the drink he was delivered.

"We've had the family background checks emailed over," Tom said.

"Yes, I've just been reading that," Jeremy said, gently shaking a sachet of sugar. "Seems you'll need to add fraud to her list of offences. Her grandad has never been registered as dead!"

"Hardly a crime, Prof!" Neil chirped, through the gap.

"It is when you've been claiming his pension and transferred the deeds of his house! Silver Mews Terrace was put into *her* name some years ago," Jeremy said, peering over his tortoiseshell glasses.

"Do we actually know that Charles Maxwell is dead? The fact that nobody's seen the guy for a while.." Neil said.

"*Ten years!*" Tom Broad, interrupted. "Nobody's seen the fella for ten years now. Clearly he doesn't live at the derelict house that we searched. And the pension payments, which are substantial, have gone into an account in *her name!*"

"Maybe she's just taken control of his finances, on his behalf. Power of Attorney, isn't it?" Neil said. "Nothing unusual there."

"God, you're starting to sound like Spencer. What is it with everybody defending Maxwell? The woman's a criminal!" Tom said, with brows arched.

"How is DI Spencer now?" Jeremy said, to interject.

"Insisting that she's fine and ready to get back to work," Neil said. "According to the text that she sent me, anyway."

"She's been examined and interviewed," Tom said, with a heavy exhale. "And yeah, she's determined to get back to it and find the guy that assaulted her, and the bastard who paid for her abduction."

"If they know which yacht she was held captive on, then they'll be able to establish who owns it, surely," Jeremy said, breathily steaming his glasses.

"They've ID'd every boat off the coast of El-Marney, but haven't released that information to us yet," Neil said. "And don't call me Shirley!" he added with a subtle wink.

"This might be a lot bigger than we ever anticipated," Tom said, stirring his coffee. "Rumour has it that some major players in international finance had a stake in all this!" he added, dunking a thin biscuit.

"As I said earlier, Tom, this is just the tip of the iceberg, and a number of individuals will be holding their breath beneath it. With Darcy gone, these sadistic narcissists will battle for ownership, to continue the business elsewhere. It seems our three chaps, the TipToeThree, were just a front," Jeremy said.

"The *TikTokTrio*," Neil said, beaming at the elderly expert, through the gap between seats.

"Yes, quite," Jeremy continued. "They were merely the shopfront, the puppets, facilitating their masters. To have the clout to bribe a High Court

Judge, and manipulate a twelve person Jury, there always had to be more to it."

"Now we don't know about that, Jeremy. That's all just speculation," Tom said, before slurping his coffee.

"Yeah, but what about the statement from the Jury's deputy foreman, Tom?" Neil said, appearing above the headrests. "She's still under police protection."

"Listen, let's just park that for the moment, shall we!" Tom said, under a hushed tone. "The IT geeks are all over Darcy's laptop, so we'll soon get a picture of who's at the summit of all this.."

"But what if there are more girls being held captive back there," Neil interjected. "I told you about the other island they bought; Makam-Raja!"

"Yes, yes I know. But we need to focus on one thing at a time. Our brief is very much focussed on Arabella Maxwell. Catching her is our priority right now!" Tom said.

"You can't just ignore it though, Tom. Given the damage Maxwell's caused to their operation we have to expect them to be tracking her," Neil said.

"Look, this underground network of sadistic narcissists., or whatever they are," Tom said, seeing the professor's eyebrows bristling clear of his frames. "As far as we're concerned, they can wait. The international authorities will follow the papertrail and pursue them.."

Three shrill beeps interrupted him. Neil glugged his coffee, whilst Tom attended to a message on his iPhone.

"Here we go.. right on queue!" Tom said, sharply. "We've had a possible sighting of Maxwell at Heathrow Airport."

"It's shocking that she's managed to escape airport security. They were specifically told that Maxwell was on that London-bound flight!" Neil said.

"It's amazing that she managed to flee Indonesia, let alone get back into the UK," Jeremy said, quietly chuckling to himself.

Tom continued, scanning the communication from BAA. Neil sprang from his seat to crouch in the aisle alongside him.

"They've reported a security breach at err.. Here we are, '*Cargo hold 3*' and have closed circuit TV footage of the woman," Tom said, tapping the attachment. A grainy video flickered reluctantly into life.

CHAPTER 86

The double decker to Marylebone had almost emptied. Bella, now with the top floor to herself, relaxed, gazing down at the rush of passengers scurrying from the bus; like revellers pouring from the bottleneck entrance into Worthy Farm.

The capital's slate-grey sky and grimy streets were in stark contrast to her last few days. Since emerging from the underground, Bella had journeyed with her head ducked, weaving and jostling through a flocking mass of commuters. Sat towards the rear of the bus, she stood to release the window latch, shoving it as wide as its safety bar would allow and sucked in the cool air.

Two more stops and she could take the alleyway at the side of Barton's bakery which led through to Gilmore street. From there, she would cut across the courtyard that linked to the back of Marylebone Heights, via the underpass. If Carl wasn't there she could maybe blag Mrs Machin to let her in. Although given the level of media coverage Bella had received, that was risky. But Carl was a creature of habit, and he didn't start until midday on a Wednesday, so he'd still be in bed.

Then came the thud of boots on the curved metal stairwell. Bella slumped into the window seat, tugging the rim of her cap low. A guy in a branded white tee under an open-zipped puffa and low-slung trackies swaggered down the aisle. Bella felt his dark stare. She could hear his nasally breaths and angry snorting, as if trumpeting his arrival.

"Alwight, bitch."

Oh fuck, no. I don't need this! Just ignore the twat, Bella. You'll be out of here soon.

He swung in, sliding across the seat directly behind her, shuffling to lean forward at her shoulder.

"Said, alright pussy, didn't I."

Bella half nodded at him with expressionless face as the bus lurched to the curbside. Five passengers alighted from the lower deck as two stepped onboard. *One more stop to go.*

"Don't talk much, do ya, bitch?"

Five more minutes, less if the lights change. Ahead she could see roadworks and a line of traffic at a standstill. *Maybe I should make my way downstairs, get away from this neanderthal.* Bella's head was spinning, a warming sensation filling her eyes.

"Ain't very friendly now, innit!"

The sound of heels clattered the metal stairs, before the shiny bobbed hair of its fresh faced owner appeared, glancing over. Bella side-eyed her as she froze for a second, then disappeared, bob bouncing quickly back down. He grabbed the handrail and swung forward, the crook of his elbow wrapping the pole, to land alongside Bella. She remained with face fixed on the window, watching shoppers darting in and out of a convenience store. The bus jerked forward, horn-blasting at an unhelmeted cyclist, who hand-gestured back.

"Yoos gonna pass me your coin, bitch." The padded arm of his puffa slid the seat-rail, creeping across her shoulders. "Then we is gonna get it on some," he said, his tongue flapping quickly between his lips.

His grubby fingers curled Bella's shoulder, squeezing her arm as she turned to face him, poking the peak of her cap clear of her eyes. There he was in all his glory, the wannabe mobster, a pasty-faced gangster-boy. The mafioso kid, all attitude and angst; a pimple pricked delinquent.

"Yeah, thas more like it, pretty little pussy-fuck aint ya."

"You wanna stop talking now, you're making me wet," Bella said, laying her hand in his.

She leaned into his shoulder, sliding her thigh over his. Her head tilted open-mouthed, inviting him in. He obliged, his tongue wrapping hers. Bella tugged, finger-knotting his thick greasy hair, her elbow clamping his arm. In a panicked flicker of his eyes, they bulged capillary-shot in their sockets, as blood spurted, escaping the seal of their lips. A bolognese red instantly coating his chin, as she bit down ever harder.

She slid to his lap, as his flailing arm jousted her interlocking fingers as claret streamed his neck; her incisors slicing deep into the tough fleshy muscle. In head-jerking violence she ripped, tearing like a lion at the innards of a buffalo's carcass. With her mouth inside his, she bit down again, severing his tongue from its core.

His head snatched back sharply, spurting a fountain of red. Bella leapt clear to the aisle, unsaddled from her raging bull, spitting the gristly organ to the floor. He lurched toward her, and that's when he felt it, much lower, where his fingers explored a stomach wrenching agony. He gazed in horror at his middle, where the bloodsoaked handles of scissors now stuck.

Bella sleeve-wiped her blood-splattered face sneering down at him as he staggered half to his feet, tumbling from the seat, as she took a step back. He fell with a childlike cry clutching his belly, as he lay at her feet. His pristine white tee, now velvety red. The stump of his tongue wobbled furiously, speckling the air red.

"This shit stops now, *Corleone.* Choose another seat next time. *Enough!*"

Bella bound the top deck, clutching a handrail as the bus pitched suddenly to the curb. She hurtled the curling steps, dipping her cap in exiting. The driver sat ghostfaced, finger-punching his phone.

CHAPTER 87

The stiff breeze billowing the warehouse was accompanied by the constant whirring of machinery. Neil Turvey, still in a short-sleeve shirt, having come straight from his flight, buttoned-up.

"Yeah, it's Ben..err," he said, peeping over the top of the police officer's notepad. "Benjamin Thornton."

"Now I knew you weren't Ben-Hur, coz I've seen the movie!" Neil said, to the nervous looking young man.

An industrial whiff of oil and diesel caught the occasional gust. Raucous laughter burst clear of the whispered chatter of his co-workers on the far side.

"Is there an office or somewhere a little quieter that we could go, Ben?" Neil asked, surveying the premises.

Ben pointed vaguely in the direction of a small portacabin and trudged reluctantly towards it, as if being escorted into court. The little office space that overlooked the baggage control area was bright with waist to ceiling windows on three sides. More importantly, they were now sheltered from the icy blast. A large screen monitor sat on a veneer desk which had been begrudgingly vacated by the operations manager. He mouthed, five minutes to Ben as he exited with coffee mug in hand.

"We've seen the footage and it very much looks like the person we're looking for. But I'm hoping you could tell me a little about her, Ben?" Neil said, sidestepping the desk to slump behind it, into the moulded plastic seat. "What did she sound like, any accent?"

"Not really, bit posh I suppose. That's probably why I believed her!" Ben said, standing obediently on the other side of the desk. "You do know that she said she was a Health and Safety Inspector."

"Look, there's no criticism of you here, Ben," Neil said. "We just need to make sure it is who we think it is and locate her."

"Yeah-yeah, Sorry. It's just that, well, there's been a bit of banter about it. You know, from the guys here!" Ben said, head-nodding over his shoulder.

Ten or so male staff were stood around a baggage loading belt, staring over at them with smug looks etched on their faces.

"Don't worry about it fella. This woman has managed to trick plenty of people; you're not the first and won't be the last, I'm sure," Neil said, tugging at the cords dangling from one side of the larger window. "Did you gauge from anything said, where she might be heading?"

"Not really," Ben said, scratching his head. "The only address mentioned was mine."

"Yours.. how so?" Neil said, tugging his notebook from his back pocket.

"Yeah, you know, checking up on who I was and that!" Ben said. "I can see it now. It was all just part of her act."

Neil Turvey took Ben's address and mobile number. He established that he lived at home with his mum and elderly grandmother. Maxwell had chatted to Ben about that, saying how lucky he was to have a loving family around him. Neil gave him his card, stressing that Ben should contact him if he thought of anything else.

"I did notice that she had some cash, a pretty large wad was bulging from the pocket of her shorts. Funny notes though, not pounds, maybe dollars. I remember thinking she must have confiscated it from someone found stealing from luggage. It happens quite a lot you know," Ben said. "I honestly feel so stupid about it all now. I even told her how to work the security door and how often we do fire drills and all that stuff!"

"Well please don't Ben," Neil said. "How long have you been working here?"

"Err, well eighteen months on and off, what wiv doing the training courses and that," Ben said, still standing with hands behind his back, army parade-like.

Neil marched with Ben Thornton over to the group of men that lay slouched around the main conveyor belt. They sat idle with a mountain of multi-coloured suitcases around them. One guy was lying across two huge cases that he had positioned lengthways, z-bed-style.

"DI Turvey, Met Police," he said sharply, flashing his badge as he got to within twenty feet of them. "You were all working here earlier, when a woman posing as a Health and Safety Executive managed to exit the airport from tarmac to terminal, via this luggage hanger?"

The group nodded, mumbling in affirmation whilst straightening up a little.

"Speak up!" Neil snapped, hooding his eyes.

"Yeah well we woz, but we weren't the one escorting her to the food court," a man in a flat cap said, to some sniggering behind him.

"No, of course not," Neil said. "You were the idiots who just sat watching as a woman dressed in shorts and denim jacket strolled right past you, without uttering a word!"

"Look, we didn't know who she was, did we!"

"Well Ben here was told that she was part of a covert H and S check," Neil said. "He has a reasonable excuse; what's yours?" he added, finger pointing at the flat capped man.

"We under arrest or summut!" he grumbled.

"Unauthorised female, potentially a bomb carrying terrorist, walks past the lot of you and nobody says a word. Totally unchallenged by anyone, incredible!" Neil said. "Ben's only been here five minutes compared to most of you."

"We was actually workin' at the time, mate," z-bed man said.

"Oh, working, were you!" Neil said with a widening grin. "I've seen the footage boys and there wasn't one of you that didn't clock her as she strutted by. Pound to a penny if the clip had sound I'd have heard more than a few catcalls. Misogyny is a crime you know!"

"Alright, fair enough, we should have maybe said something, but there's no need to shred us for it, pal," flat cap man said.

"Shred you!" Neil said, with a burst of laughter. "What like you've been shredding this guy," he added, with a hand on Ben's shoulder. "Grow the fuck up people, and try challenging something that doesn't look right next time, ehh!"

Disgruntled mumbling merged with eyebrow nods from the men as they turned, shuffling away. One man punched a large red button on a silver box and the conveyor clattered into life as they began tossing the assorted mass of cases onto the trundling belt.

"And, by the way," Neil yelled. "That hat. It's non-compliant with H and S! Get rid of it."

The man swiped his flat cap from his blotchy bald head, rolling it quickly in his fist.

"There you go, mister pigeon-fancier " Neil said. "Easily fooled, aren't you!"

Ben Thornton joined the rest of the team, belly-laughing at the man, who with a firm jerk, returned his cloth cap to his head.

CHAPTER 88

The tapping was soft but insistent. "Carl," she whispered.

She added another knuckle to it. "Carl baby, it's me!" The knocking echoed back off the doorframe into the corridor around her.

The door creaked open a crack for a second, before a bleary eye peered around it. Clearing his floppy blonde curls, Carl's jaw dropped as he flung the door wide.

"Bella.. What the hell!"

He wrapped an arm around her and hauled her inside, clunking the door behind him.

"Jeez, Bel, I've been out of my mind. I've had the police round, asking me all sorts. I thought you might be dead, babe," Carl said, instantly watery eyed.

"I'm so sorry Carl, but I couldn't tell you.."

"What the hell happened to you!" he said, slowly peeling off her baseball cap.

"Don't panic hun, I'm okay," Bella said, smiling up at him. Side-stepping Carl she leaned into the little halfway mirror. "I know it looks bad!"

"No kidding babe.. you're covered in blood!" Carl said, wiping teary sleep from the corner of his eye. "We've gotta get you to a hospital, right?"

"Honestly Carl I'm fine, it's not even my blood," she said, disappearing into the toilet and running the tap. "I just need to get cleaned up."

"You've been all over the telly, and the papers. I'm guessing this is about that bleedin' trial. You gotta tell me what's going on, babe?" he said, crossing his arms. "You look terrible."

Bella stepped out of the washroom with towel in hand, beaming at her dishevelled looking boyfriend, who stood bare chested with his pyjama bottoms barely hanging from his hips.

"How's that, any better?" she said, with a wink.

"Ok, I take it back, you clean up real good," he said, with a soppy grin. "Lovin' the new hairdo by the way. Kinda suits!"

"Yeah, it's not exactly Toni and Guy and I'm not sure about the colour. But hey, needs must," Bella said, running her finger through it to spike it. "Now how about I take a shower and you go get us some food., Chinese?" She tugged at the cord of his PJ's, wrapping it around her finger, pulling him close.

"You gonna tell me what you've been up to these last few days?" he said, thumb-hooking a loop of her shorts. "I know those bastards got what was coming, but I can't believe.."

"All," she said, kissing him softly. "In." She wrapped her arms around his neck. "Good." She kissed him again. "Time!"

"God, I've missed you, Bella Maxwell!" Carl scooped Bella up to a whoop of delight, carrying her to the shower, where they had sex until the water ran cold.

CHAPTER 89

DI Turvey flashed his badge and a wide grin at the passport control officer as he strode past his booth and pinned his iPhone to his ear.

"Guv?" Neil said, striding towards the luggage carousel. "Nothing of any great interest here at Heathrow. She had a wad of cash, possibly dollars in her shorts and was carrying an average sized green rucksack with no distinguishing marks. Her facial appearance he described as; *pretty with blue eyes and weird coloured spiky hair.* Otherwise, it's as per the snowy footage we got from the hangar."

"Nothing else? They looked to be chatting for quite a time," SIO Tom Broad said.

"The lad said she was totally believable, stern-faced with an accent that was on the posh side. Apparently she asked a lot of questions about him, which seems a bit odd," Neil said.

Neil leaned over the conveyor belt, grabbing the handle of a sky blue suitcase with Hawaii stickers emblazoned across one side.

"Ok, well get yourself back to base aysap. We've had another possible sighting following an incident on the tube at Holborn earlier," Tom said. "The timeline fits, but it sounds a bit gruesome, even for our girl! Apparently some guy had his dick cut off while trying to exit the train! We're waiting on TfL for the footage."

"Don't hold your breath with that lot," Neil said. "But sounds more like a domestic that one, boss!" he added, whilst bounding through the green customs corridor.

"*Ha-fuckin-ha*, great spelling buddy!" Neil muttered, whilst waggling two fingers at a suited guy that stood holding a back flipped A4 pad marked; *Inspecta Turdy*.

"Look, I've gotta dash, see you in a bit, Turvs," Tom said, to a rising cacophony.

"I've not missed your birthday there, have I guv!" Neil said, hearing clapping and cheering down the phone.

"Nope, but we do have something of a celebrity here. Our very own superhero is back!"

A watery-eyed DI Sarah Spencer, with a queen-like wave crisscrossed the open-plan office, collecting a number of brightly coloured envelopes along the way. Declining offers of coffee and cake, she weaved between her fellow officers toward the little office at the far end.

"Ok folks, let's settle down now," Tom said firmly. "Spence, come on through."

He ushered her into the cluttered room, clearing papers from a chair and closed the door. With a heavy sigh, tears flowed as she took a chair alongside Tom's file-filled desk.

"It's too soon, Spence," Tom said, lip-biting. "You've been through so much. You can't.."

"I'm fine, Tom," she said, tugging a tissue from a box on the corner of the desk. "It was just all that. I didn't expect it, that's all." She laid the pile of envelopes on her lap.

"Well, you know how much everyone thinks of you.. but you're not fine,

Spen.."

"Please don't, Tom," she said, staring across at him, blinking her eyes clear. "I just want to get back to it," she said sternly, turning her iPhone to face him. "Have you seen this yet?"

"No-err, we were waiting for it to come through from.."

"TfL sent it through twelve minutes ago, Tom!" Spencer said, tapping the email attachment.

CCTV footage from the eastbound platform of Holborn tube station, burst noisily into life. A quarter of the way down it, a number of travellers were taking a wider berth from the platform's edge, swerving to avoid someone.

The train remained stationary, but the suited man couldn't seem to decide whether he was exiting or boarding. As commuters cleared from the platform, the video showed that his trousers lay crumpled around his ankles.

"Looks like a flasher incident more than anything," Tom said. "And, no sign of Maxwell."

"Keep your eyes on the sliding doors, Tom," Spencer said, leaning over the desk.

The guy took half-a-step backwards but with his hips thrust toward the open door, as if pissing into the train. His back was arching, as if limbo dancing.

"This is just a gross indecency, or possibly some disgruntled TfL employee," Tom said, with a puff of his cheeks. "I hope they're not wasting our time here!"

The man jerked his waist and someone's arm appeared, their hand was clamped around his penis. A face in profile, under a baseball cap came momentarily into view. Tom dabbed the pause button. Young, short cropped hair, dark bomber jacket. With her fist wrapped around his manhood she yanked it back inside, just as the doors swished across, trapping it.

Tom winced, jolting his head back, his wrinkling face sinking into his neck. Spencer eye-pointed his attention back to the screen. The guy's panic was evident by the frantic thumping on the windowed doors, his arm waving toward the driver's end of the train. He bounced in side-steps daintily alongside it for a few seconds as it began rolling.

Tom side-eyed in grimace as the man tumbled in a jerky ripped-release from the accelerating tube. A shower sprung from his stumped penis, repainting the carriage as he crashed to the ground. He lay doubled-up, clasping his groin, as the platform's yellow safety line quickly darkened.

"Fuckin hell!" Tom said, reclining in his seat. "I'd say the description matches, but it seems she's graduated. Assaulting an innocent member of the public! It's one thing targeting the men that she tried for murder and that she believes should have been imprisoned.."

"We *all* believe that, Tom."

"Yeah maybe. But this, come on!" Tom said. "What possible motive can she.."

"I take it you've not read the witness statement, then," Spencer interrupted, reclaiming her iPhone.

"Yeah, of course I have," Tom said, firing through a pile of papers.

"Repeatedly groping, molesting and.. are, here we are, '*despite her moving away, the guy kept following her down the carriage*', the witness says," Spencer said.

"Ahh, no I've not seen that one yet.."

"The witness was in an aisle seat, next to the perspex. She saw it all, Tom. *He* assaulted Maxwell; this guy had it coming!" Spencer said, shakily laying her phone on the desk.

"Yeah, but come on Spence, you can't condone what she's done to this man, just because he's brushed her arse on a crowded train," Tom said, staring open-faced across his desk.

Spencer's neck flushed a little in a moment of silence between them. Tom rolled his pen in the palm of his hand, before throwing it with the others into his football mug.

"We need to catch Maxwell, I know that, and I'm not excusing her actions, I'm just saying I understand them," Spencer said, with a deep inhale. "Along with every other woman I just know that this is all part of the same thing. It's just not right!"

"Spence, come on, this is not in the same category as., I don't know.."

"*Rape!*" Spencer said, exhaling heavily. "If this guy can get away with this, it escalates Tom.. so what's next?"

"But we have to keep things in perspective.."

"*Stalking* is a known precursor to murder, in *94% of cases!*" Spencer stood up abruptly, tucking her mobile into her pocket. Tom noticed her hand was trembling. "So where does this guy's shit lead to?"

Tom shifted awkwardly in his seat, sucking his lips to his teeth. "Look, I'm sorry Spence, you're right, of course."

She stood at the door, her face to the floor, holding its handle. "Action on CCTV from the tube station, boss?" she said, turned from him, wet-eyed.

"Err, yes yes. Let's do a closed-circuit track and trace from all exit points around Holborn and let's get some obs back in place on the boyfriend, err.."

"Carl Turner," Spencer said, halfway through the door.

"Yes, and on Silver Mews Terrace. Maxwell has to be heading to one of the two," he said, shuffling papers untidily into a manilla file. "And Spence, I really am sorry. It's good to have you back, we're going to need you.."

His trailing words were met by the clunk of his office door.

CHAPTER 90

Bella devoured another forkful of noodles whilst stood at the window surveying the road below. It was dusk and the lines of headlight-beaming traffic were building as rush hour approached. The rain that had speckled the window now thudded it, sparkling car noses.

"I need to go," Bella said, turning and passing her carton to Carl.

"Can you see them, are they here?" Carl said, dumping the pot onto a wooden stool that doubled as a table. Dabbing the mute button, he lurched from the couch.

Over the last few hours Bella had confessed nearly everything to Carl. He sat open-mouthed as she began by explaining that Bernadette Bateman, Jamal Johnson's grandmother, had managed to get sworn-in as a member of the Jury at his trial.

Carl had witnessed Bella's extraordinary dedication to securing a successful prosecution. Committing tirelessly to months of preparation where her paperwork was regularly strewn across his living room floor. But his jaw widened in hearing of her exploits in killing Jamal Johnson and pursuing Roman Darcy.

Whilst shocked by her actions, Carl knew full well of the depravity of these men, as she recited grisly details of their sickening sex trafficking operation. Bella's disappointment at the Court's verdict had been immeasurable, a deepening depression took her in the weeks that followed; a dark emptiness swamped her every thought.

"I'm not sure, but they'll probably come here," Bella said, striding the room.

"They know I'm in London now. That tube guy is all over the news!" She slid on her black jacket. "Once the Police get onto the bus incident they'll know exactly where I was headed."

Carl joined Bella at the window, staring down at the parked cars below his block. "A lot of these buses don't have operational cameras on board, they're just duds, deterrents," he said, wrapping an arm around her. "Besides, those pricks had it coming!"

"I know, but there's always another one crawling out from under its stone," Bella said, standing furtively at one side of the thin-curtained window "I'm starting to shock myself!"

"I'm with you now, and once you're safe you can speak to someone," he said, pecking a kiss on her head. "But until then, we stick to the plan."

"Do you think you can pick up the van early, like in the next hour or so?" she said, zipping her coat to the top.

"I can be at the garage in half an hour, I'll sign the keys out under a job I'm doing tomorrow. I tanked up the Luton yesterday, so you're good to go," he said, drawing the curtains too.

Carl had witnessed Bella's daily torment in painstakingly teasing evidence from the survivor, Marcie Stone, taking a blow by blow account of the inhumane abuses she had suffered. Marcie was damaged further by the recollection of these atrocities, suppressed memories, boxed and sealed, to protect her own mental wellbeing.

Bella had gone through personal turmoil in each of her many trips to Haversham Hall to visit Marcie, cautious of the damage she might cause in unpicking these events. Following the verdict Marcie had suffered a catastrophic relapse, falling into a permanent vegetative state. That changed everything for Bella, forever.

"This might be it for some time, you know. I hope you're not too disappointed in me?"

"Only that you went to that bloody island alone, knowing what you knew about Darcy and what went on there!"

"I know, but I just had to see the place for myself. I had no idea that they had been allowed to continue, things just spiralled," she said, locking eyes.

Carl had often been a calming influence for Bella, dampening her raging anger against the three men on trial. At one stage he had pleaded with her to seek counselling or withdraw from the case, fearing for her health. Bella was clearly damaged by her role, but in truth a volatility was already there from when he first met her, at the building site.

It was perhaps that incident which caused the spark, igniting an inferno that burned furnace-like within her. At one time dormant, it would no longer be quelled; its fiery lava coated her every thought.

"Hey, what you did out there was incredible, you saved lives and I'm so proud of you for that!" Carl said, wrapping his arms around her.

But there was so much more that he didn't know, from her past, of a childhood lost. Something deeper that shaped her anger, fuelled its growth. Carl had pried on occasion, to the same stony-faced answer; taboo subject, do not enter. It was off-limits, concealed beneath the label of 'dysfunctional family, devoid of love'.

"I know how hard you worked to get them put away!" he said, holding her close. "I just wish you'd asked me to help you, I would have gone with you."

"I know and I love you for that, I really do," she said, looking sparkly eyed at him. "But I'm happy to go to prison for what I've done and I don't want that for you."

He cupped her beautiful face, kissing her tenderly as she slid her fingers through his hair. They kissed passionately, in a desperate last time, way. Bella hid a tear, burying her head into his chest, as they clung to each other.

"There it is!" Bella said, with one eye peering over his shoulder.

"Oh, shit," Carl said, half turning to see the breaking news headline. He slumped to the couch, reaching for the remote. "That's a bit harsh, that!"

The banner read: 'Two men maimed by suspected serial killer, Arabella Maxwell.' The words rolling across the screen described her as: 'Armed and dangerous, not to be approached.' A blurry cell phone screenshot of Bella exiting a double decker bus appeared above the breaking news reel.

"Hey, at least you've managed to change your clothes and hair, babe," Carl said, glancing over his shoulder. The front door was ajar, Bella was gone.

CHAPTER 91

"Don't mind if I use your loo?" DI Spencer asked, head-nodding toward the corridor beyond the tight flat's galley kitchen.

"Yeah, yeah., go ahead," Carl Turner said. "Door on the left. Might still be a bit steamy in there, I just showered."

Carl had thought about denying the Police officers entry; they were without a warrant. But given Bella had only just left he felt it better to invite them in, delaying their search and giving her time to escape.

DI Turvey stood at the window peering down at the street, some floors below. The constant patter distorted his view, the bright lights merging with blurry traffic.

"Did you see us coming, Carl?" Neil said, flicking back the curtain.

"Nope, why.. should I have been expecting you?" Carl said, slumping onto the thready sofa.

"So, you haven't seen or heard from Miss Maxwell since..?" Neil said.

"I told you, nearly a week ago, before she went on some work trip," Carl said, tucking his phone into his trackie bottoms.

"Don't mind if I check your messages then," Neil said, with an outstretched arm.

"Fine, but you're not gonna find anything on there!"

He slapped the phone into Neil's hand, who tapped at the green icon.

"You guys want some tea or coffee?" Carl said, fidgeting with a patch on the arm of the sofa.

"That's very hospitable of you," Neil said, with widening eyes.

"Like I said, I want to find Bella as much as you do," Carl said, staring up at the officer. "I'm really worried about her. I can't believe what they're saying on the news. And that woman on the bus, c'mon, that didn't look anything like her!"

"Different hair colour was it Carl!" DI Spencer said, marching into the room. "Raucous red, is it, now?" she added, waving a box of hair dye.

"Shit, she *was* here!" Neil said, grabbing it from Spencer. He tossed the box with a glossy picture of a woman with thick red hair, to the floor. "When did she leave, Carl?" he barked.

"She's not been here!" Carl said. "That's been in there forever, I'm just a bit slack at tidying."

"The fluid's still wet on the box, Carl. And there's a woman's top in your laundry basket, matching the one in the image from the bus," Spence said, pointing at the telly. The news story was still running.

Carl got to his feet, grabbing the remote and stabbed its top button. "Look, I've had another girl around while Bella's been away, so what," Carl said, with open arms.

"Got a picture of this *Ginger Spice,* have you Carl?" Neil said.

"Err, I err.. no, but.."

"Bullshit!" Neil said. "Aiding and abetting is what you're going to get done for Carl, unless you start cooperating."

416

"Look, I'm telling you it's not Bella's hair dye, or clothes," Carl said, scooping up the box.

"Let's go Turvs," Spence said, eye-nodding at the door. "We can send another officer up to deal with Mr Turner."

The two police officers departed, with Turvey speaking into his shoulder velcroed radio.

Carl pocketed a large-ringed bundle of keys, slipped on trainers and a hoodie and exited immediately afterwards. Taking the rear firedoor, he bound the spiral staircase to the car park below.

CHAPTER 92

The constant drone of traffic was all around her, a whirring hum filling the capital's snarled streets, amidst a drizzled dimness. The tinnitus-like pitch was broken only by the sirens that burst, screeching through the concrete jungle.

An electric blue flashed off shiny roads, twinking across car bonnets and blinking back from the window-dotted walls of the ogreish buildings that towered over her.

Bella wiped the dampness from the tip of her nose and flexed her numbing fingers as a crisp chill bit, pinking her cheeks. It was a stark contrast to the tropical island's all-enveloping warmth, a strength sapping heat. She wished for an instant that she was back there, to lay upon its white sands; she could sleep for a week.

It would be an island again where only birdsong pierced its crystal skies, where a gentle ripple foamed its soft sanded shores. A paradise returned to its former beauty, its demons removed. Bella shuddered at the thought of what went before, as she ran on at pace.

Tucked almost invisibly between high walled department stores, Bella took a sharp right that didn't seem to be there. Sprinting the handlebar width alleyway that ran to the delivery area at the back. The lots were mostly empty, aside from two tailgate flapped trailers that stood idle. She scuttled past shuttered bays, before darting between lorries on the far side.

Clambering through bushes and wire fencing behind them, she stepped gingerly on to an asphalt pathway that ran alongside a straight stretch of waterway. The path was clear as she sped to a canter toward a wooden arched bridge that she bound quickly. Swivelling left on the opposite towpath, she sprinted a few hundred yards, before climbing up the raised bank.

Bella kicked hard at the weather-aged horizontal plank, at the centre of three. It splintered, first kick, and tumbled at the second. She bent, squeezing through, emerging from the bushes on the other side, beyond which it was quiet.

She jogged softly, hugging close to a row of flat roofed garages that sat beneath a lowrise block of apartments. At the end garage, Bella darted right before veering off left into a narrow passageway that led out to a small parade of shops and the council estate opposite. She could smell the grease from the Fryer Tuck-Inn.

Halfway down, the footpath split and she took a right that led into a myriad of pathways that ran the rear boundaries of private properties. Puddle-splatting, she pounded on. Where it forked three ways, Bella ran the middle one a good way, weaving a chicane, before sprinting on. Here the maize-like run of guinells channelled between high walls of proud-red brick.

She slowed to a trot, stopping at a hardwood black gate and checked her shoulders; the steady drizzle still kept the coast clear. Bella picked to ease loose a brick from the wall at her heel, pulling from behind it a gold chubb key that she slotted into the gate's padlock.

Bella closed the gate on the latch and crossed the small courtyard. Fingertip picking, she dug a silver yale from a crack below the curved lip of a large urn. At the top of three stone steps she opened the kitchen door to 35 Silver Mews Terrace, Bella was home. Closing the door with barely a sound, she stood rigid for a moment, breathless in silence. But in the blackness surrounding her, not a whisper came back; it was safe.

Twelve minutes later, with a rucksack taut to her back, Bella backed out through the kitchen door, hauling a bulky load strapped tight to an aluminium trolley. The sizable parcel was bound in taped sealed plastic bags. It bounced awkwardly with each step, rocking its weight that heaved to one side and then the other as its wheels manoeuvred slowly.

Bella spun it to face forward, pushing it across the yard and into the alley, leaving the gate flapping behind her. The thick-treaded wheels of the trolley travelled smoothly the tarmacadam pathways that led from the property. Suddenly an explosive air gusting blast and eruption of *crackling* shattering glass boomed. A yellowy hue momentarily lit the skies, illuminating the gloomy alleys.

Bella ploughed on, arriving moments later at a gravelly makeshift parking area, where she turned the trolley again, hauling it backwards. She bumped the load towards a white van parked on the nearside, by the exit. Feeling the inner tread of the driver's side rear wheel, she found its key. Unlocking the van, Bella zipped across the side-sliding door and tipped-up the load, to fall halfway inside. Lifting it clear of the trolley, she heaved, pushing it onboard and swished the door closed.

Cheek puffing, Bella stood for a second brow-wiping before shoving the trolley into the bushy ground on one side of the parking space. She jumped behind the wheel, slotted the key and went to close the door. She saw the glow of his fag before his angular features and snide expression. The door was propped wide by a tall man leant against it, sucking a cigarette.

"Looks like you might need a hand with something in there, sweetcheeks?" he said, pluming a tobacco cloud into the cab.

CHAPTER 93

"I would recommend leaving it a couple of hours before you go in," the fire Chief said, easing his peaked helmet from his head. "If it's absolutely essential that you get in there immediately, then you'll need full PPE."

The three engines sprawling the end of Silver Mews Terrace were each being re-equipped by firefighters. Some were tugging off fire retardant jackets and removing masks. Deflated hoses slid like sidewinder desert snakes across the sopping pavement, recoiling to be racked in the side of firetrucks. The rain had finally subsided, leaving a clear moonless sky.

"No sign of life?" DCI Tom Broad said, staring at the smouldering end of terrace property. It looked like something from a horror movie, with ghostly grey smoke trails drifting from its windows.

"Not on the ground or first floor," he said. "There is a basement that remains flooded, but nothing registered on the PatSav monitor down there."

The chatter of neighbourhood voices came into focus as Tom turned to face his opposite number from the fire service. "Basement, you say?" Tom said, before lifting his hand. "Err, excuse me one second, Chief. Turvs, can you get everyone back another ten metres, take contact details of residents only, then send everyone home!"

"Will do guv," Neil said, adding with a wink, "Nothing to see here!"

"Sorry Chief, you were saying, there's a basement? Only we've searched this house previously and I don't recall that," Tom said. "Land registry records log all properties on this avenue as having former coal cellars filled to preserve their post war structure. The whole area was heavily bombed."

"Well they have one here!" the Chief said, wedging his hat between elbow and midriff. "There's an access route to it off the hallway behind one of the panels. Easily missed I suppose; the entire halfway was clad in them. Late 19th century mahogany.. it went up like a tinderbox!"

"Shit!" Tom said, head-scratching. "And you've not been down there?" he added, with eyebrows rising.

"Our priority was the fire, sir. It's not a huge problem if an area is flooded," he said sternly.

"Sorry, yes! Of course, I understand that," Tom said. "But can we get down there?"

"Well as I say, I wouldn't recommend it, certainly not without a decent pair of waders!"

"But, you're pumping the basement out now, I assume?" Tom said, tapping at his iPhone.

"Engine number one, there," he said pointing at the fire truck parked directly outside the house. "It may take a while.."

"Spence, this place has a basement!" Tom said. "S-sorry Chief, thanks for your help!"

"No problem, sir. Good luck with your investigation," he said, before striding away.

"Spence, it's submerged at the moment, so I'm going to need some waders brought down here," Tom said. "They're long, fishing-like, waterproof trousers."

"Yes, I do know what they are, guv! And no, we don't have any here," Spencer said.

"Ok, ok, just bring my wellington boots. They're behind the filing cabinet in my office."

"Wellies, boss? I've got a pair in the boot, if you need them," Neil said, arriving at Tom's side.

"Great. Grab them and meet me in the hallway Turvs, and get a mask on, will you," Tom said. "I don't want any more smoke inhalation claims."

CHAPTER 94

The council estate dated back to the seventies. White plastic strips strapped across the middle of every house, sandwiched between huge windows on the ground and upper floors.

Bella slowed the Luton to a crawl, trundling as she peered at house numbers. Many didn't seem to have one, whilst others had whitewashed metre-length digits on garage doors. Nearly every property had a van of some sort, parked on their strip of tarmac. The Luton was well placed here, camouflaged amidst the trades community.

Sixty two had a people-carrier, with signage on its front and side; Tommo's Taxi. Bella trundled on, past a woman in a fluffy dressing gown dumping a bin bag beside a lampost at the foot of her drive. She cast a cursory glance over before laying a fag on her lip, and disappeared into the yellowy light inside her front door.

A red truck with a triple-folded ladder on its roof rack was parked on the front lawn of *seventy four*. Its driveway, already occupied by a washing machine and fridge freezer. A hooded guy strode in sync with a quick shuffling pitbull, obedient at his side. *Eighty six* still had a metal-plated sign hung in its window; 'Santa Claus - Please Stop!'

And there it was, *ninety*. Neatly hand painted in cherry red, with a curly nine and ruby ball O, above a rusty letterbox flap. Bella pulled into the curb outside the house and switched off the engine. She loosened the cord pulley on her rucksack and rummaged inside before strolling to the front door. Poking its doorbell, she cast an eye over her shoulders whilst waiting.

"Mrs Thornton?" she said, to the frail looking woman who answered.

The wrinkly-eyed pensioner peered up at Bella. "Yes, that's right, dear," she said, in a sing-songy, sweet voice. A silver linked-chain dangled across the narrow gap between the door and its frame.

"Hi, I'm Stacey. I'm a friend of Ben's. I know he's on the late shift at Heathrow tonight, so he asked me to stop by and check on you," Bella said, flashing a soft smile. "I hope he's mentioned me?"

"Well, not really, dear. I'm afraid he never tells me about any of his girlfriend's." Mrs Thornton's face narrowed, squinting, peering closely at the young woman.

"Well I brought his Spurs cap back. He left it at mine, the daft sod," Bella said, slipping it off her head and passing it through the gap.

Taking the hat, she smiled, thanking the girl, as a flash of recognition twinkled in her eyes.

"Well Ben's told me all about you, Mrs T, so, *dada*.. it's your favourite - fish and chips!" Bella swung a thin white plastic bag from behind her back. "I won't come in, as you don't know me yet," she said, passing the warm food parcel between the door and frame.

"Oh, don't be silly dear, any friend of Ben's is a friend of mine," she said softly. "Besides, you'll need to help me with this." She beamed up at her visitor enjoying her childlike excitement in presenting the bulging bag. "My appetite isn't what it was."

"Well, only if you're sure that I'm not a mad axe murderer," Bella said, beaming at the old lady as she closed, then widened the door.

"Oh, at my age, I think I can tell. We're not all as stupid as we look, you know!" she said, with a subtle wink. "Come on in, out of the cold."

"Ahh, it's lovely and warm in here," Bella said, dropping to one knee. "Oh, I love your tabby." The thick furred feline's head poked from the living room doorway.

"Now that's Geraldine, she's a bit fussy with people. Likes to get to know someone before deciding if they're allowed to stroke her!" she said.

"Bit of company for you, I'll bet?" Bella said, slipping the hood of her windbreaker onto one of the three coat hooks below an oval mirror in the hallway.

"I prefer the talking sort dear, and I don't get much of that at my age," Mrs Thornton said, whilst tottering down the corridor towards the boxy little kitchen at the end.

"I'm sure it must get lonely at times," Bella said, following her with the warm bag dangling at her side.

"It does, and that's why I want to hear all about you, Tracey," she said, opening the cupboard at her shoulder. "Now let me get some plates. Fish and Chips, how lovely."

"It's Stacey, Mrs T," Bella said, with a warm smile. "Yep, Cod and chips," she added, laying the bag on the little round table and pulling out a chair.

"Cod, you say.. not Haddock?" Mrs Thornton said, with a quizzical look at her guest.

"Err-yes, sorry, I thought Ben said Cod," Bella said, lip biting.

"Oh, that's fine, Stacey. Why don't you go into the living room and I'll bring the plates through. It's much cosier in there, dear," she said.

"Ok, if you're sure," Bella said, settling in the front room.

After their supper the old lady took the dishes into the kitchen, humming softly whilst she washed them. Bella rifled the draws of her bureau, having earlier checked the bedroom dresser when excusing herself to the bathroom. Finally, she had what she needed and joined Mrs Thornton at the sink, where she stood drying the tea cups.

"I had better be off now. It's been lovely to meet you," Bella said, cupping her thin skinned hand. "I hope to see you again soon."

"Now now, I wouldn't want to end our lovely dinner with a lie," she said, with a widening gaze. "You could have asked for whatever it was you needed, you know. Passport, was it?"

"How did you.."

"*Old*, but not senile," she said. "I do watch the news, you know. There's not a lot else in my life, except watching that thing."

"I'm so sorry, I didn't mean to scare you.."

"*Scare me!*" she said, with a little chortle. "You are, *Arabella Maxwell*, aren't you!"

Bella nodded slowly, her lower lip dropping.

"Then I know that I'm not in any danger," she said, beaming at Bella. "You do realise that half the country is on your side, my dear?"

"You knew.. all this time?" Bella said, with a hesitant grin.

"I was more than happy to play along until you said, or took, what you needed," she said. "It's been something of a thrill having a celebrity in the house!"

"Was it me not knowing your favourite supper; bringing cod, not haddock?" Bella said, laying her hand on the little old lady's shoulder. "I guess I slipped up there!"

"That was one thing, yes, but I knew it was you, at the door. You've very distinctive eyes my dear, beautiful but recognisable," she said, smiling sweetly. "Maybe try using contact lenses., different colours, you know."

Bella laughed, hugging Martha Thornton.

"Besides that, Benjamin did tell me about a strange incident with a woman at the airport," she said. "Mind you, they haven't mentioned that on the news yet!" She put a finger to her lips.

"I hate to have used you both like this, and I'll post it back, by the way," Bella said, waving the passport. "Ben mentioned the trip to Florida that you've got planned for your 80th! That's when I knew you'd have an up to date passport."

"Please don't worry about that, my dear," Martha said.

"I really didn't want to upset your plans, and it sounds like you deserve a good holiday," Bella said. "Ben told me that you've brought him up single-handedly, since his mum died."

"Gosh, you've got more out of Benjamin in one conversation than I do in a month. Didn't mention his father, I'll bet!" she said, cussing.

"Nope, he was just glowing about you, Martha, he shied away at any Dad talk."

"Well, that is a whole other story. That lowlife just upped and left, disappeared somewhere up north, without a bye-your-leave. Not a thought for his little boy," she said, her hand trembling. "And what he did to my poor daughter! I said from day one, he was a wrong-un!"

A tiny tear trickled from her watery eyes, trailing the fine wrinkles of her wafer thin cheek. She untucked a tissue from the sleeve of her cardigan and dabbed her face gently.

"I'm so sorry to hear that, Martha," Bella said, putting an arm around her. "Why don't we sit back down and you can tell me all about it?"

Despite Martha's protestations that Bella should make her escape, they settled back into the front room, where Martha brought a fresh pot of tea and her best china on a tray. They chatted for quite a while before she pottered back into the kitchen, returning with a tartan flask and tupperware box.

"Now you get yourself somewhere safe," Martha said, helping Bella with the arm of her coat. "After what you've done, saving all those young women and standing up to those men, you deserve a medal, never mind being chased by the police!"

Bella shuddered in stepping from her door into the frosty air, the temperature had dropped considerably. Blowing Martha a kiss from the van, she drove off, headed out of London, heading North.

CHAPTER 95

"Are you at the bottom, boss.. Is it still flooded down there?" Neil asked, without a response.

Neil was surrounded by blackened, blistered wood panelling that still smouldered. Despite the constant heavy dripping above him, the air remained thick with lung clogging smoke.

"I'm gonna try and get you a better torch," Neil shouted down, through the slight rectangular ingress, where a single panel had been removed.

Neil peered into the dark space that had lay hidden behind the hallway wall. Beyond its entrance was a narrow concrete stairwell, just a few feet from where he stood. At the foot of the steps was a flicker of light from Tom Broad's pen torch as he scanned the basement.

"There's five steps, maybe another below the waterline, I'm not sure," Tom said, squinting to follow his light. "There's a cramped low ceilinged passage, with two doorways off it, presumably with rooms behind them." He waded-on towards them.

His head-jerked back, instantly recognised the foul odour that drifted like a toxic mist over the murky water, penetrating his mask. The putrid stench of decomposing flesh swamped the cramped space. Tom pinched his 3M a little tighter to his nostrils as he sloshed slowly forward. There was an eeriness, a sense of foreboding at what lay ahead.

"Can you get inside them?" Neil yelled.

"Yes, I think so, the door nearest to me looks ajar," Tom said, puffing as he waded gingerly on, ducking his head in avoiding a weight-bowed beam. "The floor feels uneven here, so I'm not sure how deep the water is.. Oh SHIT!"

"Boss?" Neil shouted. "You found something?"

"No, I haven't!" he bellowed back. "These boots have just flooded over, and I've dropped the bloody torch!"

Shrill, broken-laughter echoed into the concrete dungeon. "Well they did say you'd need waders!" Neil said, cackling.

"Just get some proper lighting rigged up down here!" Tom barked, turning back with one hand on the low ceiling. "And chase SOCO, will you. I don't want to mess this up, before they get started!"

"Will do, guv," Neil said.

"And Turvs., find out what the hell happened to the obs I ordered on this place?" Tom said, stumbling through the narrow corridor in the darkness.

"Yep, already been on it, boss," Neil said, leaning into the recess. "They've said, 'front of house only' was the brief. Apparently it's something of a rat run, the alleys at the back, so there wasn't the personnel to monitor all exit points."

"I don't give a shit if it's Hampton Court at the back!" Tom boomed. "If they'd done the job they were asked to do, we'd have Maxwell and possibly Pierre Lebouf right now!"

"You think that she kept him down there?" Neil said.

"Of course she did. We know she kept him alive somewhere because the money's still disappearing from his accounts. It's password access only remember with fingertip and eyeball ID. Unless she's dismembered Lebouf too."

"I wouldn't put it past her, guv!" Neil said, waving smoke clear, to peer into the hole. He pinned a sleeve to his nose as a strange vegetative pungency fogged the hatchway.

A high pitched ring suddenly echoed in the cave-like crawlspace, followed by a hefty thud and barrage of foul language. "You okay, boss!"

"Spence, I can't speak right now. I'm literally up to my eyes in it!" Tom said.

"It's just that we've pulled Carl Turner in, we're holding him in the soft interview suite. In the last two hours he accessed the Council plant and took a van out. We picked him up at his flat in Marylebone Heights, but the vehicle is missing."

"Check CCTV from the depot and from around the back of this place, Silver Mews Terrace, will you Spence?" Tom said, grabbing a metal pipe that ran the length of the basement.

"Will do," Spencer said, nodding at Jeremy Forsythe as he ambled into the office. "By the way, the team is meeting shortly for Jeremy's evidence. Do you want us to delay it?"

"No., but hold fire on Turner," Tom said, wading to the steps. "There's not a lot we can do here without SOCO. As soon as I'm out of these blasted Wellington's we'll be with you."

"Wellington's, boss?" Spence said, smiling across at the professor.

"Never mind," Tom said, hauling his waterlogged foot onto a submerged step. "Crack on with the profiling meeting, get what you can from Forsythe. And, I want traffic monitors focused on the M25 belt with that van's reg."

"Will do, boss."

"Oh and Spence. Stick Carl Turner in the hard room will you. Me and Neil will take it from there," Tom said, finding the next step on the tight stairway with water slopping from the lip of his boots. "That guy's had his fucking chance!"

"Ok, I'll keep you posted," Spence said, hanging up. "One minute please, Jeremy," she whispered, tapping two digits on the inter-office telephone.

DI Spencer gave instructions to traffic officers to widen the search parameters of their monitoring, within the two-hour time band from Turner having taken the vehicle from the depot. Locating the white Luton van was a priority.

"Jeremy.. apologies," Spence said softly, smiling at professor Forsythe, just as the external phone rang.

Spencer fielded the call from Douglas Stewart MD at Finance International, a close colleague of Pierre Lebouf. Stewart confirmed that another code-authorised payment, at the maximum daily allowance of one million dollars, had cleared his account in the last hour.

With a finger in the air, Spencer mouthed one minute as she stepped from the office to speak with one of the Maxwell-team, requesting that he inform all that the Forsythe briefing was postponed.

"So sorry, lot's happening on this one!" Spencer said, closing the office door and bouncing back into the chair behind the desk.

"Not at all, my dear," Jeremy Forsythe said, settling into a seat opposite the young detective. "I do appreciate this is a fast moving investigation."

"It certainly is, and given that, we feel it best that you let me know your findings. The team is somewhat, otherwise occupied, you understand" she said, smiling. "Can I get you some tea?"

CHAPTER 96

"With Maxwell, we're dealing with someone with a deep-rooted disturbance," the senior profiler said, peering over the top of his horn rimmed glasses. "A psychopathy that would have laid dormant for years, festering."

Spencer, flipped a faint lined notepad and clicked her pen. "Her psychopathy?"

"In Maxwell's case, a severe mental illness, an undiagnosed disorder," Jeremy said.

"But we're talking about a high-functioning, academically gifted young woman," Spencer said, with fingers clasping her pad.

"Quite, and that makes it all the more worrying," Jeremy said, scratching his eyebrow. "Matters appear to be escalating, and quickly. Are you sure you wouldn't prefer that I speak to the group, or wait for Tom?"

"No-no. Please press on, professor."

"I have now received a full background check on Arabella Maxwell. That is to say, as complete as records would allow!"

"You're missing stuff?"

"I'm afraid so, yes. Arabella was brought up by her grandfather, Charles, and the tracing department has struggled to locate any record of the mother, Selina Maxwell. And yet she isn't registered as deceased and has never been reported as a missing person."

"How strange, but what about Grandad, could he still be around? We received a HMRC report that his pension was still being claimed," Spencer said, leaning back in her chair.

"Aside from movement in his finances, which led to a bogus account, there is absolutely no evidence that he is alive. Nobody has seen or heard from Charles Maxwell for nearly ten years," Jeremy said, with spiky eyebrows arching his frames.

"You don't think he could have been held captive in that basement, surely?" Spencer said, to a knowing shrug from the wily profiler. "So, we're aware of the basic facts set out in your preliminary report," she continued swiftly, peeling open a thick blue folder. "Ahh yes, here we are;"

Selina Maxwell, reported as having been drugged and raped on the evening of her sixteenth birthday, following a night out at Citycatz nightclub. A venue owned by a young financier, Pierre Lebouf.

Selina reported the incident to Police, but no charges were brought against anyone and the accusation was later withdrawn. As a result of the assault she fell pregnant, and Arabella was born nine months later.

The papertrail relating to Selina dries up a few years later at which point her father, Charles Maxwell, files for custody of his grandchild, Arabella, then age four. She remained under his care, residing at Silver Mews Terrace until she turned eighteen.

Deeds to the property were transferred to Arabella Maxwell shortly before she left to take up residence in University halls at Manchester Uni. She studied Law over a three year period before returning to Silver Mews. Blah, blah, blah..

She took up permanent employment at a Barristers Chambers in London.. Her first role being part of the prosecution team in the trial of the TikTokTrio last year.

"Did I miss anything?" Spencer said, folding the report's cover.

"Not a thing my dear, but, *Everything*!" Jeremy said, placing his spectacles on the desk. "Arabella was a product of rape, the most heinous of crimes that would have significantly altered her psychology, believing herself *different; a mistake, abnormal, unwanted.*"

"Tough start, agreed," Spencer said, crossing her arms. "She lost her mum, at age four. No father, of course, and grandmother had died of cancer before she was born, chronic smoker. So she was parented by her grandfather.."

Jeremy said, "Yes, Charles Maxwell, a former scion of the financial establishment, but a man with a police record for paedophilia!"

"But Jeremy, the only thing we ever had on him, related to minor banking corruption charges."

"That was in his later years, working in the international markets. But we dug a little deeper than that, my dear," Jeremy said, with a wry smile tickling his lips. "He was caught up in a police raid in south London in his late teens. Only paper records back then of course. They were buried along with others, never manually transferred onto the criminal database."

"And this was a paedophile ring raid?" Spencer said, with elbows poking the desk.

"Yes, to be precise, he was part of Sidney Cook's gang," he said, with a little headshake. "Maxwell should have been red flagged as soon as Cook and his cohorts were convicted."

"*Sid Cook..* Jesus Christ, how did they miss that!"

"There were seven young men in Cook's flat; mostly late teens. They were his goffer's; his chicken run boys he called them," Jeremy said, removing his spectacles and breathing heavily into the glass.

"*Chicken run?*"

"Cook's preferred demographic was three to six year olds. He referred to them as his *Chicken*. He recruited men of a similar persuasion to his, sending them out to pick up *Chicken*," Jeremy said, tugging an oversized yellowing handkerchief from his pocket.

"I remember the case.. I thought they were all sent down?" Spencer said, twiddling her pen.

"The main culprits were. But there was no evidence against Charles Maxwell, he only stood accused of loitering outside schools, they couldn't pin anything else on him and charges were dismissed." Jeremy, de-smearing his glasses added, "You can't prosecute someone for being *acquainted* with a paedophile."

"So you're suggesting that Charles Maxwell went on to abuse his granddaughter, Arabella, and this was a *trigger for vengeance* for her, when it came to Darcy and other men?"

"Abused her, *yes*, more than likely," Jeremy said. "We have witness evidence from neighbours that Charles Maxwell invited many, shall we say, unsavoury characters to the house. One source., the gay chap.."

"Is his sexuality relevant, Jeremy?" Spencer said, headshaking slowly, clasping the report.

Sliding his frames to the bridge of his nose, Jeremy continued. "Sorry., *the nosey neighbour* from Silver Mews terrace, took photographs of the men toing and froing at the property. He presented them to the police, as part of his noise complaint, at the time."

Spencer, rifled the pages, arriving at some grainy black and white images, whilst the professor noisily drained his tea. "There are better pictures toward the back of my report," he said, tapping the blue bound folder with a stubby finger. "There was little the police could do, of course."

"Surely, they should have investigated, and informed social services," Spencer said, staring daggers. "There was a vulnerable young girl in that house!"

"One officer ran the pictures through the photofit T-match system and found a fifty-five point comparable to a registered sex offender. But sixty plus was the cut off on imagery evidence, as it still is today," Jeremy said, with an eye-roll. "Besides, social services were never far away. There were regular, 'pre-booked' visits."

"They never fucking learn, do they!" Spencer snapped. "Excuse my language, Professor."

"No-no, quite justified, my dear," he said, with a little nod. "It's a bit like an Ofsted inspection, where forewarned is forearmed!"

"Jesus, that poor little girl, she was like a lamb to the slaughter," Spencer said, edging on her chair. "It's a miracle she got through childhood, let alone go on to University. And then working in Barristers Chambers, on *that* case.. Christ, of all the cases!"

"And it was Arabella alone who was charged with meeting the victims," Jeremy said, opening a little brown notebook. "You will recall that two of the three survivors were trapped in mutism. At trial they referred to them as *The Tender Dead*, rather apt I felt."

"Yes, it was only Marcie Stone that provided evidence in Court, I cried when I heard it," Spencer said, with a breathy sigh. "I remember her parents' impact statement, Marcie was a shadow of her former self. You can understand Arabella's bubbling hatred of men."

"I quite agree. Maxwell was already harbouring an overwhelming loathing. It would have been unleashed when the men that she worked so hard to put behind bars, walked free, to resume their trafficking business."

"I think we can safely say that there was a lot more than just sex-trafficking going on out there, Jeremy!" Spencer said, with a frosty glare.

"Whatever it is, our Miss Maxwell was changed irrevocably by the Court's decision to release these men," Jeremy said, removing his spectacles. "Her dormant, hitherto controlled psychopathy, was finally untethered. It reached a tipping point, flicked a switch."

"But you're not actually saying that she's a psychopath. This is purely vengeance, vigilantism for women's rights, stuff?" Spencer said, cocking her head.

"The removal of body parts tells us otherwise, these are calculated, egregious crimes," Jeremy said, his eyes peering over the rim of his spectacles. "The head of Jamal Johnson was removed and placed in the refrigerator of his aged grandmother. Recently reported incidents involve the severing of one man's penis and biting through the tongue of another. The speed of escalation here is quite staggering."

"Crazy I know, but there's logic here, some justification. Surely you can see that given what you've said about her life, what she's been through?"

"Abnormal and extremely violent behaviour, these are clear indicators of a person severely affected by a chronic mental disorder," Jeremy said, tapping the tip of his finger on the desk. "I do appreciate that she has engendered the support of half the population, *but*," he sighed softly.

"But..?" Spencer said, leaning over the desk. The chair creaked loudly in a moment of silence between them.

"*But..* Arabella Maxwell fits the bill entirely, there's no doubt about it," he said, laying his glasses on the report. "She *is* a psychopath."

CHAPTER 97

The little Indian restaurant nearly emptied as the last of the large parties filed out. With bellies now filled, the droopy-eyed men stumbled into the chilling air.

She had watched them for the last hour. Hordes of alcohol-fuelled zombies shovelling poppadoms between mouthfuls of lager. Trolley's stacked with steam-rising pots were scattered all about them, filling tables that were too small for their load. In the dumb-struck pauses between their drunken slurring, heads were bowed, faces disappearing into plates.

The curry-munching morons, only lifted from their gluttonous feed to demand more amber-frothed drinks, before the *banter* resumes. It boomed to her vantage, right across the street, their boastful yammer, punctuated only by the raucous burst of laughter.

The groups staggered off towards the clubbing areas of town, swaying with arms across shoulders, before disappearing down the darker side roads, where the house music thudded.

But *he* was still there, at a table in the corner, tucked from prying eyes and the attention of others. He was just as Martha Thornton had described him, with more than a hint of Tom Selleck. Unmistakable from his profile picture, with thatch of greasy black hair and matching eyebrows, arching his ghostly pale face. He was fidgeting a little, waiting for his date to return from the ladies, perhaps fearing she wouldn't.

He sat stroking his 70's moustache, that aged him in both style and years. And there she was, a sweet looking girl, at least twenty years his junior. He stood before she'd joined him, not in manners, but impatient to exit and pay. Tossing notes to the white clothed table, he slung an arm around her waist, steering her out. Another butterfly, trapped in his web of deceit.

With cursory searches of Linkedin and Facebook, he was easy to find. Plumber arrives from out of town, sets up a business and buys property in his own name (with the money he stole from his late wife). Add in the bonus of a mate that loves to *tag* him, and you've pretty much got his routine scheduled. This loser wasn't hard to track down and the visual ID check was a formality given he was the only Magnum PI fan in town.

Bella had parked the Luton a few streets away with its cargo still safely secured inside, tied to the back wall, barely conscious. The final pouch of Saline read only 3%, but she'd squeezed it hard and he was gurgling like a baby when she changed his face strapping. She'd gone full Pulp Fiction on him, with a leather strapped helmet rounding his cheeks to a saliva-dripping pink ball, bulging out of his thin lipped mouth. Lebouf could wait for now, whilst she dealt with this other guy.

She watched intently as Magnum marched ahead of the girl, skirting the pavement and arm-waving at the traffic. Within seconds a taxi pulled-in, he swung its back door open, ushering her inside. A word or two was exchanged before he slammed it closed, and she was gone. He walked on briskly, alone.

Her first date excuses, or maybe he changed his mind, certainly she'd had a lucky escape. Either way, this would be easier now. Bella zipped high, flipped her hood and yanked the cords, barely her eyes showing as a burning warmth grew behind them. His time was up.

CHAPTER 98

Tom Broad, strode into his office with a tea towel draping his damp shirted shoulder. He was barefoot, with a face that warned; Keep Clear. Spencer leapt up from behind his desk.

"Why didn't the team meeting go ahead, hearing Forsythe's evidence?" he snapped, pausing at the corner of his desk, to allow Spencer to squeeze past him.

"Well, I can explain that.."

"And, why on earth has Carl Turner been released from custody, when I specifically told you to hold him!"

"If you'll let me, I can explain.."

"Honestly Spence, I need to be able to trust you," Tom said, easing between desk and chair.

There was a soft tutting behind her, where DI Turvey, with shoulder to the doorframe, cast her a little headshake. "Sir," she said, in an elevated tone, fleeting him a face full of scorn.

"The team were fielding calls from Lebouf's company. A significant monetary transfer has been made, but the transaction registered from a different geographical signal this time. Maxwell's probably on the move and possibly got Lebouf with her."

"Are you having a giraffe, Spence," Tom said, whilst drying between his toes. "We all know she's on the move!"

Turvey's grin widened, "That's why she torched the house, and the basement's now empty!"

"Oh, is that the same basement you didn't find, despite searching the property, twice!" she sniped, with pulled-grin.

"Alright, alright," Tom said, swapping foot and resuming towelling. "What else?"

"Comms officers and CCTV tracers have confirmed reg-plate recognition bleeps for the van. They've triangulated it somewhere just north of Birmingham," she said, smirking at Turvey.

"Great, do we have any patrol teams up there?" Tom said, tugging socks on.

"Two currently on their way. Mapping is struggling with signals through the Peak District, but we've narrowed it to within 80-square, with four forces awaiting strategic placement."

"Well Carl Turner might have known where she was headed," Neil said, arm-crossing. "You should never have let him go!"

"On that, sir. A senior Brief from Maxwell's Chambers turned up, with credible grounds for Turner's immediate release," Spencer said.

"What possible grounds could he have had?" Neil said, smirking.

"She," Spencer said loudly, in Neil's direction. "Had a letter from Turner's employers, confirming his authority vis-a-vis use of the van. And aside from disputing our flimsy grounds for holding him, she had medical records, evidencing his predisposition to stress, citing concern for Carl's wellbeing under duress. She already had a Court sealed application!"

"Christ, that's quick work," Tom said, tossing his towel to the filing cabinet. "It seems Maxwell has people in her corner."

"That's not the half of it," Spencer said. "His brief even produced footage showing that Turner had legitimately parked the Luton in readiness to attend his next scheduled job. We had zero choice, boss."

"Just coincidence then, that the van was parked a stone's throw from Maxwell's house!" Neil said, with an arched Roger Moore-like eyebrow.

The internal phone rang, breaking a building tension. "Err, excuse me," Tom said, snatching the phone. Spencer's face wrinkled, having reached for the handset. "I am still in charge here!" he added, with palm across the receiver. "Yes, go ahead."

The two officers stood in silence, watching as Tom's expression turned slowly to that of a wrinkly pug. He tapped furiously at his laptop keyboard, scanning the monitor. Pinning the phone between shoulder and jaw he leaned forwards, fumbling in a draw before slapping a piece of paper in front of him.

"Could you repeat the location; precisely where was he found? Only on my screen that isn't actually a car park," Tom said, scribbling frantically.

Spencer and Turvey shuffled into seats, opening their pocket books. Tom slammed the phone down after a cursory, thanks.

"Right!" Tom said, folding the paper. "A body's been discovered in bushes, near to where Turner left the van. Neil, I want you on that," Tom said, passing him the note. "Spence, we're going North, so get us the latest trace update. And let's try and find where that last Lebouf payment went, get Winks on it."

"You want me to get SOCO on this, body?" Neil said, waving the note.

"Nope, I want you on the victim," Tom said, getting to his feet and rounding the desk. "Apparently he's been filleted from throat to crotch!"

446

"The victim, guv.. he's alive?"

"Yep, and fighting to stay that way. He might not have long! Spence., let's walk and talk," Tom said, leading her out of the office. "Now tell me about Forsythe; what's his verdict on this girl?"

"Err, Guv," Neil yelled, as they walked away. "You might wanna put some shoes on!"

CHAPTER 99

Bella was crouched twenty feet from the block flats, half hidden behind some bushes. He flung the entrance door wide and entered the building. The entry system buzzing was her signal to move, catching the door before its re-engagement with its auto-locking frame. She was inside.

Silently she followed his stomping of the metal staircase and exit towards his apartment. Bella released the velcro strap inside her jacket pocket, clasping her flicknife. He was just a few doors down; she strode swiftly, as he bent to slot his yale.

Wrist-twisting he scraped metal into metal and pushed the soft creaking door, before being shoved forcefully from behind. He crashed through the doorway, his face smashing into the door from the speed of thrust, sending him sprawling to the carpeted hallway. Before he could move, she was on him, with the blade cold to his throat.

"One fucking word and this slits you open," she hissed.

His bulging eyes nodded his compliance. Tugging a pool ball from her pocket she ordered him to open wide, and shoved it into his mouth.

"You make a sound, and this baby goes in," she whispered into his ear, poking the tip of the knife into his neck, barely resisting puncture. "Now face the floor, there's a good boy."

Bella slid cable ties from her jacket and pinned his wrists to meet at the small of his back, lassoing them before jerking the tie taut. She looped a second strap around his ankles, probing the steel at his spine as she tugged the strap too.

Bella stood and closed the door, watching his eel-like struggle as he twisted and turned, before she hauled him up. Peeling back her hood, she shuffled him into the living room which doubled as a kitchen. The familiar stench of nicotine was dense, not the branded cigars of her grandfather, but cheaper dried leaves that were Rizla bound.

Thrusting him onto one of the two uprights, she unravelled a length of rope from her rucksack, wrapping it tight around him. Now disabled, Bella searched him, throwing his wallet and iPhone onto the nearby half-moon folding table. His head shook and eyes blooded in fury. Rounding him and grabbing his wrist, she finger-id'd his cell. Flopping to the opposite chair she scrolled, checked his last messages and dating app interactions.

Bella sat with legs akimbo, tutting at the drooling man. "Ahh, here it is!" she said, bouncing up and circling him again.

This time he wriggled harder, tugging rigidly at each restraint, before he felt the knife's tip at the back of his neck. Instantly settling, his thumb was pushed against his iPhone once more.

"I knew you plumbers make a lot," she said, tapping digits into his banking app. "And you, with a child to care for, and always pleading poverty.. shame on you!"

Bella stood over him, fixing eye contact as the glint of silver reflected back. He rocked in his chair, eyes twitching somewhere between anger and fear, his saliva trail thickening.

"Now, this," she whispered, leaning to his ear. "Is for Tracy Thornton."

Bella thrust the blade into his abdomen, plunging easily through the soft flesh, piercing his organs. With a near-silent scream, his head jerked in violent convulsion, spittle fired the edges of the juddering pink ball. Bella finger-poked the shiny gag deeper into his mouth, as his face exploded in pain, his eyes blistered bloodshot .

"And, this," she said, waving the iPhone. "Is for Benjamin Thornton, your son!" Bella slid the bank cards and cash from his wallet, pocketing them along with the mobile. "I've heard all about you from Ben's gran; you remember Martha don't you, sweet old lady?"

Tossing the wallet to the floor she strode to the fridge, tutting whilst examining its contents. He remained writhing in the chair as the open wound from his stomach pulsed, his shirt now a glistening claret.

"Oh, do stop your moaning," she said, popping the tab of a cola can. "It's only a flesh wound, it won't kill you as long as someone finds you.. if not, tough luck!"

Bella gulped at the drink as she strolled across the living space. From the ruffled centre of the curtains she snuck a peek down at the quiet road below. Parked cars lined one side.

"You treated Tracy like a piece of shit, every day of the six years you were together. Roughed her up a bit too didn't you, hey, enjoy that did you?" she said, striding over to him. "I've seen the pictures, you sick scumbag!"

Defeated, pleading eyes now stared up at her. She poked the pink ball a little deeper with the tip of her finger. It spun a little, sparkling like a glitter ball as he choked, spluttering and flaring his nostrils.

"There's a standing order going out to your son, Ben, every month. A reasonable amount, given what he's been through, losing his mum, and not having a father!"

She noticed a sideboard in the corner with a glass tray on it with ash overflowing from it. Bella rifled its drawers, emptying the contents, pausing to read some papers, before discarding them to the floor. Tugging the sleeve from her wrist, she clicked at the TV remote, dabbing the mute button before finding the news channel.

"You default on any of these payments and I'll be back," she said, striding the room. "I will find you and finish you. Trust me on that."

Glancing at the telly, she beamed, turning slowly back to him, his face flickering between the TV and his assailant. It was Bella's face above a rolling banner; Three men brutally attacked in the last 24 hours.

"Better make that four," she said, with a wink. With begging eyes, his face shook desperately, umming at her. "I had best be going now."

The TV now showed an excitable young news reporter, standing on the top deck of a London bus. The camera panned down the aisle to an area of dark staining, before a photo of a young male filled the screen above the words; Teenage boy attacked.

Bella closed the living room door quietly behind her, wiping a smear of red from her finger onto a coat that was hung in the hall. Silently turning the door-latch just a quarter, she stopped as she heard it, and froze. So faint at first that she almost dismissed it. Statuesque, in breath-held silence, it was imaginary surely, that sweet babbling innocence.

A sound that awakened something within, swamping all else, tugging her every fibre; that vulnerable soft gurgle. Then a momentary pause, before the shrill scream of abandon exploded all around her.

CHAPTER 100

Tom Broad pulled a tupperware box out of his holdall, wedging it between his legs, he peeled the cover off. "Cheese or Chicken?"

Spencer threw him a head shaking side-eye and refocused on the road.

"You should eat, this could be a long night." He eased a sandwich out and threw the box onto the back seat. "Right, I'm going with the chicken."

The bluetooth blasted and Spencer swiftly turned the dial, halving its volume at the second ring. "Broad, go ahead."

"McGiven, from SOCO at Silver Mews Terrace, sir," came the somewhat robotic response.

"What have you got, Mac?"

"Cellar-like space situated below the property's front living room. An area split by breeze block walls, dividing it into three, a narrow corridor and two six by four doored rooms. The renovations look to have been made around thirty years ago, sir," McGiven said.

"Mac, we're not buying the place, you can drop the estate agent patter," Tom said, with an eyebrow lift at Spencer, who's focus remained on the heavying traffic.

"Sorry, sir, just wanted to give you some perspective and scale, you know.."

"Yes-yes, I have been down there myself! What have you found in the rooms?"

"Room one, nearest the entrance steps, was empty. But we discovered trace

DNA, from blood on the walls, which has been confirmed as a 99% match for Mr Pierre Lebouf.."

"*Yes!*" Tom said, fistpumping the dashboard. "So he *was* held down there, and must be alive; she wouldn't have bothered shifting him otherwise?"

"Held captive for quite some time it seems. We found medical equipment and supplies including saline pouches, and what appears to be vials of drugs, unidentifiable at present.."

"Appears?"

"Yes, sir. Unfortunately, as you would have seen yourself, the basement was completely flooded. Items were only recovered following infrared scanning of the concrete floor, which remains, even as we speak, under many inches of water."

"Room two?"

"Intriguing, sir. But we'll need more time to establish what we have exactly. It might require some considerable work back at the lab..

"*Mac!* What have you found?"

"A partially decomposed body and severed bones. All confirmed as human, sir."

"Could you elaborate a little on that, for me?"

"Well, analysis from bone drilling will date the remains, but initial estimates place the body at late teens, certainly no older than thirty years, and female. Remarkably there's partial clothing attachment and the skull and bones are in reasonable condition to suggest.."

"Wait-wait, *female* you said., and how *old?*"

"Well, it's difficult to say with great accuracy at present, but possibly around twenty years."

"*Jesus,*" Tom said, staring across at Spencer. "Teeth, Mac?"

"Yes, reasonable condition. There's a good chance of identification from dental records."

"Good-good, get that to me asap will you, Mac," Tom said, lifting the sandwich from his lap. "And keep me posted with anything else," he added, taking a large bite.

His finger went to dab the red button on the dash just as Spencer took a hard left, cutting across a lane of traffic, and upped the wiper speed against the worsening downpour.

"*Err bones, sir?*" came a small robotic voice.

"*What?*" Tom muttered, picking a piece of chicken from his teeth.

"The other bones we found," McGiven said. "Did you want anything on them?"

"You mean you found *other bones* floating around down there, that don't belong to the woman?" Tom said, returning his sandwich to his knee.

"Well not floating, sir, given human bones are denser than water. These were discovered in the far corner, beside some metal work that was fixed to the back wall. We took some photographs that I can send over?"

"Yes, please do, text them to me."

"We located them when soft raking the cellar floor. Water damage hasn't helped of course, DNA and compound collection will be significantly impeded."

"Yes of course., but what *can* you tell us, Mac?" Tom said, sharing a smile with Spence.

"Well sir, they're definitely male, and the stage of decomposition is considerably less than that of the female we found."

"So he was killed *more recently*! But how can the remains of old bones be more recent than a partially clothed corpse that still holds its teeth?" Tom said, open-faced sharing his confusion.

"Oh, there is still fatty matter attached to them, sir, one limb in particular, the left femur we put through the bone scanner in the trailer," McGiven said matter-of-factly. "It looks as if the male victim was dismembered and his body parts were partially burnt down there."

"Age and ID possible, Mac?" Tom said, with a heavy sigh.

"Senior chap, this one. Again, best guesstimate only sir. But I would suggest between seventy and eighty."

"*Grandad*," Tom uttered, staring to his right.

"Sir?"

"Sorry Mac. Don't suppose you found any teeth to make dental identification a possibility?"

"Afraid not, sir. Rather interesting that there's no skull down there."

"And you've searched the entire basement?"

"Yes, rather unusual, but it seems this man was decapitated and his head disposed of elsewhere," McGiven said. "Bit of a grizzly end for the poor chap."

A coin-sized circle on the dashboard flashed green. Spencer nodded urgently at it as Tom's finger hovered over the red button alongside it.

"Great, thanks for the feedback, Mac, speak soon," Tom said, poking the button.

"Can you do this one, Spence, I've gotta eat!" Tom said, squeezing his chicken sandwich in one hand, and punched the green button.

"Spencer here, go ahead please."

"Spence, it's Turvs. Is the boss with you?" Neil Turvey said.

"Yeahh, but munchin.., watchagot Turvss," Tom mumbled, with a mouthful.

"Well this guy's hanging on literally, *by a thread*. They've repaired internal organ lacerations and stitched him back up," Neil said. "Top to tail, you might say!"

"That's some impressive stitching, I bet!" Spence said, grinning.

"No kidding, the nurse here mentioned 149 stitches, it's a new record for St. Thomas'," Neil said. "But from his account, it was our girl, Maxwell. She may have cut him open, but it's as if she wanted him alive to tell the tale!"

"What did he say, Neil?" Spence said, swerving between lorries to hit the fast lane of the M1.

"His name's Gerry Fornals, a low level criminal. He's got a couple of minors for burglary and one for assault and a live injunction relating to stalking an ex. Anyway, he says, and I quote from his statement;

'It looked suspicious, her wheeling something heavy through the alleyways behind the estate. She loaded it into a van and that's when I approached her. Before I said a word, she flicked a blade and skewered me. As I hit the deck I felt my head crack. She dragged me into the bushes, tough little bitch she was.*

She looked me square in the eyes with the blade at my throat, like she was gonna finish me. But she just smiled and walked away, like some sort of psycho."

"And his description of her, Neil?" Spence said, dismissively.

"White, twenties, around five-six, slim build. Fornals said she was head to toe in black. Sneakers, leggings and leather jacket over a dark hoodie, with hood up and over," Neil said.

"Good work Turvs," Tom said, screwing up his sandwich wrapper. "Get back to base and onto traffic will you, we've not had anything from track and trace for a while."

"Will do, boss. Speak soon."

The concrete skies above them seemed to have darkened quickly. Tom tugged his water bottle from the side hold of the passenger seat. The windscreen blurred from a sudden chattering downpour that lit a sea of red lights ahead. Spencer flicked again at the stick beneath the wheel and the wipers swept excitedly to work. Tom's iPhone pinged. Dabbing and squinting, he held it in front of his face.

"You've had a request from the authorities in Indonesia, Spence. They think they've got the guy, that-err., you know," Tom said, with lips pulled to his teeth. "They-err, they would like you to *'return to provide witness evidence and formally identify him'*. So that's good news?"

The traffic slowed amidst another dazzle of brake lights. Spencer punched the yellow triangle on the dash, the siren wailed and blue lights danced across their bonnet.

PART XIII — VENGEANCE

CHAPTER 101

She spun the dial and music blasted, thudding inside the back of the van that rocked as she stomped across its metallic floor. The baby was safe, changed, warm and asleep in the front seat after its feed.

"Gloria.. Gloria!"

Outside, barely a sound resonated from the foam-insulated cargo hold. Parked at the very end of a woodland trail, it was surrounded by trees and bushy-massed vegetation. A chill breeze whispered in the fast blackening forest, thorny branches gently brushed the side of the swaying van.

"You're always on the run now.."

In the distance an owl hooted its awakening and readiness to hunt. Bella sang out as if fueled by Champagne at her twenty-first birthday. But she was stone-cold-sober, bellowing into Pierre Lebouf's face.

".. you gotta get him somehow.."

She danced to the centre of the van, with arms waving over her head, then strutted towards him, in time with the thumping beat.

"..I think you're headed for a breakdown.."

Grabbing its long handle, she swung the machete in front of him.

"..are the voices in your head calling.."

She tapped the top button of the radio and silence fell instantly around them.

"I don't suppose you even remember Gloria, do you.. the Italian lady who bit the cock off one of your clients?"

Lebouf's angry, piggy-eyes flitted with her every movement, his ball-gagged mouth bulged.

"Do you know, I think I might be.." Bella said, head shaking. "Heading for a breakdown, that is. You see, I wasn't always like this, you know."

She strolled to the back of the Luton, peeling off her jacket, tossing it to a corner.

"I mean, I tried my absolute best to hold it in, I really did! I gave you, and yours, every chance. But, you just kept letting me down.. didn't you," she said, spinning to face him.

He tugged harder at the cable ties that pinned his reddened wrists to the batons on the back wall of the van. With arms stretching nearly the width of the van, and ankles bound together and fixed as one, Lebouf shaped a crucifix.

"I do appreciate all the money, but I need names now. Or this, really is sayonara for us."

Lebouf looked to have aged twenty years since he was first taken. His usual oily pitted cheeks, now flaky, dry white skin. Wrinkles creased his once smooth brow, even his hair appeared to be greying at the sides. His sweat-soaked shirt hung wide off his scrawny neck, his trousers were heavily soiled.

Bella tightened her clasp on the axe, leaning into him, within an inch of his trembling eyes.

"Jesus, you stink!" she said, stepping back with a face full of grimace. "We really are at the end of the road. You've got one chance to survive; name, name's. Or you die, here and now."

He nodded shakily, saliva flowing freely from the pink ball wedged tight in his mouth, re-soaking his discoloured shirt. Needles, vials and saline pouches lay discarded on the dusty floor around him. His skinny arms bore clouds of blue and yellow, blooming from pinpricks.

"Remember, no one's going to hear you out here, there's only forest around us and moorland beyond that. So don't bother calling out," she said, reaching to the back of his head. "Just give me the names and you'll live."

She unclipped the strapping, eased it from around his head and plucked the ball from his mouth, his lips torn on either side. His head flopped as he gasped at the air, wheezing to speak without words. A croaking built before his head dropped again to his chest, coughing heavily.

"Help, help!" he spluttered, head-lifting.

Bella stood, with machete swinging at her side, scowling at him. "Jesus, you're loyal, I'll give you that. But it won't help you, dickhead," she barked, with narrowing eyes.

"Help me. Help, somebody help!" he shouted softly, with the hoarseness of a throat infection.

Bella bellowed into his face, with capillaries popping in the whites of her eyes, "Someone has to pay, for the gang rape of my mother. It's either them, or you. Your choice?"

"Fuck you, Maxwell," came his gravelly response. "There's too many of them to name, they all had a piece of her, and she fucking loved it!"

Lebouf's head rocked from side to side as she reattached the mask. The ball cracked the tips of his front teeth as she rammed it in. Striding to the other end of the van she picked up the laptop, tapping the keyboard, whilst propped to her middle.

"Ok, given it's past midnight, I'll take one last payday," she said, grabbing his hand and twisting it back hard at the wrist, his thumb touching the screen.

Bella opened an app on the homescreen and tapped at the keys again. "Open wide," she said, lifting the screen in front of his face.

Lebouf squeezed his eyes tight, until he felt the familiar tip of the machete at his already bloodsoaked side. "Thank you!"

Pattering away, she entered the payee account and digits of the daily maximum, confirming; transfer. Bella laid the laptop down and ripped at a shallow boxed package, pulling the contents from their plastic covering.

"Ok, I'm the Judge, shall we say?" Bella said, with a widening smile. "You've shown absolutely no remorse for your crimes. You've destroyed the lives of countless young women and their families. I hereby sentence you to death!"

She shuffled into white coveralls and masked her face. Rummaging in the pocket of her coat, she released the blade of her flick knife and poked its tip on the button of the radio.

"Oh, yes!" she said, excitedly. The sweet yodel of Cyndi Lauper blasted out. "This is bloody perfect."

'When you gonna live your life right?'

Bella fixed a darkening gaze and burning hatred upon him.

'..Oh momma dear, we're not the fortunate ones..'

She strode with an air of abandon toward him, singing her heart out, echoing Cyndi's words. The machete rising with every step.

'And girls, they wanna have fun..' "Oh, girls just wanna have fun!"

CHAPTER 102

"The Chief Super thinks Forsythe's on track with this Ripper-copy-cat stuff, he's given us the thumbs up to engage with Yorkshire Police! ..Oh, and the tech guys have found something, guv," Neil said. "They hadn't flagged it earlier.."

"You mean they fucked up, and are now dressing it up as a find!" Tom shared an eye-roll with Spencer, as they weaved through the traffic around an intersection north of Birmingham.

"I guess you could say that," Neil said. "But as me mam always says, better late than never!"

"Ok, what have you got, Turvs?" Tom said, tapping the sat-nav screen; 'Alternative Routes'.

"Well, the bank accounts that the money has been transferred into.. these feminist groups.."

"Female Support Charities!" Spencer snapped.

"Yeah well, whatever you wanna call them.," Neil said.

"How about we call them, Women's Aid, or Refuge, or Protect a Girl, or.."

"Alright Spence, he gets the message!" Tom barked. "We've already established that they've been receiving millions from the associated accounts of Lebouf's brokerage. But they'll apply and recover the majority of those monies, so.. what else?"

"Well, it's just that-err," Neil said, before an extended pause. "Every one of these groups made *policy* clause changes to their *T and C's*. The alterations are traceable to the law chambers that Maxwell worked for. She must have been planning this for some time. These are legally watertight frameworks, with approved certification.."

"*English,* please Turvs," Tom said, under a heavy exhale.

"Basically they won't get a penny back. Any contribution, charitable donation, whatever you want to call it, is strictly non-refundable. Every box has been ticked, certifying the donors' understanding and consent; contractually it's legally binding."

"Clever girl," Spencer murmured.

"Couldn't Lebouf's corporation have just frozen, or closed this holding account?

"Not without his authority, they can't even access it without him. Investments continue to pour in via their hedge fund operators, who they don't want to spook and crash the market."

"Well that's down to the NCA and Serious Fraud Office, it's not our problem," Tom said.

"Ahh yeah, but it's these *other accounts* that the techies have unearthed," Neil said, rustling papers. "They didn't spot them initially because the sums were tiny in comparison to the millions being transferred from Lebouf Trading into the *Female Charities.*"

"Have they identified the account holders?" Tom said, grabbing his handrest.

The vehicles in front of them had grounded to a sudden halt, the shiny road disappearing beneath building traffic. Spencer poked the yellow triangle on the dash. Flicking the wiper to full speed she swerved between vehicles across the three lanes.

"They're all fake accounts, boss. Set up within the last twelve months in the names of murdered women," Neil said. "Access codes and passwords are security encrypted. The banks can't override them, *client confidentiality*, and all that bollocks!"

"So, what are we saying here, that Maxwell has access to these accounts?" Tom said.

"Yep, she set them all up. Each one can be traced back to the same IP address," Neil said. "She only needed a name, address and two pieces of identification, which she could have got from her role at the Barristers. Maxwell had level 2 security clearance to the Central Registry, giving her access via the census database to private records."

"She wouldn't have needed that," Spencer interjected. "The families of the deceased would have helped her anyway, think about it!"

Tom looked across at her, finger-rubbing his chin. His mobile was flashing on his lap, he opened the message whilst glugging his water.

"Listen-up Turvs, we've just received an incident flag of *'potential interest'* north of Nottingham," Tom said, slotting the bottle in the central holder. "Can you speak to East Mids and check it out? I-A number D746K."

"Will do, boss," Neil said.

"Oh and Turvs," Tom said. "How much are we talking about., with these accounts?"

"Ahh yeah, here's the thing, boss. She's already cleaned-out nine of them.."

"*Nine!* Bloody hell, how many were there?"

"Fifteen, in total.. well, that they've found so far."

"Christamighty, why are we always behind the fucking curve!" Tom snarled. "And ballpark, how much is in them?"

"Around £1.2 million, guv," Neil said.

"Fuck me Turvs. You said they were small amounts!" Tom looked across at Spencer whose grin was widening.

"Well it is only around, eighty k an account. You can see how they didn't focus on it, it's FSA protection level, small fry compared to the Charities that have had millions."

"Yeah-yeah, bullshit.. they fucked up. And they'll blame lack of manpower, time restraints or some other bollocks!" Tom said, barking, "When was the last transaction?"

"They had an authorised transfer to *White Ribbon UK* of the maximum daily limit; £12 million," Neil said, pausing. "That was-err, just over an hour ago."

"I don't suppose we've got any more accurate with the location finder, now that Maxwell's on the move?" Tom said, casting a stern glance at Spencer, who remained with fixed grin.

"Just reading a message from the guys at Lebouf Trading, as we speak, boss; 'The wired payment to WRUK released a transmission signal from, *the North Eastern quadrant*'," Neil said. "Not particularly helpful."

"Well Lebouf's team might do a better job than our lot!" Tom said. "Traffic obs registered a sighting at a fuel station just outside Sheffield, so we'll keep going north. You get onto that incident near Nottingham," he added, cutting the call abruptly.

"You've got to admire her, Tom. She's certainly a force of nature," Spencer said, glancing across at him. "Look what she's managed to do for all those charities; that'll save countless lives!"

"Listen, I know what you've been through personally Spence, but please do try and remain objective here," Tom said. "We're dealing with an extremely dangerous individual, our criminal profiler, Forsythe has told us - Maxwell *is* a psychopath!"

"But there was no gratuitous pleasure or torture involved in these attacks; they're always defensive or functional, revenge based. In some ways, she's heroic." Spencer said, tapping a finger on the steering wheel, "And I've never heard of a psychopath wearing a cape!"

CHAPTER 103

Swathes of the woodland floor were carpeted in bluebells. The first shards pierced the oak-leafed canopy, illuminating their well trodden pathway through the centre of the wood. Duke, as ever, was way ahead and out of sight, sniffing the tree-hugging daffodils.

Just under twenty miles away, Yorkshire's Chief of Police slurped from his chipped Leeds United mug. He stood, scanning the whiteboards that his team had set up. The briefing room was ready for the arrival of Tom Broad and his team from the Met. Datapacks were stacked on each of the eight tables that horse-shoed the display boards.

Duke barking wasn't unusual, but something had raised its excitable woofing, to a deeper decibel. It scattered ground nesting birds, twittering their annoyance at the disruption. Beams sharpened on the bushes ahead, a glorious morning looked set as he peeled his windbreaker, arm-tying it to his waist. The howl of his ageing Labrador sounded a little shrill up ahead.

The left-hand side held photographs of the dead, faces of men discovered in the county, none of whom were local to it. In fact all were southerners, mostly from the capital, who for some reason had ended up here, in Yorkshire. The criminologist had been keen to explain that each had been murdered elsewhere and the bodies dumped strategically. Their locations, referenced on the central display, matched sites of the Ripper murders of decades earlier.

"Duke, Duke.. here boy. DUKE!" His command being ignored was more than odd, something wasn't right. He wasn't a pet owner that allowed his dog to be anything other than obedient. Duke knew the reprimand he would receive if he didn't return after a few calls and more importantly, he knew the button-bikky treat that awaited a prompt return.

Their facial features at death were unusual, intriguing. Twelve young faces stared back at the Chief, with anger, disdain, even hatred filling their eyes. Each deposited at mirrored locations, their bodies humiliatingly posed with clothing removed, or pulled to their ankles, imitating the work of the Ripper. Everyone in the Yorkshire constabulary knew Peter Sutcliffe's numbers; 13 dead, and seven survivors.

The humming was audible from a fair distance. The dog's now hoarse barking and refusal to depart the scene was completely out of character. He sped from the path, lengthening stride as he rounded Rhododendron, his boots flattening surrounding bracken. He bound on, toward Duke's distressed bay, arm clearing bushes and weaving trees. Stomping soft vegetation, he swatted all around him, as the buzzing intensified. Ahead lay something peculiar, tree mounted or hung hammock-like between trunks.

The Chief paced quietly around the empty room, with dampening fists clenched at the small of his back. The stigma still haunted his force. Their failings set out for all the world to see; glaring flaws, lit-up. Sutcliffe had been interviewed on nine occasions before his chance capture, a pure stroke of luck. The toe-curling quote, 'not of ill repute' dismissive of the slaying of sex workers. The 'wearside-Jack' red-herring swallowed hook, line and sinker.

He bellowed for Duke's attention whilst unstrapping his mobile from his vest. The dog remained lapping at the fleshy mass that stretched above it. He strode closer, his phone swinging limply at his side, forgotten as he tried to calibrate the gruesome sight. With a sharp recoil the back of his hand flattened to his mouth.

"Tom.. delighted to meet you?" Yorkshire's Chief of police said, with a warm beam. "We're all ready for you."

"Actually, I'm Jeremy, Jeremy Forsythe, criminal psychologist," the little, mustard waistcoated man said. "A colleague and I flew up, given the urgency of the situation. Our SIO Tom Broad and DI Spencer shouldn't be too far behind."

Forsythe squinted up from his bottle-bottom glasses at the impressively tall, shiny buttoned commander. The Chief offered Forsythe a refreshment as he shook the tubby professor's hand. He looked like Toad, from Wind in the Willows, he thought to himself.

DI Neil Turvey strode in moments late. "Bit thin on the ground up here, Chief!" he said with a wink, eyeing the empty briefing room.

The Chief met him with a stern glare, reassuring the quick-witted detective that his team would be joining them as soon as Tom arrived. Turvey advised that the boss was currently stuck in traffic, with an eta of seven minutes. The three men hovered awkwardly, staring at the whiteboards.

"I can provide a fair bit more here," Jeremy said, pointing a stubby finger at the photograph of Arabella Maxwell.

"I think we have everything from your reports that are annexed to the briefing packs," the Chief said, lifting one of the chunky booklets from the table nearest him.

"Family, education, career and her work on the trial," Neil said, flicking through a copy. "It's all in here, Prof. Even her time at Haversham Hall, taking evidence from Marcie Stone."

"Ahh well, we've had a little more in of late, education-wise especially," he said, breathing heavily into his glasses.

"I thought we had everything to date on that," the Chief said, fanning his briefing pack.

"Yes, I thought so too," Neil said, turning to the profiler. "Besides, I don't think her GCSE grades are that important at this point, Prof."

"Quite!" the Chief added, with fingers pinched either side of his watchface.

"Details matter, gentlemen, and we've only just heard back from her local college," Jeremy said, easing his tortoiseshell glasses to the bridge of his nose. "Maxwell attended night classes last year, St. Matthews in Bethnal Green.."

"I'm not sure hearing how impressive her pottery and cake-making skills are really gets us anywhere. With respect, Professor," the Chief said, with an eyebrow raised.

"I gotta agree with you there, Chief. Maxwell might be completely potty, but you can't bring her Art teacher in as an accessory," Neil said, beaming at the Chief. "I used to struggle in origami classes.. I had to fold in the end!"

Neil's wink was met by a glare from the Chief that could crush a melon. Neil's face dipped, crumpling in wordless apology.

"How about knife skills, and advanced butchery.. both of which Maxwell passed with distinction," Jeremy said, stepping between the two. "Or a twelve week course in Taekwondo, a specialised martial art that uses an attacker's size and weight against them." Flicking the page of his pocketbook, he continued, "Ahh, here we are, Maxwell also achieved tactical mastery, stage five, in Krav Maga.."

"Kravawhata?" Neil said, with widening eyes.

"It's a fitness based masterclass, with a syllabus that includes military and combat defence techniques," Jeremy said, peering up at the open-mouthed

471

officers. "She's been in training for quite some time it seems."

Duke lapped at the arc of what looked possibly the sole of a foot that had been painted red. At his master's increasingly aggressive demand, the labrador dropped to all fours and peeled away. A widening burst of sunlight lit the unearthly scene.

Stepping closer, it appeared to be an animal, its hide outstretched from four limbs, defleshed and hung taught between silver birch. The translucent skin looked to have been slashed open vertically from neck to anus and pinned to the tree trunks.

"P-police, please," he said into his phone, with the dryness of croak.

Two steps closer, he froze. A bloodsoaked mound, a mass of organs and bones, filleted from their fatty flesh, lay below the skinned corpse. A fog of feasting insects enveloped the pile. Heart, lungs and stomach, slopped in shiny greys and pinks amidst an endless snaking coil of intestines on the forest floor. The putrid stench hit him, turning his stomach.

"Emergency. I-I err, I've found a dead body, in the woods," he said, half-turned from the grotesque sight.

Mesmerised in gaze he stepped closer, into the incessant humming, that rounded his head; like a caged motorcyclist. Duke, with his golden face bloodied, barked at his side, keen to get to the butchered meat. The cloud of flies in a tinnitus-like buzzing, blurred as evermore amassed on the soft fleshy banquet.

"Sorry, Heading.. Headingley woods," he said, transfixed by his horrifying discovery. "North-east entrance, about a half a mile in."

The defleshed remains had been stretched to extremity and nailed to the tree trunks; hung like rawhide to be tanned.

"No, I c-can assure you, they-they're definitely d-dead," he said, spitting flies.

He bent, reclipping the lead as the stench flooded him in the breeze; the fetid odour of death. Its noxious pungency swamped his senses; his gut churned, folding him in two.

Planting a hand to a tree, he pinned the phone back to his ear, "No-no, I can't check for a p-pulse," he puffed, and dry-retched to one side.

Tugging hard at the lead, he pulled Duke away from the pile. "Iya-I am quite sure," he said, gulping for a drift of fresh air that wasn't there. The rancid waft was all around him.

"Because it hasn't g-gotta fucking, head!" he spat, before throwing up.

CHAPTER 104

"Ok, the last deposition site, anybody?" Tom Broad said, scanning the room.

"New Street, Headingley," came a deep Yorkshire tone from the back. "Jaqueline Hill, found 17th November 1980, Sir," he continued.

"That's great, thanks.."

"Found in the back garden of a house, sir," he continued.

"Ok, yes, thank you," Tom said, palm signalling that the man lower his still vertical arm.

The briefing room was packed, but was without the usual low-level chatter that Tom had come to expect at the Met. Attention was impeccable, possibly due to the Chief of Yorkshire police being in the building. Tom threw him a smiling nod.

"Ok, we need that area of Leeds swamped with coppers. All plain clothed, cars and foot patrols," the Chief said, stepping alongside the Met's senior investigating officer.

It had been a relatively short meeting, partly due to the nature of the fast moving case that had captured both public and media interest. It remained of fascination to the local force, some of whom had family living in the area at the time of the Ripper murders. Other officers had relatives that had worked the case.

"Twelve innocent victims, let's not let Maxwell take another," Tom said. "We know the vehicle she's driving. IT surveillance crews will keep us updated on sightings, but she's in this county."

A fresh faced copper sidestepped between officers to the front, signalling to the Chief, who took a couple of paces forward.

"And please, radio anything you get, into me. Maxwell may look harmless, but I can assure you she is not," Tom said, side eyeing DI Turvey who was leaning against the wall. "We're not looking for any hero's today."

The Chief's face was the colour of the ash from the bottom of a barbeque drum. He nodded at the young copper who slid away between colleagues.

"One minute, if you would please, Tom," the Chief whispered, folding the piece of paper he had been handed. "Unfortunately, it appears we have been beaten to the punch!" he added, with hooded eyes.

"Yes, of course," Tom said, with a face-screwed frown.

The Chief stepped front and centre, scanning the room with a stare that could sour grapes. "A thirteenth victim has been discovered by a dog walker in Headingley woods."

A few gasps were exchanged between the assembled officers, along with one, almost triumphant murmur of, '*I told you, Headingley*'.

"I have ordered our scene of crime operatives to the scene, where I will accompany our colleagues from the Met," the Chief said.

"Excuse me. May I ask, were there any unusual features to the murder?" came a husky voiced question, buried centrally in the room.

"I'll need to discuss that with SIO Broad, before we.."

"Sorry Chief, this is our profiler, Jeremy Forsythe," Tom said, stepping forward and pointing at the short man who was somehow sitting at a table surrounded by standing officers. "I should have introduced you earlier, apologies Jeremy."

"No apology necessary, Tom," Jeremy said, slowly getting to his feet. He didn't look notably taller as he did so. Squeezing between the two burly men, he offered his hand to the Chief who aided his release. "The Chief and I did meet earlier."

"I just wonder if Maxwell might have taken mementos, or posed the body in a certain way, it might help us. Particularly with regard to her current mindset and possibly direction of travel," Jeremy said.

The senior Met officers joined them at the front. Others assembled could barely hear the aged professor, let alone see him, and drifted into boisterous chatter.

"Settle down," the Chief barked, passing the professor the incident form he had been given.

"Ahh, this is interesting, you see," Jeremy said, giving the note to Tom. "Removal of the head, now we've seen that before!"

"Have we?" Neil said, with eyebrows haunched.

"The Cheveley estate murder, Neil," Spencer said, with tongue poking out. "*Jamal Jackson!*"

"*Exactly,* and where did we find the head?" Jeremy said.

"In his grandmother's fridge! But Jeremy, with respect, we don't have time for twenty questions here," Tom said. "If you have a theory can we just hear it?"

The rising chatter around the meeting room was beyond that which allowed the professor's reply to be heard by the senior police in front of him, let alone other officers.

"Ok, enough now!" the Chief bellowed. "Everyone back to your desks and await instruction. Read the data-pack, if you haven't already done so."

The room was emptying quickly as the Chief turned to apologise to the elderly expert.

"Not at all, enthusiastic staff, that's to be encouraged," Jeremy said. "Could you possibly ask that chap, the one with the local knowledge, to remain?"

"You mean our young Ripper boffin," the Chief said, with a long crooked smile. It changed his face entirely, he looked like a friendly crocodile.

His grin disappeared instantly when hollering over the profiler's head. "*Hawkins*, not you, over here please," he barked with a hooked-finger in the air, as if beckoning a waiter for a dressing down about a sub-standard dining experience.

"It's establishing what's important to *her*, you see," Jeremy said softly. "Crucial that we understand what makes her tick. Now.. with the head of that footballer chap.."

"Jamal Jackson," Neil said.

"Yes, that's it, and Jackson's grandmother, Bernadette Bateman infiltrated the Jury system to protect him. Bateman helped the three men get acquitted," Jeremy said, with a sweet smile.

"And if it's Pierre Lebouf's head that's missing, what's your hunch?" Tom said, gritting teeth.

"*Significance*, my good chap! Batemen was significant. The bodies of these young men.." Jeremy said, strolling to the whiteboards. "Were found at locations similar to the Ripper's victims, it sent a message, a rallying cry. So where is she going to leave his head?"

"One of Lebouf's relatives?" Neil offered, shrugging.

"More of a statement than that, my boy. From a female perspective, what was the most frustrating thing about the Ripper case?"

"Police failings," Hawkins said, before dropping his head, at the glare of his superior.

"Correct, and the officer in charge at the time, was?" Jeremy said, peeking over his thick rimmed spectacles, eyeing Hawkins.

"George Oldfield," Hawkins said. "But he died in 1983, following a heart attack, partially due to the stress of the case, sir. I don't think she'll target his family," he added.

"No, quite, Oldfield did his utmost!" the Chief said, whilst removing his hat and sleeve-wiping its shiny peak. "You can't blame someone for trying to stop crime, it's the perpetrator that's responsible."

"She's making a point; an eye-for-an-eye," DI Spencer said, nudging her way into the male circle. "For every woman Sutcliffe murdered, she's killed a man."

"Ultimately, it's Peter Sutcliffe's head that she wants on a spike," Tom said.

"But these aren't just random men, each one abused her in some way. Maxwell was more than a victim of misogyny," Spencer said, staring at the wall of male photos. "From those on the building site humiliating her, the overtly sexist bus driver and cabbie, to sexually inappropriate co-workers. The vile innuendo, constant touching and verbal abuse, became her daily life." She turned to face the officers. "And her harassment complaints were dismissed!"

"Ok Spence, I think we get the picture," Neil said, flashing a smirk at the others.

"Oh, I very much doubt *you* do!" Spencer said, stepping away from the group to take a call.

"*Yes*, now then, Peter Sutcliffe.." Tom interjected

"Sutcliffe's dead, sir," Hawkins said. "Died in Durham prison of Covid, refused treatment."

"Is there anywhere else of significance that would bring attention to Sutcliffe's crimes.. where he worked, or lived?" Jeremy said, peering over his tortoiseshell glasses. "Maxwell's looking to remind people of what that man did."

"He moved about a fair bit, workwise. Started out as a gravedigger, then a truck driver," Hawkins said, excitedly. "But he lived at the same address with his wife, throughout his five year killing spree."

"Now, didn't she benefit financially somehow from his crimes?" the Chief said, poking a finger in the direction of Hawkins.

"That's right sir, Sonia Sutcliffe pocketed from book sales and from suing the newspapers," Hawkins said. "One barrister's described her as, '*dancing on the graves of her husband's victims.*'"

"And *her husband* was interviewed nine times! What was their home address?" Tom said, flashing a glance at the professor.

"6 Garden Lane, Bradford. It's in the Heaton area, sir," Hawkins said.

"Bloody hell, you're good," Neil said, scribbling in his pocketbook.

CHAPTER 105

The greying sky looked ominous as the teenage mother hurriedly wheeled her buggy along the uneven pavement towards the top of the road. Neve was headed toward the larger, bay-windowed houses on the brow of the hill; perched like crows on the tallest branch. They stood proud of sloping gardens that skirted them, at a gradient of a Tour de France climb.

Her rushing was at odds with the meandering couple opposite and teenagers lounging on the graffitied wall at the foot of Garden Lane. But Neve Bishop was panicked, and seemingly intent on achieving a record sprint with a double buggy in hand. The giggling twins, Cairon and Luke, bounced along, enjoying the change from the usual strolled pace.

Ahead, two neighbours paused their over-the-fence gossip at the sight of their red-faced friend approaching. "Jesus-wept woman, what's the hurry?" one said, unfolding her tattooed forearms.

"It's, it's that van," Neve said, under heavy exhale. "Get them kids away from it will yous!"

On the crest of the hill a muddied abandoned-looking van sat strewn across the kerb. Two youths stood alongside it, whilst another circled, checking its handles.

"Ahh, they're only messin' Neve," the larger woman said. "Don't be panicking about them lot. I knows who they are!"

"No, it-it's wh-what's inside," Neve panted, as she pushed on up the hill, reaching the two of them. "There's a ba-be crying, it's been left locked inside!"

"Now, how on earth can you be hearin tha from down here?"

Neve stopped, with a clenched fist around the handle of the pram, and the other hand propped on her hip.

"It was the old lady, at the bottom of the street. Said she heard a bairn screamin' when she walked by it. Come on now ladies, you gonna give me a hand and get this van open?" Neve said, returning to her hill climb.

"Calling my Tony, I am," the high-bunned blonde woman said.

"Ark, don't be mithering him, jus' grab me some tools!" Neve shouted.

Ignoring the soft drizzle she bound-on, before planting her boot on the pram's lever and peeling a rain cover over, press-studding it to the buggy. The wide eyed twins followed her every move, before the resumption of their rollercoaster ride.

"The cops are already on their way," the large woman bellowed. "Somebody phoned it in, they said not to touch anything, Neve!"

The house stood hauntingly at the top of the road, with steep shelved steps to one side. A broken-hinged gate lay buckled at the bottom of the garden, its fence panels either missing or snapped. The work of vandals that had returned for the umteenth time.

The dark bricked property with boarded windows shadowed the van that now stadled the street below it, and the community around it, as it had for many decades. The penny-pinching council steadfast in their refusal to destroy it, despite its lure to the unsavoury, and being unsellable.

"Just fuck off now, yous lot," Neve said, stamping on the brake pedal.

The boys meandered off, muttering expletives at the young mother. There wasn't a sound coming from the vehicle as Neve side-shuffled the slither of pavement between the van and splintered fencing of number six. From the passenger window, she couldn't see anything on the seat.

Neve stepped onto the footplate. Peering into the footwell, there was a cardboard box filled with what looked like a colourful assortment of tea towels. The deep dashboard had the usual white van-man fast food cartons scattered amidst a week's worth of local papers. The central area held crumpled drinks cans, crisp packets and a mix of sweet wrappers.

She dropped down and walked around the van, yanking the handle of its side sliding door. It was unmoved, but that's when she heard it. A dull whimper at first and then a moment of silence, before an eruption of unbridled desperation. Wailing its woe at abandon, pleading for the comfort of contact.

Neve shimmied back, putting a foot on the footplate to see the slightest movement of tea cloth from the box. And then another. Then came the soft plump-cheek of a baby, then its chubby hand with tiny fingers in wiggled angst.

She scampered through the gateway of number 6 Garden Lane, former home of the Yorkshire Ripper, where Sutcliffe and his wife were interviewed by police. Where he housed his arsenal of weapons. Neve grabbed a large stone from the ground below the boarded bay window.

The baby's cries were louder as she rushed to the driver's door window and tapped the rock against it. The sound of distant sirens echoed from nearby streets as she wielded it again, but the glass resisted. At her third, arm-swinging clout, it cracked. The sound of her smashing the splintered glass was drowned by police cars racing up Garden lane; more frantic than on previous visits.

Blue lights rebounded the van, in advance of the arrival of several siren-bleeding squad cars. Gingerly, between finger and thumb, Neve squeezed to lift the lock, catching her wrist on a shard as she pulled her arm back free of the window.

"Move away from the vehicle! Move away from the vehicle!"

Neve stepped back from the footplate and turned to the police, her face filled with flashing blue. Then the baby wailed again and Neve poked her middle finger high. She tugged at the handle and flung the door wide, diving across the seat of the van.

CHAPTER 106

"We can't be far behind her now," Tom said, clamping his fingers a little tighter around the passenger seat's grab handle. "She can't have long left Heaton!"

The young officer's foot-pumping acceleration through the city streets was considerably more than Tom was used to. Accepting the offer of an egg sandwich at Leeds police station was a mistake.

"Text Spence to find out what they've found over there," Tom added.

In the last few minutes an incident call had reported an abandoned vehicle in Garden lane, resembling the Luton van, Tom and Neil were on route. Spencer and Forsythe were dispatched to the site of the human remains discovered in Headingley woods.

"Will do. By the way, we've received the data from the yacht, where Spencer was held.." Neil said, waving his mobile around the headrest.

The driver's road hugging focus was distracted as a message boomed from his intercom box. He thumb-wheeled the dial of the volume control. The crackled message interrupting Neil.

'Vehicle at Garden lane, Heaton; located and secured. Repeat vehicle at Garden lane, Heaton; located and secured, over.'

"Well, that's a relief," Tom said. "There's no rush now officer, thank you."

The driver nodded with a, 'sir', slowing fast as they sped toward the rear of a lime green bus. Neil shuffled to the edge of the back seat, leaning on the shoulders of the front ones.

484

"It's an email from interpol," Neil said, turning his iPhone to Tom. "They've recovered files from the software on board the boat she was on. It was the largest yacht, moored off the island of Makam-Raja."

"El-Mar-ney, you mean?" Tom said, enjoying his pronunciation.

"No, it was anchored off the other one, the smaller neighbouring island," Neil said. "It says there's a list of names and they've asked us to identify any British girls from it. Boss, it's attached; it's nearly three hundred long!"

"What the hell!"

"Yep. And the owner of the yacht sounds like a main player. They've got evidence of multi-million pound transactions between him and Lebouf, over a period of ten years!" Neil said, spreading his feet before a sharp left hand turn.

"Get base onto it straight away. I want a list of all UK missing females, fifteen to thirty years, and merge-match it with their data," Tom said.

"That ain't all, boss!" Neil said, still scrolling the email. "They found a guest list on board, used by the crew to ensure their service was up to scratch. You know what these celebrity sorts are like; all manner of foibles!"

"Celebrities?"

"You wouldn't believe it! We've got everything from political heavyweights, to rock and roll stars!" Neil said.

"Get all UK based persons from that list and let Interpol know we'll be bringing them in in the next twenty four hours. Before they have a chance to leave the country!"

"This is it, sir," the driver said, pointing up a residential street.

The houses were sixties built, with bay windows and pebbledash frontage. The road swept right before a climb to the top, where squad cars already sat, their lights blinking either side of an off-white Luton van that straddled the curb.

"Good, good. Steady as you go, pal," Tom said, feeling his stomach turn as they climbed steadily.

The windscreen speckled and the driver dabbed the wiper blades into life. He slowed to a crawl toward the crest of the hill, amidst growing numbers of residents lining the street. It looked as if the van had crashed through the boundary fence of a property. A crowd spilled onto the pavement at the top of the road.

"This is going to be interesting," Neil said, leaning back.

"Turvs," Tom said, twisting between the front seats. "Can you ask base to check that Interpol list of names against our own Maxwell list."

"Maxwell list?"

"Sorry yeah, Spencer put it together, it's in the case files. It's known associates of Maxwell, friends, family," Tom said. "I'm just wondering if there might be a link here. Someone that's on the missing person list that Maxwell might know."

"You're thinking a mate of her's might have been sextrafficked?" Neil said.

"It's possible, and might begin to explain her motivation for all of this."

"Bit of a longshot, considering what that crazy bitch has done, but worth a try boss."

"Don't let Spence hear you say that!" Tom said, returning to face the front. "By the way, that millionaire's Yacht. What's the name of the owner?"

"It's some Yank, err, here we go." Neil said. "Not heard of him myself, boss. A guy named Richmond. Theodore Richmond, from Houston, Texas. Yeehaa!"

"Me neither, but there's a lot of money in that part of the world; oil, cattle," Tom said, unbuckling his belt.

"Maybe JR's back from the dead!" Neil said, winking in the rearview mirror at the driver, who remained expressionless.

They pulled up at the curbside and sat watching as a stocky officer ushered the public down the street, beyond where they had just parked-up. Another cop ran yellow police tape across the road. An eerie silence gripped the car for an instant as they gazed up to their left, at the tall house perched on the hill.

"The last attachment from Interpol, boss!" Neil said, staring into his phone. "It's a charge sheet against one, Miguel Hernandez."

"Who?"

"It's that little waiter at the hotel, you know, the bastard who.. you know.."

"Yeah, yeah. I know," Tom said, lip sucking.

"He's being tried by the local judiciary next week," Neil added, speed-reading the document.

"Shit. Locally, that's not good!" Tom said, glancing over his shoulder. "You know what that means, don't you!"

"Yep. He walks!" Neil said, headshaking. "His dad's probably the Judge!"

"Shit. Does Spence know?" Tom said, his hand clasping the back of his head.

"Yep, she's been copied in!" Neil said, his brow wrinkling. "So she's probably reading it right now."

CHAPTER 107

The warming carriage was quieter now, many having exited at the last stop. With a few seats to herself now, Bella peeled off her trench coat. The rain-swept moorland landscape was breathtaking, dotted only by mysterious lone-standing houses. Her escape had been timed well, catching the fast train out gave her every chance of making the connection she needed.

Minutes later they were at York, where more baggage-clutching passengers disembarked. The young girl sat two rows up remained, with earpods in, windowgazing. She still had chubby, *baby-like* cheeks, barely an adult.

The guy in dark casualwear swooshed through the doorway between carriages again, strutting down the aisle. A weak bladder seemed implausible, given his youthfulness. He lingered a little in passing the girl before striding swiftly-on past the elderly lady sat further back.

Bella undid the top button of her blouse, the relentless warm waft was becoming unbearable. Her eyelids were drooping, she felt like she could sleep for a week. *He was back.* A prominent brow shadowed his sunken eyes, and the dark-ringed bags of a seventy year old. This time he stopped at the girl's row, his arm laid across the headrest of the seat beside her.

"What you listenin' to?" he said, aggressive in tone, yet with the softness of whisper.

From her window seat she half-turned, grinning her nervousness, not catching his eye. Bella eased across to her aisle seat for a closer view.

"I said, what you got on that thing?" he said, slumping to the seat alongside her.

The girl, so young, pinked instantly. Her hands dived together, clamping childlike across her lap. "Just D-drake," she mumbled, as if questioned by the headteacher. A nervousness, a sense of foreboding gripped her, her movements jerky and unsure.

He glanced up, feeling Bella's hardening glare and spun away, headed back down the passageway, fist bouncing seat tops as he strutted through the carriage. Stopping at the far bay by the end door, he elbow-swung on the silver pole, staring back. Bella tugged the narrow window flap pulley, without success as the train thundered on through a sweeping vista of rolling hills. Head-leaning between headrest and window she stifled a yawn.

He was back again. The girl's eyes were stiffly fixed on the window, rigid at his presence. Wordless he stood, with an arm across the headrest, staring at her. His pinched features reflected in the fading light on the window, his scent, his movement and bull-like nasal breathing, closing her space. His baggy-crotched trackies swung in alongside her, blocking escape.

"You wanna hang?"

Her bush-baby eyes turned almost to face him, before dropping to her knees. "Err, no-no thank you. I-Iye, I've gotta get off in a minute." Passive-souled, she had the face of a cherub.

"You best not be lyin'!"

He lurched away, offended, shoulder-swaying in patrolling up and down the empty carriage. But the next station came and went, and the girl remained seated.

Bella dabbed at her temples, refixing her mask tight despite the sheen of sweat. She smoothed the skin down at the bridge of her nose and secured the blue-vein wrinkles to the back of her hands. *He was coming back, fast.* With the juddered movement of a pensioner, Bella hauled herself from her seat, stepping into the passage. His face was the colour of his faded grey hoodie, his white trainers bouncing the aisle.

"*Ginny?* Ginny Rogers?" she said, with a croaky cackle. "I thought it was you, but I couldn't be sure!"

Bella shuffled three steps towards her, before he could take six. A dismissive glare at the vulgar young man was enough to halt him in his tracks. He held still for a moment, face wrinkling, unsure, before he heard the girl's words.

"H-hi, h-how are you?" she said softly, her face full of fear.

Bella flopped into the seat alongside her and tapped her knee, offering a subtle wink that said, 'you're okay now'.

"I'm very well. Now what about you and that big brother of yours?" Bella said, with a warmth of smile that belied the years of the craggy faced woman.

"He-he's f-fine-thank you," she said, watery-eyed.

"It's just great to see you and we'll be getting off at the same stop. I can see you home, honey," Bella said, with an assuring nod.

"Th-thank you so, so m-much," she said, a tear spilling from her right eye.

Bella scanned the carriage; he was nowhere to be seen.

CHAPTER 108

"We had better wait for SOCO," the Chief of Yorkshire police said sternly.

Tom Broad and Neil Turvey flanked him at the rear doors of the Luton that had been verified as belonging to an east London council. Maxwell had been seen loading a large object into the back of the vehicle in an area behind her registered address, Silver Mews Terrace.

"I don't think so," Neil said, before a pause. "With respect sir."

"Do excuse my colleague, Chief," Tom said, flashing a furrowed brow at his young DI. "But we will need to take a look, without going inside, save for preservation of life, of course."

A baby had been pulled from the front passenger footwell of the van moments earlier by a neighbour and was now with the paramedics. Police enquiries were underway to establish the identity of the child's parents, whilst emergency fostering arrangements were being put in place.

"I don't think there'll be anyone alive in there, after what was found in the woods!" Neil said.

A duplicate set of keys lay in Neil's blue gloved hands. The Chief nodded at Tom, who eye-pointed Neil to the lock in the handle of the door. With a twist and tug, he unfolded the rear doors, staggering back with a sharp head jerk, burying his face in his elbow.

"Sweet Jesus!"

A putrid stench was released from the back of the van, like steam released from a boiling pot. The raw, fetid odour seized their senses in an instant, each of them spun away, mouth-covering from the stomach churning reek.

"Get those people further back," the Chief bellowed at a copper stood idle with yellow tape at his back. He jumped straight, nearly saluting.

"What the hell is that?" Tom said, squinting into the gloomy van, finger-pinching his nostrils.

The grooved metal flooring shone in a slimy blend of reds and greys; like Van Gogh's studio floor. A barbaric act of human butchery had taken place here. Fleshy entrails were strewn, amidst the mass of bodily fluids that had been spilt. And on the back wall, staring hauntingly back, a head, somehow fixed to it, seemingly floating. A gory mix of flesh and veins trailed below it.

"Lebouf, boss?" Neil squeaked nasally, stepping alongside Tom.

"More than likely, but impossible to tell from here!" Tom said, squeezing his eyelids a little tighter. "What's that in the mouth?"

Its blood splattered face, with life-drained eyes glared vacantly back at the coppers, its mouth wide, forming an 'O'; something had been wedged inside it.

"*It's his dick, sir!*" Neil said, in a pitchy voice, pinching harder at his nose.

"Yes, thank you Neil!" Tom said, with a little head shake at the Chief, "I think we can leave it for scene of crimes to determine matters from here."

"What's that, boss?" Neil said, pointing to a small rectangular box in the far corner. "Looks like some sort of phone or a camera."

"Could be a burner, or-err, some sort of tape recorder," Tom said, peering in. "Looks like we might have been left a message!"

"You want me to get it?" Neil said.

"Let's get a grabber and lift it out," Tom said, turning to the Chief.

Nausea welled in the Chief, whose complexion had paled. "Yes, I'll get one from the squad car," he said, moving from the van. The pit of his stomach rocked like a rowboat on high seas.

Forsythe, the psychologist, emerged from the latest squad car to arrive. Its flashing added to the blue-white lighting display illuminating the tall house.

"Thought you and Spence were investigating the body in the woods?" Neil shouted over.

"DI Spencer had other plans, I'm afraid," Jeremy said, hurriedly waddling over.

"I'll deal with Jeremy, Turvs," Tom said, stepping clear of the van. "Can you go and speak to the woman who reported the vehicle.. we'll need a statement."

"Sure. I think she was the one speaking to Hawkins when we arrived. *Neve*, I think I heard him say," Neil said, peeling his gloves.

"Good, good. I'll take those if you don't mind," Tom said.

Neil tugged his notebook from his breast pocket and strode in the direction of the crowd of onlookers. Tom stared back at the van, headshaking as he tapped his iPhone, slipping it to his ear. There was no answer, so he left a voicemail for Spencer to call him.

"Neve, is it?" Neil said, approaching a young woman that was stood chatting with neighbours either side of her. "I understand you discovered the baby in the van and phoned us. Do you mind if I take a quick statement? "

"I only *rescued* the ba-be, love," Neve said. "I was *told* that it was in there!"

"Told," Neil said, with a slight headcock. "By who, who first found it?"

"The old-bird that passed me at the bottom of Garden lane," she said, pointing down the hill.

"An older woman, you say.. did you know her?"

"Nope, never seen her before!"

"Not a local then?"

"Don't think so. I know everyone on the estate and I've no idea who she was, or why she was cutting through Garden lane!"

"Another fuckin grief tourist, I'll bet ya!" a large, arm-crossing lady interrupted.

"What about her accent.. northern?" Neil said, with a pulled grin.

"Definitely not local, sounded southern to me, but a bit posh-like!"

"Her age?" Neil said, pen hovering his pad.

"Yeah, she looked about ninety, but moved like a twenty year old," Neve said, wrapping her open coat across her middle. "Bit rushed, she was."

"Description?"

"She had one of those long trench coat type macs, grey or.., or dark green. Scruffy looking cow, had a headscarf on even though it wasn't rainin."

Neil scribbled into his notebook, jumping at the blast of a horn. "Her face, and ethnicity?" he continued, stepping onto the pavement, avoiding a large police vehicle.

"Oh-err, white. Hooked nose, wrinkly mare she was, like I said, probably nineties. She had a couple of hairs poking from a mole on her chin!" Neve said, stroking her jaw.

"Sure it wasn't me grandma, Neve!" the large lady said, with a bellowing laugh.

"*Err,* thank you, Miss!" Neil snapped, extinguishing the woman's soppy smile.

"Well she's hardly Britain's most wanted, is she," the woman said softly, refolding her tattooed forearms. "Why all the fuss? Neve woz the one that saved the bairn!"

"Is there anything else you can tell me about her?" Neil said, open-faced at Neve.

"I don't think so. It was only a short convo'. She just said that she'd seen a ba-be crying inside the van," Neve said, scratching her head. "It wasn't crying when I got there, but maybe.."

"She definitely said that she'd *seen it,* did she?" Neil pressed.

"Yeah, that's right."

"And when you found the baby, it was in the footwell on the passenger's side," Neil said. "So the old woman would have had to have stepped up on the footplate to have seen it, like you did?"

"I doubt the ol' gal coulda climbed up to take a gander, but she defo said she saw it, she did."

Neil thanked Neve and headed back to the Luton, now shielded by a large vehicle housing the Scene of Crime team and their equipment. A white tent had been erected over the van, protruding three metres from its rear doors, which remained open. Beside it, the stumpy figure of Jeremy Forsythe stood, with glasses perched on the tip of his nose, peering inside.

CHAPTER 109

The girl on the train was safe; the train-stalker had been dealt with.

Bella missing her train wasn't the end of the world, but it had meant her taking a National Express coach that was now stuck in a town bedevilled by roadworks. The tiresome stop-start journey was slower than a hotel toaster.

It could have been coincidental that he was also getting off at Stamford. And possible that he was always going to turn left out of the station, and cross the same road. Even to follow the same footpath toward the Pembroke estate. But when he also cut through the green space near the swings, it more than fortuity could bear. Bella had no choice but to act.

A triangular thatch of trees provided perfect cover to ambush the stalker, who trailed Bella and the girl at fifty feet. Despite the fading light, his eyes lit-up in seeing the girl unaccompanied; the old woman gone. The girl continued across the park alone, vulnerable. His pace sped.

Poor boy. He didn't know what hit him, and nor would he ever as he laid unconscious with blood streaming from a fractured skull. His resting place, the dark wet undergrowth, was fitting for the diseased vermin that he was.

Finally traffic was moving, clear of the green lights that had stood defiantly red. There weren't more than twenty onboard, mostly couples with heads resting on shoulders. Bella clocked the time from the digital display at the front of the coach and slouched to one side. Behind her the few single travellers were ear-budded with faces over their iPhones.

The warmth of the quiet coach felt comforting against the dark silhouette of the countryside outside. Bella head-nuzzled her rucksack that she propped up at the window. Car lights flashed across her, mesmeric in their waves, her heavying eyelids folded.

Some hours later, Bella was awoken into brightness by a gentle rocking at her shoulder. Shocked, she sat bolt upright, blinking the woman's features into focus. Soft, smiling but with frowning eyes; trouble.

"Hi," she whispered, in a hush barely audible.

"Hi, thanks for waking me," Bella said, tugging the rucksack to her lap.

"You err., might want to take a look at that," she said, finger-tapping her forehead.

Bella planted her hand to her brow, feeling the prosthetic flapping either side of her temples.

"Shit. Th-thanks, that's very kind of you," Bella said, palm-tapping across her forehead, as if checking a feverish temperature.

"We've not long arrived at Heathrow, but the coach driver's been shouting down for you to get off," she said, with a concerned-face smile.

"Thanks for the heads up," Bella said, sliding across her seat.

"Good luck, honey," the woman said, with a wide-eyed nod, before quickly walking down the aisle.

Bella knotted her headscarf tight to her chin. A stiff breeze greeted her as she stepped from the coach. Facing the bright lights of Terminal 5, Bella swung her rucksack to her shoulder; now for the tough bit!

CHAPTER 110

"Boss!" Neil yelled, racing over. "I think I might have something here.. boss?"

Tom turned, waving his number two away dismissively, with index finger raised.

"For fucks sake, Turvs. I was just speaking to Spence about the guy that attacked her!" Tom said, finger-punching his phone. "She's talking about flying over there to deal with him!"

"Sorry guv, but-err it *was her*," Neil said, peeling the cover of his pocketbook. "It's the same old lady description that we had from the Cheveley estate, after Jackson's murder."

"What.. who are you talking about?"

"*Crumpled face, hooked nose, wart on her chin, wearing a pale headscarf and dark trench coat!*" Neil said, flicking hard at his notes. "*That* was my record, taken at the time of Jackson's murder."

Tom's face tilted to one side, "And?"

"Here we are.., 'Hooked nose, wrinkly face with hairs poking from a mole on her chin' and err, 'long trench coat type mac, grey or dark greenish. Scruffy looking with a headscarf'. That is the description provided to me just now. It's the *same woman*, boss; it's Maxwell!" Neil said, staring at his SIO.

"Neil, you're describing just about every old lady in this country!" Tom said, nodding at Yorkshire's Chief of police, who strode across to join them.

"This is for you," the Chief said, handing Tom a clear bag with the recording device inside. "It's been dusted and tape-scraped. They've got everything they need, so it's all yours."

"Thanks, Chief," Tom said, finger pinching the top of it.

"Chief, could I just ask, is there CCTV in operation in this area?" Neil said.

The Chief turned to Neil, pursing his lips, "There will certainly be some on the high street, but not on the residential roads off it. Although.," he paused. "*Hawkins!*"

Constable Hawkins trotted over. Behind him high voltage lighting illuminated slow moving Scene of Crime operatives in their puffy white overalls, resembling images from the moon landings.

"DI Turvey is enquiring about CCTV in this area, am I right in recalling there was something put in place at some point, or was it taken down?" the Chief said.

"They removed the old system two years back, Chief, but installed new equipment six weeks ago following an escalation in grief tourism and another attempt to torch the property," Hawkins said, with chest puffed.

"Excellent, well there you have it detective!" the Chief said.

"And, err, what sort of range would it cover?" Neil asked Hawkins.

"They fitted the new high-def smooth frame kit, so around two hundred metres either side of the pod station. So the entire length of Garden Lane, I'd wager sir," Hawkins said.

"Fantastic, and where is this piece of techie kit, exactly?" Neil said, scanning the street.

"The camera? Well it's right here, sir," Hawkins said, waving a finger above his head.

The men craned their necks as one, like synchronised swimmers emerging to surface a pool. Gazing up, high above them, an alien-like half-glazed sphere, perched at the top of a silver post. It looked like ET sat on a street light, protecting the house below from intruders.

Jeremy Forsythe sidled over to join them, slipping his spectacles down his nose as he peered skywards. The base of the post was anchored in the pavement outside number 6, the Ripper's former home. The Luton van had only just missed hitting it.

CHAPTER 111

The reflection that greeted her wasn't a pretty sight. The disguise was useless, peeling in sweeping curls from her face, its adhesive quality lost. Either ruined in her confrontation at Stamford or by the vent blasting heat beside her as she slept on the coach.

Bella picked, detaching the mask's remnants, clearing them from her pink skin. She palm-wiped the back of her hands removing the blue veined mapping, like peeling sunburnt skin. Bended over the basin she massaged in the QwikDye solution, colouring her hair back to blonde.

At the sound of mother and child entering the restroom Bella scooped everything and darted into a cubicle, Clunk. Bella flushed twice before the toilet bowl filled and the wrinkly grey plastic disappeared. A face covering that had served her so well, now gone. Without it she felt exposed, unprotected.

Bella stepped from the cubicle, checking her fresh-face in the mirror, mask and makeup free. She looked so young, like a snake that had shed its skin; born again, rejuvenated. She washed a trail of gluey residue from her jawline.

"Hiya,"

Bella returned the smile of the woman who arrived at the sink next to her.

"Do I know you from somewhere?"

Bella's face screwed, realising the obvious answer to that question. "I don't think so, I've just got one of those faces!"

Slinging her rucksack to her back she exited quickly, striding swiftly to merge amongst the more boisterous groups in the airport's check-in hall. She needed to somehow get through security. The passport of pensioner Martha Thornton was no longer usable.

"Sorry! My fault, not looking where I was going," Bella said, barging heavily into the back of a young blonde girl, stood clutching her travel documents.

"No problem," she said, bending to retrieve them. "These early-flights are a killer!"

She'd mistakenly just picked up Mrs Thornton's passport from the shiny floor, her own now lay under the heel of Bella's sneaker. Martha's passport had been strategically placed.

Not a lookalike, but blonde, blue eyed and of similar age; it should work. Her enemy was time, the girl would be at the luggage desk shortly. Bella bound off towards security.

At an ever quickening pace she crossed the concourse and hovered her boarding passover the reader, and the glass gate parted. Bella joined the lengthy queues leading to the bag and body scanners. She slid off her jacket and squeezed down the line apologising as she eased past.

"There's a fuckin' queue here, love!" a portly, bare-armed woman shouted.

"Do you mind if I go first," Bella said, loudly, with a grimace. "Only I'm not feeling great. Something I ate, I think," she added, stomach-clutching.

"Sure, yeah-yeah, you go on!" Families parted like the waves of the Red Sea.

Bella, half smiling at the grumpy faces still ahead, said, "So sorry, my child just ran through!"

Dragging a storage tray from below the conveyor, she slung her rucksack and jacket in it, slid off her trainers and threw them on top.

"Watch, jewellery, belt, madam," a burly voice ordered.

"Nothing!" Bella said, lifting her sleeves.

She went through the body scanner without incident. Reunited with her tray, she arm wrestled her jacket on and slung a rucksack strap over her shoulder. She was aware of receiving more than a few odd stares, including from airport staff.

Despite her relief in passing security, there were yet more lingering looks cast her way as she walked the perfumed hall of duty free shops. There again, a woman with scent tester in hand, peering a little longer than polite, it was as if she were of celebrity status.

Bella flipped the hood of her jacket and darted toward the restroom. At WHSmith she stopped in her tracks, doubling back two steps to examine a little closer the row of newspapers. Her face stared back, there for all to see.

The young blue-eyed, blonde girl, a picture of innocence, emblazoned across every paper. A face that sat in stark contrast to the gruesome headlines that surrounded the photos: Ripper Revenge Killer, The Bloodbath Butcher, Maxwell's Massacre, Britain's Most Wanted. With a growing sense of unease, she shot off.

CHAPTER 112

Jeremy Forsythe poured slowly from the balloon Cafetiere that was steaming his spectacles. "Coffee, Tom?" he said, offering to pour.

"No-no. Thank you, Jeremy," Tom said, tapping his watch.

"Ahh, yes of course," Jeremy said, returning the jug to its hotplate.

The two left the kitchenette, headed for the briefing room where the huge team now assigned to the Maxwell case had been assembled.

"So, we have a confirmed sighting of Maxwell exiting the Luton van!" Neil said softly, shuffling up behind them. "It's definitely her, boss," he added, unfolding a piece of paper.

A photograph of the elderly woman described earlier by the witness in Garden Lane, covered half the page. The other side featured a grainy image of a similarly dressed pensioner captured from footage at the Cheveley estate, near the bin storage unit, where the butchered body of Jamal Jackson was discovered.

"The crew here have traced her movements on CCTV, boarding a southbound train, alighting at Stamford and disappearing from shot for twenty five minutes. They picked her up again boarding a coach headed for London," Neil whispered his excitement. "Destination, Heathrow!"

The three men took seats around a table at the front. Yorkshire's Chief of Police, had begun addressing his troops. Behind him was a blown up picture of Arabella Maxwell above some grainier images from the camera footage, believed to be her disguised as an elderly woman.

"Ahh, now then Professor Forsythe, if you would," the Chief said, with an outstretched arm.

The criminal psychologist offered a little grin as he waddled over, swapping positions with the Chief. He squinted across the room at the mix of young and old faces in front of him.

"With a grievance, we are all dangerous people," he said, lifting his spectacles from his face. "But suffering an abusive childhood, being the product of rape, losing your mother at a young age, would be a challenge beyond most.."

The muttering of officers at the back ceased instantly at the raised hand of the Chief, who nodded at the Professor. The profiler looked very different without his glasses, hardened.

"Charles Maxwell, her grandfather and carer, was a paedophile. For Arabella, it was a life lived in anxiety and fear; she would never be completely sane of mind."

"Any one of us has the propensity to harm another, and without love and nurture, devoid of kindness, one's psychology will change," he said, replacing his tortoise-shell frames. "There are the harbourers; grudge holders. And there are the releasers; forgive and forget'ers. Undoubtedly we all know some of these," he said with a little grin, as the chatter returned.

"Settle down, people!" the Chief barked.

"Thank you," Jeremy said, sipping his coffee before placing it on a cabinet behind him.

"Maxwell is a highly intelligent woman, graduating with an Honorary first in Law amongst a host of other achievements; she was fast-tracked to the bar. But at some point there was a 'Trigger', an incident that flicked a switch and that darkness lying dormant was lit."

"Jeremy," Tom whispered, with eyebrows raised, twisting at his wrist.

"Of course, yes." Jeremy said, softly. "Whilst there was, it has to be said, rationale for her earlier planned murders of Jackson and Darcy, it is fair to say she has now lost all control. A likely consequence of the sheer weight of her mental trauma that has misaligned amygdala in the prefrontal cortex, the brains seat of fear and dubiety."

Tom's eyebrows met his hairline as he tugged his iPhone from his trouser pocket and pinned it to his ear. "Maxwell acts now without forethought," Jeremy said, and took a slurp of coffee.

"The bodily slaughter of Lebouf and her suspected involvement in the murders of twelve other men, is evidence of a deranged psychosis. You are dealing with an extremely dangerous individual, capable of killing without conscience."

"Killing men only though prof, women are safe?" Neil Turvey said.

"Her targets have been male, given her perception of injustices against women. But Maxwell will not hesitate to kill anyone hindering her in rectifying such wrongs," Jeremy said, before waddling over to join Tom and Neil at their table.

A frozen video image filled the wall as the six-switch light panel was clicked and the room plunged into darkness, all eyes focussed on the footage that burst into noisy life.

"Is this that tape that was in the van?" Neil whispered to Tom.

"Yeah, I've seen it, so I'll step outside," Tom said, his iPhone in hand. "See if you think there's any clue to her next move in there?"

"Will do. Anything I can help with there, boss?" Neil said, eye pointing at

Tom's phone.

"It's Spence, she's leaving for Indonesia to attend the trial. You know, of that waiter.." Tom said, with lips sucked to his teeth. "I need to speak to her before she flies out."

Two or three shhh'es were fired at them as an eerie hush descended. Birdsong was the only sound as the video panned from the treetops of Headingley woods to a dirty white van.

Hi, I'm Bella Maxwell, but I'm guessing you already know that…

CHAPTER 113

To the south, fields of dust stretched for as far as the eye could see, only broken by shallow hills that swept the rural Texas landscape. The stillness and building humidity of the day prickled the foreheads of the ranch hands that were working the livestock.

Market day came twice-weekly now to Richmonds, such was their dominance in the state. A formidable cartel that had suppressed all rivalry in the region over the last few years.

The pounding of hooves was thunderous as the posse rode up from the outbuildings, leaving a dust trail running a hundred metres in their wake. A stub-nosed tractor revved, bouncing the long grit driveway, and met the saddled men under the fancy 'R' of the ranch gates.

"Been calling you for the last hour or more, Teddy," she hollered. "What in the hell you got that cell strapped to your hip for, if you ain't ever gonna use it?"

The riders yanked hard on their reins, the horses' heads rocking as they circled the mini tractor, as dust plumed around it. One of the hands dismounted in a graceful leap, scooping the leashes of two, then three animals, lashing them to the three-beamed boundary fence. Wrought ironwork, arched above them; 'Welcome to Richmond'.

"What, in the name of the good lord, could be so urgent to disturb a man's enjoyment of God's country?" Ted said, sat in the fleece-lined saddle of his huge steed.

509

Another hand lashed the other horses as the men began dismounting. Theodore Richmond's horse twisted sharply, head turned from the spit of the engine. He tightened his grip and dug his heels, edging his animal closer to the tractor.

"Now don't you take that tone with me!" she said, silencing the juddering motor.

"You guys get on over to the barn and help out with the auction arena for this afternoon," Ted said, pointing at a large red wood building beyond the main house.

The men strode off through the gates, each with head dipped, finger-tapping hats as they passed by Mrs Richmond; *Maam*.

"I'm sorry Kasey, but we've been kinda busy down in the basin you know, what with the extra orders coming in," Ted said, towering over his wife.

"Well we ain't exactly beena slacking up here. Market day ain't exactly a breeze for me either, you know," she said, jumping from the tractor and taking the reins of his jetblack stallion.

"Well okay, I'm sorry honey," Ted said, dismounting with a heavy booted thud. "I guess I just 'aint heard it ringing, what with all the animal bleating, an all."

He hung an arm around her shoulder and planted a peck on her lips. "I'm not sure I got this new one set right," Ted said, plucking his cell from its holster.

"Give me that thing!" she said, snatching it from him. "Well, you sure as hell shouldn't have gone and lost the other one now, should you!" Kasey was considerably younger and smaller, both in height and girth, than her man-mountain of a husband.

"Who is it that's after me in anyways, honeycup?" Ted said, removing his stetson.

"Some gal, says she's from the IRS, insistin' on speaking with you. Said you got into some business dealings you ain't yet declared or somesuch!" Kasey said, stroking the horse's nose. "Gotta say it sounded kinda important, Teddy."

"She left a number for me to call her?" Ted said, peeling off his sunshades.

"On the kitchen table. Said her name's Brown, *Josie Brown*," Kasey said, tickling the horse's cheeks.

Ted unknotted the bandana from his neck and wiped the glisten from his forehead. "Probably just some confusion about our cattle and oil revenues, again!"

"Well, apparently she spoke with you before, said about when you were off *doing business* over in Indonesia, or somesuch," Kasey said, with question mark eyes.

Ted's face dropped. "Best I deal with her right away then," he said.

CHAPTER 114

Bella had made the call she needed to make, having spent the last twenty minutes hid in a toilet cubicle. She splashed water on her face, trying to clear the tiredness that overwhelmed her.

"Boarding pass, please," the red-lipsticked attendant said robotically, for the hundredth time.

Bella stood stifling a yawn, near to last in the line of passengers waiting to board flight 740 to Houston. She handed the woman her iPhone, its screen showing the QR code.

The woman paused for a moment longer than she had done for other passengers. She looked into the face of Bella Maxwell a little closer than she had the others.

"*Problem?*" Bella said, with a soft smile.

"Err yes, *sorry*. Could I just ask that you, err, step to one side for a moment, please, Miss Hughes," she said, her voice anxious.

From behind her little desk she pulled a beige phone to her ear, whispered something into it, whilst Bella stepped to one side. The guy behind her in a tracksuit, sneakers and Nike holdall, took his turn at the boarding gate as she replaced the receiver.

Bella scanned the departure area, the seating around gate 62 was empty. Further down at 64 they were queuing to board. There were families sitting on the hard seats behind her at gate 60. Beyond that, at the drinks bar, there were three men on stools drinking beer.

And then she saw *them*, two of them, weaving the crowded lounge further down. They split to pass families with over-excited youngsters, then realigned to pace the concourse as one.

With peaked caps and dark suits, they almost resembled pilots, save for the waist holstered handguns that flashed as they strode toward her. One had an oversized silver hooped keyring hung low from his belt, bouncing his thigh with every stride.

The older of the two said, at more than ten metres, "*Miss Hughes*, is it?" His blotchy complexion came quickly into focus.

"Hi, yes. Is everything ok?"

The senior man, with a face like curdled cream, placed his hand on his hip, making sure to peel his jacket a little further to reveal his armour. A statement of authority and control, a warning of power; unfiltered masculinity. His body language oozed arrogance.

"Yes, I hope it will be," he said, as they moved to flank her. "We just need you to accompany us, to answer a few questions."

"Sure, but I wouldn't want to miss my flight."

The younger, slim guy, held a smirk-filled face. The collar of his pale blue shirt looped well wide of his scrawny neck. His bony long fingers pinched at her forearm.

"I don't think you need to worry about that!" he said, with a widening smirk, almost releasing a snigger.

CHAPTER 115

The video recording that Maxwell had left in the Luton van continued on the large screen, holding the packed police briefing room in silence.

"I believe these were all cases brought by the Met?" the Chief of police said softly, shaking his head. "Terrible prosecution rates in crimes against women you've got down there!"

"Yeah, but these were cases where Maxwell's law firm represented the victims. They lost them all!" Neil whispered, to Yorkshire's Chief, who cast him a deep frown. Neil turned back to the screen, refocusing on Maxwell's taped montage.

The third clip showed a young woman walking a little unsteadily along a well-lit high street as two men approached from the opposite direction. When they reach her, there's an altercation and she is seen trying to push them away before her arms are clamped behind her, by the men. She stumbles, losing a shoe before being dragged into a side street, out of shot.

The digital time recording on the CCTV footage records the time at 03:43 am The men re-emerge at 04:26 am. One man is seen buttoning his jeans as the other flips the hood of his jacket.

At 04:34 am, the girl emerges in a state of undress, clearly distressed as she attempts to flag down a passing motorist. The image freezes and, as with the previous incidents, the screen scrolls the reported outcome;

'CASE DISMISSED: Insufficient evidence. WITNESS TESTIMONY: Unreliable. ACCUSED: Released without charge.'

The soundless footage continues. This one is from a tree-lined terrace, where a man is seen standing behind a bush; just under six foot, medium build, wearing dark cargo-type trousers, bomber jacket and pumps with a colourful logo. In checking his shoulder, his face is to the camera, it's clear to see; white, middle aged, high receding hairline. A woman of around thirty approaches from the other side..

"Sweet Jesus, how many of these are there gonna be!" Neil said, head-cocking at the Chief, sitting alongside him.

"Do you actually remember any of these cases, DI Turvey!" the Chief snapped.

'When you walk through a storm, hold your head up..' Turvey's iPhone boomed out to a mix of jeers and shhing.

"Can you take that outside!" the Chief ordered.

Neil dabbed his phone, halting the dulcet tones of Gerry Marsden, and crouched in a scuttled exit from the briefing room. Shutting the door firmly behind him, he took the call from the Met comms team, strolling into the kitchenette as he spoke. Tom was there, having just come off the phone with Spencer, he flicked the switch on the coffee machine.

"Okay thanks, that could be useful," Neil said, poking the red button.

"What, 'could be useful', Turvs?"

"Comms.. they did that cross check you asked for," Neil said, tucking his phone into his pocket.

He pulled a Leeds United mug from the shelf in front of him, placing it alongside Tom's cup. "You know, UK missing persons, the cross-match with the list they found on the boat that Spence was on?" he said, to Tom's screwed face

"Yeah-yeah, Richmond's Yacht anchored off El-Machey."

"El-Marney you mean, although it was actually the other one.." Neil said, lifting a carton of milk from the fridge.

"Yes! Get to it, Neil," Tom snapped. "We've got a man that's been disembowelled!

"Well, they got a match," Neil said, sniffing the carton. "Several UK hits in fact, but just the one with a link to Maxwell.."

"And..!?"

"It's a-err, a Sadie Barlow," Neil said, pouring a dab of milk in their mugs. "Barlow went missing from the UK in the last few years, she was on Richmond's list. It's possible the old oil baron bought Barlow, in one of Darcy's sextraffic sales.."

"And the link, is?" Tom said, eye-bulging.

"Link, boss?"

"To Maxwell!" Tom spluttered. "Christ Neil, is there a tangible link between Barlow and Maxwell! Do we actually have anything on her motive and objectives?"

"Yeah-yeah, sorry boss," Neil said, pouring his coffee. "They were best friends at Manchester University. Like, thick as thieves, apparently!"

"Christ that's it, then; it's Richmond she's after," Tom said, bolting out of the room. "She'll be headed for Texas!"

"That'd be Heathrow then, wouldn't it?" Neil said, half-turning, as coffee spilled his mug's sides. "Actually, I think Manchester flies direct."

CHAPTER 116

Bella's left wrist was cuffed to a metal bar that ran along the underside of the table, that sat central in the tight-walled room. The table was bolted to the floor. Opposite her was the man with a face that reminded her of cottage cheese.

The skinny guy in an oversized suit stood behind him, wearing the same excited sneer that he had earlier. "We all know who you are!" he said, with a child-like grin.

He flung a newspaper onto the desk in front of her, her own face staring back. "Bella fuckin' Maxwell!" he chortled.

"Yeah, alright Joe!" the older guy said, pissed that Joe had stolen his line. "Let's keep this calm shall we and wait for the Police to arrive," he added, with a glare at Bella that said, I'm in charge.

Bella scanned the room, which was surprisingly close to the departure gates. The security men had pushed a handleless door, set within a beach-scene mural wall, that you wouldn't know was there. Behind it was the small interview room, which was windowless and vanilla.

"Now, is there anything that you'd like to tell us?" he said, his fat fingers interlocking.

Bella shrugged her head, leaned back in the chair and said nothing.

"Not going to deny this is you, are you?" he said, poking a sausage-like finger at the newspaper that was between them.

"I think half the airport knew it was you, rumours were flying. More than

517

when that Kardshian flew in," Joe said, failing to suppress a chortle. "And once you stole that passport that was game over, luv!"

"That was a bit of a silly move, wasn't it," the larger man said, a little grin creasing his face. "We do have cameras monitoring everything, you know!"

The men's shared amusement was broken as the door burst open and a woman strode in, flapping a police warrant. "Great work, chaps!" she said, flashing the shiny badge.

"Wow, that was quick," the big man said, getting to his feet. "We only just called it in!"

"We already had obs monitoring Heathrow, but you guys got to Maxwell first, congrats," she said. "Uncuff her, I have my own set."

She clipped one side of her handcuffs to Bella's free wrist, the other to herself. Mottle-faced Joe rounded the table, slid a key from the jangling bunch on his belt, and released her other wrist.

"Shouldn't we deal with the paperwork before you take her?" Joe said, lifting a manilla file to his chest. "The transfer from us, to you guys."

She tugged hard at Maxwell's wrist, hauling her to her feet. "We don't need to do any of that right now; this is a Cat A case," she said, frowning at the nodding men.

"Yeah, yeah, we knew that," the big guy said, snatching the file from his partner. "This is high profile, the media are all over it. We can deal with paperwork later, Joe!"

She walked Bella to the door, before turning sharply. "I will need a full statement from each of you, setting out your role in Maxwell's capture?"

"No problem," the big man said. "We're proud to be the ones that finally apprehended her!"

"Ideally sooner rather than later, if you don't mind fellas," she said, nose-pointing at the desk. "Let's get this wrapped up quickly, shall we?"

"Of course, yes-yes," the senior security man said, ushering Joe to sit at the table.

Joe slid a silver ballpoint from his jacket pocket, clicking its head several times whilst settling behind the desk. The policewoman exited the airport's hidden security area, pushing the adjacent fibreglass door to step into the departure lounge, opposite gate 62.

CHAPTER 117

The briefing room emptied slowly, in an eerie silence, with heads hung. The coppers stunned by the demonstrated repeated failings of the police, clear miscarriages of justice. Cases where, on the basis of Maxwell's tape, there was no room for doubt; guilty men had walked free.

"We've got her boss!" Neil said, jumping into the passenger seat, alongside Tom.

Dangerous predators, released back into the community where, in '85%' of cases they would re-offend, as Maxwell's final graphic demonstrated. The accuracy of what they had seen needed to be verified, but the officers leaving the room were in no doubt of their horrendous failings.

"What, where?" Tom said, sliding his seatbelt clip into its buckle.

Failures to prosecute cases of rape, assault and stalking were all highlighted in Maxwell's video, alongside workplace sexual harassment claims, all of which were dismissed.

"*Heathrow!*" Neil said, beaming at Jeremy Forsythe who was already buckled into the back seat, cleaning his spectacles. "As predicted she was headed to the States, Houston to be precise."

"Do we actually have her in custody?" Tom said, slotting the key.

"Yep, Airport security has her under lock and key. I've told our guys to send three squad cars over," Neil said, with rising excitement.

"For one woman!" Tom said, with a wrinkled brow. "Bit over the top isn't it?"

"Show of strength and authority. Several members of the public reported seeing Maxwell, it'll be out there! The place will be crawling with TV crews. This'll play well, boss," Neil said.

"It will look like overkill! Just make sure there are plenty of female officers in attendance at the transfer," Tom said, eye rolling

"Remember what our esteemed expert said about Maxwell," Neil said, winking over his shoulder. "She is '*out of all control with deranged psychosis*' and, '*capable of killing without thought of consequence*'. Am I right Prof, or am I right?"

Jeremy shuffled forwards in his seat, just as the car echoed with the ringing of a bluetooth call. The dashboard flashed, *DI Spencer*.

"Go ahead, Spence?" Neil said. "I thought you were leaving us."

"Err, yes I am." she said. "Is Tom there?"

"Hi Spence, I'm with Neil and Jeremy, we're heading south. They've got Maxwell at Heathrow!" Tom said. "All ok with you?"

"Yeah, I heard about that! I'm actually outside Heathrow, and wondered if you could verify me for airport staff? It's crazy down here now, after Maxwell nearly got through. They're not allowing anyone in or out," Spencer said. "Could you confirm my CIN pin for them?"

"Yep no problem. Turvs, could you deal?" Tom said.

"It's probably my loungewear throwing them!" she said. "But I don't want to miss my flight."

"Sure Spence, put them on., The *staff*, not your loungewear, I mean!" Neil said, with a cackle and wink at Tom. It met with a ploughed face.

There was a moment of silence before a squeaky voice requested verification of DI Spencer's criminal investigation number. Neil read the details, and confirmed the police support number, before the silence returned.

"Thanks guys, wish me luck!" Spence said, ending the call abruptly.

Spencer waited as the attendant pulled a phone from beneath the admission stand at gate 62 and dialled the number given to her by DI Turvey. Moments later she replaced the receiver.

"That's fine, please go ahead and board immediately. The flight is already running late for its slot," she said, with a tilted smile.

Spencer marched down the long white tunnel behind the departure desk, with Bella Maxwell alongside her. The corridor bent left after forty yards, where she stopped. Further on, two red uniformed stewards stood either side of the plane's door.

"*Take this,*" Spence said, digging her hand into her jacket pocket.

Spencer slid her passport, police warrant card and driver's licence into the front pocket of Bella's rucksack, that drooped from her shoulder. She released the handcuffs from their wrists, tucking them into her back pocket.

"Aren't you going to arrest me?" Bella said wide-eyed, rubbing her red wrists.

"*What..* lock up a woman that stands up for women.. I was never going to do that! In case you don't know it, you've started something, Bella Maxwell!" Spence said, whilst rummaging in her pocket. "You've inspired half the nation with what you've done."

Bella's watery eyes glistened, the colour of the ocean that laps the shores of El-Marney. "Thanks so, so much for this, I had no idea that you.." she said softly.

"Don't you dare thank *me*, after all you've done, rescuing all those women from that lowlife Darcy!" Spence said, squeezing Bella's arm. "And the millions you've put into women's charities across the world, that will save countless lives!" Her bottom lip wobbled.

The two shared a nod that said so much, both lip-biting. "We owe you, big time!" Spence said, as a tear flew from her eye, barely skimming her cheek.

"I just hope things change for the better.. it's so long overdue!" Bella said, tugging her backpack high to her shoulder.

"Well you've certainly unleashed a tsunami, Bella!" Spence said, patting her pockets. "Oh, and you might need this."

She pulled a tiny plastic bag from the thigh pocket of her cargo pants, shoving the sachet into the pouch of Bella's hoodie. "It's Auburn Mist, not the greatest colour, but the nearest fit I could find," Spencer said. "We're not exactly twins, but it might help."

"*Err, Miss, if you wouldn't mind please,*" one of the stewards called, with an arm aloft.

DI Spencer waved a finger in the air, mouthing *one-minute.*

Bella said, "But you are actually with the police?"

"More importantly, like half of the population right now, Bella.. I'm with you!" Spence said, finger-wiping her eyelid. "You might find you have more supporters out there than enemies!"

"It was just my friend, Sadie, that I was desperate to find," Bella said as they walked. "I found evidence on Darcy's boat that she.."

"*I know,* and I'm hoping there will be people that can help you over there," Spence interrupted. "You have my police ID, use it."

"But what about you, how are you going to.."

"Don't worry about me. I'm going to nail the bastard who attacked me in Indonesia," Spence said, tear-blinking. "You'll be my strength and inspiration, Bella."

"*Please madam, we don't want to miss our slot,*" the steward said, firmly.

"I'm so sorry to hear about that.. *God,* I don't even know your name.. Spencer, is it?"

"It's actually, *Sarah,*" she said, beaming. "Not that anyone's ever called me that!"

"Thanks for everything, Sarah, and good luck in Indonesia. If they don't lock him up, just let me know" Bella whispered, with a wink. "I hope we meet again." She squeezed her hand.

"*Miss please. Take off in three minutes!*"

The two paced swiftly towards the stewards, Spencer placed a hand on Bella's shoulder as they approached them. "Please escort this passenger to her seat," Spencer said, to one of the flight attendants.

The steward walked Bella to a row of seats near the tail, passing more than a few smiley women sat alongside frown-faced men.

"Now, as I believe has been explained to your colleagues, she is to fly unfettered to the US," Spencer said, assertively.

"*Understood!*" the stewardess said, with a Dorothy-like heel-click. "It's like having royalty onboard," she whispered, with a long-lashed wink.

Spencer beamed a Cheshire cat grin as she bounced back up the ramp.

Bella buckled herself into the window seat as the plane immediately began taxiing. The flight was barely half full, so she had the row to herself. A hostess stopped her march down the aisle and leaned over, dropping a bag of make-up onto the seat beside her.

"If you need too.. *you know!*" she said, with her index finger circling her own face. Bella smiled, mouthing, *thank you.*

Moments later they were in the air and another steward sporting a cheeky grin lowered the seat-table next to Bella. He placed a hot tray down alongside an ice-filled tumbler and a can of drink.

"Special service, for a special lady!" he said, with pursed lips. "You need a *G and T* any time, you just holler hun!" he added, before pirouetting away.

Bella welled-up as she trawled through her bag of makeup, discovering Earbuds that she paired with the iPhone Sarah had slid into her rucksack. She *clicked* open the can and poured it fizzing over the ice, enjoying the refreshing sound, before taking a sip.

Slipping a *U*-cushion behind her head, Bella settled into her seat and tapped play on the phone. The saltiness of her tear-dampened cheeks met the lips of her beaming smile, as Laura Branigan's ballad *Gloria* filled her ears.

ACKNOWLEDGEMENTS

The voyage of storytelling is a truly magical one, allowing one's imagination to run free, to create and explore a different world. To park yourself in the midst of peril and venture into places that exhibit the darkest of human behaviours. *Cold Justice* took me there.

The journey from draft manuscript to book however, is a long and sometimes arduous one. My laptop died during this process (simply refusing to wake one morning)! The word by word, page-by-page analysis of editing is certainly testing. This was made considerably easier thanks to the skilled assistance I received from my editor (and eldest daughter), Charlotte. My eternal gratitude to her and her unwavering diligence and keen eye for detail.

The book's beautiful cover was designed by Usama Champbajwa.

And of course, for their love and support, my thanks to my family who have to live with me when often deeply immersed in another world, often jolting me from its terrors, for dinner! To my wonderful children, Charlotte, Georgia, Mia and Jack (the inner circle!). You are my greatest achievement, and make me proud every day. My love, always.

Not forgetting, the huge thank you that must also go to my readers. The fantastic response I received to my debut novel, *Chameleon*, was overwhelming. Your feedback and reviews were all greatly appreciated.

Book formatted by Usama Champbajwa.

Printed in Great Britain
by Amazon

50107493R00293